D0561754

JASON

A powerhouse [...] out of his sla[...] with the Ville[...] [...]ed him but gave him what he wanted.

ANDREA WHITBY
Jason's daughter. Incredibly beautiful and headstrong. She broke her father's heart when she fell in love with Riley Villette.

RILEY VILLETTE
He was determined to be better than his family—especially after his affair with Andrea.

PATSY
Andrea's daughter. She was the ugly duckling who became a swan. Now every man wanted her, including Joseph Villette.

JOSEPH
A charismatic young man whose associates were rather unsavory. But he wanted Patsy above all. . . .

JASON'S PEOPLE

Fawcett Gold Medal Books
by Beverly Byrne:

JEMMA

FIERY SPLENDOR

The Griffin Saga
THE OUTCAST (#1)

THE ADVENTURER (#2)

JASON'S PEOPLE

Beverly Byrne

FAWCETT GOLD MEDAL • NEW YORK

A Fawcett Gold Medal Book
Published by Ballantine Books
Copyright © 1985 by Beverly Byrne

All rights reserved under International and Pan-American Copyright
Conventions. Published in the United States by Ballantine Books,
a division of Random House, Inc., New York, and simultaneously
in Canada by Random House of Canada Limited, Toronto.

Library of Congress Catalog Card Number: 84-91713

ISBN 0-449-12455-X

All the characters in this book are fictitious and any resemblance
to actual persons living or dead is purely coincidental.

Manufactured in the United States of America

First Edition: March 1985

1850 . . .

Millicent

Chapter One

1.

The fog didn't lift; it came apart in shreds. From his place on the schooner's deck Lliam Murray could make out the shabby, soot-stained shacks and warehouses of the Dolgellau wharf but not the approaching dinghy. That he heard. The oars made a soft splashing sound, too gentle for the March-cold Atlantic waters, a deception.

"Be this the ship from America, the *Half Century*?" The singsong Welsh voice drifted through the mist.

"It is." Murray's words sounded distorted in his ears, strange in a strange place.

"You be Lliam Murray, then? Of Vermont?"

"I am. Are you Gareth Jones?"

"Himself." The dinghy slapped against the side of the schooner; wood rasped against wood. "Sorry we're late," the Welshman said. "Bloody fog."

"It's all right. Is everyone here?"

"Everyone that's coming. The Edwards brothers from Llanfyllin changed their minds." The speaker clambered up the rope ladder and swung onto the deck. The dinghy turned shoreward. "Couple of others backed out, too. 'Tis a big step, emigrating. Your Mr. Whitby, he'll have to understand."

Murray shrugged, the gesture lost in the gray dimness. "How many in all?"

"One hundred and three. Twenty-seven of 'em is quarry men. Rest is kin."

"We'll bring the women and children aboard first. Will they manage the rope ladder?"

"They'll manage. They're good Welsh stock." Jones looked the length of the deck, arching his neck to peer into the rigging.

In the distance Murray heard the sound of the returning dinghy. "They're coming back."

"Yes. This is a fine ship. Are you the captain?"

3

"No, I'm Mr. Whitby's attorney. The captain's gone ashore to arrange supplies."

"How long before we reach Vermont?" Jones asked.

"We'll be in New York in about two months. Then a week to ten days overland to reach Whitby Falls."

"Whitby Falls, Vermont," Jones repeated softly. "We sail today?"

"Yes, today."

A voice called a question from the water; the dinghy bumped against the side again. The Welshman leaned over the rail, then turned to look at Murray. "March the first, eighteen hundred and fifty," he said solemnly. " 'Tis a good day for beginning. St. David's Day."

The American smiled. St. David, legendary patron of Wales. Who, he wondered, was the patron of Vermont? He chuckled softly. Jason Whitby, perhaps, but no one would ever put saint before his name.

Millicent Turner saw Jason Whitby for the first time on the eleventh of April.

Missie—no one called her Millicent—was celebrating her seventeenth birthday at a luncheon in the dining room of Parker's Hotel in Boston. She sat between her father and her fifteen-year-old sister Susan, in the place of honor on the red velvet banquette, and was the first to see the strange man approach their table.

"Papa, that man seems to be coming over here. Do you know him?"

Edgar Turner glanced over his shoulder with a hesitant smile of welcome. When he turned back to his daughter, the smile was gone. "I know him."

"But who is he, Papa? He's terribly handsome. And he *is* coming over here."

The stranger arrived before her father could answer. Turner rose with obvious reluctance and performed the introductions. "This is Jason Whitby of Whitby Falls, Vermont, girls. My daughters." He didn't pronounce their names.

"Edgar, ladies." Whitby bowed gracefully.

Missie guessed him to be about thirty. He was thirty-four, she learned later, and the silver streaks in his black hair had been there since his early twenties. So had the fine lines around his pale blue eyes. Her attention was arrested by the full lips and even white teeth that showed when he smiled and by his tall, slender build. She realized that he was studying her just as avidly, and she dropped her eyes and felt her cheeks redden.

"I didn't think to meet you in Boston." Turner didn't ask the stranger to sit down.

"Business takes a man where he will and where he will not," Whitby said. If he noticed the other man's coolness, he didn't show it. "And you, Edgar, what brings you to the hub?"

"It's Missie's birthday." Turner inclined his head to his eldest daughter. "Since my wife died some years past, I always take the girls out for a celebration luncheon on their birthdays. Missie wanted to come to Boston . . ." He let his voice trail away. He was talking too much, showing his nervousness.

"Missie . . ." Whitby smiled at the girl. She raised her eyes. They were startling eyes, an intense violet color, dramatic with her honey blond hair. "Are you called Miss Missie?"

"Millicent," she said softly.

"Oh, I see. Miss Millicent, then. Happy birthday. You must allow me to order a bottle of champagne, Edgar. I insist."

It was done before Turner could protest. The modest claret he had provided was whisked away, the grander wine opened and poured with due solemnity.

"Happy birthday, Miss Millicent," Jason Whitby said, raising his glass in a toast.

Four days later, Whitby called at the house in Nashua. The Turners kept only one servant, and she was out marketing when the man from Vermont lifted the tarnished brass knocker. It was Susan who came to the door. "Mr. Whitby." She gasped in surprise. "Come in. I'll tell Papa you're here."

"No need. Just show me to his laboratory, Miss Susan. He is there, isn't he?"

She nodded and led the way along a corridor of faded wallpaper and threadbare carpet. When they reached the heavy oak door of her father's private sanctum, her knock was tentative. "Papa," she called softly, "it's Mr. Whitby to see you."

She opened the door as she spoke, and her father turned to see the other man already in the room. Turner was holding a fragile glass test tube. It dropped and shattered on the bare floorboards. "What are you doing here?"

"I want to speak with you, Edgar. I believe we've business to discuss."

Susan ran away to find Missie and tell her of the extraordinary visit. Few people called at the old house, certainly not tall, handsome strangers.

"Perhaps he's a scientist, too," Susan offered by way of explanation. "Maybe he's come to discuss an experiment with Papa."

"I don't think so," Missie said thoughtfully. "He doesn't look like a scientist." The occasional colleague her father received was always ancient and bent and dusty and bewhiskered. "Besides, I don't think Papa likes him."

Susan was about to answer when their father came into the sitting room. He merely nodded at the girls and went to the piano. He always played Haydn when he was troubled.

"Is Mr. Whitby gone?" Missie asked boldly.

"Yes, he's gone."

Nothing further was said until after supper.

"Step outside with me, Missie. It's a lovely evening."

"It's warm for April, isn't it?" Then, reaching for his hand the way she had when she was a little girl, she asked, "What's wrong, Papa? It's something to do with that man from Vermont, isn't it?"

"Yes." Edgar Turner looked at his daughter and sighed. "You are very like your mother, you know," he said softly.

"Yes, I know. I remember her. I wish she'd lived." Missie's voice was a faint whisper.

"So do I. Particularly for your sakes, yours and Susan's. She'd know what to do."

"About what, Papa?"

"Mr. Whitby's first wife is dead. He wants to marry you. He came today to ask for your hand."

Missie gasped. "But I hardly know him! We just met the other day."

"Yes, I said that, too."

"And why does he want to marry me? He's much older and handsome as anything. There must be dozens of other girls—"

"He's a wealthy man, Missie," her father interrupted. "He could give you things I can never hope to provide."

The violet eyes widened. "Do you want me to marry him, Papa?"

"I don't feel I've a right to deny you this opportunity." His voice was husky with strain.

"I don't understand. There's something you're not telling me, Papa."

Turner's shoulders sagged. "Five years ago," he said quietly, "I thought I'd found a new process for tanning leather, a chemical process that would shorten the time involved by half. I thought it would revolutionize the industry, make my fortune. A number of men invested in the scheme. Mr. Whitby was one of them."

"It didn't work, did it?"

"It didn't work. All the investors lost every cent. I've been trying to repay the money, but it's been hard. There's only the income from your mother's trust and the little bit my father left me. I haven't reduced the debt to Mr. Whitby by much. Lately, he's been pressing hard."

"Before we met him in Boston?"

"Yes, before that."

"And if I marry him?"

"He'll forgive the debt, even pay off the other creditors. Missie"—he put his hand on her arm and turned her toward him—"you mustn't do it for that. I've only told you because I want to be honest. If it were just the debt, I'd never have mentioned the whole affair. I'd have sent him away."

"But you didn't." She moved away, embarrassed by the tears on her father's cheeks, not wanting him to know that her heart was hammering with excitement.

"No, because I've no right to deny you an opportunity that may never come again. He's a keen businessman, very well thought of not only in New England but in New York. He owns all kinds of land in Vermont. Even the town is named for his family, Whitby Falls."

"That's where we'd live? Whitby Falls?"

"I expect so."

"You didn't answer my earlier question. Why does he want to marry me?"

"Missie, Missie . . . How young you are, how innocent. You're very beautiful, child. Any man would want you for a wife."

She looked at him. "You're sweet to think that, Papa."
She was afraid to say more.

"He's coming back day after tomorrow. He wants an answer then."

All night she lay and listened to Susan's breathing in the next bed. She didn't think about her sister or her father or even about Jason Whitby, but about the house where she'd been born and grown up. She could see every shabby inch of it as clearly as if she were walking through the rooms. It hadn't always been thus; the decline had come gradually since her mother's death. Missie hated the peeling paint, the faded carpets. She hated the pitying looks of the neighbors and the overheard comments about "those poor motherless girls."

When she was little, she'd dreamed of a fairy godmother who would change everything with a magic wand. Later, the fantasy became a Prince Charming who would whisk her off to an enchanted kingdom. Now, when she was old enough to know that fairy stories weren't real, maybe the Prince Charming had arrived. "An opportunity that might never come again," Papa had said. She recognized the truth of the statement.

Missie suggested a June wedding, but Jason insisted it must be earlier. Business affairs, he explained. They should be wed as soon as possible. The date of the marriage was set for two weeks hence, the second of May. As it turned out, that was the day the schooner *Half Century* docked in New York.

2.

There was no sign of Jason's first wife in the house; Missie looked, but she could see nothing. "She died most unfortunately," Jason explained. "I'd prefer she not be mentioned again. I'm telling you only so you won't be shocked by some village busybody."

Missie didn't see how that could come to pass. There were too few people in Whitby Falls for there to be a village gossip. The place reminded her of a toy she and Susan loved when they were children, a paper stage set of a small town devoid of inhabitants except for the dolls the little girls supplied.

"Where is everybody?" she asked her husband of a week. It was her first day in her new home, a sunny May morning.

"I wondered if you'd noticed," Jason answered, laughing. He had a charming laugh, deep and hearty, with nothing of the timidity that had always marked her father's humor. "They've gone West, pursuing the American dream." The last words were bitter.

"Just left, you mean?" Her eyes widened, and she glanced across the rolling lawn to the deserted street.

"Exactly that. People have been doing it for decades, but back when the only transport was a covered wagon, it took some courage. Now all that's needed is the price of a railway ticket."

"But their homes, their work . . ." Missie gestured vaguely at the row of houses on either side of the Village Green.

"Not theirs," Jason said quietly. "All of Whitby Falls is mine, Millicent. Built by my father and grandfather and great-grandfather."

She didn't know what comment to make to this. How could a man own a whole town? The porch on which they stood was small, a simple but elegant frontage to the three-story brick house. Missie leaned against the classic white pillar and turned to look at her husband. "What am I to do here, Jason?"

Jason laughed again. "There'll be plenty for you to do; you'll see. To begin with, there's the house." He stepped closer and put a hand on her shoulder. His skin looked very dark against the pale ivory wool of her dress. "In a few days there are people arriving. Some thirty families. I've brought them from Wales."

It sounded to her as if he meant he'd purchased them. Dolls to fill up his stage set. "I don't understand."

"The Welshmen are slate workers," Jason said. "Experienced, good at the job. I've a quarry up there." He gestured to the looming shadow of Herrick Mountain behind the town. "It's just a small one my father started to meet local needs. I'm going to make it the biggest in Vermont. There's money to be made in slate, Millicent." He smiled at her. "The

Welshmen are bringing their families to live in those houses."
He pointed down the street.

"Did the people who lived there before work in the quarry?"
Millicent asked.

"Only a few; it's a small quarry now, as I said." He
sounded impatient. "The others farmed."

"And they left their farms behind when they went West?"

"My farm," he corrected. "My grandfather's, my father's,
and then mine. Time was when the Whitby dairy herd was the
largest in the East."

She strained to see the cows of which he spoke. Jason
chuckled. "They're all gone. Sold off last month. There's no
profit in dairying in Vermont anymore. That's why I'm enlarg-
ing the quarry."

A sense of unreality was settling over Missie, a feeling that
the universe she inhabited now was totally different from the
one she'd known in New Hampshire. "I see," she said
nonetheless. "At least I think I do."

"Good." Jason had left his hand on her shoulder all this
while. Now he increased the pressure, and his eyes looked
insistently into hers. "I expect you to be a good wife, a
perfect one. I knew it the first time I saw you."

"I'll try, Jason." Her voice was a whisper. She had not the
least idea of what he meant by "a good wife."

"I'm the last of the Whitbys, Millicent," he said fiercely.
"Give me sons." Then he reddened, the first time she'd seen
him show embarrassment, and abruptly turned away. "I've
things to see to. Why don't you take a walk? Stay out of the
hills, though. There's still a lot of snow."

She stretched out her hand to prevent his going. He'd
talked of future plans, but she still knew nothing of her duties
that day and the next. "Jason . . . What about dinner? Will
you be coming home? Am I to prepare a meal?"

"Dinner? Oh, you mean lunch. We dine at eight in the
evening, Millicent. Lunch is at noon. Yes, you'll have to do
it for the next few days. When the Welsh arrive, I'll hire
some of the women to staff the house."

Missie watched him stride off down the deserted street,
then turned and went back into the house.

Nothing was faded or threadbare there. It was all mahogany and velvet and brass, all shiny and perfect. The flocked
wallpapers glowed with color; the turkey carpets were spotless.

Who had made it so? Jason's first wife? Was she perhaps still warm in her grave, watching from some world beyond the replacement whom her husband had quickly and unceremoniously chosen? Missie shivered.

That morning, breakfast had been waiting on the dining-room table when they descended the stairs. But whatever mysterious agency had provided the meal had not cleared it away.

She gathered the dirty dishes and carried them through the swinging door to the butler's pantry. The kitchen was in the back where she expected it to be. It was well equipped: two soapstone sinks, a big ice chest, shelves full of crockery and glass, a door that led to a pantry, a great cooking fireplace with two ovens beside, and even a coal stove. Friends in Nashua had purchased such a stove the year before. It was the latest thing. Missie had envied it then, marveled at its shiny efficiency. Now, possessed of one of her own, or at least of her husband's, she was terrified by it. She left the dirty dishes in the sink and ran out the back door.

Sons, he'd said. He'd married her to acquire sons. Why should she be shocked at that? Didn't children inevitably follow marriage?

The sun shone brighter; it was nearly eleven. Missie walked the length of the road that skirted the Village Green. She studied her surroundings, struggling to dispel the sense of unreality. Houses marched either side of the street, uniform in their pitched roofs and white clapboard and small picket fences. Saltboxes, they were called.

Scattered among them were shops. But there were no people in them. There was a church, white wood like almost everything else, and one red brick building that looked to be a school. When she produced her sons, would they be educated there? Would they be alone? In all of Whitby Falls she heard no child's voice, saw no evidence of a toy or a carriage.

Two big houses, not as grand as Jason's but finer than the saltboxes, marked the end of the street. Each had a shingle hanging outside. The one on the right said, "Josiah Sills, M.D."; that on the left, "Lliam Murray, Attorney at Law." Both houses were as silent and empty as the rest of Whitby Falls.

Where the road ended, there was a stone marker with the words "Main Street" etched in amateur letters. Fields stretched beyond—and a long row of barns she now knew to be empty. Behind them were wooded hills. Everything was still except for the sound, sudden and unexpected, of running water.

She picked her way carefully toward the stream. It was hidden by stands of pine and maple on either side. A few of the yet leafless trees had buckets hanging on wooden pegs. Sugaring off. The phrase leaped into her mind from some long-ago school lesson. Maple trees produced sap that became syrup and sugar. Delicious, and an important factor in the economy of the state of Vermont, according to her teacher. But there weren't enough buckets there to be important to any economy, just three tapped trees lazily yielding a trickle of colorless liquid. Missie touched the stuff gingerly and raised her finger to her tongue.

"Is no taste yet. Boil it down first; then it's good."

The voice startled her, and she guiltily thrust the tasting finger behind her back. "I just wanted to try," she said quickly. "I didn't mean to take any."

The man laughed. He stood with his back to the sun, and Missie could see nothing but the bulky outline of his form. "You can do what you wish. You're her, no? The new wife of Mr. Whitby?"

"Yes." His accent was peculiar; she couldn't place it at first. "I'm Mrs. Whitby." The title was unfamiliar, like everything else. "May I know your name?"

"Why not? Maybe that, too, belongs to your husband, like everything here, like the sap from the maple tree. I'm Jacques Villette. Me and my family, we live by the covered bridge over there."

"Jacques . . . That's a French name, isn't it?"

"Canadian. *Quebecois*. We are ten years in the town of Mr. Whitby. Now I am called Jack."

"By whom?" She looked back toward the deserted village. "I haven't seen anyone but you."

"No." He hooted with laughter, but there was no mirth in it. "You have not. Nobody left. They go West, go where they can buy their own land. No more be only Whitby tenants."

Missie sensed that he was broaching a subject she dare not discuss. "You said you had a family?"

"Yes, a wife and three boys. Soon we have another baby."

On cue, a woman stepped out of the trees. Her enormous

belly thrust forward beneath her shapeless, colorless cloak. A small boy clung to her hand. "So, you are the new wife," she said by way of greeting. "Why you come down here?"

"I took a walk," Missie said defensively. "I wanted to see the town."

"Not much to see." The woman pushed a strand of dank black hair from her forehead and absent-mindedly cuffed the little boy, who was tugging at her hand.

"This is my wife, Eve," the man said. "And that's our oldest boy, Hugh." He stepped to the tree while he spoke and retrieved a bucket of sap.

Missie could smell him. He was sour and dirty, and he had a matted black beard as unkempt as his wife's hair. She moved away and gathered close the full skirt of her ivory dress. Jack Villette seemed not to notice the gesture, but his wife did.

"You liked your breakfast?" she asked.

"It was fine. Delicious. Did you—"

"*Oui*, all the cooking and cleaning of the big house I do since the others left. If you want, I continue. There is nobody else." She spoke the words defiantly.

To Missie, the opportunity was heaven sent. "Oh, yes! If you could. Mr. Whitby, my husband, that is, he said he would hire some of the Welsh ladies. But they're not here yet, and there's dinner, I mean lunch, to fix . . ."

"*Oui*." The woman smiled in triumph. "I'll go now and fix the lunch. I know what is liked by Mr. Jason Whitby." She pushed the little boy toward his father, but the child sidled up to Missie.

"Do not bother the lady," Jacques said.

The boy ignored him. He was staring up at Missie, and she found herself staring back. One pudgy little hand reached out and stroked the soft wool of her dress. "Pretty," he lisped. "Hugh likes pretty . . ."

Jacques reached out and pulled the child away. "Sorry," he muttered. "Is stubborn, this one. I will beat sense into him."

"Oh, no! You mustn't beat the child on my account. He's done no harm." He had, in fact, left a muddied imprint of his fingers on her dress. Missie quickly adjusted the folds so that the stain didn't show. "No harm at all," she repeated.

The other woman grunted with something half humor, half scorn. "Jacques don't beat the boys. All talk. Only talk."

Missie was embarrassed for the husband, but he seemed to pay little attention to his wife's words. "About lunch . . ." Missie stammered.

"I don't forget," Eve Villette said. "At noon, it is ready, Mrs. Whitby." The title sounded somehow evil in her mouth.

Eve trudged away toward the village, her huge belly going before her like a warning. Soon the man left, too, carrying the bucket of sap, and the little boy followed in his wake. No one said good-bye. Missie stood alone by the rushing stream and listened to the sound of water and the wind in the leafless trees. She pressed her hands over her flat stomach and pondered what it would be like when she, too, was swollen with child. It struck her as outrageous that she must display a souvenir of all that sweating and straining and groaning in the dark.

"How did she get here?" Jason asked, tight-lipped, when Eve Villette deposited the platter of pork chops on the table and returned to the kitchen.

"I met her this morning. I went for a walk like you said, Jason. She said she worked here since the other people left. And she offered to go on, at least until the Welsh women arrive. It seemed a good idea . . ." Her voice trailed off, and she stared at the polished wood of the table.

Jason didn't answer right away. When he did, his voice was expressionless. "Very well. Until the others come. They're due the end of the week."

That night, while she sat at the dressing table in the bedroom and brushed her long blond hair, he stood behind her, staring at her face in the glass, and said, "Don't have any more to do with those Canadians than you can help. They're troublemakers, and they're filthy."

Missie put down the pearl-handled brush and turned to her husband. "Are they your tenants? Don't you own the land down by the river?"

"Of course I do. Their cabin, too."

"Then if you don't like them, why don't you send them away?" She knew it was a dangerous question, but she couldn't keep from uttering it. For a moment she saw rage on Jason's face. She thought he was going to strike her. Then his hand dropped back by his side.

"Come to bed," he said quietly. "It's late."

She climbed in beside him and waited while he turned down the wick of the oil lamp. Then he moved toward her in the dark, and she felt his hands sliding up the soft linen of her nightdress. She lay still, frightened and angry because she understood so little.

"Spread your legs," he commanded when she made no motion to receive him.

She did as she was told. The sheets were cold, and even his body felt icy as he rolled on top of her. For a few seconds nothing happened. Then she felt the turgid thrust of his male organ, and he was pounding his hips into hers. She lay quiet until he was finished.

"In the future," Jason said when he had caught his breath, "don't make decisions without consulting me."

3.

At the end of the week, the Welsh arrived. They came in wagons heavy with trunks and boxes and blanket rolls, drawn by tired, sweaty horses. When the extraordinary caravan lumbered into Whitby Falls, Jason was standing on his elegant porch. He remained there as the tall man riding in the lead wagon jumped down and went to join him.

"Evening, Jason."

"Evening, Lliam. All present and accounted for?"

"Every man jack of them. I should say man Jones. Half the people of Wales are named Jones; other half, Edwards."

"It'll keep things simple, then," Jason said, grinning. He moved away from the pillar against which he was leaning and called into the house, "Millicent, come here a moment, please. There's someone I want you to meet." Then, when she'd stepped out the door, "My dear, this is Lliam Murray, my attorney and business associate. He's brought the Welshmen, as you can see. Lliam, my new wife, Millicent Turner Whitby."

Murray bowed and took her hand. His surprise was obvious. "Delighted, ma'am, and astounded. I've been gone less than four months, Jason; you've obviously been both busy and lucky." He surveyed the young woman appreciatively but with deference.

"So have you," Jason rejoined. He turned to his wife. "Lliam and Sarah live at the end of Main Street. That big white house with the green shutters."

"Yes, I've admired it many times since I came, Mr. Murray. Your wife traveled to Wales with you, I take it?"

"No, ma'am. Sarah and the children have been with her parents in Rutland while I was away. They'll be returning tomorrow. I'm sure the two of you will be great friends."

"I'd like that. And please, call me Missie. At least that's what everyone called me back home in New Hampshire."

"This is your home now, my dear," Jason interrupted. "And Missie was all right for a child, not a married lady."

There was an edge to his voice, and Murray shot him a strange look before he said quickly, "Millicent, then. Now, if you'll excuse me, we've come a long way. I'll see to getting these people bedded down for the night."

Jason withdrew a folded sheet of paper from his pocket. "I've assigned the houses. Thirty families, isn't it?"

"Twenty-seven. Three backed out at the last minute."

"No matter," Whitby said. "Get them settled and tell them to be on the Green tomorrow morning nine sharp. I'll speak to them then."

She wanted to stay and watch them unload, but Jason led her inside. "I'm delighted to have met you, Lliam," she called over her shoulder. "Please tell your wife I'll call in a few days when she's had a chance to settle."

"Thank you." He was halfway down the path before he turned back and asked, "Did you say New Hampshire? Are you Edgar Turner's daughter, ma'am?"

"Yes!" Her voice was gay for the first time in many days. It was wonderful to be recognized, to be a person again. "You know my father, then?"

Murray didn't answer. It was possible he didn't hear her; the wagons and the horses were making a lot of noise, but the look he gave Whitby belied it. In the house, Jason said sternly, "It's not your place to call on Sarah Murray, Millicent. She will call on you. I'm sure she knows that even if you don't."

*   *   *

Some hundred and fifty people gathered on the Green the next morning. Missie had been afraid she wouldn't be allowed to attend, but it turned out that Jason expected her to go with him. "Wear your dark blue gown today," he said to her first thing after they woke. "It's appropriate to the occasion."

Dutifully, she donned the serge with its highbutton neck and black velvet trim, but it didn't suit her mood. Missie was gay. With people in Whitby Falls it would be more like Nashua; she would begin to feel like a normal wife—at least as she imagined a normal wife must feel. She was disappointed when she saw the platform erected for her and Jason and Lliam Murray. It had three stiff chairs and was separated from the throngs of people. She'd have preferred to mingle.

"Good morning, ladies and gentlemen," Murray began as soon as the three took their places on the shaky podium. He had brown hair slick with pomade and a neat brown moustache. The sun winked on his rimless glasses. "Glad to see you back, Hiram, and you, Willis," he said. Two men acknowledged the greetings from somewhere toward the back of the crowd. "Now, folks, for the benefit of the newcomers from Wales, let me say a few things obvious to the rest of us. This town is Whitby Falls, in the state of Vermont. We're about two hundred miles north of New York City and eight miles southwest of Rutland, a slightly smaller place." There were chuckles from a few of the natives. The Welsh didn't laugh; they continued to look attentively at Murray.

"That rather large hill behind us is Herrick Mountain. It's some twenty-five hundred feet tall and belongs to the Taconic range. Herrick can be friend or foe, as you'll come to find out. About a quarter mile down this road is the Little Whitby river. It rises up on Herrick and empties into the Poultney four miles southwest of here. Apart from the slate, this isn't bad soil. That ornery-looking gent standing by himself over there is Jeb Stuart."

A number of folks turned to look where Murray was pointing, but the man so identified continued to stare at his boots. "Jeb runs Sugarbush Farm." Missie noted that Lliam said "runs," not owns. "He has a fine herd of dairy cows and grows good wheat and barley. We've a gristmill, too, so you ladies won't want for flour to bake your bread. And we've everything else needed. Hiram, take a step forward, will you?"

"That's Hiram Howard, runs the clothing and dry goods store just across the road. And the fellow next to him is Willis Phillips, the boot maker. Our grocery store is without a manager at the moment. Frank Anderson, who ran it up till now, died last winter. But it looks as if his wife, Phoebe, is coming home, and she'll be opening up by the end of the week."

Murray paused and looked around. The unseasonably warm spring air had been replaced by a more typical chill. A number of people were stamping their feet and clapping their hands to keep warm.

"Now I want to introduce the man who has hired you, brought you from Wales, and will make it possible for you to have good lives here in America. His great-grandfather bought this land from the governor of New York when such grants were being sold. Before Vermont was even a name, let alone a state. That was in 1778. Today, seventy-two years later, the family tradition is upheld. Ladies and gentlemen, Mr. Jason Whitby." Murray himself began the applause.

Missie thought Jason looked more handsome than she'd ever seen him. He wore no coat despite the cold, and his black suit was cut to accentuate his tall slimness. A breeze ruffled his black and silver hair, and he looked tanned and healthy compared to the pasty, tired faces staring up at him from the Green.

"Lliam's told you all the basics," Jason began. "I want to tell you about the slate. Little of it has been dug in this country until now. Most of what we use here in America has come from your native Wales. But it's there"—he gestured toward the west—"and we're going to quarry it."

"Are you sure, sir?" The voice that interrupted from the crowd had the gentle cadence of Wales, but the question was tinged with fear. "Sure there's slate, that is?"

"I'm sure, lad," Whitby answered. "I wouldn't have transported a hundred-plus people across the Atlantic if I weren't. And I've already made contact with some of the biggest roofing contractors in the East. So all that remains is to dig the stuff out of the earth. As we agreed by correspondence some months ago, you'll be paid twelve dollars a month. Your houses are rent free, part of your wages, and the shops here in Whitby Falls will give you as much credit as you need. Now, are there any questions?"

There was silence for some seconds. The wind picked up; the leafless trees around the Green sighed and creaked. Jason was about to dismiss the assembly when a short, stocky man raised his hand.

"I'm Gareth Jones, sir. 'Tis I that made the arrangements with Mr. Murray and brought the lads over. I wanted to ask about the children, sir."

Jason looked at the crowd. There were many children present. "Those old enough and strong enough to work will be given jobs either in the quarry or here in town. As for the little ones, that brick building across from the church is a school. Come September, there will be a teacher."

A few of the women murmured appreciatively, and one or two even called out a thank you. "There's something else," Whitby said. "I understand that most of you folks are of the Methodist faith. I've arranged for a minister of your persuasion to call here once every two months." A ripple of pleasure passed through the crowd. Missie felt her heart swell with pride. He was good to them, thoughtful. It wasn't just a matter of buying dolls to stock his play town, after all.

"Now it's getting cold, and we've all work to do. This afternoon I'll meet with the slate workers at the quarry site. We start digging tomorrow."

The sound of erupting black powder became the background of Millicent's days. The noise punctuated the things she learned, the way she changed. When she decided she must be Millicent, not Missie, even in her own mind, the thought was confirmed by the loudest explosion yet heard in Whitby Falls.

To enlarge the quarry, the men had moved as much earth as possible with shovels and barrows, but the scar they opened was shallow. It exposed only something called "freak slate" or "golden pheasants." They weren't workable or profitable, because they wouldn't split evenly into the small squares needed to make roofs. To find that precious stuff, they must go deeper, blast away the worthless layers and find the mother lode. Millicent decided her life was like that, too.

Gradually, a few natives of Whitby Falls returned; not those who'd joined the westward migration, only those who'd been left behind and believed the town dead. With the coming of the Welsh and the opening of the quarry, they came home.

By summer, the shops were open again. Even Dr. Sills had moved back to his house on Main Street. His wife, Tessa, came to call on the new Mrs. Whitby. So did Lliam Murray's wife, Sarah. They were the only two women in town more or less her social equals; the others she met less formally. But none of them provided her with the information that furthered her education. That came from Eve Villette.

Millicent hired Martha and Nelly Jones, two Welsh women, to work in the house, as Jason instructed, but she kept the Canadian on, too. Jason was too busy at the pit to notice, or at least too busy to comment. Eve didn't cook or clean; she just came to get the laundry, which she took home to wash and iron. Millicent said little to her until one hot September day.

She took a bundle of clean linen from the other woman's hands and put it on the table. Eve had borne her baby, a girl, some weeks earlier, and Millicent found herself staring at the transformation in the French woman's shape. That she wore no corsets or petticoats was obvious from the way her breasts and buttocks jiggled beneath her ragged dress. Millicent was fascinated and repelled. She was envious, too. On such a warm day the freedom from such clothing must be blissful. "Have a glass of lemonade before you go," she said impulsively.

"Don't mind," Eve said.

"How's your baby? What's her name, anyway?"

"Maryann. Jack wanted Marie, but I tell him no more French names. No one pronounce them right. My second boy, Raoul, everyone call him Riley. Like Irish. For young Jacques, they say Jackie."

Millicent ignored most of this. "Eve," she said slowly, "when your babies were born, did you have a doctor?" Both Tessa and Sarah were mothers, but she'd never had the nerve to question them about childbirth.

"Course not. What for I need doctor? Is natural . . . Why you ask? *Alors!* I guess. You're pregnant, no?"

"Yes, I think so."

"Think so! Must be yes or no. If you no bleed every month, then you are pregnant."

Millicent dropped her eyes. No one she knew ever talked like that, not even she and Susan. "Yes," she said finally. "I'm expecting in February."

"Ah, that is why you do not yet show. But is lucky that you are pregnant. The other one, the first wife, she hanged herself from right here." Eve pointed to one of the beams overhead.

Millicent gasped and stared at the spot.

"You didn't know that, eh?" The French woman laughed softly, a tired, bitter sound. "Was beautiful, the first one, like you, but barren. Four years married to Jason and no baby starts. Not even the miscarriage. She could stand it no more, so . . ." Eve clasped her hands to her throat expressively.

Later, a strange idea struck Millicent. How come the Villette woman called him Jason? Almost everyone else said Mr. Whitby. Somehow that thought was more disturbing than the suicide of her predecessor.

4.

In January, when Millicent's first baby was born a month premature, it was snowing. She watched the great white flakes plummeting down outside her bedroom window as Dr. Sills told her gently that the child, a little boy, was dead. "Stillborn, my dear. I'm so sorry."

Millicent was sorry, too, and she felt guilty, because she'd insisted on going for a walk in the heavy snow the afternoon of the day she went into labor. "That's got nothing to do with it, Mrs. Whitby. You mustn't blame yourself. Besides, you're very young. Not eighteen until April, isn't it? You've plenty of time for more babies. A whole houseful of them."

She tried to keep those calm, sensible comments in mind, tried not to brood and to ignore the look of disappointment on Jason's face. She even tried to avoid looking at the spot in the kitchen where the first Mrs. Whitby had hung herself.

Sills told Whitby he must forego his marital rights for at least six weeks, but it was less than a month after the delivery when he rolled on top of her and poured his seed into her belly once more. He seemed angry, as if he wanted to punish her, and it occurred to Millicent that he wasn't enjoying the act as much as he usually did. Still she lay beneath him, silent and immobile, and told herself it was natural. This was the way marriage was. Besides, she wanted another baby as much as he did.

When spring came, she was pregnant again. This time she showed earlier and was bigger than she had been before. Maybe it was twins. That would be wonderful.

At the quarry they'd begun taking out real slate, and the first shipment was floated down the Little Whitby toward New York in early June. In the beginning they'd planned to transport all the slate that way, but Jason announced a startling bit of news on the afternoon of the big "bee" to raise a barn at the quarry site.

They needed the barn to stable the horses and mules that pulled the wagonloads of slate up from the pit. That first summer and autumn they'd been busy just opening the new veins; then the winter came, and the snow made barn raising impossible. Now, in June of 1851, the barn was completed with the help of every able-bodied man and boy in the town. When the last nail was in place, the women went to join the men, carrying baskets of home-baked beans, breads and cakes, and leading a cart loaded with hard cider and rum.

They'd all had a few glasses by the time Jason swung up to the hayloft and called out to everyone to be quiet and listen. "I've been in Rutland this past week," he said when he finally had their attention. "And I can tell you now that the news is definite. We've gotten together, couple of slatemen like myself and those fellows quarrying marble a few miles north. We're going to have a railroad from Rutland to Salem, New York. Going to be called the Rutland and Washington Railroad."

Everyone cheered and drank some more, and the new barn looked splendid. So did the three shanties where "slitters," as the Welsh called them, sat and carved the great blocks of rock into the proper size and shape for roof tiles. Millicent thought it all appeared invincible in the moonlight. When they walked home, she took Jason's hand.

That night, he turned to her with a slightly more relaxed air, and it took him longer than usual to finish. Millicent felt a stirring of pleasure between her legs, and she heard herself breathe a tiny little moan and felt her hips bounce gently once or twice.

Jason rolled away and sat on the edge of the bed. He was

breathing hard and fast, and it didn't seem the result of his exertions. "Don't do that," he said softly. "Don't ever do that again. Decent women don't."

She didn't understand what was so terrible about her tiny reaction, compared to his much greater one, but she was too frightened by his tone not to comply. After that, she made sure that she lay very still and she bit her lips to be sure no sound would escape. It wasn't difficult. She never again felt those slight stirrings of enjoyment. But she didn't comprehend any of it until a day in August when she was walking along by the river because she thought she'd suffocate if she stayed in the house one more minute.

"Damn you . . . Damn you to hell! Stop it, no, don't . . . Ahh . . ."

She recognized Jason's voice, but she could make no sense of the words or the tone. Millicent knew she should turn around and walk home and pretend it had never happened, but she couldn't. She moved a little closer to the sound, terrified lest she be caught, trying to be silent despite her bulky, pregnant body.

They were lying behind a stand of ferns deep in a glen of pines. Jason was naked, and so was Eve Villette. Their clothes made an untidy heap a few feet from their bodies. Millicent stared, unable to believe what she saw.

Eve had her head buried between Jason's legs. She was doing something to him, something incredible. For a moment, Millicent thought she was biting off his male organ, and she gasped aloud, then clapped her hand over her lips. Neither of them heard her. Later, she realized they were so intent on their pleasure that they would not have heard her had she blown a bugle. She wanted to run, but she couldn't. The mixture of horror and fascination was akin to what she felt every time she went into the kitchen and stared at the spot of the suicide.

"Now, for God's sake!" Jason moaned aloud. "I want you now."

Eve didn't answer, but she changed her position. When he mounted her, her hips writhed as vigorously as his own, and her strong tanned legs were clasped around his buttocks. She was moaning as loud as he did and shuddering. Millicent knew instinctively it was almost over. If she stayed now they would see her, as soon as their passion was spent. The thought of being discovered was too terrible to contemplate. She moved away, and when she heard their final scream of pleasure, it was from a distance.

For the next few days she made sure she wasn't at home when Eve came to collect or deliver laundry, and she pleaded her condition as reason for going to bed before dinner. Once, at the end of the week, Jason made a gesture implying he intended to take her. She moaned aloud and clasped her head and complained of how ill she was feeling.

It wasn't wholly false. She felt sick in body and soul and mind, and she spent many hours sitting in the small summer house at the bottom of the garden attempting to catalogue her feelings and understand them.

The effort was ended before it reached fruition. Two weeks to the day from the afternoon in which she'd observed her husband in his perverse and animallike infidelity, she went into premature labor. When this son, too, was stillborn, Millicent wasn't sorry. She looked at Jason's disappointed face and thought, It serves you right. But later, when she was alone, she cried. The tears wouldn't stop. They came and came, and she knew she was crying for much that had nothing to do with losing another baby.

Jason knew she knew; Millicent was sure of it. He shot guilty looks in her direction when he thought she wouldn't notice, and at night they lay in frozen, heavy isolation next to each other in the big four-poster bed. When he announced the first week in October that he was going to New York, it was a relief. Business, he said; five days or so.

Millicent changed her tack. While Jason was gone, she sought out every opportunity to be with Eve Villette. The other woman didn't seem to notice anything. Millicent watched her carefully, studying the jiggling breasts and bouncing buttocks evident beneath her flimsy, ill-fitting clothes. Eve, she decided, was homely. Her skin was sallow, her hair limp and without sheen. When she talked, her full mouth distorted the shapes and sounds of the words. Her French accent wasn't charming; it was a bastardization of the language.

Millicent thought about that word. Bastardization, bastard . . . Were Eve's sons Jason's bastards? Was Maryann? And Eve mentioned one afterooon that she was pregnant again. She said it casually, with no hidden meanings or innuendo.

Another bastard, most likely. What did Jason see in her? Why did he break his marriage vows on her behalf?

The girl remembered the scene often, with every detail vivid in her mind—the writhing bodies, the patterns and shadows of the leaves in the dappled sunlight, the distant sound of the falls. Eve was shameless. She made those responses that angered Jason. Hadn't he been repelled the one night Millicent involuntarily took pleasure in the marriage bed? But he must not feel that way about Eve Villette. On the contrary, his fondness for her—was that the proper word? —made him tolerate the Villettes' tenancy in the tumble-down log cabin; the idle, slovenly behavior he would allow no other resident of Whitby Falls.

While she pondered these strangenesses, Millicent looked poorly. Dr. Sills gave her a tonic; his wife, Tessa, and Sarah Murray both remarked on how thin and pale she seemed. Everyone attributed the condition to her two failed pregnancies. She confided the true cause to no one.

Jason's stay in New York was prolonged. When he'd been gone ten days, Lliam Murray called at the big house. "Sarah and I are going to Rutland for the day, Millicent. Come with us; the trip will do you good."

The journey took a couple of hours at this time of year, when the roads were open and hard-packed. The two chest-nuts pulling Murray's carriage knew the way and didn't mind the twisting, turning route dictated by the mountains and the streams. The three riders spoke little. The countryside was aflame with autumn splendor.

Millicent breathed in the pure fresh air and didn't think about her problems. The Murrays seemed content with the quick results of their prescription for her well-being.

"It's your first visit to Rutland, isn't it?" Lliam asked when they neared the town.

"Yes. Is it much like Nashua?" Millicent regretted the touch of homesickness in her voice.

"A bit, perhaps. Smaller, though. But that won't last long, I warrant. Take a look at that." He gestured with his whip, and both ladies peered in the direction he indicated.

"It's just a half-built building, Lliam," Sarah Murray complained. "What's so special about that?"

Murray laughed. "Wait a bit, ladies. Just you wait a bit and see."

They were on West Street, a cemetery at their backs and a row of fine houses ahead of them. Murray turned the carriage down Merchant's Row, then reined in. "I've business here. Have a look round the shops, ladies. Later, we'll meet for luncheon at Bardwell House."

Sarah bought some lace and a lovely gray silk bonnet trimmed with pink roses. "The color suits you," Millicent said. Sarah had eyes the same soft color as the silk and roses in her cheeks that rivaled those on the hat. She was a small, stocky woman, not pretty in the usual sense but appealing.

Millicent bought nothing, just looked. She didn't mention that she had no money. Jason never gave her any, and until then it hadn't occurred to her she might need it. In Whitby Falls, the shopkeepers automatically marked down on her account anything she purchased.

By one they were seated at a table in Bardwells.

"I've a surprise for you, Millicent," Lliam said, eyes sparkling. "Two, in fact."

"Oh, I love surprises! Tell me."

"Well, the first has to do with all of us. But it'll make you specially proud, I think. My business this morning was with the owners of that unfinished building you girls thought so little of—Rutland's new railroad depot. It's now decided, the place will have a roof of Whitby slate. Not even Jason knows yet. You can tell him soon as he gets home."

At the mention of her husband, Millicent lowered her eyes. Both her friends pretended not to notice. "That's fine, Lliam," she said as warmly as she could manage. "But it's your cap that wears the feather. You tell Jason."

"Very well. Here's the second surprise." He withdrew an envelope from his pocket. "Letter for you. I picked it up at the post office." Murray made a trip to Rutland to collect the mail for Whitby Falls twice a month. He knew that Millicent received few communications from her family.

"It's from Susan, my sister," Millicent said. "Her hand is very distinctive. You can't miss it."

"Go ahead, Milly dear." Sarah was the only person alive who called her Milly. "Read it. We won't take any notice."

"No, that's all right. I'll save it for later, if you don't mind." She tucked the envelope into her silk drawstring bag and looked at her companions. They all seemed to be searching for something to talk about. Fortunately, the soup arrived just then and created a diversion.

5.

Susan was going to be married. Millicent read the news in the privacy of the drawing room at dusk. A fire leaped in the grate and cast sparkling reflections from the crystal wall sconces and the polished mahogany floor. There was a gilt-framed mirror over the marble mantel, and she could see herself in it, oddly distorted by the dancing flames. She looked hard, brittle even.

Her sister's fiancé was Tom Mulberry, a boy they'd both known since childhood, a nice boy. He wasn't wealthy and probably never would be. Susan would have no room like Millicent's. She wouldn't rest her feet on a fabulous turkey carpet or recline in a slipper chair of exquisite brocade. Millicent had no cause to envy Susan.

Had it not been for Millicent's spectacular gesture of selflessness, agreeing to marry a man she hardly knew, there would have been a scandal. Susan's wedding would not be taking place. That's why she'd done it, wasn't it? To make the future safe and secure for Papa and Susan?

"No, for myself." The words startled her. She spoke them aloud in the empty room, repeated them. "I married Jason Whitby because I wanted to." It was the first time she had admitted the truth, though she'd known it all along deep inside herself. It came as a surprise.

I married Jason—she was careful just to think the words this time; she mustn't start mumbling to shadows like some daft old woman—because I wanted to be rich. I wanted to share the world of a man who looked and sounded as sophisticated and sure of himself as Jason Whitby did. In the bargain, I got to feel noble about it. Now there's no sense acting like a martyr because the idol has feet of clay and the dreamworld is tarnished and rather lonely.

She rose and went to the kitchen to eat her solitary supper. It wasn't dinner unless Jason was with her and they ate in the dining room.

*   *   *

The following day he returned from New York, excited and happy. "You won't believe the things I've accomplished," he said. "Sold tons of roofs! Everyone's saying the Whitby Quarry produces the best slate in the country. With this railroad, we're going to make a fortune!"

"The railroad depot in Rutland," she said softly, made shy by his uncustomary high spirits, "it's going to have a slate roof, too. Lliam Murray arranged it and told me to tell you."

"Hah!" He picked her up by the waist and swung her around the room. "The quarry's a winner, Millicent. A genuine, bona fide American success. Despite all the Cassandras who said it couldn't be done."

"I'm glad for you, Jason. Truly glad." Her violet eyes glistened with unshed tears, though she didn't know why.

"Millicent"—he set her down but kept his hands on her delicate, narrow hips—"I'm sorry the way things have been between us, your losing the babies and all."

"So am I, Jason."

He led her upstairs to their bedroom, despite its being not yet eight o'clock, and undressed her. It was the first time her naked body had been exposed to him—she had always undressed in the privacy of her dressing room and worn her nightgown to bed—and Millicent trembled with the strangeness of it all. I can't be like her, she thought in sudden panic. I can't be like Eve; he mustn't expect it.

He didn't. The act was as formal and quick as always. Still, given all the things she had finally admitted to herself and the unusual boyishness of his mood, Millicent felt a kind of satisfaction when it was over.

The railroad began operating in December, and the quarry changed its shipping pattern. No longer did they float their heavy cargo down the Little Whitby river on cumbersome barges. Now they hauled the squares of carefully cut tiles of slate cross-country to Castleton, where it was loaded on the freight train. It meant harder work, more labor for men and animals, but it was cheaper and faster in the long run, Jason said. His elation continued until February of the new year of 1852.

The snows came late but with a vengeance; a relentless, steady fall coupled with temperatures so low it should have been too cold to snow. The small gauge trains with their woodburning engines were no match for the weather. The

Little Whitby froze over. There was no way to get the slate to the buyers.

The great blocks they cut from the open pit came up with no more difficulty than usual. The brawny, clever Welshmen carved them out of the earth and slung the gray-green blocks into the wagons. The teamsters, some of the older Welsh lads and some locals, bullied and cajoled the horses and mules up the steep sides of the quarry and brought the hard-won bounty to the shanties where the skilled craftsmen waited. But the slitters needed damp slate to work. At the right temperature and moisture the stuff would split into perfect sheets with each carefully directed blow of the chisel and mallet. Frozen rock shattered into useless fragments, becoming just so much rubble to add to the growing heaps surrounding the quarry.

Jason grew tense and short-tempered. The faces of everyone in Whitby Falls showed strain. One night, Willis Phillips, the boot maker, led a delegation of tradesmen to the big house.

"Mr. Whitby, the accounts is gettin' out of hand."

"I know, Willis," Jacob said. "I review the books every month."

"Yes, sir, we know that." Hiram Howard was a small man, crippled since birth by a too short leg, but his voice was astonishingly big and booming. Millicent could hear him plainly out in the hall. "But beggin' your pardon, sir, it don't make no sense to keep giving credit when there's no money to pay."

"The quarry workers aren't paid if there's no way to cut the slate and no way to ship it," Jason said. "They need to eat and clothe their families all the same. You have to extend their credit. Come spring, they'll catch up."

"No way they can catch up," Willis said. "Not on their pay."

"But that's not your problem, is it?" Jason's voice was calm and reasonable. "As long as cash is passing through your hands, it doesn't matter about the accounts."

"That's just it," said Phoebe Anderson, who ran the grocery. "There is no cash. We got to pay our suppliers, Mr. Whitby. And we got to pay you our rent, if it comes to that."

"Well, Phoebe, the last is easy to remedy. Let's say you all have three months' free rent this winter. Nothing due again until May. As for your suppliers, tell them to contact me if they have problems. Meanwhile, you let the quarry workers charge up as much as they need to. Understood?''

There were murmurs of assent, but the tradespeople didn't look happy as they filed out into the bitter, snowy night. Millicent thought Jason's offer more than fair, and she didn't see why the others weren't satisfied.

Spring came with a rush of full, churning waters hurtling down from Herrick Mountain. There were floods. The falls became treacherous. A three-year-old Welsh lad was carried away and drowned as his mother gathered spring greens a few feet away.

Eventually, the elements subsided. Summer was gentle and dry, and the town relaxed. The sound of blasting resumed at the pit, and Millicent moved slowly through the days and nights, waiting.

This baby was more active than either of the other two. It kicked and squirmed constantly. At least she knew it was alive.

Jason urged her to get more involved with the town. "It's your rightful place, my dear," he insisted. "Simple people like these need someone to look up to."

She didn't know why the others should look up to her, a woman who couldn't even keep her own husband faithful, but she dared not disobey him. Besides, she was convinced that no one in Whitby Falls knew about Jason and Eve. No one but her. The lovers were very discreet. There was no hint, no suggestion of scandal.

Millicent took to visiting the Welsh women in their homes. She called after lunch every Wendesday and Friday. It became a regular routine. She carried a basket of something special, some luxury the workers were unlikely to be able to afford, and left little tokens behind her in selected houses.

The visits were not outwardly remarkable. Mostly, Millicent simply exchanged greetings and gossip with the women. Sometimes she was able to do something she saw as "true charity"—report a problem back to Jason, perhaps help to arrange housing for a youngster being married. Once in a while she could make an effort at nursing someone who was ill or mind a baby while the mother went to the store. It all seemed quite natural once she got the hang of it. And everyone approved. Even Jason.

Millicent always tried to make her presence calming. "Simple people get excited easily," Jason had warned her. But when she heard about Eve Villette's new daughter—"A fine healthy baby, ma'am. Beautiful too . . ."—she turned away. Jealousy wasn't the name for it, not anymore. She hated Eve. Hated all the Villettes. Even the newborn infant. Canucks—that's what they were. Dirty, ignorant Canucks.

"That's nice," she managed to say finally. "I'm glad they're both well. Though it does seem that a woman shouldn't just go on having children, then taking such poor care of them."

The informant nodded her head. A hardworking Welsh woman, she shared Mrs. Whitby's opinion of the Villettes. "It does that, ma'am. Still, they're Catholics, you know. Got to expect something like that."

Millicent did not wish to seem guilty of religious prejudice. "I don't think that's the reason," she said quietly. "There are Catholic families in Rutland who behave quite decently, I'm told. Besides, I don't believe the Villettes practice any faith. They're just . . ."

"Just Canucks," the other woman supplied. "We've learned about them since we came. Not much good for anything, are they?"

Good for writhing in the grass and acting like an animal, Millicent thought. She smiled and took her leave. Later, she studied her swollen body in the glass in her room. A fine, healthy baby, that's what Eve had produced. "Please," she prayed aloud. "Don't let her have everything. It isn't fair."

She dared not confront Jason, accuse him of fathering yet another bastard. Indeed, she had no desire to do so. It wasn't his fault, she decided. It was that woman's doing. She had bewitched him.

A week later, on the seventeenth of July 1852, she felt a rush of water down her legs as she descended the stairs for breakfast. Millicent returned to her bed and sent for Dr. Sills.

It was all over before he reached the house. Martha Jones, one of the Welsh serving women, assisted at the birth of Millicent's daughter. The baby came into the world red-faced and squalling and very much alive. "A girl?" Jason said incredulously when a neighbor ran to the quarry with the news.

He had ordered sons. Millicent had disobeyed him.

"What shall we call her?" the new mother asked when he dutifully stood by her bed and looked at the nursing infant.

"I don't know. I never thought of any girls' names."

"What do you think of Andrea? Andrea Whitby—it has a nice ring to it." The house shook with the echo of yet another explosion of black powder.

6.

For the first five years of her life Jason took little note of his daughter's existence. He still hoped. He watched each of Millicent's subsequent pregnancies with the belief that this one would be different; this time she'd give him a living, breathing heir. Millicent conceived five times more. Each time she bore a dead son, one for each year of Andrea's life. That made seven all told, including the two that preceded the little girl.

After the last one, when labor started at seven months and went on for three harrowing, scream-filled days, Josiah Sills came to see Jason. "I've found an article in this journal I think you should read," the doctor said.

It was a medical journal full of words Jason didn't know and diagrams he thought disgusting. "What's any of this to do with me?"

"It explains Millicent's condition."

"Her condition? What the hell are you talking about! Millicent's a fine, healthy girl."

"She's had seven miscarriages, Whitby! For God's sake, what does it take to convince you something's wrong? This last time you almost lost her. Doesn't that matter?"

"Naturally it matters. But Millicent's young. She's only twenty-four. We can expect more children."

Sills sighed and sank into a chair, then picked up the learned journal and tapped it on the edge of Whitby's polished mahogany desk. "Your wife has a rare condition, so rare it doesn't even have a name. Chap named Randolph down in Boston has observed it in a number of his patients. Male children are aborted. What laymen call miscarriages or stillbirths. It never changes, Jason. Millicent can't have a son.''

They talked a little more, and eventually Whitby was forced to recognize the truth. He never touched his wife again. After a few months he moved to a separate bedroom and remained there.

Millicent didn't miss his physical attentions, and she wasn't sorry to be free of the constant, sterile pregnancies. She felt aggrieved all the same. It was Eve's fault, of course. Eve had stolen her husband's affections.

Her eyes developed a haunted, sad expression, and all Whitby Falls became aware of some tragic flaw in Millicent's life. ''What good's all that money? It don't make her babies live, does it?'' Naturally they assumed the stillborn infants to be the cause of Millicent's sorrow, her increasing vagueness. She was aware of it but too frightened of Jason to explain to folks that they were mistaken.

Except that once she did say something to Sarah Murray. Sarah had become her best friend. Millicent spent more and more time in bed, but the two women met frequently. Sarah would sit beside the younger woman, sewing or knitting while her friend's pale hands lay idle on the coverlet, growing more blue-veined and fragile-looking with each month that passed. Usually, the two women spoke of village gossip, other people's doings, not their own. However, on one occasion, a remark of Sarah's provoked Millicent to speak.

''So I told Effie,'' Sarah was saying, ''she didn't have to let Dennis get drunk every Saturday night and come home and beat her. But these working-class women, they simply don't understand. . . .''

''Don't they?'' Millicent's tone was bitter. ''I think they understand better than you and me. Better than so-called ladies. They don't fool themselves about what men are, the kind of things they do. . . .''

Sarah looked hard at the frail figure in the bed. ''Most men, most gentlemen, that is, aren't like that, Milly. They don't abuse their wives. Any that do aren't gentlemen at all, for all they pretend to be.''

Millicent realized she'd been misunderstood but didn't bother to correct the impression. ''Maybe,'' she murmured. ''Maybe you're right. Not really gentlemen, that's it.''

Sarah pursed her lips and said no more. Soon there was a

common opinion in the town that somehow Jason abused his wife. Maybe he'd even caused her miscarriages. It never spread as far as the men, but it remained an unspoken knowledge among the Whitby Falls women. Millicent knew of it and gleaned a measure of satisfaction. She even allowed a few more hints to surface in her conversations with Sarah. The older woman eventually understood that in addition to his other sins Jason wasn't faithful. She spoke of this to no one. But she never forgot.

Once he accepted the fact that there would never be a son, Jason Whitby began to notice Andrea. By the time she was seven, he adored her. The child was a beauty, an exquisitely perfect little creature, and bright, too. Jason looked at her and knew hope once more. Andrea would grow up and give him grandsons. He began to groom her for the role.

There was one relatively brief period when it appeared that the heritage he expected to pass on might cease to exist. It began in 1860 with the election of Lincoln and the War Between the States. Fortunately, Jason saw what was happening and took steps to protect what was his.

Washington charged Vermont with the task of raising a regiment of seven hundred and eighty men, the state's quota as fixed by Mr. Lincoln's secretary of war. Jason thought it madness. Men who went to fight left jobs behind them, work that wouldn't be done, profits unearned. Few saw this as clearly as did Jason Whitby.

Young and old alike rushed to volunteer. Vermont raised enough men for five regiments. Whitby money helped to outfit and arm them, the women of Whitby Falls spent endless hours sewing uniforms, and Sugarbush Farm supplied foodstuffs. Jason Whitby was seen as a loyal citizen whose patriotism was second to none.

Only the most astute realized that not a man from Jason's town left to fight. Natural resources mustn't be abandoned in wartime, he told the workmen. The North would need every bit of building material she could produce, every nickel of capital she could raise. If any man closed his eyes to those facts, Jason Whitby would remember his name. He needn't come home looking for work when the conflict ended.

Maneuvering his way through the war took all Jason's energy for the next few years. He spent less time thinking about

Andrea and her future, none at all about his wife and her increasing withdrawal. What's more, he broke off his meetings with Eve Villette. She was getting old, while his horizons were widening. The raw crudeness of Eve didn't excite him as once it had. Besides, he had increasing opportunities to satisfy his appetites of late.

During the early sixties Jason spent more time traveling. He was a businessman of renown, a power to be reckoned with where power was the only currency that mattered. And in Boston, New York, and Washington a man could find suitable ways to relax once his business was done. Jason availed himself of such pleasures. Sometimes he'd come home so refreshed and renewed that he was a changed man, almost a younger one.

"Well, and how's my little girl!"

She was always his little girl. Andrea understood that even when she was thirteen. "Fine, Papa, just fine. Mama's feeling poorly, though. She's been in bed all week."

"Yes, well, your mother needs her rest." He dismissed Millicent with a wave of his hand. "How about your music lessons? Are you practicing regularly, as you promised?"

Andrea nodded and went to the piano. Jason watched her, smiling. He poured himself a drink while she arranged her music; then he sat down to listen while she played. The sound of Chopin filled the big house. To Jason, it was the sweet sound of success.

Eve didn't much mind when Jason stopped wanting her. Their relationship had always been more for his satisfaction than for hers. And it had achieved more than she'd hoped it would. Jason felt responsible for her and her children.

Eve always kept careful count of the days of the month, the times she conceived, but what she knew she told neither her husband nor her lover. She considered it appropriate that Jason charged them no rent for the cabin and gave her boys jobs in the quarry as soon as they were old enough to wield a pickax. It was no more than his duty, as Eve saw it. That he no longer used her body changed nothing. What had been, and its consequences, made her able to shrug off the abuse of the town and to ignore Jason's high-handed ways.

The other Villettes didn't share Eve's attitudes toward Whitby. Jacques was drunk most of the time, so he didn't count, but Eve's children surprised her. They displayed minds of their own early on. Hugh and Riley, for instance, both hated Jason. They never spoke their feelings aloud, but Eve knew. Sometimes she watched Hugh, and she saw in her eldest boy a hunger that frightened her. He had dreams of glory that were no part of his world. And she didn't know what he might do to make them come true.

"Is going to end his days swinging from a tree, that Hugh," she sometimes muttered to Jacques. "Fancy ideas, too big ideas."

"You are a stupid woman," her husband always answered. "You speak things where the devil can hear."

Eve hooted with laughter at such remarks. "You are the stupid one. You are old, superstitious Canuck. Hugh drives himself. Is locked up inside, Hugh's devil."

Jacques preferred to ignore her insults and her premonitions. Hugh didn't interest him; neither did Jackie, the youngest son. But the middle boy, Riley, was different. Riley was clever. He read books. Sometimes he talked to his father about them. Strange words came from Riley's mouth. He spoke of the rights of workers and of justice. Jacques knew these ideas to be fantasy, but he liked to listen. Imagine a son of his able to speak such words. The school in Whitby Falls had made all the Villette children free of *Quebeçois* accents. For Riley it had apparently done more.

For Jacques that made the rest of it tolerable. He'd always known about Jason and Eve, but he knew, too, what his wife had bought by lying down and opening her legs. Jacques preferred not to dwell on the fact. Most of the time he could blot it out with drink. When that didn't work, there was Riley and the marvel of his quick brain and glib tongue. It followed that he never allowed himself to question who had fathered Eve's children.

"Riley says there should be a law about how much a man has to pay folks what work for him. I heard him telling Pa." Maryann, the eldest girl, was Eve's confidante. She knew things none of the others suspected.

"Riley's got the big mouth and the crazy thoughts," Eve said. She turned to swat her daughter for no other reason than that she was near and Riley wasn't. "Crazy thoughts make trouble. You hear good, Maryann Villette! And forget nothing."

The girl evaded her mother's blow with ease. "It ain't me

what's saying them things, it's Riley. What you hitting me for?''

''The dishes are not washed.'' Eve searched for an explanation and found one. ''Three days, they're not washed. They stink.''

''You wash 'em,'' Maryann said sullenly. ''Or get Betty or Celia to do it. I ain't your maid.''

Eve looked around for the two younger girls, but neither of them was in sight. ''Hell with the dishes,'' she said finally. ''Later we wash them. Come, we go for the walk.''

Life in the Villette cabin was for the most part easy. The family liked it that way.

1868 . . .

Riley

Chapter Two

1.

The year 1868 was an important one for America. It was the year Andrew Johnson was almost impeached, retaining his office by one vote. It was the year the Republicans nominated Ulysses S. Grant to be president because he'd been such a damned good general in the Civil War. The Democrats met at a place called Tammany Hall in New York City to choose their nominee. It took them twenty-one ballots, and they could have saved themselves the trouble. He lost.

It was the year that seven former Confederate states were readmitted to the union and the year that the transcontinental railroad was completed. Other things happened, too—not so well marked or easily identified, perhaps. People were beginning to talk about the rights of the working class, and in Philadelphia, Uriah Stephens was attempting to form a fraternity called the Knights of Labor.

Most of those events roused only temporary interest in Whitby Falls. People knew they could rely on Jason Whitby to protect their future. Politics didn't have much to do with quarrying slate or looking after a family.

Not everyone was indifferent, however. In that summer of 1868, the second Villette boy, Raoul, whom everyone called Riley, was nineteen. He was a tall, quiet-spoken lad, unlike the rest of his family. They were all short and tough and noisy, except for Hugh, the eldest at twenty, who was short and tough and silent. Riley felt some affection for his clan but little kinship with them; he saw the world differently. Even his father, who listened to him talk, didn't really understand. Riley knew that in all Whitby Falls only he recognized the shape of the coming new order.

Those differing perceptions came in part because he walked into Rutland once a month and borrowed books from the library, and in part from the fact that he was a critical observer of the town and its people. The books gave him clear notions of social justice, the stirrings in the land of something called *trade unionism*; what he saw around him was more complex and more disturbing.

On this first Sunday in July, Riley left the crowded log cabin early in the morning, before any of the others were awake. He waded through the familiar debris and sleeping bodies to the table by the wood stove, took a loaf of bread and a slab of cheddar cheese, and went to the door. There was no need to be quiet. The previous night, his father had brought in a jug of applejack. Jack Villette's still was famous, albeit illegal. Everyone around brought their cider there, to be turned into headier brew. They all knew Jack skimmed a bonus from their stock, but they didn't complain.

Riley stood over his mother. Eve's slack mouth and heavy snores bore witness to her enjoyment of the Saturday-night drunk. The others, even Celia, thirteen and the youngest of the six Villette children, were in the same condition. Riley took one disgusted look around and left. It was nearly nine o'clock. Other people would be up and about. Skirting the town, he made his way through the pines to the foot of Herrick and hiked up about two hundred feet to a rocky outcropping that was his favorite perch winter and summer. From there he could see everything.

The village, nestled into its crevice between the river and the mountain, sparkled below. It had changed little since his earliest memories. There were two white steeples now, the Congregational church having recently been joined by a Methodist chapel. The Welsh had clung to their religion despite being assimilated in so many other ways. While Riley watched, people moved in a steady stream toward the two churches. They looked like ants from that distance, or rather like puppets. Riley knew who pulled the strings.

His glance turned to the quarry. Riley could remember when there had been only one pit; now there were three, stretching west of the town like an ugly ulcer. The heaps of rubble and waste around them were raw wounds, and the boy cursed softly when he looked at them. At least the oldest mountain of rubbish was no longer such an eyesore. Sycamores and weed grasses had sewn themselves into its seams. That always happened as soon as they stopped dumping. But Mr. Whitby never ordered a heap abandoned until he was sure the last possible wagonload of splintered rock had been hauled to the top. No one knew that better than Riley. He was a teamster.

"Ain't got no feeling for the stone," the others said. "Hugh, now, he's different. He understands." At twelve, Hugh had started in the pit. Until the previous year he'd been a blaster. His squat, square fingers knew instinctively how many sticks of the miraculous new explosive, dynamite, were needed to cleave a ledge of slate. Recently Hugh had requested a transfer to the shanties. Now he was an apprentice slitter, as deft with a chisel and a mallet as he'd been at every other operation in the quarry.

Riley didn't envy his older brother his better pay or his status or even his silent but real ambition. Nor did Riley envy Jackie, his junior by one year. Jackie wasn't good for much, and little was demanded of him. He had a sometime job tending the wood-fired pumps that kept the water out of the base of the pit, and he earned the least of the three of them. But as far as Riley could see, he and his brothers shared places in hell. He hated slate. He hated the look of it and the smell of it and the constant noise that accompanied its production. The mules and the horses he tended weren't much, perhaps, but at least they were alive.

He looked away from the quarry. He spent six days a week with its dust in his eyes and nose; today he would pretend it wasn't there. In the town the streets were empty; everyone was in church. Except Andrea Whitby.

She walked along Main Street by herself, slowly, as if she didn't know she was late. Riley knew it was she. No other female in Whitby Falls was that tall and slim or had that same elegant stride. She was carrying her bonnet in her hand, and the sun made silver splendor of her hair. Andrea's hair was incredible. It was so pale a color that to call it blond seemed ridiculous. Other girls had blond hair, but Andrea's was like the underside of a poplar leaf. Her skin was tanned gold— winter and summer it never faded—and her eyes were violet with black streaks.

When she reached the steps of the Congregational church Andrea paused for a moment, tied on her bonnet with unhurried gestures, then went inside. When she opened the door, Riley caught the faint strains of the organ and the sound of the congregation singing "Jesus Lover of My Soul." Riley had been to the services once. He tried the Methodists once, too, and liked them better. At least they sang spirited songs like "Amazing Grace" and "Rock of Ages." The Welsh loved to sing; they had a choir that met every Tuesday night. Riley thought that part of religion acceptable, but he could stand the sermons in neither church.

If the ministers had preached the truth to the people, told them Jason Whitby was their jailer, that their company-owned houses and company-backed credit were traps to keep them enslaved, he might have felt differently. As it was, both reverend gentlemen were lackeys who licked the Whitby boots just like everyone else. Riley never went back, not even to be near Andrea.

The girl, three years younger than he, would be sixteen in a couple of weeks. Everyone in town knew Andrea's age. Each year on the seventeenth of July her father gave a big party on the Green. There were lemonade and ice cream for the children and applejack and rum for the adults. Two years earlier, Riley had stopped attending the parties. He was probably the only person in Whitby Falls who didn't go, but no one seemed to notice his absence.

Before that, Riley and Andrea had been friends of a sort and went out of their way to exchange greetings when they passed in the street. When they were small children, they'd sometimes played together. It was an unlikely alliance, but in Whitby Falls no one paid much attention to the very young. Only as he grew older did Riley come to understand the gap between himself and Andrea Whitby. Now he pointedly avoided her. Riley told himself it was because he despised her family and the system they kept alive.

Riley came down from the ledge late in the day. Main Street was empty, and Whitby Falls drowsed peacefully in the summer Sunday afternoon. He didn't see Andrea until she rounded a corner and crossed in front of him.

"Hello, Riley," she said quickly.

He couldn't avoid talking to her now. "Hi," he mumbled, quickening his pace.

Andrea fell into step beside him. "Where have you been?"

"No place special."

"You aren't very talkative," she teased.

He shot her a sideways look. Her smile was dazzling. "Where are you going?" he asked. "I thought you'd be home with your ma and pa at this time. I thought a princess had to stay in her castle.''

"Princess! Is that what you think I am?''

"Well, aren't you? In this town, at any rate.''

"Maybe,'' she said softly. Her voice was strangely sad, and unconsciously he slowed his steps so she could keep pace. "If that's what I am, I don't recommend it,'' she added.

Riley stopped walking and turned to face her. They had reached the end of Main Street and were almost at the river. "Why not?'' he demanded.

The intensity of his tone frightened her. Whatever confiding she might have done seemed suddenly impossible. "Nothing,'' she said. "I don't think anything about it. I was just chattering.''

Riley shrugged. "Okay, I thought maybe you understood. I'm not surprised you don't. It's natural for your class.''

"I don't know what you're talking about.''

He began walking again and would have outdistanced her if she hadn't trotted beside him. "Listen, Riley, wait a minute. It wasn't an accident, meeting you today. I've seen you going home at this time lots of Sundays. I want to talk to you.''

"About what?'' he inquired gruffly. "What's the famous Andrea Whitby want to talk to one of the Villette Canucks about?''

"Oh, stop that! You're always so difficult, Riley. You have a chip on your shoulder. Everyone says so.'' Before he could defend himself, she continued. "I want to ask if you're coming to my birthday party the week after next.''

"I haven't come to your birthday party for two years,'' he said.

"I know.''

They were at the covered bridge. He stepped into its shadow and looked at Andrea standing in the sunlight. Her straw bonnet hung down her back, and her silver hair sparkled as if bejeweled. "I didn't think you noticed whether I was there or not,'' he said.

"I noticed.'' She had spent all her courage; now she dropped her eyes in shyness.

He felt loutish and cruel. "Listen, it's not personal. It's just that your father—''

"It's my birthday, not my father's,'' she interrupted.

"Yes, but . . . I can't explain. How come you care, anyway? Everyone else goes."

"I want you to come. Say you will. Promise me you'll come this year."

He shook his head sadly. "I'm sorry, Andrea. I just can't."

Andrea felt humiliated. When they were children, she'd thought Riley was her friend. She liked him better than any other youngster in the village. Riley never seemed to envy her or try to use her. He just acted as if he liked her for herself. Apparently she'd misread his feelings. "Forget I asked," she said stiffly. "I'm sure you're free to do as you like. It makes no difference to me."

He stretched out one hand and laid it lightly on her arm. He could feel her trembling through the thin cotton of her summer dress. It wasn't her fault she was Jason Whitby's daughter. "Andrea, listen. Don't be hurt. It's nothing to do with you, really."

"I told you," she said. "I don't care." She half turned to walk away, but he tightened his hold on her arm and restrained her.

"I'm real proud you care about my coming," he said. "I mean it. Thank you for asking me."

She looked up at him and smiled. His breath caught with the beauty of her. "Look," he said. "I won't be there, but I wish you a happy birthday, anyway. You remember that. Here, I'll see you do." Swiftly, he leaned forward and brushed her lips with his own. Andrea gasped, then stood quite still. "Happy birthday, princess," Riley repeated.

The violet eyes met his for a moment; then Andrea turned and hurried back toward town. Riley stayed where he was for a long time.

"Mr. Whitby, may I speak with you a moment?"

"Of course, lad, come in." Jason ignored the boy's neglect of "sir." This particular Villette was always a bit odd. He didn't seem like one of Eve's kids at all. Whitby flinched away from that thought and asked, "What's on your mind, Riley?"

"I want to earn a bit of extra money."

"I see. You're a teamster, aren't you? Getting thirteen dollars a month. I suppose you want a job in the pit. Quarry apprentices start at nine, you know. Though they can get to seventeen once they're trained.''

"I know that, but I don't want a job in the pit. I want to go on being a teamster. What I had in mind was something extra. Something out of normal working hours.''

Whitby raised his eyebrows. "Sounds like you've given the notion some thought. What sort of something extra?''

"The big house. The trim could use a coat of paint. I could do it in a month working evenings and Sundays. Charge you ten dollars and the cost of the paint.''

Jason leaned back in his chair and eyed the boy. One of Eve's brats with a yen to get ahead? The thought of her tempered Jason's other thoughts. He kept the Villettes on in the cabin for old times' sake; ignored their slovenly ways, the strumpets the three little girls were fast becoming. For that same reason he'd give in to this strange request.

"All right, but not ten dollars. Eight. I can hire an experienced painter from Rutland for ten. And get the paint from Anderson's. Tell Phoebe to put it on my bill. White, same as always.''

Riley nodded and left. He'd kept his promise to himself; he'd not said "sir" once. Moreover, the money would be useful. He could give his mother half and put the rest in his secret fund. Escape would be four dollars closer.

Andrea came out on the porch the third evening Riley was there. "The pillars look nice freshly painted.''

"Yeah.'' He kept his brush going and didn't look at her. Beneath his homespun shirt his heart was beating uncontrollably, and his trousers felt tight and uncomfortable. He reminded himself that he'd arranged the episode just to test his willpower, the strength of his convictions.

Andrea might have said something else, but Jason came out just then and asked her something about practicing the piano. She went inside dutifully.

Jason wondered why he allowed himself to get so nervous every time Andrea exhibited the fact that she was growing into a young lady, with a natural interest in boys. He poured himself a brandy and noted with some surprise that his hand was trembling.

The girl was such a beauty, no wonder he worried. But she

was always obedient. Jason felt secure in his plans for Andrea, lucky that she'd turned out so well. Especially since to all intents and purposes she didn't have a mother. Millicent had grown stranger and more withdrawn with each passing year.

He poured himself another brandy and lay back with his eyes closed. The sound of the music from the drawing room gave him a sense of well-being.

2.

Andrea usually visited her mother before going to bed. She changed into her nightdress and wrapped a thin woolen shawl around her shoulders.

"Evening, Mama." She kissed the frail woman lightly on the forehead. Her mother's skin felt like tissue paper, dry and thin and fragile. "Have you seen the porch? Riley's made it all clean and sparkling."

Millicent turned her face to the wall. "It can't be a good job. Those Villettes are good for nothing."

"But it is a good job! And I heard Papa say that Hugh, the oldest boy, is a natural genius with dynamite."

Painting the house trim had nothing to do with quarrying slate. Andrea didn't know why she mentioned it. Besides, it was silly to defend the Villettes to her mother. The girl didn't know why Millicent was so hostile to them. Andrea had never told her mother that she liked Riley Villette better than anyone in Whitby Falls, but she feared that for some reason it would be terrible if she did.

"It's your birthday next week," Millicent said, changing the subject.

"Yes. Mama, do you think you could ask Papa not to give a party? Not on the Green, I mean."

"Why ever not?"

"It's embarrassing. I'm too old for it."

"You're sixteen this year. That's a special birthday. Your father will particularly want to mark the occasion."

"A party here, then. In the house. Not on the Green," she repeated.

The blue-veined hand lying on the lace coverlet fluttered once in protest, then fell limp with the effort. "If you want to change the arrangements, you'll have to speak to your father."

Andrea bit her lip and played with the fringe of the shawl where it crossed her breasts. "I thought you might do that."

"No, it's up to you."

Later, lying in bed with the new moon streaming through the window and lighting the delicate pink and white china of her washbowl and pitcher, Andrea thought about it. Why was Mama so distant, so weak? Had she always been like that, even as a girl?

Andrea knew little about her mother's past. Only once had she been taken to New Hampshire. Four years earlier, the grandfather she'd never seen had died, and Andrea had accompanied her mother to Nashua for the funeral.

"This is your Aunt Susan." Mama had said when a pleasant little woman joined them at the funeral parlor. Until then, Andrea had never seen her mother's sister. Why not? she wondered. Susan Mulberry didn't look like someone to be hidden away and ignored, not even with her eyes red from weeping. Mama didn't weep for her father, but Aunt Susan did.

After the burial they all went together to the house where Mama and her sister were born and raised. It seemed to Andrea a dismal place.

"That's my mother's portrait," Millicent told her daughter. "She died when Susan and I were small children."

"Your Andrea looks a bit like her, Missie," the aunt had said. Andrea looked at the picture and was glad. She thought her grandmother beautiful. She was surprised, too, to hear her mother called Missie.

"Is that your nickname? Missie? Did Papa ever call you that?"

"No, not Papa. I was only called Missie here when I was a girl."

It was difficult to imagine Mama a girl. "Was the house always like this?"

"Like what?" Aunt Susan asked.

"I don't know . . . so . . . ."

"She means so shabby," Millicent supplied. "Yes, it was always like this. We never had much money."

"We were happy," Susan said quickly. "It didn't matter.

Our father was an inventor, Andrea. He had lots of dreams. They didn't always work out as he hoped.''

Andrea had said nothing, but she had noted the looks the two older women exchanged.

"I wish we saw more of you," Susan had said to her sister. "I wish Papa had seen more of you before he died.''

"Yes, well, I'm very busy in Vermont. Jason's affairs keep me very busy.''

Andrea couldn't understand that. Mama seldom did anything, certainly nothing that related to Papa's business.

"Besides," Millicent had continued, "I haven't been well.''

"Poor darling.'' Susan had reached for her sister's hand. "I know. I grieved with you. So did Papa. All those miscarriages . . .''

Andrea had wandered off and left the two women talking about pregnancy. Aunt Susan had five children, all girls. She must know a lot about it. Andrea preferred to examine the house. She passed from one dusty, ill-furnished room to another, and eventually came to a big evil-smelling chamber filled with glass bottles and strange apparatus.

"This was my father's laboratory," Millicent said, coming up behind her. "He did his experiments here.''

"Did any of them work?''

"Not many.'' A ghost of a smile played around Millicent's mouth. "If they had, perhaps I—''

"What?''

"Nothing. Come into the parlor. Aunt Susan's husband and her daughters have arrived. I want you to get to know your cousins.''

Andrea didn't like them much. They were loud, and they laughed all the time. It seemed to her inappropriate to laugh in this place. When she and Mama left to return to Whitby Falls, she was very much relieved. Everything about Nashua depressed her. And Mama seemed strange there.

Lying in her bed on this summer night, Andrea examined the memory, as she'd often done. Maybe there was some clue in New Hampshire, something in Mama's childhood that explained the way she was now. It didn't help, however; it never did. The only lasting impression Andrea had retained was a wonderment that Millicent saw so little of her sister and a lasting conviction that being an inventor was perhaps the worst profession a man could choose. It meant failing all the time. And it was somehow related to Mama's weakness, her vagueness. "Missie," she whispered aloud. "I wonder why she didn't prefer that to Millicent."

She felt her own strong arms and legs where they pressed against the mattress and clasped her hands over her taut-muscled, flat stomach. Since she was a tiny child she'd wished she could give some of her physical strength to her mother. After the trip to Nashua, she had understood that what Millicent lacked was strength of a different sort.

Andrea studied the intricately intertwined rosebuds decorating the china washbowl. There were no thorns on those painted roses. Should she ask Papa not to give the party? He'd be angry, disappointed. He loved the seventeenth of July. Andrea sighed. It would have been so much better if she'd had brothers and sisters. She wouldn't feel this terrible weight, the burden of being all his hopes and dreams. She knew the other young people in town envied her. If they only knew.

In the end she said nothing, and the celebration took place as usual. Andrea wore a pale lilac dress of silky percale with white organdy trim. Papa had brought the pattern and the material home from New York and had a dressmaker in Rutland sew the frock. There was even a straw bonnet trimmed with the bows and streamers to match the dress. She hated the outfit. It was childish and overdone for Whitby Falls.

Except for Riley, everyone in town was on the Green. She glanced toward her house, and she could see him painting, as he had every evening for a week. Her father called her, and Andrea turned to him with a guilty start.

By eight in the evening it was growing dark. The party had lasted its customary two hours. The drinks and the food were nearly gone. So were most of the guests. Hiram Howard toasted her silently with one last glass of Applejack, and she smiled and nodded. Her face felt stiff with smiling. Andrea looked for her father and saw him deep in conversation with Lliam Murray.

"Papa." She approached the two men over a wealth of paper streamers that had fallen to the grass, picking her way carefully so as not to soil her white kid slippers. "Everyone's just about gone. I'm going back to the house and see if Mother's all right."

"Millicent wasn't feeling well enough to come, I take it?" Lliam Murray directed his question to Jason.

"The warm weather makes her feel poorly," Andrea said quickly.

"So does the cold." Jason's voice was bitter. He resented it when Millicent didn't make an appearance at public gatherings.

"I'll see if there's some lemonade left to bring her," Andrea said.

There wasn't. The barrels were all empty, and so were the heavy glass pitchers. Surprisingly, there was a bit of applejack left in the bottom of one keg. Impulsively, Andrea ladled it into a cup and took a sip. She grimaced. It was awful, and it burned. She started to tip the drink out, then had another idea. Carrying it carefully, she walked up the road to the big brick house, now obscured in the dusk.

"Are you still here, Riley? I brought you something."

He was arranging his paintbrushes in a wooden trough of turpentine. He didn't look up when he answered. "I'm just going. The party's over, I see."

"Yes, you missed it, like you said you would. You could have had the evening off, anyway. Papa wouldn't have minded."

"It's nothing to do with him. I make my own time. All I promised was to get the work done." Riley went on cleaning the brushes.

Andrea shrugged. This was only the second time they'd talked since the day he kissed her. She was trying hard not to show her nervousness. "I brought you some applejack."

She held out the cup, and he stared at her a moment before he took it. Andrea wondered if he was remembering the kiss. She dropped her eyes. When he finally reached for the drink, their fingers brushed, stayed in contact for a brief moment. Then he yanked the cup from her hand and raised it to his lips in a swift, jerky motion. Part of the liquid spilled down his shirtfront. The mark was invisible on the dark, sweat-stained cloth.

That night Andrea thought about Riley before she fell asleep. The way he looked, the way he smelled. Sweaty because he worked hard and it was hot. She liked the way he looked, though, the way his thick black hair swept back from his forehead and the way his eyes were dark and crinkly at the corners. What she thought of most was the way the curly hair of his chest showed beneath his open workshirt and the way he'd wiped it with his big, capable hands when he spilled the applejack.

That night she dreamed about Riley, but in the morning she couldn't recall the details of the dream.

Riley finished painting the house, and she didn't see him again for weeks. Once, when she went to the quarry to bring Papa a letter from New York marked "urgent," she spotted Riley leading a team of mules toward the company barn, and she smiled brightly and waved, but he acted as if he hadn't seen her.

In September there was some talk of her going to New York to a finishing school for girls. Andrea thought it a wonderful idea, and she begged her father to make the arrangements.

"No," he said finally. "I've thought it over, my dear, but it's not a wise idea. You must trust me with decisions like this. I want the best for you. You know that. Besides," he added, seeing her crestfallen look, "your mother needs you. She's been very ill this summer. We don't want to upset her by sending you away."

Andrea pursed her lips into a thin line. She wanted to say that he was concerned about Mother's health only when it suited his needs, but she didn't. "Very well, Papa," she said softly instead.

"Good girl. And I tell you what. You shall have a trip to New York, after all. Somewhere around Thanksgiving I'm due there on business. You'll go with me and see all the sights of the big city. You'll like that." It occurred to Jason that bringing his daughter with him would curtail his own pleasures in New York.

About the middle of October people complained that the autumn colors weren't up to standard. Just the right number of warm days and frosty nights were needed to produce Vermont's spectacular fall show, and this year it didn't materialize. Andrea didn't mind. She liked the subdued russets and browns lightened by the clear yellow of the birch. She liked, too, the way the fallen leaves crunched beneath her feet and the way the woods smelled so strongly of pine and pitch when she took long, dreamy walks by herself.

She usually went along the bank of the river, ending up by the falls, revisiting the spot where Riley had kissed her, half hoping to meet him. After some weeks she decided she didn't care if she never saw Riley Villette again. One afternoon, to prove to herself that she meant it, she set out in a different direction—west, toward the mountain.

Herrick Mountain cast its shadows over everything, creating subtle differences in the pattern of light and shade. Suddenly, it seemed to Andrea that the world had grown a dark and fearsome place. She felt a small panic knot in her stomach. Ridiculous. There was no way she could be lost, not a stone's throw from Whitby Falls. She turned to try and locate the village, but there was nothing to see except looming trees.

She took a step or two back in the direction she'd come, then changed her mind. The walk had become a challenge. Gathering her skirt and petticoats tighter around her body, she strode on. A bird chirped loudly, and when she looked toward the sound, she spotted a clearing. Turning, she went toward it. Seconds later, she was standing on a rocky precipice jutting out from the side of the mountain.

She was higher than she'd thought. The town and the quarry and the river were spread out before her, far away and remote. Her heart was pounding with exertion and the foolish fear she hadn't been able to stifle. The sun, reflected on the rock face behind her, was warmer than when she set out. Andrea unbuttoned her coat and slipped it off.

"What are you doing here?"

The angry voice startled her, and she nearly lost her footing. She grabbed a sapling struggling to grow out of a cleft in the rock. "You frightened me, Riley! You'd no call to do that. I just came for a walk. I've as much right here as you."

"More," he said sarcastically. "You're a Whitby. You've a right to the whole world."

Andrea flushed with anger and glanced toward the quarry. "How come you're not working?"

"I didn't feel like it. I took the day off."

"Shame on you. That's why you Villettes never get ahead. You're all lazy and shiftless." She knew it wasn't true; she just wanted to wound him, reject him as he had rejected her.

"That's the gospel according to Whitby, isn't it?" He laughed, but he sounded hurt all the same.

"Everyone knows it." She wouldn't apologize; nothing could make her. Andrea let go of the little tree and sat down on her coat. He needn't think he could drive her off the mountain. The moss-covered stones felt cold even through the thick wool. "Why do you live in that awful cabin?" she demanded suddenly. "Why must you Villettes be so peculiar? You could live in a house like everyone else, you know."

"Sure," the boy said softly. "We could live in one of your father's better houses, but we'd still be beholden to him for everything but the air we breathe. Just like everyone else, as you say."

"You're talking rubbish, Riley. I don't even understand you."

He clambered to his feet and moved toward her from the back of the ledge. He seemed very tall. The wind was blowing his hair back, and she could see his dark eyes, fixed on her face. She turned away so he wouldn't see that he made her blush.

"Andrea." His voice had changed. It was less hostile. "Tell me the truth. Just this once, just you and me alone up here. You don't approve of the things your father does, do you?"

"I don't know what you're talking about," she insisted. "Besides, I love my father."

"That's got nothing to do with it." He sat down beside her. "I love my father, too. All the same, I know he drinks too much and doesn't do anything but talk and dream. He doesn't work to make his dreams come true."

"That's just what I said before." His hand was inches from hers on the ground. She was staring at his fingers while she spoke. "If people work, they get ahead; otherwise, they don't. It's simple."

"Getting ahead in Whitby Falls just means being more in debt to Jason Whitby. He owns the town and everyone in it, Andrea. He gives them credit so they can never afford to leave. They can't even own their own houses, no matter how long they live in them."

"Rubbish," she said again. It didn't come out firm and decisive as she intended, however.

"It's the truth. You're a smart girl; you must see it."

She shook her head. "I don't know about that, but what you said that time about my being a princess, it's not true. At least I don't feel like one. Everyone expects me to be a certain way, to do certain things. I used to think you were the only one who didn't, that you liked me for myself. Now it seems you only care about my father."

"I do like you," he said hoarsely. "I like you a lot, always have. I've got principles, though. A man's got to have principles."

"And these 'principles,' as you call them, mean you can't care about me anymore?"

His hand had inched closer to hers. While she watched, he drew one of his square, blunt fingers along the back of her tanned skin. "I care." The words were barely audible.

Andrea held her breath and waited, but he said nothing more. He left his hand on top of hers until she pulled it away and stood up. He rose then, too. They were almost the same height, and their eyes met. "I have to go now," she said. "My mother expects me to bring her tea."

"I'll walk down with you."

They didn't touch during most of the swift descent. Once he led her to the edge of a rushing stream, explaining it was a shortcut, and when she stepped onto the big stones that forded it, he took her arm to steady her. "I always go up there on Sundays," he said suddenly.

"Up to that cliff, you mean?"

"Yes. Every week, if the weather's not too bad. Come some Sunday if you can."

"I go to church."

"After church, then."

"After lunch," she amended. "About two-thirty."

They didn't speak again. When they neared the town, he hung back and let her walk alone.

3.

Riley and Andrea did not again discuss the economics of Whitby Falls. They talked about people in general—Phoebe Anderson's habit of clicking her store-bought teeth, the funny accents still retained by the older folks from Wales—and about music and books.

Riley brought her a few volumes from the Rutland library. *Romeo and Juliet* and *The Tempest; Oliver Twist* and *The Old Curiosity Shop*. Later, he gave her Shakespeare's *Sonnets*.

"I don't care for these, I must say," she told him when she returned the volume the following week. "There's no story, just poems. And besides, a lot of it's . . . well, shameless." She dropped her eyes, and he turned his face away so she wouldn't notice his grin. Sometimes Andrea was very young despite her elegant manners and royal upbringing.

"As you like," he said. He decided not to give her *The Arabian Nights*, only *Wuthering Heights*. He'd earlier rejected *Jane Eyre*. A mad wife in the attic was a theme too close to home.

Andrea was the pupil in matters of literature, but she knew more about music than Riley did. "I liked it when I heard you playing," he told her. "When I was working at your house, I mean. You always play in the evening, don't you?"

"I practice after dinner, from seven to eight."

"There's one piece in particular I like," he said. He hummed a bit of a tune.

"You mean this," she corrected, singing the melody line of a Chopin nocturne. She tapped it out on his arm as if he were a piano, and Riley watched her fingers intently. Her hands were long and slim, and she wore a small gold ring with a little blue stone. The jewel flashed in the autumn sunlight.

Riley usually told himself he was just being kind to Andrea, recognizing that Jason's daughter was lonely on her pedestal. But sometimes he glimpsed his true feelings, and

57

they frightened him. It'll be okay, he told himself. She's just a kid. When I've got enough money saved, I'll leave, like I've always planned, and neither of us will ever remember the other.

Andrea was oblivious to his struggle. She relaxed with him when they were together and allowed herself to laugh and be spontaneous as she was with no one else.

"You're king of the mountain," she cried aloud on the ledge one Sunday afternoon. "And I'm the queen!"

The wind was blowing. It whipped her hair around her face. Riley stood a few feet above her on an outcropping, his arms outspread and his face tipped back into the October sun. "Right!" he shouted. "Their majesties, the king and queen of Herrick Mountain." He leaped down to stand beside her and execute an exaggerated bow. "Your wish is my command, milady. What dragon will you have me slay?"

Andrea cocked her head. "The green dragon of the north, I believe. The one that spits fire and devours elephants."

"Silly! There can't be elephants in the north."

"Riley, whose dragon is this, yours or mine?"

He laughed. "Have it your way, a northern dragon that eats northern elephants." Suddenly he cupped her face in his hands. "You're beautiful, you know," he said softly. "I don't think there can be a more beautiful girl in the world."

"I like it that you think so," she whispered.

Riley bent his head and kissed her. He had not intended it; he'd disciplined himself never to kiss Andrea again. Since that first time by the river he had recognized that allowing himself to do so was to cross a rubicon, and there would be no return. This time his discipline failed.

He still held her face in his hands. She couldn't pull away. She didn't want to. Andrea tasted his mouth with delight. Riley made her feel safe and excited at the same time. She stepped closer to him, put her hands on his shoulders. The kiss went on for a long time. Riley was the first to break the contact.

"I'm sorry," he said. "I shouldn't have done that."

"Don't be sorry. I'm not."

"Andrea, listen to me. . . . . There's things you don't know about." He struggled with the need to tell her he planned to leave Whitby Falls and the inability to make himself say the words.

"What things?" she asked.

"Me, the past, the way things are here . . ."

She smiled at him. "You mean what people would say? I don't care, Riley. I made up my mind to that weeks ago. We do have to be a little careful about my parents, though. Just for now. Later, we'll make them understand."

"Little girl," he said softly. "Sweet, beautiful little girl who has so much and wants so much and knows so little."

She took hold of his hand and raised his palm to her lips. "I know about you and me," she whispered. "And I'm not a little girl anymore."

"C'mon," he said gruffly. "We'd better be getting back."

Andrea allowed him to lead her down the mountain.

Millicent noted that Andrea seemed preoccupied of late, but her vague, half-phrased questions produced no information. She put it down to the girl's age. Sixteen was a moody time, a foolish time. She remembered it well. Once she tried to say something to Jason, but he paid no attention. He was intent on a difficult business matter. He had to make several unplanned trips to New York as a result, and, forgetting his earlier promise, he didn't take Andrea on any of them.

November was unseasonably warm. The ground was still bare of snow, and it didn't rain despite gray, overcast skies. Sometimes Millicent walked in the long garden behind the big house. Years before, she had planted roses at the bottom of the property, by the gazebo. They had romped all over the structure since she stopped pruning and caring for them. Now she would go down there once in a while and look at the shrubs and think about the early years of her marriage.

She liked to say the names of the roses. Tuscany and Queen of Denmark and Madame Hardy seemed romantic and fraught with possibilities, and in summer they produced a few lush blossoms and heady scent despite her neglect of them. In November, they were brittle and ugly, and all the thorns showed. "Like me," Millicent whispered. "Just like me."

"Come up to the house, Mama." Andrea appeared and took her arm. "It's starting to snow."

There were only a few flakes, and the ground stayed bare until Thanksgiving day.

Mother and daughter ate their meal alone. Jason was in New York. He had apologized for being away at the holiday but pleaded business too important to wait. In the village, most of the families either went to visit parents and grandparents or had relatives visiting them.

Lliam and Sarah Murray had invited the Whitbys to Thanksgiving dinner, but Millicent declined. The house would be full of people, not only the numerous children, whom she knew, but the Rutland cousins, whom she didn't. There was another invitation, from Susan in New Hampshire. The two sisters wrote to each other at least once every month, but they had not seen each other in years. Millicent didn't want to visit Susan now. The younger sister's letters were full of the happenings of a busy, happy household.

Andrea had a hearty appetite despite being tall and thin. She ate huge amounts of turkey and stuffing and pumpkin pie and sat back and sighed when she could eat no more. "That was good. I do miss Papa, though, don't you?"

"Yes." Millicent pushed away the sliver of untouched pie on her plate. She never missed Jason in his absences, and she suspected Andrea knew it, but they kept up the pretense. "I'm tired, dear," she said softly. "I think I'll go up for a nap."

"Yes, Mama. I'll bring you tea later."

Andrea watched her mother walk slowly and carefully from the table and listened to her climb the stairs. Only when she heard Millicent's door close did she rise. She wished she'd agreed to meet Riley on the ledge. He'd suggested it, but she refused, saying that since her father was to be away, she couldn't leave her mother on the holiday. She could have, though. Millicent would sleep for three or four hours.

Andrea strolled into the drawing room and sat down at the piano. A bit of Schubert first, then the Chopin nocturne that Riley liked. She heard the tapping at the window when its last notes died away.

"What are you doing here? Are you crazy?" Andrea tried to close the window, but Riley put his hand beneath the sash and prevented it.

"I missed you," he said. "Come for a walk."

"I can't."

"Why not? Doesn't look like there's anyone here."

"Mama's upstairs, sleeping. And Papa's away. I can't leave her."

"Just come down the garden, then. The old summer house. I'll wait for you there."

Andrea looked around her. The servants had been told they could take the rest of the day off, but she was nervous, anyway. "All right," she whispered. "Just go. I'll come soon as I can."

She closed the lid of the piano and put away her music, then went upstairs and listened at Millicent's door. The only sound was of deep, even breathing.

The kitchen and the pantry were empty when she checked. Everything had been washed and wrapped and stored away in the ice chests and cupboards, except for a platter of sliced turkey and cheese left out for their supper. Satisfied that the two serving women were indeed gone for the day, Andrea took her coat from the hall and went out.

Riley was waiting for her behind the hedge of roses that screened the gazebo from the house. "Are you mad at me? I wasn't going to let you know I was there. Then I heard you playing and saw you were alone."

She shook her head, and the silvery hair made a swinging veil around her bronzed face. She still wore it loose down her back, like a little girl's. Papa preferred it that way. "I'm not angry," she said. "You startled me, that's all. I don't want Mama or Papa to know, Riley." Her voice was barely a whisper. "Not yet. They wouldn't understand."

"No, they wouldn't. Come in here. It's all right. I checked."

He'd examined the summer house for rats or mice and found none. There was a lot of dust, since no one came there anymore, but it was sound of floor and even cozy inside. At least it seemed so until the damp chill of the place became apparent.

"Are you cold? I'd have brought a blanket if I'd thought of it."

"I'm not cold."

"Yes, you are. You're shivering. Here, take my coat." He stripped the heavy jacket off before she could protest and wrapped it around her shoulders.

"You'll be cold now," Andrea said, looking up at him.

"No, I won't." He stared at her intently and didn't remove his hand from her shoulders. "Your eyes are like violets," he said. "I've never seen such eyes before."

She didn't reply, and when he bent his head, she knew he was going to kiss her again.

"I've wanted to ask you for a long time," he whispered when their lips parted. "Has anyone but me ever done that?"

"No one." She was trembling again, but not from cold; so was he. She could feel his hands shaking where they still rested on her shoulders.

They sat down on the floor, because the bench that ran around the room was piled with debris and rusted garden tools. They were very close together, but they couldn't feel each other's body through the layers of clothing Andrea wore. "I don't need this," she said, shrugging off his jacket. "We can use it to sit on." They made a blanket of the jacket, and without saying a word she removed her coat and folded it to act as a pillow. Neither of them was cold any longer.

Riley propped his head on his elbow and kept looking at her.

"Kiss me again," she said, astounded at her own words.

He bent his face to hers, and their mouths met. He could taste her tongue and her breath, and the hunger of the caress shocked and surprised him.

Andrea wanted to suck his lips; she wanted to bite them. She had been dreaming of him more and more frequently of late, and in every dream she was biting and sucking at his flesh. She felt his hand on her hip, and she put her own over it to increase the pressure so she could feel it through her petticoats. When he started to raise his lips from hers, she gave a little cry and put her other arm around his neck and pressed his head down again. This time she did bite his lips, but if she hurt him, he didn't say so.

She was squirming beneath him, and it was more her doing than his that he was finally stretched full-length on top of her. She could feel every hard-muscled inch of him, because her skirt and petticoats were up around her waist and only the thin material of her pantaloons separated her skin from his breeches.

"Oh, God," Riley moaned. She felt his hand fumbling somewhere below her belly. It wasn't her he was touching—it was himself—and in a few seconds she realized he'd loosened the buttons of his trousers. His gropings brought the back of his hand in contact with the soft place between her thighs.

"Touch me," she whispered.

He lifted his face from where it was buried in the sweet flesh of her neck and looked at her. The pale hair was spread like a halo, gleaming in the dusky seclusion of the gazebo. "I love you, Andrea," he said.

"I love you," she answered.

He moaned again and kissed her harder than before. He was supporting his weight with one arm, afraid to crush her delicate bones, and with the other he fumbled with the ties of her pantaloons until he had freed them and slipped the little garment down her hips and thighs. Her skin felt like velvet, and her tongue tasted of apples and sweet, fresh cider.

A vision flitted through Riley's mind. He could see himself doing fantastic things to her, things beyond imagination. He wanted to kiss not just her mouth but her whole body, all the intimate cracks and crevices. Her breasts were thrusting at him, and he knew from the feel that she wore no corsets and laces. He wanted to unbutton her frock and see those naked breasts. He had a picture of himself putting his mouth over Andrea's breast and sucking at the nipple. The thought terrified him; he was shocked by his perversity. But the idea made him breathe even faster.

Andrea arched her hips, pressing herself closer to him. She felt something hard and hot thrusting against her belly, and she was aware of a pulse beating in the moist, secret spot between her thighs.

When the hard, hot thing slid down her belly to that same secret place, she began to cry, but not from sadness. The tears kept coming when she felt him inside her.

There was a moment of sharp, stabbing pain, and she gasped. Then the pain was past, and Riley was working up and down over her hips, biting her neck, moaning and saying her name over and over. Each time he moved, he touched some part of her she hadn't known existed and sent dizzying waves of pleasure all through her body. Suddenly, he stopped.

Andrea, unwilling to let the pleasure end, kept squirming beneath him. A corner of the rough wool of his trousers made contact with her pulsing, wet flesh, and she jerked her body beneath his, rubbing as fast as she could against that hard, satisfying fabric. The pleasure mounted and exploded inside her, and she didn't know she was shuddering and screaming until he pressed a gentle hand over her lips and whispered, "Quiet, my darling, quiet."

They lay together in silence for a few minutes. Then Riley wiped her thighs with his handkerchief and pulled up her pantaloons and tied them. They sat up. Andrea shook her hair back from her face and replaced the velvet ribbon that had come undone. Riley buttoned his pants and tried to put his jacket back around her shoulders, but she shook her head and shrugged it off.

"I didn't mean that to happen," he said finally.

"No," she answered. "I know that."

"I meant what I said, though." He was afraid to look at her when he spoke. "I love you, Andrea. I've loved you as long as I can remember. I made your father give me the job at the house just so I could be near you."

She put her hands on his cheeks and turned his face to hers. "I know. I meant it, too. I love you, Riley."

He wanted to kiss her again, but she stood up and smoothed her skirt and shook the wrinkles from the coat that had been their pillow. "I have to go now. Mama will be expecting her tea."

"You'll come to the ledge on Sunday?" he asked tremulously.

"Of course. Until Sunday, then."

He watched her walk up the garden and disappear into the big brick house with the freshly painted white shutters. When he went home, he buried the wet, bloodstained handkerchief with which he had wiped her clean. He put it in an old box he kept secreted beneath the gnarled roots of a very old oak.

In her pink and white room with its girlish rosebuds and dimity curtains and bedspread, Andrea removed her pantaloons and studied the rust-colored stains. The garment had a strange smell, the scent of Riley. She pressed it to her nose before consigning it to the fire.

4.

Jason came back from New York full of news. He had been talking with a man named Jay Gould off and on for months now. Mr. Gould was brilliant, a prophet of a new age; he was going to buy the Rutland and Washington Railroad. Jason would put up part of the money and own a piece of it, too. Once he and Mr. Gould took over, they would modernize the line, replace the wood burners with steam engines, and widen the track.

"You're sure about this man Gold, Jason?" Lliam Murray sounded worried.

"Not Gold, Gould. I'm sure. It's the best thing that's happened since we opened the first pit."

Andrea stood in the hall and eavesdropped. She did that often, but never admitted to anyone that business fascinated her. There was something intensely satisfying about the way her father made things happen. She could never explain it, not even to Riley. Perhaps least of all to him. She loved the sense of power that emanated from her father. She could imagine the way he looked, sure and God-like, while he made the lawyer understand.

"What you say about bringing in outsiders, Lliam, is right, of course, but I've taken care of that. As I told you, I'm to have a large share of the stock. It's going to be marvelous, you'll see. With steam, we can keep the railroad running all winter."

In December, the snows came, and it was impossible to meet on the ledge. Riley suggested the gazebo. "It's dangerous, I know, but I can't think of anyplace else. We'll just have to be careful."

His idea of caution was that they wouldn't do the things they'd been doing together since Thanksgiving. That abstinence made Andrea nervous and unhappy.

Their relationship had changed. At first it was she who pursued him; since they lay together in the gazebo, Riley had stopped fighting her and himself. Andrea knew that, but she suspected her hold on him remained fragile. If she were not careful, he'd revert to the old ways, say again those queer things about her not knowing how it really was and how they had to be just friends.

The Sunday after Christmas, when he kissed her, she thrust hard against him and unbuttoned the front of his trousers.

"No, not here. We mustn't . . ." he whispered.

"I don't care," she said. "I love you." She stepped back then, only a tiny step, and looked at his turgid male organ in the blue afternoon light. "I've never actually seen how a man was made before," she said softly.

Riley pulled her close with a groan. "It isn't right, not like this, Andrea. We have to get married. Somehow I've got to make your father agree."

She didn't answer. She was doing things to him instead, things she dreamed of frequently. Her fingers played over his swollen member, and she hiked up her petticoats and rubbed against it. Andrea wore no pantaloons. Riley realized she'd planned all along to resume their forbidden pleasures that day. He was angry; such forwardness was his prerogative, not hers. But he was marvelously excited nonetheless. He let his hand stray to her bodice and fumbled with the buttons.

"Yes," she murmured. "Yes, yes." She helped him with the dress, and when her breasts were exposed, she pushed his head down so he could kiss them.

They were just as he'd imagined, high and round and soft. He kissed the warm flesh and licked tentatively at the firm little nipples. She pulled him down to the floor. They twisted together in hunger.

Andrea worked herself on top of him and rubbed her secret, sensitive place on his thigh. He let his hand rest on her buttocks, pressing hard to keep up the pressure he knew she wanted. Then, when she was gasping and moaning so much he was terrified that someone would hear, he rolled over so that she was underneath. That way he could silence her mouth with his own. His hand was between her thighs, and he did the thing he'd been wanting to do for weeks but hadn't dared—he allowed his fingers to explore the hidden woman crevices. One kind of touch made her body arch and caused stifled whimpers to echo in her throat.

He felt the master of her, perhaps for the first time. It had nothing to do with loving her; it was the product of years of knowing she was Andrea Whitby and he was Riley Villette. He rubbed harder, and when he knew she could bear no more, he plunged himself into her. Their screams came together then, and neither of them thought of the proximity of the house.

"God," he breathed when it was over. "That was crazy, Andrea. That could have brought him down here."

She watched while he hastily buttoned his trousers and tucked in his shirt. Finally, she said, "They're not home. They went to the Murrays together. Mama does go out sometimes."

Riley stared at her. "Why didn't you tell me?"

She shrugged. "You didn't give me a chance. Besides, I don't care."

"Are you crazy!" He was really angry now. "You've got to care. Andrea, for God's sake, don't you realize anything? You could have a baby."

"I know," she said calmly. "I've thought about that. What if I do? Papa will have to let us marry then. Don't you want to marry me, Riley?"

"Want to . . ." His voice softened, and he touched her cheek. "I want to so much, but—"

"But what?"

"Nothing." He shook his head and said no more. He didn't think Jason Whitby would be so easily bested, but he couldn't tell that to Andrea.

Eve was waiting for Riley two nights later when he returned from work. "Something for you," she said. "From Hugh." She handed him a folded piece of paper.

"What's this?"

His mother couldn't read. She shrugged and said, "Don't know. This afternoon Hugh come home early. I thought he was sick, but he only take some things and tell me to give you this note."

Riley held the message in his hand. He was afraid to look at what it said. He looked at the cabin instead. It was filthy, as always. With four women in the house, why couldn't they keep it clean? Nobody minded but him, that's why. And now Hugh must be in some kind of trouble, wanting Riley to get him out of it.

"Read it," Eve said. "Tell me what it says."

She had grown fat in recent years. Her dress hung shapelessly from her shoulders, and there was an egg stain across her broad bosom. Riley didn't want to look at her. In the back he could hear his father and Jackie laughing together about something to do with the still. "Where are the girls?" he asked.

"Don't know. Out." Eve shrugged again.

"You shouldn't let them run loose," Riley said. "They're going to get into trouble."

"Celia, maybe," his mother answered, laughing. "And Betty sure. But Maryann, she is smart. Smarter than me, maybe." The oldest girl remained Eve's favorite and the one to whom she told things kept secret from the others.

The mention of his sixteen-year-old sister made Riley think

of Andrea, and he flinched. Eve didn't notice. "*Alors*," she said. "You read that thing. I want to know. If you won't read it, I give it to Jackie."

"That's what Jason Whitby did for the Villette brats, isn't it," Riley said. "We all went to his school, so we can read and write. Wonderful man, Jason Whitby."

"Jesus Christ! Don't again start that." Eve was angry, and she made a move to snatch the letter away from him.

"I'll read it." Riley twisted out of her reach. He opened the paper and studied the words in Hugh's careful hand. "Perfect penmanship," Riley said. "He gets an 'A' for that."

"What he say?" Eve repeated.

"Jesus . . ." Riley muttered under his breath. "I don't believe it."

"Gone, no?" Eve sat down heavily at the rickety table. "Gone away and left us."

"How did you know? Did he say anything to you?" Riley demanded.

"Nothing, he say nothing. I guess. All these years I guess something like this happen."

"He's gone to Canada to join a logging camp. They're paying good wages according to him. He says when he's saved enough money, he'll come home."

"Money enough for what?" his mother asked.

"He doesn't say. Mama, you really expected him to do this?" She nodded her head. "What about me? Do you expect me to go away?"

Eve looked at him and didn't answer. Then she sighed and started for the still to tell Jacques and Jackie. Riley watched her go and thought about his secret cache of escape money under the oak tree—along with the handkerchief stained with Andrea's blood.

Two weeks later, Jason received a visit from the fabled Mr. Jay Gould. The short, spare New Yorker came unannounced. Andrea let him in and asked him to wait in the study. "Papa's at the quarry," she explained. "I'll send someone to tell him you're here."

"Someone speedy, please, Miss Whitby," the man said coolly.

Jason was home in less than half an hour. He and Mr.

Gould remained closeted in the study a long time. When the undersized stranger came out, his host didn't accompany him. Andrea watched from her bedroom window while Mr. Gould stood for a moment staring around the town; then he got into his waiting carriage and drove away. A few minutes later, her father left the house and headed toward Lliam Murray's.

Dinner was over before Jason returned. Andrea was waiting for him. "I kept some food warm for you, Papa. I can bring you a tray in your study if you like."

"Thank you, my dear, but I'm not hungry."

He looked gray and tired and suddenly a great deal older. Andrea felt sympathy for him and anger at Jay Gould. "Mama's gone to bed," she said. "And Nelly and Martha have gone home." Her words were designed to assure him that the two of them were alone, that he could confide in her if he wished.

"Come into the drawing room, then," Jason said quietly. "Play something for me, Andrea. I'll have a drink."

She played Schubert, Haydn, and Chopin but not the nocturne Riley specially liked. Finally, she turned and said, "What's happened, Papa? You can tell me."

He smiled a little. The brandy and the music had relaxed him. "I lost a battle, Andrea, that's all. Not the war, just a battle."

"With Mr. Gould?"

"Yes. He's bought the railroad outright. It was devious and unscrupulous." Whitby laughed aloud. "And damned clever. He floated bonds, raised all the capital he needed without me. So now he owns the Rutland and Washington. Lock, stock, and barrel, as they say."

"Will he charge more to ship our slate?" Andrea asked.

Jason looked at her incredulously. It never occurred to him that the girl would understand the issue so swiftly. "That's the chief danger. You're right. But I won't let him do it, child. Don't worry your pretty head about that."

"I'm not worried," she said, turning the piano stool so she faced him directly. "I just want to know how you're going to stop him."

He couldn't avoid her direct gaze. "The line's no good to him without freight," he explained. "What I will do is see to it that all the shippers stick together and demand a fair price."

Andrea nodded her head. "You can do that, Papa. You're

Jason Whitby. People around here will listen to you more than to puny little Mr. Jay Gould from New York.''

Her father crossed the room and laid his hand on her silver hair. ''You're a remarkable young lady, Andrea,'' he said. ''I'm lucky to have you.''

''Even though I'm not a boy?'' she demanded. ''Not the son you always wanted?''

''Your mother's been saying silly things to you.'' Jason turned aside. ''You're my daughter. That's the only thing that matters.''

''When I have sons, Papa, they'll be your heirs. They will, won't they?''

''Andrea!'' He was shocked. ''No unmarried girl should say such things.''

She ignored his displeasure. ''But it's true, isn't it? My sons will be your grandsons, and they will inherit.''

''Yes,'' he said finally. ''That's my dream, too, Andrea. As soon as you're old enough to marry.''

''I'm not a child anymore, Papa.''

''No. I'm starting to realize that. We've a great future ahead, you and I, Andrea.''

''I know.'' She nodded solemnly.

The next day, Andrea began wearing her hair piled up on her head. Jason noticed, but he didn't say anything.

5.

''Andrea, I want to talk to you.'' Riley swallowed hard.

''Very well,'' she said. ''I'm listening.''

''Not here.'' He waved his arm around the dim gazebo with its cast-off rubble. ''This place is getting me down. Could we walk up to the ledge, do you think? It's not too cold today.''

The weather had turned mild, a typical late-January thaw. Andrea set out first, then waited for Riley to join her at the base of Herrick. When he came, they climbed the familiar trail together. Neither spoke. Nor did they touch until they reached the ledge. The rocky outcrop was snow-laden, icy.

They leaned back against the stone face of the mountain, and Riley pulled off Andrea's mitten and secreted her hand in the roomy pocket of his jacket. Fingers intertwined, breathing hard, they stood for some minutes.

"I've got to go away," Riley said finally.

She felt a pain grip her chest. "What do you mean? Go away where? For how long?"

"I can't say exactly how long. I'm going to New York. If I don't, we'll never be able to get married."

"I don't know what you're talking about. How can we get married if you're in New York?"

"I'm going so I can make some money. Then I'll come home, and we'll get married."

Andrea pulled her hand away from his. "You aren't making any sense, Riley. What makes you think you can earn money in New York?"

"It's the big city," he said stubbornly. "It's where everything's happening, Andrea. I've saved enough to see me through a time, long enough to get work, anyway."

"Are you going to join those trade unionists—that man Stephens you keep talking about?"

"Uriah S. Stephens," Riley amended. "No, he's in Philadelphia, not New York. There's no money to be made with the labor men, Andrea." He sounded sad but resigned.

She faced him for the first time since they began talking. "What's money to do with it, anyway? My father has enough."

"Your father . . ." He was stupefied to think she would presume so much.

"Yes, my father. Don't you see, once we're married, it won't matter. You'll be family. Our children will be Whitby heirs." She stopped and held her breath, waiting to see how much he understood.

Riley moved to the edge of the cliff, where he knew she didn't like to follow. "I intend to support my own wife. I don't plan on Jason Whitby doing it for me."

"Riley." There was no longer anger in her voice. "Step back here beside me. Please. You know it makes me nervous to be on the edge."

Andrea waited until he'd done as she asked; then he put her hand on his arm. "Very well, I'll go with you," she said. "We'll leave together and get married before anyone knows we're gone." He didn't answer, and she found herself warming to the romance of an elopement. "I can help you in New York," she said quickly. "There's a man who sees Papa sometimes. He's very powerful. His name's Jay Gould. We can find him. I'll introduce you, and when he realizes you're Jason Whitby's son-in-law, he'll give you a job and—"

"Jay Gould is a bastard," Riley said quietly. He didn't apologize for swearing. "I'd die before I'd work for him. Or be more beholden to your father than I already am." When he turned to face her, his eyes were wet with tears. "Andrea, I've got to do it my way, darling. Trust me; be patient, please. . . . I'll never ask you anything else."

She looked away, embarrassed by his being so close to crying and puzzled by the cold, dead feeling inside herself. "Very well, Riley," she said. "You do it your way."

He was gone before the week was out. Jason mentioned it casually at the dinner table. "Second one of those Villette lads has taken off. Riley, the teamster." He shook his head and reached for another of the hot crusty rolls he liked so well. "Don't know why those boys couldn't make something of themselves. I tried. Heaven knows I tried."

Millicent stared at her plate and gritted her teeth. Her once-generous mouth was a narrow white gash in her drawn face. Andrea quietly went on eating.

Three weeks later, Andrea announced, "Mama, I have to tell you something. Just stay calm and listen to me, please. I'm—" Her voice broke once; then she continued. "I'm going to have a baby."

Millicent stared at her daughter. Andrea was standing at the window of her mother's bedroom. Weak February sunshine outlined the girl's graceful figure and highlighted her silvery hair. "What did you say? I don't think I heard you right."

"Oh, Mama, please! Don't make it harder. I'm expecting a baby." Andrea set the tea tray on the table. She had steeled herself for such a moment. In many ways it was the solution to all problems. "I'm sorry if I disappoint you, Mama, but it's all going to work out fine, long before the baby comes in September."

"I don't believe you. You're making this up."

"No, I'm not. It's true." The girl sat down on the edge of the bed and folded her hands in her lap.

"Why . . . ? Who . . . ?" Millicent couldn't form a coherent sentence.

"I'm sorry to upset you, Mama." Andrea's composure began to crumble at the edges. "I know you're hurt and angry. But it's not so bad. We love each other, and we've planned all along to be married."

"Who—" Millicent demanded with sudden urgency. "Who do you love? Who is the father of this child?"

Andrea dropped her eyes. This was the hardest part of all. "Riley Villette," she whispered.

Millicent didn't say anything. Her tongue was swollen and dry, and her throat was constricting so that she couldn't breathe. For some seconds she stared at the top of her daughter's bent head. Finally, she said, "That is impossible. It's an abomination, too ugly to be true."

The girl straightened, and angry sparks showed in her eyes. "It's not ugly! Don't you say it again. I love Riley, and he loves me."

Millicent fell back on the pillows and pressed her hands to her cheeks. They felt hot, and she couldn't stop trembling. "You don't know, Andrea." Her voice was a low wail of anguish. "You can't know, and I can't tell you. But—"

"Mama, listen." Andrea got to her knees beside her mother's bed and took those frail white hands in her own. "It's not necessary to be so dramatic. Riley went to New York to earn enough money so Papa would agree to our getting married. I thought then I might be going to have a baby, but I didn't say. I wasn't sure, and I was mad at him for wanting to leave and— That doesn't matter. Papa can find him in New York, and he'll come home, and we'll get married. That's all there is to it."

Millicent struggled to sit upright, to free her hands from her daughter's grip. Then she was clasping the girl to her. "My baby, my poor little girl. It's all her fault, that awful Canadian woman. And Jason, it's his fault, too. But it will be all right. I know how to make it all right. I was just too startled at first. My poor baby . . ."

"It will be all right," Andrea agreed, too preoccupied with her own concerns to take in what Millicent was babbling. "I wanted you to know before I told Papa. I thought maybe you'd tell him with me."

"No!" Millicent pushed her away so she could look into

her eyes. "That's the one thing you must never do, never tell your father. You can't understand, Andrea, but you must obey me in this."

The girl's violet eyes widened. "But that's impossible. How can Papa not know?"

"Listen to me, child. . . . Get me those smelling salts over there." She took the crystal vial from her daughter's hand and inhaled deeply. "That's better. I'm feeling so strange, and I do want to make sense. It's important."

Millicent wiped her face with a bit of lavender chiffon.

"Sit down, my darling," she said, "and listen. There are things a lady can do in situations like this. Men don't understand; they're all beasts, anyhow. But women have ways. They have to. There are lady physicians who can make all this just a bad dream. We'll send you to your Aunt Susan in New Hampshire. No one will question that. Then she'll make the arrangements and take you down to Boston. Susan will do it if I ask her. I know she will. . . ."

"Mama." The voice that interrupted this breathy flow of information was expressionless, as cold as an east wind. "Are you suggesting I murder my baby? Do you mean for me to kill Riley's child?"

"It's not a child!" Millicent protested. "Not till it quickens. September, you said. That means you're only three months along, maybe less. It's not a child, Andrea." She grabbed for the girl's hand once more, but Andrea backed away.

"I won't do it," she said. "I'd never do such a thing. Papa wouldn't want me to. He wants heirs. Grandsons! You never gave him sons, but I will!"

She started toward the door, but Millicent stopped her. "Andrea, for the love of God, wait! Listen to me, this isn't a baby. It will be a monster, an abomination. You must listen. . . ."

Andrea ran from the room.

The thought of her father was uppermost in her mind. It pushed away the memory of the things Millicent said. Papa would be angry, of course; he'd rant and fume. But then he'd realize that she was carrying a Whitby heir, and he would make sense. Not like her mother. Papa wouldn't want to murder her child.

She grabbed a coat when she passed through the hall,

struggling to put it on while she stumbled and ran toward the quarry. She couldn't wait until he came home. She had to see Papa now.

"Sorry, Miss Andrea," old Gareth Jones told her. "Mr. Whitby left early today. Didn't say where he was goin'."

It was after three. It would be dark before four-thirty. Andrea sped back toward town, but when she reached Main Street, she didn't know where to go next. Lliam Murray's house—that was it. Papa must have gone to see Mr. Murray.

Sarah opened the door. "Andrea! Come in, child. What's wrong? Is it your mother?"

"No, Mrs. Murray. Mama's fine. So am I. I just need to find my father. He's not at the quarry. I thought he might be here."

"No. Lliam's in Rutland today. I haven't seen your father. . . ." Sarah suddenly clasped a hand to her forehead. "Yes, I did! I just remembered. I was in Howard's looking at some new calico, and I saw him walking toward the river— just out of the corner of my eye, you understand."

Andrea murmured a thank you and hurried off.

She composed herself as she walked through the fading light toward the Little Whitby. She mustn't let those crazy things Mama said disturb her at a time when she needed all her wits. The scene with Papa was going to be difficult. But he'd come around in the end. They thought alike. They always had.

When she came to the embankment, Andrea stopped. The woods were thick there, and dark. The snow was deep, too. And she hadn't stopped to put on galoshes. Her feet were soaked, her shoes ruined.

To her left was the path leading to the Villette cabin. Why should Papa have gone there? If he had business with the Villettes, he'd have summoned them to the house or the quarry. On the right lay another, less traveled path. It snaked away from the river to a less frequented part of the forest. Once, when she was a small child, Papa had taken her for a walk along that path. Andrea remembered a glen and a natural clearing. That must be where he'd gone. Funny day for it, though. She shivered and turned right.

Footprints appeared in the snow before she'd gone ten yards. One set belonged to a man and could very well be her father's; the others were made by a woman. There was no reason to think they'd come along the path together, however. In some places the two sets of prints overlapped. Andrea watched the ground and walked on.

It was just as well that Papa decided to take a walk that day. There in the woods was the right place to confront him with her news. They could have it all out with no one to hear, and by the time they went home, they'd have made it up and reached an agreement. There was only one possible solution. The next day Papa must send to New York to find Riley.

She was so busy planning what she'd say and watching the path that she almost missed the clearing. It was small and isolated, just as she remembered, and at first she thought it was empty. Then she saw a man and a woman. She edged a little closer. It was her father and Maryann Villette.

Andrea stood still, afraid despite all her brave thoughts. What was Papa doing there? Why was he talking to Riley's sister?

She stood still, trying to decide what to do; then she heard the girl laugh. It was the sound of mockery and triumph. A few seconds passed. Andrea held her breath.

"You need horsewhipping," she heard her father say.

"This is what I need," Maryann said. She tucked a folded wad of bills into the front of her dress. "And I'll keep my mouth shut, which is what you need. Wouldn't do to let folks know the great Mr. Whitby was fucking Eve Villette for years and years and now he's fucking her daughter, who probably is *his* daughter, too."

He looked as if he were going to strike her, but he didn't. "You're filthy," he said. "You've got an ugly mouth."

The girl stepped forward and thrust her aggressive breasts toward him. "Why don't you beat me, then? Don't I deserve it?" She threw back her head and laughed. "I know why. 'Cause you'd rather fuck me. Isn't that it?"

"I want to be rid of you," he muttered.

"You want your cock in me, Jason Whitby," Maryann repeated. "I know it, and you know it. My ma knows it, too. I tell her everything. She thinks it's real funny that you know that maybe you got sons, after all. Only they's bastards, which ain't how you planned it."

"No more," Jason said. "This is the last time I meet you here." He turned to walk away.

Maryann stood her ground. Andrea shrank further back into the shelter of the trees, her heart pounding. She thought he must have heard it, but Jason passed the place where she stood and kept walking.

Andrea watched Maryann. When Jason was out of sight, the smile on the other girl's face faded and became a pout. She took the roll of bills out of her dress and counted them, then put them back. Finally, she shrugged and headed away from the clearing toward the cabin.

Abomination. The word hammered at the fringe of Andrea's mind as she walked home, and remained there after she locked herself in her bedroom.

Papa and Eve Villette—her children are Jason's bastards. Papa and Maryann—who is my sister, but he lies with her, anyway. Andrea put her fist into her mouth to keep from screaming. Just as I lie with Riley, who is my brother. Only I didn't know, but Papa does. So does Maryann, and—oh, God! —Riley knows! That's what he meant when he said I didn't understand about him. That's why he went away.

Andrea pressed her hand to her head to stop the pounding, but the terrible thoughts wouldn't disappear. Mama knows, too. That's why she called my baby an abomination. Because Riley is my brother. Once more she had to stuff her hands in her mouth and bite the knuckles to keep from shouting.

The little brass gong sounded for dinner, but Andrea didn't go downstairs. A few minutes later the maid knocked on the door. "Your father's waiting on you, Miss Andrea."

"I'm ill," she said. "I'm not coming down."

"Shall I tell Mr. Whitby to send for the doctor?"

Andrea struggled for her normal voice. "No, that's not necessary. It's just a headache—just ordinary."

"Oh, I understand," Nelly said. She knew all about monthly headaches. "I'll tell Mr. Whitby."

Around nine someone tapped on the door. "Andrea, it's me, darling." Millicent's presence outside her daughter's bedroom was a sign of the extraordinary.

"Go away, Mama. I have a headache."

There was silence for a few seconds. "Very well. We can talk again in the morning."

By morning the girl was gone. She left with a single suitcase that she pulled behind her on a small sled and thirty-six dollars removed from the strongbox in her father's study. She left no note and returned the empty strongbox and its key to their customary positions. She also made her bed, neatly and carefully, before leaving.

It took her nearly three hours to walk into Poultney. She was there in time to catch the early-morning train to New York.

Chapter Three

She had to change at Fort Edward and again at Troy.
Andrea went through the motions benumbed. She kept won-
dering if she would see Riley as soon as she arrived. Ridiculous,
New York was a big place. But he was one of the only two
people she knew in the city. The other was Jay Gould.
Somehow it seemed she must see one of them.

Towns like Redbrook, Cleremont, Hyde Park, and Fishkill
drifted across the landscape. The cities looked something like
Rutland, except that there were no mountains. She found
herself searching for them, feeling the lack of their looming
presence as a personal loss.

When they approached New York, it had grown dark, and
she could see nothing but pinpoints of yellow gaslight in the
blackness. Finally, the conductor walked through, calling,
"New York City. Hudson River Depot, New York City."

Andrea took her bag, her coat, and her muff and stumbled
to the door. She was groggy with exhaustion and suddenly
afraid. The step down to the platform was very low, and she
was grateful when the conductor took her things and handed
her down. "You'll want to put this on, miss," he said kindly,
holding her coat so she could shrug into it. "Mighty cold out
there."

She managed a smile to accompany her thanks.

"You being met?" he asked. "Got somebody waiting for
you here?"

"I'm expected at my aunt's," she lied quickly. She could
sense the other questions in his mind. "I know where it is."

"That's all right, then," the conductor said. "Just go out
that big door." He pointed along a seemingly endless platform.
"There's plenty of hansoms out there."

She nodded and moved away, carrying her bag and her
muff and trying not to lose her footing in the jostling crowds.

The depot was hot, made so by milling humanity and potbellied stoves scattered along the platforms. Overhead a big clock said eight-thirty, and Andrea had to search her mind to decide if it was night or morning. Night, of course; she'd left Poultney early in the morning. It seemed a lifetime ago.

A man fell into step next to her. He was portly and bewhiskered, and his top hat was tilted back on his head. He had to struggle to stay beside her, but he managed it. "Excuse me, little lady. Heard you say you were going to your aunt's. If you'll just tell me where that is, perhaps I can escort you. I'm taking a cab myself. Glad to drop you."

"No, thank you." She mumbled the words and walked as fast as she could. Finally, she came to the doors. Outside, the cold air washed over her. She lost her breath and had to stand still for a moment and get adjusted. She searched out of the corner of her eye for her would-be escort but didn't see him. Andrea sighed with relief. She wished she'd worn warmer gloves. It was impossible to use her muff and carry the suitcase, too.

A line of horse-drawn cabs was just ahead on the corner. People were hiring them as quickly as they poured out the doors of the depot. They'd all be taken soon. Andrea mentally fingered the money pinned into her pocket. The railway ticket had cost $3.75, so she had $32.25 left. She decided against the cab.

There was a frightful din in the vicinity of the station. When she walked some distance from the building, the sound decreased. Dirty snow covered the ground, and there were bits of paper and glass and rubbish everywhere. She pursed her lips in distaste. A gaslight cast a pale yellow glow on the corner where she stood. She looked up and saw a sign saying Ninth Avenue and another, at right angles to it, that said Twenty-ninth Street.

She knew of the Brunswick Hotel at Fifth Avenue and Twenty-sixth Street, that was where her father always stayed. The thought of him was like a pain in her belly. She sucked in her breath and shook her head and forced the thought from her mind. A couple came toward her. They were young and walked arm in arm, looking at each other and laughing.

"Excuse me," Andrea said. "Could you tell me which direction is Fifth Avenue?"

They told her and explained that Twenty-sixth Street was three blocks downtown from where they stood. "Downtown and east. You sure you've got that?" the man asked.

"Thank you. Yes, I've got it." Andrea began walking.

It was after nine when she reached the hotel. She stood on the pavement and peered in at the elegant lobby, filled with elegant people. Thirty-two dollars and twenty-five cents. The Brunswick Hotel was out of the question. She kept walking.

She came to a street of houses with BOARD AND LODGING signs in the window. Andrea climbed the stairs of the nearest one. The heavy brass knocker made a loud, demanding sound.

The streets of New York were full of people and carriages and horse-drawn buses that raced everywhere. For days she walked and thought. Not logical, coherent thoughts but a formless set of ideas and convictions slowly taking shape in her mind. She didn't want to find Riley. When she thought of him, of his body and the things they'd done that had produced the life growing inside her, she went red with shame. Never before had she felt anything wrong about their lovemaking. Now the memory singed her and made her tremble. She didn't want to see Riley Villette ever again.

What about the child, then? The abomination, as her mother had termed it. Did she want to do what Millicent suggested? No, that was murder; it was a sin. She reminded herself of what her mother had said. "It's not a baby until it quickens." Andrea clasped her hands across her still-flat stomach and knew she couldn't accept that reasoning.

It will be maimed, she told herself. Deformed. Insane. That's what happens when brother and sister make a baby. So be it, she decided. She would care for the poor thing. Always. That would be her penance.

Eventually, the realization dawned that she needed to find a job. She had less than twenty-five dollars left. She also began to wonder if her father was looking for her. He must be. Unless, of course, Mama told him the truth. If Jason knew, he might be content to let her disappear. She hoped Millicent had hurled the truth at him, screamed the fact that his daughter was going to have a baby and because of the evil things he had done it was an abomination. She hoped so, but she doubted it. Mama would lie silent on her bed and watch Papa with accusing eyes, but she would say nothing. So he must be looking for her.

That didn't matter. Among these thousands of people it was unlikely Jason Whitby could find his daughter. Just as it was unlikely she would see Riley. Or Jay Gould. That made her laugh. The funny, bitter little chuckle she'd adopted of late. Imagine her crossing paths with the powerful Mr. Gould. In less than two weeks in New York she had come to understand the absurdity of that notion.

The period in which she looked for work was one Andrea later blocked out of her mind. It was March, and winter was loosening its grip on the city. The dirty snow turned to dirtier slush. At night, the slush froze, and in the morning the streets were a mass of icy ruts and small, insurmountable mountains. Then it melted again and swirled in the pavements and gutters and soiled the hem of her dress no matter how careful she tried to be. Horse dung and all manner of other refuse flowed in the melting rivulets. One gown, her best blue serge, was stained beyond her ability to clean it, and she was reduced to wearing the two other dresses she'd brought with her, a pale rose silk and a lavender moiré. Neither was suitable for the weather or the conditions of her life.

She first tried for work at an agency whose sign said they supplied maids and governesses to better families. They weren't interested when they learned she had no experience. Then she went to a music school and asked about giving piano lessons.

The director took her to a small studio with a piano. When she'd been playing for a few minutes, he leaned over her shoulder as if to turn the sheet of music, and his breath nuzzled her neck, and she felt his hand creeping up her midriff. She stood up hastily and moved away from his reach, and he said he was sorry but there were no openings for piano teachers at present.

In the factories they just looked and shook their heads. She was so obviously not one of the breed of women bending over the stitching machines. Andrea understood. And she knew that in six weeks, possibly less, her pregnancy would show. She'd already let out the waist of one of her dresses.

By the time she accepted the truths implicit in these

experiences, it was nearly April, and she had three dollars left. Not enough to pay for another week in the boarding-house. She packed her suitcase and left early, before anyone was awake and could see or speak to her.

2.

Andrea found a rooming house on the Lower East Side that charged twenty cents a night. You didn't get a room, however; you got a bed in a dormitory with six other women. On one wall a shaky hand had scratched the words "Oh, God! that bread should be so dear and flesh and blood so cheap!"

She didn't sleep at all that night. She was too frightened, too conscious of the breathing and stirring of the others. There was a big, blowsy blonde who looked as if she'd been pretty once and didn't belong in this charnel house of despair. One old hag was really filthy, but her bed was far from Andrea's. The girl lay awake, stared into the darkness, and tried to make herself believe this was all really happening to her. Andrea Whitby of Whitby Falls, princess. Not anymore.

Dawn came, and the other women slept on. Andrea rose, dressed, and tiptoed to the door, carrying her suitcase. She had her hand on the knob when the once-pretty blonde came up beside her. "My name's Maggie. There's coffee and rolls downstairs. Only a nickel. You better get something to eat before you take off."

"Thank you, I will."

"No, you won't." Maggie shook her head. "You're too damned scared and shocked at being in a place like this. I seen it all before, a hundred times. C'mon, baby girl. Maggie will have breakfast with you. Like I said, you gotta eat."

They bought their food and at Maggie's suggestion took it out on the stoop. It was very early. The sun was spring warm, and the air felt fresh and clean. There was little traffic at this hour—a few milk wagons, no pedestrians. Andrea sipped the hot drink and gnawed on the stale roll and was grateful. "Thank you," she said to Maggie. "You were right. I would have left without it."

"I know. Where you going, kid?"

Andrea shrugged. "I'm not sure. I'm trying to find a job."

"How about home?" Then, when the girl looked blank, she said, "I mean, how about going back where you come from? Get out of this jungle. You don't belong here."

"I can't go home," Andrea said.

"Can't or won't? Okay, don't answer. It's none of my business, anyway." Maggie pushed her heavy blond hair off her forehead. She was about forty, maybe more, and her skin was splotchy, and her eyes red rimmed. Her smile, however, was genuine—broad and wide and warm. "What kind of work do you do?" she asked.

"That's just it." Andrea managed to laugh. "I don't seem to be able to do any."

"Poor baby." Maggie clucked softly and took another swallow of her coffee.

Andrea didn't want any more attention focused on her problems. "What about you?" she asked. "Have you a job?"

"Yeah," the other woman said. "I'm a hostess." She watched the silver-haired child out of the corner of her eye. "For important men. Gents from Tammany Hall and the like. You understand about that, kid?"

"A hostess? You mean you give parties, entertain? For politicians?"

Maggie chuckled. "Something like that. Now I suppose you're wondering what I'm doing down here in this flophouse."

"I was, sort of," Andrea admitted.

"Demon rum," Maggie said matter-of-factly. "I drink, little girl. Something fierce. Not all the time, mind you; just once in a while, when I get blue or mad or just bored. Then I drink until I can't stand up, and no one wants to know me, and eventually I come down here. Owner's a friend of mine. Did him a favor once. He takes me in and lets me recover, you might say. Took over a week this time. I'm okay now, though. Going home today. Back to my regular work."

Andrea felt horribly embarrassed but couldn't let the opportunity go by. "You wouldn't—I mean, you couldn't hire me, could you? Does hostessing involve having jobs to give to girls?"

"Oh, sweet baby." Maggie shook her head and looked at the girl with her silver hair and her violet eyes. "This town is going to eat you up and spit you out in pieces. You don't know anything, do you?''

"I'm sorry." Andrea didn't know why she was apologizing. "I just thought—"

"Listen!" The older woman moved closer to the girl and grabbed both her hands. "Isn't there anything you can do to earn a living? Anything at all?"

Andrea was taken aback by Maggie's intensity. "I've tried everything I could think of," she said. "I can't be a governess or even a maid because I've no references. And the factories won't give me a chance. They say I don't look strong enough. I applied for a position as a piano teacher, but the man was horrible. He—"

"Wait a minute!" Maggie was squeezing Andrea's hands. "You play the piano? Are you any good?"

"Not bad. I've had lessons since I was a little girl. And I can sing a bit."

The blonde hooted in triumph. "That's it, then! I know just the thing. And you'll do, baby girl. The way you look, you'll do fine!"

She made Andrea wait while she dressed and exchanged a few words with the owner of the rooming house; then they took a bus uptown. Andrea sat silently, watching the team of horses pull the heavy wooden vehicle. Maggie didn't explain any further, and Andrea hadn't the courage to ask questions. Soon they were standing on Third Avenue and Twenty-seventh Street. Maggie dragged Andrea around the corner to a tiny opening between two buildings marked Broadway Alley. "Here it is, baby. The answer to your maiden's prayer." She laughed, and Andrea had to laugh with her. There was a door and a sign over it that said, O'FLAHERTY'S BAR, and beneath that, LADIES WITH ESCORTS INVITED.

"I don't understand," Andrea said finally.

"You will, child." Maggie was beaming. She pushed open the door and walked into the deserted gloom. "Desi!" she bellowed. "Where the hell are you, you no good lazy Irish lout!"

Andrea tried to adjust to the dark after the bright sunlight of the street. There was a counter along one side and a lot of mirrors behind it, and there were booths and tables. The place was empty at this hour, but the smell of the previous night's beer and smoke hung in the air. In the far corner was a tiny raised stage surrounded by footlights, and an old upright piano.

A man came to join them from somewhere in the dark recesses behind the bar. He was yawning, and he wore an undershirt and suspenders and nothing on his bare feet. He had a shock of red hair and a red beard that gleamed even in the darkened room; when he spoke, his brogue sounded like music. "Sure if it isn't Maggie! Might have known it would be you, waking a man from his bed in the middle of the night."

"It's not the middle of the night, you fool. It's morning. And I brung you a present. This is Andrea." She pulled the girl forward like a prize steer at the county fair. "Ain't she something? And she can play the piano and sing. Now thank me proper."

Desi O'Flaherty looked the girl up and down. Then he walked around and examined her from the other side. "Andrea, is it?" he said in his soft singsong voice. "Pretty name for a pretty girl. One of yours, Maggie?"

"Course not! Can't you tell a lady when you see one? If she was one of mine, I wouldn't be bringing her here. She's an entertainer. Legitimate."

Andrea didn't have any idea what the exchange was all about, but she knew she mustn't let this opportunity go by. "I'd be glad to play for you, Mr. O'Flaherty," she said. "Is that piano tuned?"

"Mr. O'Flaherty," he repeated, and chuckled. "I like that. But it's Desi, lass. Everybody calls me Desi. As to the piano, I don't know if it's tuned. Nobody's played it since Sally got married."

"His last entertainer, Sally LaFrance," Maggie explained. "Got married a couple of months ago. Now she's Mrs. Sally Winestein from Brooklyn."

Andrea walked to the instrument and turned back the cover of the keyboard. The ivories were thick with dust, but when she fingered them lightly, they responded. "Not too bad," she said.

"Go on, kid," Maggie said. "Show Desi how great you are."

Andrea dusted off the stool, sat down, and paused for a moment. "I don't have any music with me, you understand," she said softly.

"That's all right, lass," Desi said. "Just play something you can remember. There's bits of paper with music written on sold all over New York. We can take care of that later."

Andrea thought for a moment, then began part of Schubert's song cycle *Die Winterreise*. Her confidence increased as she played, and her voice carried in the dark, low-ceilinged room. Finally, she finished, and she let her hands fall into her lap and waited.

"Hell, kid," Maggie said at last. "Don't you know anything livelier? I thought when you said you was a singer . . ." Her crestfallen voice trailed away.

"Don't listen to her, lass," Desi interposed firmly. "I'm the boss here, and I liked your song. Sure it'll give the place a bit of class. Besides, like I said, we can buy music anywhere in New York. What kinds of gowns do you have?" He gestured to her suitcase.

"Only this one," Andrea said shyly. "And another. I'm not a real entertainer."

"Forget that." Maggie had regained her sense of command. "I can lend her some gowns until she's able to buy some of her own."

"Nothing too much," Desi said softly. "I want her to look like she looks now, Maggie. Not like one of yours."

"Don't you think I know that?" the woman demanded. "Why'd you think I brought her here rather than to my place if I didn't know that? And you treat her right, Desi O'Flaherty. If you don't, I'll scratch your eyes out. And ruin some other vital parts while I'm at it."

3.

In the months that followed his daughter's departure, Jason Whitby became an old man. At first he hoped that eventually he would understand the thing and put it right. Not until those hopes died did the onslaught of age begin. His hair had been shot with gray for many years; now the silver became a sickly yellow. His skin was yellow, too, and it sagged along his jawline and under his eyes.

Millicent watched the transformation with satisfaction.

In those cold winter weeks right after Andrea left, Millicent intended to tell her husband what she knew. She would tell him Andrea was pregnant, that Riley Villette had fathered the child. Yes, she'd tell him. She was only biding her time, waiting for the right moment to make her revelations. She kept thinking about it and the way he'd look when he heard it all. She wouldn't say anything about Eve, Millicent decided. She'd let Jason see for himself the terrible fruits of his infidelity.

But the right moment to speak her truth never materialized. Instead, she witnessed the changes in Jason and came to understand that his fears were worse than the reality.

That's my daughter's vengeance for the terrible injustice he's done her, Millicent told herself. Jason must atone for the legacy of sin he's left to Andrea. She remained silent, and satisfied with her silence. As to Andrea's whereabouts, Millicent wasted little time in speculation.

"She's in God's hands," she said repeatedly to her husband, to the servants, and to Tessa Sills and Sarah Murray. In fact, Millicent began speaking more and more of God.

Jason wasn't prepared to leave the mystery to the Almighty. He went first to the police in Rutland. His daughter was missing, he reported, and because of who he was, they made every effort to find her. "An accident, maybe," they said. "Or foul play." They combed the woods and climbed the mountain and examined the open quarries. They even dislodged the hills of slate rubble and dragged the Little Whitby.

The second theory was kidnapping. "Can't be that," a tired old officer said finally. "Ten days and no ransom demands." Then a young member of the force, a lad with an eye to getting ahead, had the notion of questioning the ticket sellers and the conductors of the railway. Three days later, he came to the big house to report.

"Poultney, sir—that's where she boarded the train. Chap who sold her the ticket to New York remembers Miss Andrea—the conductor, too."

"Who was with her?" Whitby demanded. "Who was forcing her to make the journey?"

The young man squirmed. "Fact is, sir, they didn't see anyone. Both men say she was alone, traveling of her own free will."

"Rubbish," Whitby said forcefully. "Why would she do that? You don't know my daughter. I tell you, it's unthinkable."

"I'm sure, sir. That's why I'm making further inquiries. She had to change at Fort Edward and then at Troy if she went to New York. I'm looking for the train attendants on those parts of the journey."

"Good lad," Jason said. "Keep it up. I won't forget it."

At the end of the week the policeman returned. "Found him, Mr. Whitby, the conductor on the Troy–New York trip." He cleared his throat nervously. Jason waited. Eventually, the lad reported everything he'd learned. Even the bit about Andrea saying she was going to the home of an aunt who expected her.

"But it's impossible! She doesn't have an aunt in New York."

"All the same, sir, it's what she said. And the conductor was dead sure she was by herself. No one forcing her, that is."

Whitby drummed his fingers on the arm of his chair. "Get out," he said finally. "You think I don't realize you're in league with them?"

"With who, sir?" The boy was genuinely puzzled.

"With whoever abducted my daughter. Now get out of my house and out of Vermont. You'll never work again in this state."

A few days later, Sarah Murray came to see him. "Jason, I thought I might speak with you if you're not too busy."

He looked up to see her standing in the door of his study. She had grown plump with the years, but Sarah Murray still had the look of a girl about her. Whitby managed to smile. Lliam's wife was a good woman, and he'd always liked her. "Come in, Sarah. What can I do for you?"

"Nothing, Jason." She sat down gingerly at the edge of a chair, twisting her hands in her lap. "It's just that I think I'd best tell you something. I should have spoken before. I know it was my duty, but—"

He sighed. It was obviously something about Millicent. He didn't need anyone to tell him his wife was getting worse, that he should put her away. He'd been considering it for some time, thinking only that he'd wait until Andrea was married. "All right, Sarah," he said gently. "Speak your mind. I'm listening."

"It's about Andrea."

"Andrea!" Whitby rose and stood looking down at his visitor. "For the love of heaven, Sarah, if you know something about Andrea, why have you waited this long to tell me!"

"But I don't! Not really. I just know that she was looking for you."

"Looking for me the day before she disappeared, you mean?" He sank wearily to his chair once more. "I know that. Gareth Jones told me she came to the pit. If you only knew how often I've cursed myself for not being there." He ran nervous fingers through his hair, then leaned back in exhaustion.

"I don't know about her going to the quarry," Sarah said. "But she came to my house; I know that. About three in the afternoon."

Whitby leaned forward. "That would make it right after she left the quarry. Yes? Go on, Sarah, for God's sake."

"Well, like I said, she came to the door and asked if you were with Lliam. But I told her Lliam was in Rutland that day. You know, Jason, the day he went to talk to the man about a new roof for the school." He nodded, and she could see in his eyes that she was dragging the story out too much, putting off the moment she dreaded.

Sarah swallowed hard and continued. "You see, I first told her I didn't know where you were. Then I remembered—it came to me all sudden-like—that I'd seen you when I was buying some calico. Just out of the corner of my eye. I saw you walking toward the river. So I told Andrea that," she finished lamely.

Whitby sat silent for the space of ten seconds. When he stood up, no hint of despair showed in his voice. "Thank you, Sarah," he said quietly. "It probably doesn't shed much light, but thank you, anyway."

She was gratified by his calm reaction. "You're welcome, Jason. Anything I can do, anything . . ."

After she left, Jason stared after her. It was clear to him that Sarah knew about his indiscretions. About who the Villette brats were. If she didn't, she'd never have been so nervous or delayed her report so long.

He found himself hating the sight of her straight back as she hurried down Main Street. Sarah not only knew; she was the cause of Andrea's knowing. His daughter had come searching for him for whatever reason—some girlish enthusiasm, most likely—and Sarah Murray had maliciously and deliberately pointed her toward the river. Then Andrea must have come to the clearing, must have seen her father with Maryann Villette.

"Oh, my God . . ." He whispered the words into the twilight, and they hovered over his head, a sword of destruction. "Oh, my God. Andrea must have heard everything."

Soon after that, Jason hired a firm of private investigators to search for Andrea in New York. He told them she was alone, that she must have arrived with little more than thirty or forty dollars. Until then, he'd not admitted to himself that the money missing from his strongbox had been taken by Andrea. He'd kept insisting it was stolen by the same people who forced her to leave. Now he permitted himself to see the truth and to tell it to the detectives.

The second result of Sarah Murray's visit was that the aging process accelerated. He could see it himself not only in his mirror but in the eyes of everyone around him. Jason's bitterness at the blow struck by fate festered in him like an ulcer.

If he hadn't gone to meet Maryann that day, if Andrea hadn't come seeking him, if Sarah Murray hadn't seen him. If, if, if. Hate and anger oozed from his pores. They were the cause of his skin discoloring and sagging, the poison that yellowed his hair.

Millicent kept looking at him. He could feel her stare following him night and day. What had happened to her astonishing violet eyes, Jason sometimes wondered. When had they become the haunted things with which she looked at him now? As the weeks lengthened to months and the private investigators brought him no news, Millicent became an accusatory presence that permeated the big house. Jason resolved to go ahead with his plans to commit her to an asylum for the insane, but he couldn't muster enough energy to make the arrangements.

All that spring he slept at his desk, even took his meals there. Apart from that, he only traveled as far as the pit. He'd stand on the hillside, looking at the busy scene below and listening to the explosions of dynamite and black powder.

When the horses dragged the huge blocks of slate to the shanties, he watched in fascination. How could it be that all this was still going on? The Whitby Quarry was still producing; the town of Whitby Falls still paying him its rents and its homage, and all for nothing. All to die when he died. It was monstrous.

4.

In her first two weeks at O'Flaherty's Bar Andrea learned a great deal.

Her routine was quickly established. She played from six to seven for the early-evening trade, the men stopping for a bit of liquid refreshment before going home. At that time she did classical things, the music with which she was familiar. Then she took a break and had some supper out in the back kitchen.

The cook was a big Negro woman from Barbados. Her name was Delilah, and she had been in New York since she'd been brought there as a teenager by the man who owned her. "Was it when Mr. Lincoln freed the slaves, Delilah?" Andrea asked. "Is that when he let you go?"

"He letted me go when I said I was gonna cut off his cock if he didn't." Cook spoke the words matter-of-factly. "No point keepin' a whore that might cut you up when you was sleepin'. That's why he letted me go."

Eventually, Andrea learned the meaning of the word whore and of the various levels of professional behavior under which they were organized. Maggie Hoyt, Delilah explained, was the fanciest madame in the city. Her girls were famous. "She coulda took you in, honey chile. You would of fit jus' fine, with that hair and them eyes. Didn't 'cause she wanted to do you a good turn. You be real grateful to Miss Maggie. She done right by you. Mind you"—Delilah eyed Andrea critically—"she might not o' thought you pretty enough if she seen the way you is fillin' out. You better stop eatin' so much o' my cookin'. You's gettin' fat, honey chile. You truly is."

At that moment, Andrea almost told Delilah the reason she was putting on weight. Maybe the Negro woman could help her make some dresses that would conceal her pregnancy. As it happened, Desi came in just then, and Andrea didn't say anything.

The only opportunity to talk to Delilah was during that supper break. From eight-thirty until the small hours of the morning, Andrea entertained the gentlemen drinkers and their lady friends. Desi had brought her an armload of the latest sheet music, and she learned to play and sing lively songs. Andrea Adams—Desi had decided that was a better name for a professional *chanteuse*—was a popular addition to O'Flaherty's Bar.

Sometimes while she was performing, she would watch the customers and fantasize about their lives. One man who came in every night was so ugly it hurt to look at him, but he was always accompanied by a dark-haired woman of astounding, exotic beauty. "That's Sheila Briony," Delilah explained. "Was the most chased-after woman in New York a few years ago. Men was killin' themselves just 'cause she didn't smile at 'em."

"But then why—" Andrea didn't need to finish the sentence.

" 'Cause she had a kid, that's why. Had a baby without bein' married to its father. Thumbed her nose at any what didn't think it proper. Girl can't do that, honey chile; not open like that. Folks don't care what you do, long as you don' rub their noses in it."

Andrea went pale but said nothing. Later, she made an opportunity to mention Sheila Briony to Desi.

A pleasant, easygoing man, Desi was good to her. He gave her a room over the bar and all her meals and paid her five dollars a week besides. He told her jokes and laughed with her and took her on long walks. He'd never made an improper overture, and she'd never heard him say an unkind word about anyone. "Isn't it a shame," she said one afternoon while they strolled along Madison Avenue looking at the grand houses. "About Sheila Briony. She's so beautiful, and it's so tragic."

"She's a tramp," Desi said quickly. "Don't you go taking up with the likes of Sheila, lass. Had a child, she did. And her not married. Even kept the poor little waif. No decent woman would do such a thing." He dismissed the ill-fated Miss Briony with a wave of his hand. Andrea felt an icy lump forming in the pit of her stomach.

*   *   *

"Come in, baby girl." Maggie eyed Andrea suspiciously. "What you doing here at this hour?" She led the girl to her sitting room at the back of the house.

Andrea had twice before taken tea with her benefactress. Familiar with the cozy little room, its overstuffed chairs and lace antimacassars, she wasted no time examining it now. "Maggie," she said, "I'm going to have a baby."

"Desi," the older woman gasped. "That bastard! I'll kill him!"

"Don't be silly. It's not Desi. How could it be. I've only been at the bar for three weeks. My baby's due in September."

Maggie's eyes narrowed. "Stand up," she said. "Hold your skirts in." She cocked her head and examined the girl's profile. "Damn it. You're telling the truth, ain't you? So that's why you couldn't go home."

Andrea sat down and folded her hands in her lap and looked straight at her friend. "I didn't intend to come whining to you. I intended to have my child and keep it. Lately, I've come to realize that's impossible."

"It sure is, little girl. Keeping it, anyway. Your life's well over if you do a dumb thing like that." Maggie shook her head sadly. "There's homes, though. Most are run by nuns. You can go to one and have your baby, and the sisters will find someone to adopt it."

"No." Andrea said. "That won't do. No one would want my child." She closed her lips with an air of finality.

Maggie didn't require long explanations. "Okay, honey," she said softly. "I got the picture. Leastwise as much as I need to have. You want a doctor, right?"

Andrea nodded.

"Time was when that was easy." Maggie sighed. "There was female physicians advertising in every paper in New York. Then them smartasses up in Albany made it illegal. So now the only place a woman can get help is from crooks. Men!" She spat out the word. "All cocks. No brains and no hearts."

Of late, Andrea had ceased to blush at explicit language. "I can still have the operation, can't I?" she asked. "Even if it's illegal."

"I'll see that you do, sweetie. Never mind about the laws. Besides," she said, laughing loudly, "better'n half the lawmakers is regular customers at my house. They ain't likely to make any fuss about a friend of mine.''

She got up and poured a small glass of wine for Andrea. Between binges, Maggie herself was a teetotaler. "Here, it may be morning, but you need this. Now, September, you said. That means you're what . . . nearly four months gone.'' Maggie whistled through her teeth. "Makes it tougher. We better tell Desi you gonna be sick for about a week. No.'' She snapped her fingers. "I got a better idea. We'll tell him you're goin' home to visit your folks. Then you'll move in here and stay till you're recovered.'' She laid her hand on Andrea's silver hair. "Leave everything to Maggie, baby. Men make the trouble, but we women know how to get ourselves out of it.''

5.

When he first went to New York, Riley intended to write to Andrea every week. He'd start as soon as he got a position, he decided. Then he could keep her informed of how much he was making and saving. She'd be party to it all, right along with him. They would plan their future together.

But he didn't find work immediately. Riley was embarrassed to write to Andrea and tell her no one wanted to hire him. New York, it seemed, had plenty of teamsters; one more wasn't needed. Teamsters earned good money, and the jobs were given to men known by the haulage companies. When he got a job lugging crates of fish at the Fulton Street Market, he was ashamed to report such a humble beginning. He didn't want to tell Andrea that almost all the four dollars a week he earned went to pay for his room and board and that he had nothing to save toward their marriage.

"Hey, Villette! C'mon, you Canuck bastard, move your ass!''

That was the extent of his conversation with his boss. It didn't seem likely to lead to promotion. After the first few days Riley gave up trying to explain that he wasn't a Canadian, that he'd been born in Vermont. He also gave up expecting to get ahead at the Fulton Market. They were interested only in his broad shoulders and brawny arms.

The hours were long, from five in the morning until after seven in the evening, and they left him no time to look for a better opportunity. At night, when he returned to the boarding-house on Pearl Street, he was too exhausted even to dream of the future.

Because his landlady objected to the fact that he stank of fish, he had to strip off his clothes in the backyard and scrub himself with the bucket of icy water she provided. Then he was allowed to go inside and join the other lodgers at supper. It was Riley's one meal of the day, as he left too early to eat the breakfast for which he was paying. After supper, he slept until it was time to return to work.

The notion of writing a letter to Andrea became more and more remote. But the girl herself lived in his memory, a talisman against the backbreaking drudgery of his life in the big city. Andrea, who, despite all the odds, loved him and was waiting for him.

Spring came with lengthening days and warmth. Riley didn't have to fight through the snow and ice to get to Fulton Street; he could walk easily along streets made less ugly by sunrise, marveling at the early end to winter compared to what he'd known all his life. In the evening, when supper at the boardinghouse was finished, he took advantage of the long twilight to stroll along Pearl Street, studying the other men of this, the greatest city in the world.

There was one saloon where he sometimes stopped for a glass of beer. It only cost a nickel, and he had seventy cents a week left from his wages after he paid his rent. The saloon was called Barney's, but the proprietor was named Saul. "Wouldn't do to call it Saul's," the fellow explained to Riley one night. "In this town, any bar that ain't Irish might as well close down."

"Why's that?" Riley asked, sipping at the tall foamy head of his drink. " 'Cause of them?" he nodded his head toward the opposite wall, where placards proclaimed the virtues of the Democrats running for office. Every candidate was named Clancy or O'Toole or the like; each announced his support of William Marcy Tweed.

"That's right, son," Saul said, laughing. "For a greenie you learn fast. Where you from, anyway?"

"Vermont."

"Oh, nice place, I hear. Cold, though. What's your name?"

"Riley."

"Hah!" Saul slammed his fist on the counter and laughed loudly. "You do learn fast. Here, have another one. On the house."

Riley waited until Saul had drawn the beer and pushed it across the counter before he said, "Thanks, but it isn't my last name. That's Villette. Riley is a nickname for Raoul."

"You a Canuck? You don't sound like one."

"I told you, I'm from Vermont. My folks are Canadian, though."

"Yeah, well it's all the same, ain't it? Canuck, sheeny, Hebe. Only thing that matters is if you survive." Saul was polishing the mahogany counter with a rag as he spoke. Suddenly, he looked up. "That fellow over there," he said. "Take a look at him."

Riley turned and saw a man who was short but strong and fierce-looking. His black eyebrows came together over his nose, and his beardless chin jutted forward over his barrel chest. "That's Boss Fallon," Saul said. "He runs this part of town. He could help a greenie who wants to get ahead. Just say your name's Riley. Forget that Frenchie part."

"Why you telling me this?" Riley asked.

"Why not?" Saul shrugged. "We Canucks and Hebes, we gotta stick together."

In the ensuing weeks Riley came to know Boss Fallon well. Fallon's job was to size up every individual in his territory, to know every voter and potential voter—at least that's how Riley explained to himself Fallon's friendliness. As to his own part in the budding relationship, that was just common sense. He didn't want to stay a toter of dead fish all his life.

"Smart lad like you could make something of a job at Fulton's Market," Fallon said one July night.

"I don't think so," Riley said morosely. It was beastly hot, and even the beer was warm. He ran his finger through the puddle of water the glass made on the bar. "My boss doesn't seem interested in any kind of promotion. All he wants me to do is lug crates."

Fallon laughed. "Look at you. Can't say I blame him.

They don't come your size very day in the week. That's not what I meant, anyway."

"What, then?" Riley asked with genuine curiosity. He had long realized that success in New York was evading him. Other young men came to the city and made their fortunes. He simply didn't know how it was done.

"Well," Fallon said slowly. "Oysters, for instance. There's plenty of folks want oysters. Expensive, though. Costs a lot to go and buy 'em at Fulton's. Or terrapin. All the restaurants want terrapin."

He'd lowered his voice at the last words, and he was watching the boy closely. Riley was aware that something momentous had been said; he just didn't know what it was. "I don't understand," he said.

Fallon leaned closer. "Look, lad, you ain't never gonna get ahead if you don't make your own opportunities. That's the way it is in New York. For instance, some night you might see a way to slip a few boxes of oysters or terrapin or something out behind the door. Leave 'em where no one would see 'em when they was locking up. Then, later, they could be collected. Working man has to take advantage of his chances. Like I said."

Riley had the sense not to show his shock. "I'll think about it," he said finally.

"You do that. When you make up your mind, let me know. I'll arrange to have the stuff picked up. Split the profit with you fifty-fifty." Fallon moved off to speak with another subject in his empire.

Riley was trembling; not just his hands but the muscles in his back, shoulders, and legs as well. He thought he would drop the massive crate of terrapin and small diamond-backed turtles would scurry through the yard. Somehow he managed to lug the hoard to a spot behind a mountain of fish scales and gurry. The stench was horrendous. Villette gagged, then made himself remain long enough to kick some of the refuse over the top of the box.

Inside the cavernous market no one paid any attention to his five-minute absence. He waited to hear his boss yell something like "Hey, you lousy Canuck bastard, where the hell are them turtles?" Nothing happened. Sweat poured down his face and torso, but it was summer, so there was nothing unusual in that.

"Villette!" The call came at last. "Come over here. We need more flounder."

It was nearly nine that night when he got to Barney's, but the Irishman wasn't there. "Seen Fallon this evening?" Riley asked Saul.

"Not yet," the barman said nonchalantly. "Hang around. He'll be in."

He arrived a few minutes before ten, grinning broadly and signaling for Riley to join him. "You're okay, kid," Fallon said. "Everything just like you told me. All done and no one the wiser. Here," he said, slipping a bill into Riley's palm. "Fifty-fifty, like I promised. That's a twenty you got there, kid. How long you work at Fulton's before you make twenty?" He didn't wait for an answer but guffawed and slapped the boy on the back. Someone came up to ask him something, a favor most likely. Riley mumbled a few words and moved away.

He stumbled into the back alley and leaned against the wall. So now he was a thief, a crook. He had twenty dollars in his pocket that proved it. Twenty dollars. Jesus Christ! So that's how the working classes could get ahead. The rottenness of the system made him gag. Fallon was the same as Jason Whitby. He bought people body and soul, too. Only his methods were different.

He'd done it for Andrea. So they could be together. Riley closed his eyes and summoned the vision of her that pleased him most. Not the way she was alone with him on the ledge or in the summer house, but a picture of Andrea walking along the road in Whitby Falls, swinging her bonnet by its ribbons and caring not a fig that she was late for church. Andrea. The sweet memory soothed him and he returned to the smoky room.

"Here you are, kid!" Fallon called. "I thought you'd run off. We're gonna celebrate. You and me are goin' uptown, and I'll show you some of what this city offers smart lads who use their heads."

Riley didn't dare refuse. Just as he couldn't tell the boss man that he knew damned well the crate of terrapin had sold for more than forty dollars.

Fifty-fifty was a lie; friendship was a lie, too. He didn't care. He'd let Fallon play his game, let him think he owned Riley Villette. Then, when the time was right and he'd made enough money, he'd free himself from Fallon's slimy grip. He would never allow himself to be fooled again.

They were a party of seven—he and Fallon and five of the Irishman's cronies. They dragged Riley from bar to restaurant to music hall and made lewd comments that the greenie was seeing the real New York. Close to one in the morning they were in a gambling club near Madison Square. Bug-eyed, Riley watched half a dozen men in elegant evening dress gamble thousands on the turn of a card. Black tie was required only of the players. Most of the spectators, like him, wore ordinary clothes.

Fallon nudged him. "See that guy over there, the one next to the dealer? That's Jay Gould. Maybe the richest man in New York. I met him a few times. Calls me by name, Jay Gould does." Fallon puffed hard on his cigar.

"Listen, Mr. Fallon, I've got to go home. I'll have to climb in a window as it is. My landlady locks up at eleven."

"What's your hurry, kid? Tomorrow's Sunday, ain't it? You gotta get up for church?" He laughed hard at his joke, then turned to one of the others. "C'mon, Frankie, let's take the kid to O'Flaherty's for a nightcap."

6.

At first, when Andrea returned to work after her two-week absence, she was pale and withdrawn, and both Desi and Delilah watched her anxiously. Gradually, her color returned, and she seemed more like her old self.

"What happened to you up in Vermont?" Desi asked one day as they walked beside the lake in Central Park. "You seem different since you got back."

"Different in what way?" Andrea asked, running her fingers through the delicate leaves of a branch of weeping willow. "I've been a bit tired, that's all."

Desi stopped walking and turned to face her. "No, that's not all. You're . . . I don't know how to put it, lass. Harder—maybe that's the word. Some of the softness is gone out of my girl." His brown eyes searched her face with tenderness.

"Soft people don't survive, Desi," she said quietly. "Besides, I've never been soft, not really."

"Andrea, listen." Looking down at the grass, he ran his finger around the collar of his shirt. "You know how I feel about you. I just don't want anything to hurt you, that's all. I've been thinking that maybe you and I—"

"Ssh, don't, Desi. Not now, please." She pressed her gloved hand over his mouth, and he clasped it to his lips for a brief moment, then released her.

"All right, darling girl, not now. But someday. Someday soon."

After that, Andrea made a special effort to be bright and gay, and she found excuses for not spending afternoons alone with Desi. She could not have said what her plans were, but she knew Desi O'Flaherty and his Broadway Alley saloon were no part of them. At least not permanently.

Spring lengthened into summer, and the bar was hot and unbearably close at night. The papers were saying that 1869 was the hottest summer anyone could remember. Everyone who could do so fled to the country and the seaside.

Andrea remembered Whitby Falls—the cool green of the woods and the river and the shadows on Herrick Mountain. She had mixed feelings about those memories, both longing and revulsion. She'd given up wondering if her mother and father had searched for her, or how much of the truth Millicent had told Jason.

Most nights she dreamed of Maryann Villette's saying, "You like to fuck me, Jason Whitby, and you know I'm your kid. . . ." Andrea would wake up trembling and perspiring and not be able to fall back to sleep. The burning ache low down in her belly kept her awake. Because of it she couldn't forget the horror of the abortion, the way Maggie had to gag her and hold her down while the so-called doctor cut the child out of her body.

Riley and Jason seemed to be in the room with her then. Her father and her lover had done this to her. They knew the truth, and they never told her. She hated them. Riley most of all. "I love you, Andrea," he'd said. He was her brother—he had no right to love her. And she'd chased after him, confided in him, believed him to be the only one in Whitby Falls who really understood her.

Andrea would retch with the shame of it and clench her fists and pound her pillow. She pretended that it was Riley's face and that she was paying him back for everything.

The seventeenth of July came and went. Andrea told no one it was her seventeenth birthday, but she couldn't help thinking of the Green at home and the fact that the locals would miss their party that year.

On the night in August when Fallon and his friends came in for a drink just before closing, Andrea didn't notice them. They sat near the door, far from the stage and the piano. The gas footlights blurred her view. She realized only that a new party of customers had come in and decided she'd play one last number before she finished.

Extraordinary, Riley thought, looking at the entertainer. She looks enough like Andrea to be her double. He passed his hand over his eyes and tried to protest when someone brought him a whiskey. He'd drunk too much that night, more than ever before in his life. That's why he was seeing things now.

"Hey, kid, don't get sick or pass out or nothing," Fallon said, seeing his protégé's expression. "This is your celebration." He chuckled and noticed Riley staring at the pianist. "All right, ain't she? But you just get to look, not to touch. The little lady ain't available. O'Flaherty's property, they say. But she's something, ain't she? Andrea Adams. Quite a sight."

"What did you say her name was?" Riley's voice was a hoarse whisper.

"Andrea. Andrea Adams."

Riley stared at the girl sitting some ten yards away from him. Her pale silver hair was piled on her head, a few loose tendrils trailing along her neck. She wore a gown of pink lace over satin that bared her shoulders and had only brief sleeves covering her arms. At her bosom were three silk roses. In the gaslight Riley could watch them rise and fall as she sang.

It had to be a mistake, a bizarre coincidence. How could his Andrea be here in a New York saloon? She was waiting for him in Whitby Falls. Then the girl reached the end of her song, and she stood up and closed the cover of the keyboard.

Riley watched the way her hands moved. The truth was inescapable. When she turned to face the drinkers and curtsy, he knew. No one in the whole world moved just that way, had a chin tilted just so. No one but Andrea.

"C'mon, kid," Fallon said. "Closing time. We'll get you home."

"Go ahead without me," Riley said softly. "I've someone to see."

"Now look, Villette." Fallon's voice was both amused and reasonable. "The lady's not available. You want a girl? I'll take you someplace you can find one."

"It's okay," he said. "She's an old friend. We come from the same town in Vermont. I just want to say hello, that's all."

Fallon looked doubtful. "You sure, kid? You better be. Desi O'Flaherty's got connections. I don't want no trouble."

"No trouble," Riley assured him. "It's just like I said."

The other men left. Riley remained where he was, the untouched whiskey on the table in front of him. "Drink up, lad. Closing time." He looked up to see a big red-bearded man standing over him.

"I'd like to see Miss . . . er, Miss Adams." He'd almost forgotten the new name.

"Sorry," O'Flaherty said easily, "she doesn't see gentlemen privately. You come back tomorrow night if you like. She'll be at the piano then."

"I want to see her now." Riley stood up.

"I don't want trouble, lad," the older man said with quiet menace. "It's late, and I'm tired—and you're drunk. So just get yourself out that door, and we'll forget the whole thing."

Riley clenched his fists, but his arms hung at his side. "It's not what you're thinking," he said. "I know her. We're old friends."

"Is that so?" Desi cocked his head. "And how does that happen to be the case?"

"We're from the same town in Vermont, Whitby Falls. Her real name's Andrea Whitby."

O'Flaherty frowned. Suddenly, he hated this boy with his black hair and his earnest black eyes and his claim on the girl. He hated him for being part of Andrea's former world. Still, O'Flaherty wasn't a fool. Whatever might happen, it was better to get it over with. "I'll tell her," he said finally.

He started for the kitchen, not realizing the boy was right behind him. "Andrea, there's a lad out front won't leave unless he talks to you. Says he's a friend of yours from Vermont."

She was holding a glass of milk, and she lowered it slowly to the table while staring over Desi's shoulder at Riley standing in the doorway. "What are you doing here?" she asked at last. "How did you find me?"

O'Flaherty whirled and saw the boy. He remained standing between the two young people, feeling the currents of their emotion pass through him. Delilah watched for a moment, then took a step nearer the tableau.

"C'mon, mister man," she said to Desi. "I made you some of my corn fritters. You just come over here and eat 'em while they's hot." O'Flaherty ignored her. She moved closer and lay her hand on his arm. "C'mon," she repeated. "Let Andrea talk to the feller alone."

Desi made a strangled noise of assent. "You want me to leave you alone, lass?" he asked. " 'Twill be however you say."

"Just for a few minutes, Desi," the girl said. She was terrified of the truths that might be uttered there in the kitchen. When O'Flaherty moved across the room, she walked past Riley through the darkened bar until she was leaning against the front door, as far as she could get from the others.

Riley followed her and stood staring into her face in silence. A streetlamp glowed through the colored glass of the saloon door, bathing them both in an unearthly, surreal light. "What are you doing here?" he asked at last.

"I needed a job," she said tonelessly. "Desi gave me one."

"What do you mean . . ." He could make no sense of her words. "Why did you need a job?"

Andrea shrugged. "It doesn't matter."

"Oh, Christ! Oh, Jesus Christ!" He wailed the oaths, the cries of a man drowning or suffocating or dying. Then he put his hands on her bare shoulders and gripped her flesh as hard as he could.

Andrea shuddered. His fingers were burning her skin. His touch was a pain that echoed all the other pain of the thirteen months since she had climbed up to the ledge and met him.

"Don't touch me," she whispered. "Let me go. Get out of here and don't come back, Riley Villette."

He shook his head violently, as if he could force her words out of his brain. "What happened? For God's sake, Andrea, I don't understand any of this!" He was still holding her shoulders, and he could feel how icy cold her skin had become despite the heat in the dark, airless room.

Memories engulfed Andrea. She remembered all the other times he'd touched her, the things they'd done. Shame and hatred and anger choked in her throat. "I was going to have a baby," she whispered. "Your baby. It was an abomination."

"A baby," he repeated. "Where is it?"

"Dead," she said. "I killed it. I killed the abomination. I'll kill you, too, if you ever touch me again." She wrenched herself from his grip and leaned panting against the wall. Her breast rose and fell as she struggled to breathe. The three little silk roses danced a macabre rhythm.

Riley let his hands fall to his sides. His fingers clenched and unclenched again and again. "Oh, my God. Oh, Jesus. Andrea, darling . . . I didn't know. . . . Why didn't you find some way to let me know. We could have been married. You didn't have to—"

"Liar! Filthy, rotten liar!" She hurled the words at him in the same hoarse whisper. "You think I'd have married you? I know who you are. I know about your slut of a mother. Can't you get it through your thick Canuck skull? I know."

"You bitch." So that's all he was to her, just a stupid Canuck. "You bitch out of hell. I stole for you. Became a thief so you and I— Aagh . . ."

The last was a wail as hatred gagged him. Acid bile rose in his gorge, churned in his gut. He reached for her once more. For a split second he meant to take her throat between his fingers and squeeze. Then he cursed again, a string of the foulest words he knew, and threw her away from him to the floor. When he ran into the street, a gust of wind grabbed the door and hurled it against the wall. The colored glass shattered.

Whatever Desi had overheard, whatever he suspected, he said nothing. Neither did Delilah. They asked no questions, and life went on as before in Broadway Alley.

Boss Fallon wondered about Riley. He made inquiries at

the fish market and at the lodging house. The only thing he discovered was that the boy had left town. Someone said he had mentioned Philadelphia. Fallon shrugged. It was out of his territory.

1869 . . .

Hugh

Chapter Four

1.

Hugh Villette left Whitby Falls driven by a need he didn't understand. His sense of purpose was writ large by what he achieved in Canada. Hugh became important; he tasted the sweet savor of respect. His *Quebecois* origins helped for the first time; so did his bull strength and knowledge of explosives.

In the endless forests surrounding Hudson Bay, men of his stamp were useful. The rich harvest of timber required reapers willing to tolerate the sweeping silence, the penetrating cold, the paralyzing loneliness. Hugh was undaunted by any of them. He chopped and sawed and struggled and wrested the trees from the earth. After a few months he could keep pace with men who had been logging before he was born. But Villette could do more. When the enormous trunks clogged in the swift-flowing rivers, he knew just how much dynamite was required to loose the jam. Moreover, he would willingly hazard a perilous climb over tumbling trees and swirling water to set the charge. The lumbermen came to admire his skill and daring.

Nonetheless, they didn't consider Hugh Villette a friend. He did not drink with them or gamble with them or accompany them on their infrequent trips to the towns in search of whores. Neither did he remain long in any one place. Further north, always further north. The young man from Vermont moved every time he heard of a more remote camp offering higher wages.

He came to the installation on the Great Whale River in the spring of 1869, when he was twenty-three and had been in Canada a little less than a year. He had arrived at the edge of the world. To the north lay Ungava Bay and the barren lands of the tundra; to the east, the ice-bound upper tip of Newfoundland.

"Villette," the log boss repeated. "I've heard the name. Know about dynamite, don't you?"

"A bit."

"You a *Quebecois*?"

"My folks were. I'm an American. From Vermont." He never let anyone forget where he was from.

"Oh, yeah? Too bad, but we can still use you, if you can take it. Nearest settlement's thirty miles south. Nine months of the year you couldn't get there with a dogsled. Pay's thirty dollars a month plus a bed and all you can eat. Grub's the best there is this side of Montreal."

"I'll take it," Hugh said.

"Villette—one more thing. Some of our arrangements are a little unusual. Stick to the rules and you'll make out all right."

The unusual part was that the camp cook was a woman. Her name was Lise Patont, and she was tiny and dark and tough as nails. Her hair was as short as a man's, a halo of tight black curls, and her eyes were big and wide-set and brown. She had a generous, mobile mouth and small white teeth that showed when she laughed.

Lise wore breeches and jackets like the lumberjacks and the same thick-knitted sweaters that they affected. Hugh thought she might have a good figure, but it was impossible to tell and unwise to speculate. Lise belonged to Henry, the log boss. She wasn't his wife; she was his woman. They had no children and never displayed any affection, but they shared a cabin, and word was that Henry had knifed to death two men who had tried to replace him.

Hugh quickly accepted the situation and only looked at the girl when he was sure no one would notice. Soon he had other things on his mind.

The camp's isolation meant that stocks of liquor were exhausted before the supply wagon was due to return to civilization for replenishments. Hugh saw a profit opportunity.

In June, when a wagon was going south, Hugh handed a request to the driver. "Get me this stuff while you're in Kanaaupscow. I'll pay for it."

The man read the brief list. "Rubber hosepipe, jugs, sugar, and a hundredweight of potatoes. Potatoes, for Christ sake! What the hell you want with potatoes?"

"You'll see. Just get it, okay?"

The man shrugged. "Sure, why not?"

Hugh's still was operative in two weeks. In less than a

month he was selling potato whiskey for ten cents a glass. He kept the money in a well-hidden iron strongbox that also contained most of his earnings since his arrival in Canada.

Then, one day after he'd set a frighteningly delicate charge and blown free a menacing logjam, Lise Patont approached him. "That was terrific, what you did today. I watched you. You still selling your home brew?"

"If you want it." He liked her praise, but he was uneasy about her lover's reputed jealousy. Besides, he'd never seen her drink before. Still, she dressed like a man, and she cussed like one. Maybe she drank, too. Thinking of Eve and his sisters, he smiled. "First one's on the house. No charge unless you like it."

"Forget that." She thrust a coin at him. "I pay my own way."

Villette shrugged. "Suit yourself." He poured a tumblerful of whiskey and watched her toss it down. After the first swallow she was gasping and sputtering. "Where in hell did you learn to make that stuff?" she demanded.

"My father taught me."

"Did he teach you about dynamite, too?" She wiped her mouth with her sleeve and sat down on a nearby log. "You're a man of many parts, Hugh Villette. I don't understand you."

"You're not so simple yourself," he said. "And no, my father didn't teach me about explosives. I learned that in the quarry."

"What quarry?" She leaned back on her elbows, and the brown eyes watched him with friendly interest. Villette told her about Whitby Falls and about blasting slate.

"You like it," she said at last. "Digging the slate out of the earth. You really like it."

"I guess I do. It's something I grew up with. What about you? Where did you grow up?"

"Over there." She nodded her head toward Newfoundland. "But I never had a father to teach me anything useful like making whiskey."

"You sure can cook, though. Did your mother teach you that?" He was looking at her and enjoying the way her mouth moved when she spoke and as much of her body as showed beneath the heavy clothes.

"Didn't have a mother. At least not that I knew. I'm an orphan. The nuns in the orphanage taught me to cook."

"Are you a Catholic?" Her mention of nuns surprised him.

She laughed, and her white teeth sparkled in the dusk. "Do I look like a religious woman? A *putan* like me?"

"You're no whore," Hugh said quietly.

For a few seconds Lise simply looked at him. Then she got up and walked away.

A few days later, she came back, and they talked again. Soon it became a pattern. Hugh watched Henry warily and was always cautious when the log boss was near, but the other man displayed no sign of anger at the friendship between Villette and the girl.

"Don't worry about him," Lise said one night. "If I want to talk with you, it's all right with Henry."

"That's not how I heard it," he said.

"It wasn't the same. Those other men, the two he killed, they were bothering me. I didn't like either of them. Henry takes care of me, that's all."

Villette thought her casual mention of murder chilling, but he spoke no more about it. Apart from that reticence, he talked more than he ever had in his life. Lise asked him endless questions about himself and his past and his dreams for the future, and Hugh told her more than he realized.

"You want to go back, don't you?" she said one night. "Back to Whitby Falls. That's why you don't drink or gamble with the others or go into town. You're saving your money."

He was startled. If anyone suspected the existence of the strongbox, it would be in danger. "Why do you say that?" he asked, stalling.

"It's obvious. I heard they look down on *Quebecoises* in America, though. Call them Canucks and treat them like dirt."

"Not me they don't," Hugh said. "At least they won't."

"When you go back, you mean?"

"Yeah," he admitted. "When I go back."

After that he was more open, and she didn't have to drag information out of him. He told her about the quarry and the town, the mountain and the cabin where his family lived, and about Jason Whitby, who owned it all.

"All my life I've eaten Jason Whitby's dirt—choked on slate dust so he could get richer."

"And?" Lise asked softly.

"And I ain't going to do it anymore. I'm a bigger man than Jason. I seen it clear when we started using dynamite. Jason never got close enough to touch the stuff; he's afraid of it."

"But you aren't." She reached out and touched his sleeve.

"No." Hugh looked at her hand on the rough wool of his jacket. "Jason never did anything to deserve what he's got. Someday I'm going back and take the whole damn thing away from him."

"How are you going to do that?" she asked.

"I've got it all figured out." It was the only thing he would say. They remained in silence for a while. Then he turned to her and asked, "What about you? I've told you what I want. What do you want?"

Lise clasped her trousered legs to her chest and rested her little heart-shaped chin on her knees. "I can't tell you. You'd laugh at me."

"No, I wouldn't." She still didn't answer. "How old are you, anyway?" he asked at last.

"Nineteen."

"That's young to be so tough."

"I'm not tough," she whispered. "Not really." She turned to him and took his hand and put it on her head. Her hair felt like spun silk beneath his callused fingers.

"It's been like this since I was fourteen," she said.

"I don't understand. Like what?"

"This short. I had a sickness, a terrible high fever. All my hair fell out, and when it grew back, it wouldn't come any longer than a boy's. I wore a bonnet night and day after that so people wouldn't stare and laugh."

"I can't picture you in a bonnet," he admitted. "I'll bet you'd look beautiful, though."

"Not when you have to wear one. Anyway, a little while after that I met Henry, and eventually I came up here."

"And that's all you want? Just to live up here and wear men's clothes and cook for the camp?"

"I want to be a lady," she whispered. "A grand lady." Then she ran away before he could say anything.

Later, they talked again, and she told him of the women she had seen on the streets of Quebec City and Montreal. Women with elegant gowns and parasols and fans and fancy carriages waiting to take them wherever they chose to go. "Isn't that ridiculous?" she said mockingly. "Me, Lise Patont, orphan and whore, I want to be a fine lady and live in a fine house."

"Do you want to live in the house alone or with a husband and children?"

"That would depend on who he was," Lise said. She didn't look at him when she spoke, and soon she left and went back to the cabin where she slept beside her lover.

At the end of the week, she came to him with an idea. "That new fellow, the one who calls himself King Jacques, he says he can beat any lumberjack alive at arm-wrestling. He's willing to bet money on it. Take him on, Hugh. Bet a lot. You've already beaten every man here. You can beat this King Jacques, too."

"I don't gamble," he said. "It's too risky. I arm-wrestled the others for laughs, not for money."

She put her hands on his shoulders. Hugh wasn't tall, but she was so tiny she had to look up to see his face. "Do it for money this time. You could double what you've earned on the whiskey. Maybe even triple it. Jacques has plenty of money. I saw his roll."

"You're crazy."

"No, I'm not. Hugh, pretty soon we'll be snowed in. If you want to get out, you have to try now."

He remembered the way she'd looked at him the day he blew the really tough logjam, and he knew he'd do anything to see that look again. "All right," he said.

The bout was arranged for Saturday night. Everyone in camp gathered in a big circle around the level tree stump on which the contest would take place. Hugh and the stranger approached from opposite sides of the makeshift ring. It was September and the night was cold, but both men were bare from the waist up.

The stranger was covered with matted blond hair that grew even along the backs of his hands. By contrast, Villette looked hairless. Jacques was taller by more than a head, but the crowd appraised the contestants with an approving murmur. The two men were of equal brawn. The outcome would depend on the relative strength of those bulging muscles.

"Okay." Henry stepped forward. "You both know the rules. First man to bring the other's hand down to touch wood wins. Only one go. Winner takes the pot." He held up a leather pouch containing three hundred dollars. Each of the pair of wrestlers had gambled a hundred and fifty on himself. "If there are any side bets, gents, you better make 'em now." There was a flurry of activity while the others wagered.

Hugh looked around but couldn't see Lise anywhere. She'd talked him into this, and she wasn't even going to watch. He thought of the hours he'd toiled to earn the money that was now in the leather bag, and at that moment he hated Lise Patont.

If he lost, it would take him months to recoup. Maybe he never would. Some of the others had started their own stills, so he no longer had a monopoly. He envisioned fifteen months of swinging an ax and pulling a saw, fifteen months of risking his neck setting dynamite charges atop slippery, moving logs while white water rushed all around him; that's how long it would be before he made back the hundred and fifty he was risking that night.

"Take your positions," Henry shouted.

The two men knelt by the tree stump and rested their elbows on its surface. When they clasped hands, Villette could feel the stranger's strength.

"Ready. Set." There was a long pause. The spectators strained forward. "Go!"

For what seemed an eternity, nothing happened. The clasped hands were frozen, immobile. Then they began to waver. A half inch this way, an inch in the other direction. King Jacques groaned softly once, and someone shouted, "Keep the pressure on, Villette! You got 'im on the run!" Hugh was the camp's champion. The crowd's support was palpable in the cold night air.

He tried to increase his grip, but nothing happened. He had no reserve of strength to call on; this was the maximum pressure he could muster. The result would depend on which of them gave in first, on which set of rippling muscles began to quiver with exhaustion and agony, followed by defeat.

Sweat poured from Villette, but his opponent was breathing harder than he, opening his mouth to gasp for air. Hugh gritted his teeth. There was a red haze in front of his eyes, but he kept searching for Lise. She wasn't there.

The stalemate continued. Then Hugh felt the barest relaxation in the hand that gripped his. He sucked in a long breath and strained against that weakness. The hairy blond arm began to bend. Villette kept up the pressure, but Jacques didn't collapse.

Hugh could taste the salt of his own sweat, and his eyes refused to focus. The top of the tree stump was just below their clasped hands, but he couldn't make it come any closer. More seconds ticked by. Hugh's arm trembled. One more time he tried to force Jacques's hand against the wood. It wouldn't budge. Then, with a fiendish cry, Jacques reversed the position, and Villette felt his arm give way.

"King Jacques has won!" Henry shouted.

There was no enthusiasm in the crowd. They gave the stranger a smattering of applause, then turned to settle their wagers. Most had bet on Villette, and they looked at him with ill-disguised hostility as they paid up. For long minutes Hugh could see nothing. When the terrible pain in his arm and shoulder dulled somewhat and he could focus, he saw King Jacques walking away, swinging the pouch with the three hundred dollars. Silently, he shrugged into his shirt and sweater and stood up. He thought he saw Lise, but she was in the middle of a crowd of lumberjacks, and he decided he didn't want to talk to her anyway.

Villette hadn't had a drink since he came to Canada. It was one of his promises to himself when he began the venture. Now he went beyond the cabins to his still and took a long pull at a jug of potato whiskey.

"There's no time for that now," Lise's voice said behind him. "We've got to get out of here."

"You get out of here," he said. "You've made enough trouble."

She came up to him and laid her hand on his sleeve. "You don't understand," she said softly. "I'll explain, but first we've got to get clear of the camp. Some of the boys lost a lot. They'll be coming after you."

"What difference does it make to you?" he said between clenched teeth.

She stared at him for a moment, then said, "You're acting like a spoiled child. I'm going. Are you coming with me?"

"I wouldn't go to heaven with you."

The girl waited a few seconds, then moved away. She'd gone about ten feet when she turned back and called his name. "Look at me, Hugh. I've got something of yours."

When he looked, she held up his strongbox. The metal

sides gleamed in the moonlight. Villette lunged for her, and she broke into a run. The girl was incredibly fast, and, unlike him, she wasn't exhausted. They'd gone some two miles into the forest before she stopped and let him catch her.

"Give me that box, you bitch! How did you get it?"

"I just watched, and eventually I knew where you hid it," she said. They were both panting and struggling to breathe, and that was all they said for a while. Lise regained her voice first.

"Now will you listen to me?" He said nothing, so she continued. "When I took your box tonight, before the match, there was five hundred dollars in it. There's eight hundred now. That's twice as much as you lost in the arm wrestle."

He stared at her. Her chest was still rising and falling with the effort to suck in air, and he could see that beneath her heavy, shapeless clothes she had a woman's soft, round breasts. "I don't get it," he said finally.

"I knew you wanted to get out, to get back to Vermont. That's why I arranged the whole thing."

"The contest, you mean?"

She nodded. "I had to do something. Ten cents a drink, thirty dollars a month logging. How could you make any money that way? It was the only chance."

"Where did that extra three hundred come from?" He thought he knew, but he wouldn't believe it unless he heard her say it.

"From all the men in camp. I made bets."

"Against me?"

"Of course. Otherwise, I wouldn't have won. I used your money, by the way. I don't have any of my own. Henry never paid me."

He didn't say anything for a moment. Then he asked, "How could you be sure I'd lose?"

"I couldn't, but I had a hunch. I had to risk it."

She thrust the strongbox toward him. "Here, take it. I never meant to steal a penny. I thought you'd realize that. What I said is true, though. You'd better keep going south. There's no place for you back there. Not now."

"Lise . . ." He reached not for his money but for her hand. "What about you?"

She shrugged. "I'll be all right. Henry will look after me if I want him to."

"Do you? Do you want to go back to Henry?"

The girl didn't answer, but she left her hand in his. Finally, she shook her head from side to side.

"Then do you want to come with me? I mean marry me," he added hastily. "Not like you and Henry. I don't want that."

"Will we go to Whitby Falls?" she asked. "Will we fight Jason Whitby and take everything away from him?"

"If you'll help me," Hugh said. "I couldn't do it without you. I see that now."

When she smiled, it was like sunshine, and when they kissed, Hugh tasted tomorrow in her sweet, tough mouth. "Someday you'll be a fine lady in a fine house," he promised, and she arched her body against his and moaned.

2.

That same September of 1869, when the trees in Whitby Falls were just on the verge of turning, Jason Whitby made up his mind.

There was no color left in Millicent, no promise of life. She had become a reproach to him, an ever-present reminder of what might have been. Besides, Millicent was sick; she needed care. Jason was never a man to shirk his duty.

"Come in, Josiah," he said with exaggerated warmth the night the doctor answered his summons. "No one's ill, at least not in the usual sense. I just want to speak with you."

"As you like, Jason." The doctor took a seat in the great man's study and accepted a small glass of port. "How have you been feeling lately?" he asked with professional concern. "I've been worried. Since Andrea left . . . ."

Jason made a motion of dismissal with his hand. "I'll be all right. It's Millicent I want to talk to you about. All this has been too much."

Sills sighed. "I know. I see her regularly."

"Good." The host leaned forward to pour more port. "You'll understand, then, that I've no choice."

"No choice about what, Jason?" the doctor asked quietly.

"Brattleboro."

The word danced in the air between them. Both knew exactly what was meant—the Brattleboro Retreat for the Insane. "I don't know, Jason. I don't think she's quite that bad. . . ." Sills busied himself drinking his wine.

"I do know, Josiah," Whitby said. "I live with her, and I know. Believe me. It's for the best. I'd never suggest it otherwise."

Sills opened his mouth, then closed it. The house he and Tessa lived in was owned by Jason Whitby, and so was the school the Sills children attended. They were taught by a teacher Jason paid.

"No, of course you wouldn't do a thing like that," he said, and stood up to leave. "Lliam will prepare the committal papers, I presume. Tell him to bring them to me, and I'll sign them."

"Thank you, Josiah. I knew I could count on your understanding."

Jason didn't want to bring her to Brattleboro himself. He hired a carriage from Rutland to make the journey. "She'll give no trouble," he assured the driver. "The doctor will see she's quiet." Sills often dosed Millicent with laudanum.

On the day the somber black coach waited to take the woman away, Main Street was deserted. Every house had drawn curtains and closed shutters despite the October sunshine. The people granted Jason Whitby his God-given rights, but they didn't want to see them exercised.

He stood on his white-pillared front porch and waited while Nelly escorted Millicent downstairs. She was whimpering softly, her eyes glazed and her mouth slack. A dribble of spittle escaped from one corner of those pale lips. "Jason," she whispered when she saw her husband. "Jason, where are they taking me?"

"Just to a nice farm for a rest, my dear. The way Dr. Sills and I explained. It will do you good. Besides, it's in Brattleboro. That's nearer New Hampshire. You'll like that."

"Yes," she agreed. "Yes, I will. And it's in God's hands, you know. Everything is. God will reward the just and punish the guilty, Jason."

Her voice was a small singsong, without emphasis or accusation, but it made the hair rise on the back of his neck.

The driver flicked his whip, and the horses moved down the silent and empty street.

The journey from the north woods was, by contrast, a pleasure trip. Hugh and Lise moved ahead of the encroaching winter. In Kanaaupscow they bought a pair of mules, some blankets, and a few necessities for camping. By day they spoke little, concentrating their energies on the demands of the trek. At night they made love under the stars and the blankets. On the tenth of October they crossed the Saguenay River where it emptied into the St. Lawrence, and the following morning they were in Quebec City.

Lise knew exactly where to go, to a hospice run by the Grey Nuns. "The mother superior there used to be in charge of the orphanage in Newfoundland where I was raised," she explained. And to the nun she said, "We need a place to stay for a few days, *ma mère*, and a priest to marry us."

Mother Clotilde examined the young woman in her men's clothes and the boy who accompanied her. Lise had been one of the nun's failures. The girl did not grow up a devout, hardworking servant of the sort the orphanage prided itself on turning out. Lise was wild and unpredictable and a heathen. Mother Clotilde loved the girl nonetheless and berated herself for having failed the child.

"Are you a Catholic, young man?" Clotilde demanded of Hugh.

"He is from Vermont," Lise said before Hugh could answer. "His mother and father are Quebecoises."

The mother superior bit her lip and remembered the stories she had heard about Lise living in sin in the wilderness with a godless woodsman. She looked again at the girl's companion. "What is your name?"

"Hugh, *ma mère*. Hugh Villette. I'm a slateman by trade and a blaster."

"You have a job, M. Villette?"

"I have work waiting for me in Vermont. If you prefer, Lise and I can be married there."

Clotilde suppressed a shudder. She knew about the heretical clergy who performed weddings across the border. She knew, too, that these children would continue their journey south in intimacy, with or without the blessing of holy Church. "Very well," she said. "I will speak to Father."

They were married four days later. Hugh wanted Lise to have a wedding dress, so he took her to a Quebec shop that sold bolts of white satin and lace and crepe de chine. She shook her head at such frivolity and chose instead a piece of russet serge.

She appeared for the wedding ceremony in a gown of perfect fit and classic fashion, the kind of dress that would look suitable anywhere in the world. The dark orange-brown color suited her, and it was apparent that while the nuns might have failed in much they tried to teach Lise, they had made her a formidable seamstress.

Mother Clotilde approached the bride just before she entered the church. "You have no bonnet, *ma chère*. It is not permitted."

"I will not wear a bonnet ever again," Lise said quietly.

The nun remembered, and she understood. She hurried away and returned with a length of the lace the sisters made and draped it over Lise's short, dark curls. "You look like a Spanish madonna," she said, and smiled at the unlikely comparison.

That same afternoon Lise changed back into her trousers and jacket, and the newlyweds mounted their mules and headed for the border. It was nearly November when they arrived in Rutland.

Lise put on her dress before they entered the town. Then they left their animals with a farmer and walked into the city. She objected to the waste of money, but Hugh insisted on renting a room in Bardwell House and eating in the dining room there. "I said you'd be a fine lady, and I meant it," he told his wife.

"I know you did," she said. "But there's time. I can wait."

Hugh grinned. "Okay. But tonight's our honeymoon."

Lise grinned, too. During the weeks of their journey she had made him a handsome black suit, sewing it in the evenings by the light of the campfire from material she had bought in Quebec. Now he looked like a proper gentleman. No one would guess where they had come from.

"Hugh," she said when they were sipping coffee from delicate white china cups. "Maybe we should stay in Rutland. You could get work here, couldn't you?"

"Sure," he agreed. "But that's not my plan. Tomorrow I'll show you."

The next day, they reclaimed their mules and their traveling clothes. Skirting Rutland, they headed southwest toward Whitby Falls. When they'd gone about six miles, Hugh turned up into the foothills. They climbed a short distance, then halted on a windswept cliff with stunted trees clinging to the edge. "Remember the Plains of Abraham we saw in Quebec?" he asked. "Well, this is going to be our plain. This place is called the Skillet, because it's shaped like a frypan. Here's where we'll fight our battle. And we'll win."

They dismounted, and he led her to a patch of undergrowth. It was nothing but leafless twigs and branches. Hugh parted the scrub with his strong hands and motioned her to look.

There was a fissure in the earth just wide enough for Lise to get her head into, but when she peered down its depths, she could see nothing. She raised her face in questioning disbelief, and her husband smiled. Then he knelt down and scraped a bit of dirt from deep in the cleft. "Look at that."

"I don't see anything."

"What color is it?" he asked patiently.

"Sort of red," Lise said.

"Yeah," he agreed. "It's red, all right." He stood up then and drew her beside him so that they were standing together looking at the bleak corner of the world he considered so important. "There's slate here," he said. "I found this place a few years ago, and I suspected what was underground. So I came up one day and blasted that crack there. Then I knew for certain. It's a deep, wide seam of slate, Lise, and it's red."

"That's good?"

"Yes. The only red slate comes from over in New York, Hebron and Granville mostly. Whitby slate's a kind of dark gray, with a few pieces of green sometimes. Red slate, now that's something else. People pay a premium for red slate." He stopped speaking and looked at her. "You following me?"

"I think so," she said. "Who owns this land, Hugh?"

"Jason Whitby."

"Will he sell it to you?"

"Soon as I asked to buy it, he'd know there was slate

underneath. I been finding new seams for Jason Whitby since I was old enough to pick up a stick of dynamite.''

"What, then?"

"I'm going to make him give it to me.''

The cabin and his family had changed little in the eighteen months he'd been gone. He watched Lise anxiously for signs of disgust, but she betrayed none. "I've seen worse," she said laconically when the others were out of earshot. "Where will we sleep, though?''

"Not in here." Hugh glanced around the crowded hovel. "I'll make up a bed for us out in the still shack. I used to sleep there sometimes when I was a kid. It's not so bad once you get used to the smell. And it's warm and private." She nodded, and Hugh gathered up their blankets, then turned back to her. "It's going to change," he said. "Everything around here's going to change. But not right away. First we've got to get the land.''

Later, he questioned Eve about conditions in the town, and when she told him, somewhat gleefully, that Andrea had run away and Millicent had been carted off to the loony bin, he looked pensive and pressed her for details.

"What else is to say? Is a hard man, Jason Whitby. When no longer they could take him or his ways, they both leave. One way or another.''

"Did Mrs. Whitby go to Brattleboro on her own?''

"No. Jason sent her away. Made bad feeling in the town. Folks think is not right; she do no harm in her own house. But Jason, he do what he want.''

"He doesn't care what they think, then?" Hugh asked.

Eve shrugged. "Not enough to have a crazy woman around the big house. But he cares. Always he worry about scandal. Jason wants people to believe he is God.''

Her son nodded thoughtfully. "That's what I've always thought. And I'll bet he took Andrea's running off pretty bad.'' Then, as if a possible connection had just dawned on him, he asked, "Where's Riley?''

"Gone," Eve said. "Two months after you left. We don't know where, but to Jackie he send a picture card. From Philadelphia. Riley say nothing about Andrea. Always he wanted her, but he is not with her now.''

Jackie, the youngest brother, was small and wiry, like a

ferret. He had a ferret's long nose, too. The impression was mitigated by an appealing grin and a shock of curly hair that fell over his forehead. He wasn't very smart, but he was loyal. Jackie listened to Eve and Hugh, but he didn't speak. He knew things they didn't suspect, but he'd kept his mouth shut for over a year, and he wasn't going to rat on Riley now.

Hugh dismissed the subject of his absent brother. "I'm going to the big house tomorrow," he told his mother.

She smiled. "You will get back the job. Nowhere does Jason find anyone to blast like you."

"It's not exactly like that," Hugh said.

The next morning, he told Lise to put on her dress and accompany him. She was pleased that she wouldn't be left behind to wait. "Will you wear your suit?" she asked.

"No. I'll wear my work clothes. And Lise, don't say anything."

3.

"Mr. Whitby, someone to see you, sir," Nelly announced.

Jason looked up from his desk. "Who is it?"

"The Villette lad. The one what went away."

"Riley?" Whitby was surprised. He hadn't expected the boy to come back.

"No, not him. Hugh, what went to Canada. Got a girl with him. Says she's his wife."

More surprising still. "Show him in," Jason said, and waited.

"Good afternoon, Mr. Whitby. This is my wife, Lise."

Jason appraised the young couple with some interest. The girl was pretty in an unconventional way. Her dress was simple, but it suited her. And it was a better quality than anything he'd expect to see on one of the Villettes. He looked away, lest he seem overinterested, and examined Hugh. Not much changed. A little broader and more muscular, perhaps. And he'd grown a beard.

"Welcome home," Whitby said finally. "You surprise

me, Hugh. I didn't expect to see you or your brother here again.''

"I can't speak for Riley, but for me home's best." The girl nudged him, and he added, "Sir."

Whitby chuckled. "Plans to make a gentleman of you, does she?" he said. "Well, more power to you, Lise. A formidable task, though, training a Villette." Lise smiled shyly and dropped her eyes. Jason found himself liking her. She knew her place. "I suppose you want your job back," he added.

"Not exactly. I mean, it's business I've come to talk about, sir, but not the old job."

Whitby began to feel annoyance. "I do business at the pit, lad, not in my home. I'll see you there anytime you want to talk." He looked down at the papers on his desk.

"I think you'll want to hear what I've got to say, Mr. Whitby."

Something in the younger man's tone made Whitby look up. "Sit down, then," he said finally. "And if we're going to talk business, perhaps Lise would like to wait outside."

"Mrs. Villette can stay," Hugh said. Jason's eyes narrowed, but he let the comment pass.

"I've a scheme to propose, sir," the younger man continued. "For the quarry. It will save you hours of labor and increase your profits."

Whitby sat back and tapped the corner of his desk with his fingers. "Something about the blasting, I suppose. You're a natural genius with dynamite, Hugh. I never denied it. What do you have in mind?"

"I'd have to show you, sir. And"—he paused and looked at the floor in embarrassment—"I'd need to be paid for the idea."

"I treat my workers right, Hugh. You know that."

"Yes, I know," Villette agreed. "But this is different. It's my idea, Mr. Whitby, and it's all I've got to sell. I'd rather you have it than anybody in Castleton or Fair Haven. I was born in Whitby Falls. You understand." He hadn't looked up, and the sweat and trembling of his excitement could easily be mistaken for nervous deference.

"Of course I do, lad." Whitby rose and walked around the desk to stand in front of his young visitors. "Now, Hugh, man to man, how much did you have in mind? Presuming your idea works, of course.''

"Well, that's just it, sir," Hugh said earnestly. "I don't want to name a price until after you've seen my plan in operation. I know I can count on your being fair. Like you said."

"As you wish," Whitby said with some impatience. "When can you show me?"

"Beginning of next week. Tuesday, say. At number-three pit."

They shook hands on it, and when the Villettes were leaving, Jason said, "By the way, Hugh, you and your new wife will probably want a house. I'll talk to Mr. Murray and see if there's something available. It'll be part of your wages. Meanwhile, if you need anything, tell the shopkeepers I said you could charge."

Later, Hugh warned Lise, "Don't buy a thing. Not even for cash, let alone charged. Just stay in the cabin and don't talk to anybody."

The girl nodded. Hugh had explained how Jason Whitby exercised his hold on the town. In their makeshift bed in the shack that housed the still, she asked Hugh what he was planning, but he refused to tell her.

"You wouldn't understand," he said. "And Whitby's wrong, too. It's nothing to do with blasting." Then, as if he regretted sounding brusque, he said, "Lise, I'm sorry about telling you not to buy anything. And not to go into town. It's just for a little while."

"I don't mind. I don't need anything yet. Not until the time gets closer."

"What time?" He propped himself on his elbow and stared at her, incredulous, because he knew what she meant despite his question.

"We're going to have a baby in the summer," she said. "June, I think. Maybe July."

He kissed her softly, and they slept with their arms around each other. In the morning, he began his preparations by taking Jackie with him to the woods and dragging home a tall, straight pine. "You get busy and hack every branch off this thing," he told his younger brother. "I'm going into Rutland and get the other stuff we'll need."

*   *   *

A few days before the Tuesday for which the demonstration was scheduled, Hugh went out of his way to talk to the slatemen. They all respected his talent despite their opinion of the Villette clan. When he said that Jason Whitby had promised to pay him if he proved he had a workable plan to increase profits, most dared to hope the great man might be going to get a little of what he was due.

Whitby heard of the sentiments abroad among the workers and the excitement the mysterious scheme was generating. "What the hell did you promise that boy, anyway?" Lliam Murray demanded.

"Nothing specific, Lliam. Just that I'd be fair. You know me better than to think I'd do something rash. Besides, he's a clever lad. No good letting him take his idea to the competition."

"Very well, Jason, but you'd best be prepared to stand by your word. Frankly, since Millicent . . . Well, there's a lot of feeling in the town. One or two families might even be thinking of moving away. There are other quarries, you know."

"Relax," Whitby said, smiling. "People like the Villettes don't think beyond next week. Hugh will ask for some sum that sounds a king's ransom to him. A hundred dollars, maybe two. I'll pay nearly as much as he wants, and it'll be gone before a month is out. Trust me, Lliam. I know those Villettes."

Tuesday was gray and overcast and threatened snow. Hugh and Jackie were at the quarry before dawn. The first thing the others knew was the sound of a mighty blast that came while everyone was still in bed. They streamed from their houses to the pit, fearing a terrible accident. "It's all right," someone finally shouted. "Just Hugh and Jackie."

An hour later, they were staring in wonder at a tall pole embedded at the edge of the quarry, in the hole Hugh had blasted to receive it, stretching some fifty feet toward the sky. It was guyed with heavy metal cables, and an even heavier cable was threaded through the top of the pole and stretched across the open pit to where it was secured on the opposite side.

"What the hell's it for?" the onlookers demanded. "We gonna swing out on the thing like monkeys? Dig the slate with our feet?"

There were a few derisive laughs, but Jason Whitby wasn't

amused. He saw at once how it would work. Nonetheless, he asked, "What's the plan, Hugh?"

"Pulleys." Villette said. "A moving carriage made to travel the length of the cable. I've drawn the plans for it, and a blacksmith in Rutland's making the thing now. Blocks of slate or rubble or what have you get dumped in the carriage, and the horses pull it along the cable. The animals do all their work on level ground, so they don't have to struggle up the sides of the pit."

Those standing closest to the men heard Whitby commend the strange device, and word spread of his approval. Everyone waited to see what would happen next.

"Well, lad, fair's fair. How much do you want for your invention?"

Hugh drew a deep breath. He wished Lise were present, but he had insisted that she remain in the cabin this time. "I don't want money, Mr. Whitby," he said finally. "Not cash, I mean. I'd like a small piece of land."

The collective intake of breath was audible. Everyone knew Jason Whitby didn't sell land.

"Just what piece did you have in mind, boy?" Whitby asked quietly.

"The Skillet," Hugh said.

Jason had expected Villette to ask for a house he could own outright, not rent as part of his earnings. "The Skillet," he repeated in surprise. He'd thought it a worthless outcropping of stone at the very edge of the town, but now Whitby understood what the truth must be, just as Hugh had predicted he would. "So there's slate under the Skillet," he said softly. "Trust you to find it."

"Yes," Hugh admitted, "there's slate there."

Now everyone understood the dimensions of the drama. And they expected Jason Whitby to go back on his word.

"The Skillet's worth something, then, provided a man could get the slate out," Jason said. "It needs workers to do that, Hugh. And capital. Just what are you planning to do about that?"

"I figure me and Jackie can manage alone at first," Villette said honestly. "Eventually, I'll be able to hire more help."

"And go into competition with me." Jason smiled. "You think I should set you up like that, Hugh? Sounds a little foolish, doesn't it?"

"Maybe," the younger man said. "Maybe not. This here pole's going to save you a lot of money, Mr. Whitby. Make you even more. It'll be a long time before I'm any kind of competition that measures up to that."

Jason turned and surveyed the crowd. He could read what they were thinking. Finally, he turned back to the boy. "All right, lad, I'll make you a deal. I won't give you the Skillet outright, but I'll lease it to you free, for one year. With an option to purchase. Mr. Murray here will draw up the papers. We'll even agree on the price in advance. Two thousand dollars. What do you say, Hugh? You earn two thousand dollars out of your quarry in a year's time, and you can buy it. You have my word on it."

Villette stuck out his hand. "Agreed," he said. "Can Mr. Murray have the papers ready today? I want to start working before the heavy snow sets in."

"But why did he do it?" Lise asked later. "I mean once he guessed there was slate up there."

"Two reasons," Hugh explained. "One was the way people in town are feeling about him these days. I didn't count on that; it was a bonus. As to his knowing there was slate, I told you he would. What he doesn't even dream is that it's red slate. There's none ever shown up around here. It's just a freak seam on the Skillet. So Whitby thinks it's ordinary gray or green stuff."

He was pacing in his nervous excitement, patrolling the ground in front of the decrepit log cabin. "Now, knowing how hard it's going to be for me to dig out any quantity of the stuff the first year— Well, it's a safe deal from Whitby's point of view. If it weren't red slate, I wouldn't have a prayer of being able to pay him two thousand dollars at the end of a year."

Lise smiled. "Besides, he doesn't know about your stake." She nodded toward the place where they'd hidden the strongbox.

"Neither of my stakes," Hugh said, patting his wife's sweet belly.

The pole and pully contraption Hugh rigged at Whitby's number-three pit seemed at first only a clever idea. No one suspected it was a lever to move the world.

The day after the demonstration, Jason Whitby went to

Rutland to see the blacksmith who was building the carriage. He studied Hugh's plans, then requested some modifications. The smith nodded and set to work. At the quarry he instructed other men to build a big shed. A boiler house, Whitby explained to Lliam Murray.

"Same principle as running the pumps to keep the water out of the pit base," he said. "I'm not going to use horses to move that carriage up and down the line. I'm going to use steam."

Word of "the big stick" spread. Businessmen from up and down that section of Rutland County, known as Slate Valley came to see the thing. There was no way to keep it secret.

"Let 'em come," Jason Whitby said. "Having a stick isn't going to make a quarry profitable, not by itself." He was confident, and in Whitby Falls people took their security for granted. Not until some weeks later did it dawn on the teamsters that the coming of the stick meant, for most of them, the end of their jobs.

Before that tremor shook the town, Hugh Villette called his family together in the cabin.

"Jackie," Hugh began, "you and me are going to quarry some slate. Not for Jason Whitby, for ourselves. But before we do that, we've got to organize a few things around here." He glanced at his three sisters and his parents and at the cabin. Lise sat at his side and stared at her hands, folded in her lap.

"What things?" Eve asked.

"This place. The way we live. It's going to change. We're not going to stay gypsies in this town; we're going into business." The family knew about Hugh's deal with Jason Whitby, but his social concerns were beyond their comprehension.

"The way we live, it's fine," Eve said. Her anger could be ugly, and the others knew it. They squirmed and murmured assent.

"Is this all you want? All of you?" Hugh threw out his arms, and a jug of cider was knocked to the dirt floor. "Jesus! That's just what I'm talking about. A man can't move in this stinking cabin!"

Betty had been waiting her chance. "Hugh, listen," she said. "Part of the trouble is there's so many of us in here. Me and Celia got an idea.'' The younger sister nodded her agreement but didn't speak.

"What idea's that?'' Hugh asked.

Betty reached into her pocket and withdrew a crumpled newspaper clipping. "It's from the *Rutland Herald*. We seen it last month.''

Hugh studied the advertisement, then raised his head. "The Oregon Territory,'' he said softly. "That's a long way away, Betty.''

"What's this about?'' Eve demanded. "What is this Oregon?''

"It's a place out West, Mama,'' Hugh explained. "This here's an advertisement for girls to go out there and marry the settlers.''

Eve stared at him in disbelief. Even Lise gasped. Finally, Jacques said, "Is crazy to advertise for a wife.'' He dismissed the notion with a projectile of spit directed at a pile of rubbish in the corner.

"We'll talk about it later,'' Hugh said. "I'll ask some questions, Betty, and see what this is all about. Meanwhile, for God's sake let's get this pigsty cleaned up. Lise is going to have a baby. She can't sleep out in the still all winter. I'll help for a couple of days. After that me and Jackie will start work on the Skillet.''

You couldn't say the cabin sparkled, not even after they spent two days cleaning it. It was, and would remain, a hovel. When Hugh was convinced that no amount of further effort would improve things, he went into Rutland, driving Jacques's old wagon. He came home with a load so heavy he had to walk beside the mule.

"What is left in Rutland?'' Eve demanded. "Where you get all the money and all the fancy ideas, Hugh Villette?''

Her son ignored her questions and began unloading. Most of it was pickaxes and barrows and dynamite to hack the slate from the Skillet. Jackie spied lengths of metal cable. "We gonna put one of them sticks up at our quarry, Hugh?'' he asked with delight. "A real tall one?''

"Eventually,'' Hugh said. He stacked the tools of his trade beneath some trees. "Rest of this stuff is for the house.'' There were bolts of cloth that Lise would make into dresses for the women, a few pieces of crockery, and a heavy length of burlap. The last he carried into the cabin himself.

"We're going to have a bit of privacy," he told his wife. Then he proceeded to nail a drape of burlap across one corner, effectively partitioning off a third of the small living space. "This is our place. None of you come across this curtain unless you're invited."

Lise looked at the sullen faces of her in-laws and wondered how long they would permit themselves to be bullied by Hugh. He seemed oblivious to any such worry.

"Listen, everybody. I talked to some folks in Rutland. This here Oregon thing is okay. The women who've gone out have mostly done all right. It's just like it says in the advertisement; the men marry 'em as soon as they get there. A fellow from New York organizes the whole thing. The men pay him a fee."

"The white slaving," Jacques muttered. "They sell the girls into whorehouses."

"Better'n giving it away for free," Jackie said, grinning.

"Shut your mouth," his brother said fiercely. "It's up to the girls. Maryann, Betty, Celia . . . do you want to go, or don't you?"

Betty and Celia nodded their heads furiously. "Might as well," Betty said. "No chance of marrying anybody decent around here. They just call us Canucks."

"Okay." Hugh turned to the oldest girl. "You ain't said nothing, Maryann."

"I ain't going to any frontier territory with wild Indians and bears!" She shuddered. "And I ain't stayin' here, neither."

"She was the woman of Jason a little time. He give her money," Eve supplied. "Then he drop her after Andrea run away. Maryann brood ever since. I warn her what he is like."

"Jason's got nothing to do with it," the girl said angrily.

"Leave her be," Hugh commanded. "She don't have to go to Oregon if she don't want to."

He went outside and returned to his task of unloading the wagon. Then, when it was empty of all the things he'd brought for the cabin, he piled the equipment he'd need to take to the Skillet back in.

"You should have bought that stuff first," Lise said, watching him. "Then it would have been on the bottom and could have stayed where it was."

"Yes," Hugh said. He didn't bother to tell her that he'd been strangely excited by the idea of buying cloth and dishes and the appurtenances of civilized living. It had seemed to him a declaration of something important and solemn. Instead of explaining, he handed her a parcel. "I got this for you."

"Harper's Bazar." Lise read out the title of the magazine and stared at her husband.

"Comes out on Saturday," Hugh said. "Costs ten cents. I want you to have it every week. Learn about all that fancy stuff. Make some of the dresses. They got patterns for baby's things in there, too."

Lise nodded. "What's that for?" Hugh was carrying a paper-wrapped bundle over to the still.

"You'll see," was all he said.

Later, when he was busy doing something with that same mysterious bundle, Maryann joined him. The night was dark, the shack that housed the still barely visible. "I want to tell you something," his sister said without preamble. "I'm going to have a baby."

Hugh didn't look up, but he stopped what he was doing. "Jason Whitby's?"

"No. I ain't been with Jason in over a year."

"Okay," he said. "Whose kid is it?"

"I don't know whose it is," she said. "Ain't none of your business, anyway."

"Suit yourself," he said, and resumed his task.

"What are you doing?"

"You'll see."

"Hugh . . . I want to go away. Not to Oregon, to Boston."

"What the hell are you going to do in Boston? Specially now you're pregnant."

"I'll manage. I need money for the train, though. And a little to get me by until I find my way."

"It's crazy," he said without looking at her.

"It's what I want. You got your dream, and Betty and Celia got theirs. Why can't I do what I want?"

For some seconds he was silent. "I guess you can," he said at last. "I can let you have fifty dollars. No more. I can't afford it."

"That's plenty." Impulsively, she leaned forward and kissed him on the cheek. "Thanks, Hugh. It's the best way. I'd just make trouble for you if I stayed here. I know what you're planning. I wouldn't fit into all that."

"You're my sister," he said fiercely. "You'd fit in if I

said so. Anybody doesn't like it can deal with me. Go to Boston if you want, Maryann, but anytime you feel like coming home, you come ahead. We'll all be here.''

Maryann nodded, then, for the first time, looked closely at what her brother was doing. "You crazy, Hugh? That's dynamite! God Almighty, we're just a few yards from the cabin, and you're setting dynamite!"

"Isn't going to touch the cabin. Not even that tree right there." He pointed to the old oak beside them. "There's just enough here to do what I want. Move off.''

He lit a match. Maryann backed away in the dark, her eyes wide with terror. "Papa will kill you," she whispered.

"He'll be mad, but he'll get over it." Hugh set the flame to the fuse, then jumped back to stand beside his sister. "I told 'em all, things is going to change around here. I meant it."

The roar of the explosion ripped apart the silence of the night. When the dust cleared, Jacques Villette's still had ceased to exist.

1870 . . .

Andrea

Chapter Five

❦

1.

"I'm off to the Battery for a maid," Maggie announced one day in the surprisingly mild and snowless January of 1870. "Come with me, baby girl. It's worth a few laughs."

"Why the Battery?" Andrea asked as they boarded the elevated railway on Sixth Avenue.

"Because I want one that's dumb and ugly. Saves trouble." Andrea looked puzzled. "With the other girls," Maggie added. "They aren't jealous of a greenhorn, and she don't fancy herself cutting in on the action right away."

"So the pick of the greenies are on the Battery," she asked. "Is that it?"

"All the greenies, baby girl. Castle Garden. It's where they come in. They hold the ships out there by Staten Island for a couple of days." Maggie gestured to the horizon visible from Battery Park. "Check 'em for sickness and bugs and God knows what else. Then they bring 'em here."

A single-file line of assorted humankind attested to her statement. They were waiting to go through customs, and Maggie was little interested. "Be days before they're ready for work. Over this way, to the Labor Exchange."

It was a drab, dark room, cavernous, reeking of sweat and a dozen other smells Andrea couldn't identify. "One of them Germans," Maggie told the man behind the counter. "Them what don't speak English. I like my maids to mind their own business."

"Not likely to find a German," the clerk said in a bored voice. "They usually come with a bit of money and head West to buy farms. How about an Irish girl?"

Maggie bristled. "No, you clod. I said I wanted somebody dumb and quiet."

The man shrugged. "Okay, maybe a Pole, then. Lots of Poles here today."

"Yeah." Maggie nodded with satisfaction. "A Pole will do fine."

Eventually, four women were brought forward for Maggie's inspection. Andrea watched with amusement for a few minutes, then wandered off. There was much to study in Castle Garden.

"Here, Andrea! Come tell me what you think of this one." Maggie's strident voice rang out over the hum of foreign tongues. "She's not bad. Good teeth. Look." Unceremoniously Maggie yanked at the girl's jaw. Andrea looked quickly, then turned away. "Good arms, too," Maggie said. "Feel them muscles."

"For heaven's sake, you're not buying a horse." Sharing the embarrassment of the stolid lump of girl, Andrea could feel her own cheeks redden.

"Yeah," Maggie said, undaunted. "That's just what I'm buying. A workhorse. If this little chippy wants to be something else, I won't stand in her way. But for now, she's a Polack workhorse. That's the way it starts, baby girl. For all of us what come here fresh from the old country. You wouldn't know about that."

They took the Polish girl home with them. She said nothing and stared straight ahead, not even looking at the city that rolled by beneath the elevated railroad. "She's frightened," Andrea whispered to Maggie.

"Yeah, wouldn't you be? Never seen nothin' like this, probably. Riding up in the air and not a horse in sight to make the thing go."

For days Andrea pondered Maggie's views on immigrants and what she'd observed at Castle Garden. Then Jay Gould paid a visit to O'Flaherty's Bar.

After her first few days in New York, nearly a year ago now, Andrea had realized with relief that it was ridiculous to expect to see the great man on any street corner. Then, late one Tuesday night when the bar was almost empty, Gould came in alone and ordered a drink.

She spotted him as soon as he walked through the door. Swiftly, she closed the piano and slipped from the stage.

"No break now," Desi said. "That's Jay Gould. Play something."

Reluctantly, Andrea returned to her seat. She played, but she didn't sing, and she kept her face turned away from the footlights. Gould sipped his drink, then rose to leave. But instead of turning to the door, he walked straight back toward the piano. "Good evening, Miss Whitby. I'm surprised to find you here."

Andrea didn't say anything; she just kept playing. Desi watched the interchange, but he wasn't close enough to overhear.

"I'd like to speak with you," Gould continued. "Come to my house tomorrow at three." He laid his card in front of her sheet music and left.

"Stay away from him, Andrea," Desi warned. "He's nothing but trouble." Strained though the relationship between them was, Desi's sincerity was apparent.

"I know," she said. "Don't worry."

It seemed inevitable that if she failed to keep the appointment, Jay Gould would inform her father of her whereabouts. Either she went to see him, or she left O'Flaherty's Bar. She couldn't just do nothing and wait for Jason to arrive.

The house was magnificent. Marble and gilt, mahogany and stained glass—a cathedral, Andrea thought, dedicated to the great god power. That constant, vague yearning for something she couldn't name, the thing that made her continually refuse Desi, was symbolized in the templelike foyer of Jay Gould's mansion.

A servant ushered her into a paneled study where Gould sat behind an enormous desk. "I expect your father would like to know where you are," he said immediately.

"Yes, I expect he would." Andrea stood in the middle of the room, conscious that the winter sunlight from the window behind Gould illuminated her while it left the great man in shadow. "What would you gain by telling him?" she asked.

Gould stood up and came toward her. She was almost a head taller than he. "Why shouldn't I? Runaway daughters are irresponsible ingrates."

"Not always," she said.

"Are you frightened of me, Miss Whitby?"

It took her a few seconds to decide on an answer. Finally, she shook her head. "Not frightened exactly. Should I be?"

Gould chuckled. "That depends," he said. "Here, look at this."

He led her to a wall map of the United States, crisscrossed

with lines in either red or blue. "The red ones are railroads I own. The blue, railroads I intend to own."

"Yes." Andrea nodded. "I've followed your fortunes, Mr. Gould. About the Erie Railroad, and your war with Mr. Vanderbilt."

"Indeed! An extraordinary interest for a beautiful young woman."

"Perhaps." She stretched out her gloved hand and traced the outline of the small, insignificant red line that indicated the Rutland and Washington Railroad. "I'm surprised you haven't built an extension along here."

"That's through the mountains," he said. "Difficult building."

"Not necessarily. Right here, for instance. We call this flat bit the Skillet. It would lead you directly toward Woodstock. From there you could move east toward Boston."

Gould chuckled again. "Here's the future." He clapped his hands over the Midwestern states. "Here and farther west. I don't think I'll be wasting my time in Vermont."

The man cocked his head and studied her. She wore a dark purple velvet suit with a gray fur collar and a matching fur hat. It was the latest fashion. "You seem to be managing quite well," he said.

"Yes." Was he interested in her? Andrea wondered. "Why did you ask me here, Mr. Gould?" She looked at him directly.

"I wanted to make up my mind about doing Jason Whitby a favor. I don't think I will. You can go." He dismissed her with a wave of his hand.

Andrea turned, but before she reached the door, he stopped her. "Miss Whitby, that bit of land, the one you called the Skillet. Who owns it?"

"Jason Whitby," she said. "Naturally."

She didn't know why she was so sure he was going to do it, just that she was. It crystallized everything for Andrea. Thinking about a railroad spur running right by Whitby Falls made everything real. At night she lay awake shaking with excitement, and by day she frequented Castle Garden. She studied the hordes of immigrants, and she made her plan.

The fellow was Irish. She hadn't planned on an Irishman, but he seemed perfect in every other way. Tall and broad and ruggedly good-looking, he had brown curly hair, no beard, and laughing brown eyes. Mostly she was attracted by the way he moved, with grace and a certain hopefulness, as if he expected great things to happen after he took his next step.

He was studying the list of available jobs in the Labor Exchange when she approached him. "Hello, have you just arrived?"

"Indeed I have, ma'am." His eyes twinkled when he looked at her, and he had a ready smile.

"Where are you from, and what do you do?"

"From Dublin. In Ireland. And what I do depends on what there is to be done to earn a bit of brass. My real work is another matter."

"Oh? Just what is your 'real work'?"

"I'm an inventor." He made the statement, then waited for her to laugh. "You don't think that's funny," he said when she didn't smile. "Most folks think it's the best joke in the world, being an inventor."

"My grandfather was an inventor," Andrea said. "He died a pauper, or close to it. What's your name?"

"Patrick Kelly. What's yours?"

"Don't be cheeky," she cautioned. "It's Andrea Whitby. Andrea Adams professionally. Miss Whitby to you."

"And have you a job for me, Miss Whitby?"

"Not exactly. But I'll take you where there's one to be had, better than anything you'll find listed there." She gestured toward the blackboard. "And better than inventing, God knows."

She took him to Maggie's.

At the front door she paused and asked, "Can you guess what kind of house this is?"

"No, why should I . . ." He broke off and stared at her. "Do you mean—"

"Yes, that's just what I mean." Maggie herself came to the door. Andrea said, "This is Patrick Kelly. He's the right size for a bouncer, I think."

"Wait," he said when the girl started to leave. "Will I see you again?"

"I don't see why you should," she answered. When she walked away, she was smiling.

Patrick wheedled information about Andrea from the whores at Maggie's house. She was uppity, they told him, gave herself airs. One of them nearly told him about the abortion, but she knew Maggie would kill her if she did. The Irishman didn't pay any attention to undercurrents of judgment, only to the details of where Andrea worked. He couldn't go to O'Flaherty's at night when she was performing because he was required at the brothel then. Once or twice he went to Broadway Alley by day, but the bar was locked up tight, and there was no sign of the girl.

Finally, Maggie took pity on him. "Goes for a walk, she does, most afternoons around three."

He began a relentless pursuit, standing near the bar and waiting until she came out, then following her. At first, she ignored him; then she deigned to speak. Finally, it became accepted that they would spend their days together.

"I know you were never one of Maggie's girls," he said suddenly one February afternoon. "She told me."

Andrea turned to him, and the expression in her violet eyes was unreadable. "And before she did that, did you think I was?"

"I didn't know what to think."

"Did it matter?"

"You know how I feel about you, Andrea love. Of course it mattered."

"Don't feel anything about me," she said stiffly. "It's a waste of your time."

"Too late for that now," he said softly.

Andrea moved away from him and watched the pigeons feeding in Madison Square. When he joined her, she said, "You've never told me why you came to America. What do you want to do here?"

"I did tell you. I'm an inventor. America's the only place for me."

She sighed. Apparently there were things he had yet to

learn. "What kind of things do you invent?" she asked.

"Lots of things. I dream ideas, picture them in my head, and I make them work."

"I see."

Andrea knew about dreams and visions. She knew about power, too, and that the two things were incompatible. The dreamers of the world were seldom powerful. It was a truth Patrick Kelly had to accept. After that conversation she refused to allow him to accompany her in the afternoons.

A few weeks passed. Finally he lay in wait for her some distance from the bar. She came out because she believed the coast clear, but she'd walked only a short distance when Patrick accosted her. "Why won't you see me?"

"Why should I? You've no claim on me."

"I have, damn it!" He jumped in front of her, and she had to stop walking. "I love you, Andrea. You know that. I think you love me."

"No, Patrick." She shook her head. "I don't love you. Now let me pass."

He wanted to reach for her, slap her, kiss her, do something to get through the shell of her reserve. They were on a public street with dozens of other people, so he could only walk stubbornly beside her. "Why not?" he demanded at last. "Why don't you love me?"

It struck her as the most audacious question she'd ever heard. "Because," she said slowly, "I know the kind of man I want. You're not the right sort."

"You've got everything planned out, haven't you?" His voice was bitter. "Know just what you're after."

"Yes," she agreed. "At first I wasn't sure. Now I am."

"Then why did you pick me up at Castle Garden, lead me on?" he asked. "You kept me dangling, then dropped me. That was a cruel thing to do, lass."

"No," Andrea said. Her voice was pensive. "I just couldn't tell right away. I thought you might do."

"Do! Jesus God Almighty! What kind of woman are you?"

She didn't answer, and they walked almost five blocks in silence. The day turned gray, and a snowflake or two announced the coming of a storm.

"We'd best turn back," Andrea said quietly.

"Listen." He grabbed her arm so tightly she couldn't pull

away. "Tell me what it is you want. I'll do anything for you, Andrea."

She narrowed her eyes and stared at him. "I wish you meant that," she said after some seconds. "I could love you if you meant that, Patrick."

His reply was a strangled cry in his throat. "I do mean it."

"We'll see," she answered. "Maybe we can try."

Two days later they stood in Central Park, watching the skaters on the still frozen lake. "I come from Vermont," Andrea said. "It's about two hundred miles north of here. A small town."

"What's it called?" Patrick asked. He was touched; she'd never before volunteered any information about herself.

"Whitby Falls. My father owns it."

He stared at her, then looked away. "You're rich, then?" His voice was pained.

"My father is."

"That explains everything."

"Does it?" she asked. "If it was that simple, why should I be here in New York, singing for my supper in O'Flaherty's Bar? Using the name Andrea Adams?"

He shook his head. "I don't know."

"I'm an only child, my father's only heir. Something happened, and I left home. I'm never going to tell you about that, Patrick. Don't ever ask me."

"All right." He shrugged. "I don't see what it has to do with you and me, here and now."

"Everything," she said. "You think about it, and perhaps you'll come to understand."

The next day he said, "You want to go home, is that it? Claim what's yours?"

Andrea began to tremble. With that simple statement he had fulfilled all her hopes for him. "Yes," she said. "That's it. Would you care to go with me, Patrick?"

"Are you proposing to me?" His tone was mocking. "Am I some kind of stud horse you've chosen?"

"Not the way you mean." She shook her head, and the sun glinted on her pale silver hair. "But we'd have to be married."

"Do you think I want you on any other terms? What would I do in this place, this Whitby Falls?"

"We quarry slate. My father would teach you the business."

"Would he, then? You think he'd welcome me with open arms? A greenie from Dublin?"

"Yes." She laid her hand on his arm. Beneath the heavy jacket his flesh was firm and hard-muscled. "If you were my husband. And there's something else."

"What's that?"

"Your name. It can't be Kelly. Not in Whitby Falls. You must change it. Legally. Before we're married."

"Change it to what?"

"Whitby."

Patrick Michael Vincent Kelly was born in 1848 in Dublin, on Holy Lane off Moore Street. There was nothing holy about the place. It was a fissure in the earth, a ditch draining the overflow from Dublin's cesspool.

The Kelly dwelling was one of a series of two-room hovels joined together in a chain of ugly misery. "Workers Cottages," they were called by those who lived in the elegant Georgian streets and squares of the other Dublin. In the Workers Cottage where Patrick was conceived and birthed, the total living space consisted of something less than three hundred square feet. He was the tenth of thirteen children.

From the time he could walk, the boy wandered his extraordinary world with a sense of wonder. "Why?" he would ask. "How?" He wasn't discouraged by the lack of answers.

By the time he boarded the ship that took him to Castle Garden, he was twenty-three years old. In the intervening years he had produced a number of innovations and adaptations to make things work better. For most of them he was paid a few shillings or a few pounds, and the inventions themselves became the property of the chap doing the paying. But when Kelly finally scrimped together the price of steerage, he carried with him a plan for a miracle.

Patrick Kelly believed he could produce light without benefit of gas or oil, match or wick. He did not have the money to buy the components necessary to create this fantasy, but he had a journal filled with plans and sketches and a head filled with dreams.

After he left Andrea, on the day that she proposed marriage, Patrick went home to his room in the brothel and took the precious journal out of its wrappings. He held it in his hands for some minutes, not reading over his notes, just looking at the book itself. By his bed was a large wooden trunk that he'd purchased with his first week's earnings in America. Now, two months after his arrival, it was gradually being filled with the equipment he needed to build the prototype of his gasless, wickless lamp. He'd not given the thing a name yet. He just thought of it as "the light."

He had dreamed of creating his lamp, loosing it on the waiting world, and, in the glow of that adulation, winning Andrea. For now he needed only to know that she was there, present in his universe, waiting untouched until he had earned the right to claim her. Today she had changed the shape of that expectation. She was offering to become his immediately, to give her precious self to him in return for something almost insignificant—the name Kelly.

"It's not just that!" He slammed the journal onto the bed and lay back, hands folded behind his head. "It's not just my name she wants." He was speaking aloud, conducting a debate with an imaginary adversary. "She's manipulated the whole thing. Give a bit here, hold back a bit there, make me hunger for her, love her. Wheedle and twist until my head's spinning and I can't think straight for wanting her. And never admit what she wants herself."

But she has admitted it, the chimerical opponent reminded him. She wants to go back to that town of Whitby Falls, wherever it is, and claim her inheritance. You've been selected as escort. And a kingdom must have heirs, so you're to be the stallion.

Patrick groaned aloud and buried his face in the pillow. It was easy to imagine his cheek pressed against Andrea's soft breasts, to pretend that she lay beneath him. Why me? he asked himself. New York is full of men. Dozens of them would jump at the chance to marry her. She's so beautiful, so desirable. Aren't there others who feel the same? She doesn't love me. All she said was that she could love me—might love me—if I do what she wants.

"Then do it, for Christ's sake." He sat up and listened to the words echo in the empty room. Do it. Because if you do, she'll be yours, and that's worth any price at all.

3.

Maggie arranged for one of her regular clients, a judge, to marry them in the front room of the brothel. Andrea wore the purple velvet suit and matching fur hat. Patrick hadn't expected a gown and a veil, but he'd thought she might choose something more bridelike. He had a new suit, black alpaca with velvet lapels, and a carnation in his buttonhole.

A few days earlier he'd asked if she wanted to go to Niagara Falls for a honeymoon.

"No, why should we?" Then she asked, "Have you any money, Patrick? Any savings?"

He shook his head. "Not much, lass. I've been buying things I need for my work. I can manage Niagara, though. I'll borrow a bit from Maggie."

"Don't be silly. I've enough to get what we need."

He was afraid to ask her what she meant.

Patrick did, however, reserve a room at the Astor House without telling her about it. He paid three dollars, in advance, for one night's lodging and breakfast. It was a lot of money, but the Astor was the finest hotel in New York. Patrick wanted nothing less for Andrea and for their bridal night.

When he gave the address to the cabbie after they left Maggie's, she made a face of distaste. "It isn't necessary to be so extravagant, Patrick."

"Yes, it is." He smiled at her, and when she smiled back, he saw heaven in her violet eyes. "It's the most glorious day since the start of the universe, love," he said.

They arrived at the Astor in time for the six o'clock tea. Sitting in the bedraped and bevelveted dining room, they were served pickled beef and clams and thinly sliced white bread and little rice cakes with honey. Neither of them ate much.

Patrick repeatedly told himself that Andrea was nervous, that it was natural for a bride, that he was jittery because she was. In fact, he knew she was reserved and preoccupied but not nervous. It was her coolness that made his hands tremble, the sense of remove she communicated.

Patrick called for the bill and made a point of observing the new fad of leaving something extra for the waiter. The man's obsequious bow of thanks gave the Irishman confidence.

Finally, they went up the marble staircase, and Patrick unlocked the door to their room and stood aside for Andrea to enter.

She paused in the middle of the floor and looked around. It was not as nice as the room waiting for them in Whitby Falls. She had decided to claim the corner guest room, the one they called the Chinese room, for herself and her husband. She didn't want to return to the girlish rosebuds and the dimity. Andrea brought her thoughts back to the hotel chamber. "It's very nice, Patrick," she said. "You were sweet to arrange all this."

Patrick looked at her, feeling so much love and longing and wonder he thought he must burst. He wanted to tell her about the miracle of knowing she was his and he hers, about the paroxysms of joy that gripped his gut. Instead, he said, "Would you like to be alone for a bit? I could go down for a drink, come back in half an hour."

Andrea shook her head. "You needn't do that," she said quietly. She gestured to the folding screen in the corner, then took her small overnight bag and stepped behind it.

Her nightdress of pale blue chiffon and ivory lace was the grandest such thing she'd ever owned. Maggie had given it to her as a wedding present, and she smiled when she slipped the filmy gown over her head and went to join her husband.

He was already in bed with the covers drawn up to his chin. Andrea guessed that he must be naked beneath the blankets. She couldn't be sure, though; he'd closed the drapes and snuffed out all the lights except for one small gas jet on the far side of the room. It created a pale, ethereal glow.

"You're so beautiful," he whispered. "So beautiful, my love. Come here to me. Don't be afraid."

"I'm not frightened," she said. She wasn't. She was remembering Riley and the ledge and the gazebo. She hadn't intended to think of any of that, but she couldn't help it. The memories welling up inside her made her feel hot and cold all over, and when she lay down beside Patrick, she was trembling.

"My love, my love, my love." He kept whispering the words and kissing her eyes and her cheeks and her lips. He buried his face in her hair, and it smelled of lemon. Patrick didn't want to alarm her, so he moved slowly and gently. Then Andrea took his hand and guided it to her breast.

Exultation flowed through Patrick. She wanted him, too. She must love him more than he'd realized. He fumbled in an effort to remove the blue chiffon nightdress. "Please," he whispered. "Is it all right? I want us to be free together."

She didn't say anything but helped him ease the garment over her head and then turned and pressed her naked body against his. He felt her strain for more contact, thrust her pelvis against his thigh. The exultation was a roaring tide in his head now, and when she moaned, the pressure in his genitals became unbearable.

With his big hands he turned her on her back, and then he moved his body into position over hers. In the dim light he could see that her eyes were tightly shut, and suddenly he wasn't in so much of a hurry. He leaned down and kissed each closed eyelid. She didn't say anything, but she moaned again.

Patrick guided his organ between her legs. The pounding in his head was back again, and he kept telling himself to be steady, slow, not to hurt her. There was no resistance, however. His penis slipped inside, and she arched her hips to meet his and moaned again.

For a space of seconds, surprise supplanted feeling. Patrick felt disembodied, a witness of the act. *She is not a virgin.* The words were spoken in his head by a professorial voice, without emotion. She has lain like this beneath some other man.

Andrea was moaning and squirming, and she didn't seem aware of Patrick's suspended passion. His penis began to go soft inside her, and he felt something akin to panic. The joy was slipping away. Then it changed again. She was writhing and churning her hips, and Patrick's mind and his heart were no longer involved; only his body. He swelled and pounded and exploded and lay over her, shuddering with the aftermath of passion.

When it was done, Andrea murmured good night and went to sleep. Patrick realized that whatever he might be feeling, he had pleased his wife. No, he amended the thought, I satisfied her. I did what I was supposed to do.

Most of the night he lay awake. In the morning he rose and opened the drapes, and sun poured into the room. Patrick returned to the bed and looked at the sleeping woman. He lay down beside her again, and she turned to him sleepily.

Rage made him tremble. He pulled her still naked body close to his, wanting to drive himself into her and punish her for the truths that had become clear in his mind throughout the long night. Not only that he wasn't the first man to know her but that she was using him. But despite his desire for revenge, he didn't become hard, and there was no way for him to prove himself superior to her plans.

After breakfast they returned to Maggie's to claim their baggage, and Andrea went up to one of the rooms to change. She came downstairs wearing a magnificent dress of green satin with black velvet trim and a matching black velvet coat. It was a much grander costume than she had worn the day before.

Excited and happy, she chattered to Maggie about coming back to New York for a visit sometime soon. She even kissed all the whores good-bye. When they went to the depot and boarded the train for Troy, Andrea noticed his big wooden trunk for the first time.

"Whatever's in there?" she asked, laughing. "Are you taking a corpse to Vermont, Patrick?"

"It's my equipment," he said quietly. "For my work."

"Oh." She nodded and said nothing more about it. She resumed her chatter, telling him about Whitby Falls and the people he'd be meeting.

"Andrea," he said suddenly. "What if he doesn't take you back?"

For a moment she didn't understand. Then she said, "My father, you mean? Don't worry, Patrick. There's no chance of that."

He stayed silent beneath the onslaught of her gaiety as the last hope of salvaging a future slipped away with the rolling countryside. That day was Andrea's real wedding, Patrick realized. It was the day that Andrea had planned for and the rite for which she had gowned herself in splendor.

Andrea insisted on spending the night in Troy. "We don't want to arrive home after dark," she explained. "Afternoon will be better."

They were in Rutland at noon the next day. Only a handful of passengers got off the train with them. Patrick looked around at the depot and the small town, now in the grip of lunchtime quiet, and asked, "You're sure you won't miss New York? There's not much happening here."

"There's enough happening," Andrea said. "You'll see."

She pointed to a man standing beside a small carriage. "He's waiting for us, Patrick. You'll need this." She pressed an envelope into his hand and walked toward the stranger.

Patrick pointed out their luggage to the porter and followed his wife to the victoria. It was a slick and elegant little vehicle, obviously new, with a green leather top and polished wood japanned in rich mulberry. A pair of matched grays stood patiently in harness.

"Everything just like you ordered, miss," the guardian of the carriage was saying.

"Mrs. Whitby," Andrea corrected. "This is my husband." She turned to him. "They've done a fine job with the carriage, don't you think? And the horses look all right."

Patrick merely nodded. It seemed to him pointless to become involved in a discussion about the victoria. Andrea hadn't consulted him before she bought it.

"There's eighty-five dollars due, ma'am," the man said. "Allowing for your deposit of fifty."

Andrea nodded and looked at Patrick. He stared at her, uncomprehending, then remembered the envelope. "I expect you'll find it all here," he said, handing over the money without counting it. "Mrs. Whitby's taken care of everything."

Andrea ignored any undertone in his words. She motioned to the porter, and their baggage was tied onto the rear of the victoria. The man from the carriage maker's handed her up to the seat. Patrick climbed to his assigned position beside her and hesitated only a moment before he picked up the reins.

"I'll give you directions as we go," Andrea told him. "Oh, I know this road so well! I've traveled it in my dreams every day I've been away."

When they approached Whitby Falls, she made him stop and lower the top despite the cool April day. She wanted to be seen, Patrick realized; Cleopatra on the royal barge.

If Andrea got her wish, Patrick couldn't see how. The single street of Whitby Falls was deserted. His wife appeared oblivious to that. She held her head high and kept smiling while the grays pranced down the road. Patrick wondered if he was intended to do a lap of honor around the open square she identified as the Village Green.

"Doesn't seem to be anyone here," he said finally.

"Oh, yes, there is." Andrea didn't stop smiling. "We've been seen by dozens of people since we started up Main Street."

"You sure of that?"

"I'm sure. Stop just there. That's the house."

He looked at the gracious three-story brick building with its colonnaded white porch and its rolling front lawn. Snow still covered the ground. The trees were all leafless, too. Only a few pines provided color. In the distance, behind the house, he could see the top of a mountain, frozen and solitary.

A great roar suddenly shattered the silence. "What the blazes was that?" Instinctively, Patrick had tightened his hold on the reins, but the horses didn't shy.

"Dynamite," Andrea said. Her voice was shaking with excitement, not fear. "They're blasting at the quarry."

"These two seem well used to it." He nodded at the grays.

"Everyone in this part of Vermont is used to it," she said. "Wait awhile. You will be, too."

She climbed down without waiting for him to assist her and looked up at him. "Come, Patrick. It's time."

Andrea didn't knock. She merely went in and walked down the hall to the dining room. "Good afternoon, Papa."

Jason had his back to the door. At the sound of her voice he turned, his fork still in his hand. "Andrea . . . My God! Andrea . . ."

She didn't go forward when her father rose. He looked as if

he wanted to embrace her, but she stood quite still and said, "This is my husband, Patrick. Patrick, my father, Jason Whitby."

Jason was gripping the back of his chair, trying to adjust to the shock, to say something coherent, to ask the questions racing through his mind. Andrea gave him no opportunity.

"I'd like to speak with you, please," she said. "Patrick, would you mind waiting in the drawing room? Papa and I will go to the study."

Finally, they were alone, and Jason found the wit to say, "Andrea, I can't make myself believe it's you. In God's name, child! Where have you been? Why? Who is this man with you?"

"One question at a time, Papa." She took off her coat and her gloves and sat down, waiting for him to assume his customary place behind the desk. Jason did so from force of habit.

When he was seated, she said, "I've been in New York. Patrick is my husband, as I told you. Our surname is Whitby, by the way. Mr. and Mrs. Whitby."

"A coincidence," Jason said. It was an inane remark, the only one he could think of.

"No, I arranged it." Andrea sat back and folded her hands in her lap. "I told you once that I'd give you grandsons, Whitby heirs. Well, I'm home, and I'm married, and I mean to do just that."

He stared at her in disbelief. "I can't get it through my head that you're really here," he stuttered. "I worried myself sick, Andrea. I thought . . ."

"Papa"—she leaned forward and fixed him with her intent violet eyes—"I don't want to know what you thought. I have no intention of telling you what I thought. Or anything else about the last year."

"Fourteen months," Jason interrupted. "You've been gone fourteen months and six days."

"That's over, Papa, finished. We're here. We're married. Our name is Whitby. If that's not enough, then I'll go."

Jason covered his face with his hands and breathed deep. When he looked at her again, he was more composed. "It's enough," he said finally. "If you promise me you'll never go away again. Not like that. Look at me, Andrea. Can't you see what this has done to me?"

She looked at his yellow-gray hair and the sagging folds of skin beneath his eyes and jaw. "Yes." she said. "You've aged, Papa. But I owe you no apologies. I don't intend to say more than that."

"Listen to me, for God's sake! It wasn't what you thought! What you saw that day in the woods—"

Andrea stood up. "I told you, I don't intend to discuss it. Those are my terms. You can take them or leave them."

Jason closed his mouth and made a weary gesture of acceptance.

"Fine," she said, acknowledging her victory. "Now, I think it would be nice for you to spend a little time with Patrick. Take him to the quarry, perhaps. You'll find him very capable of learning. I will go and see Mama."

She was taking off her hat and moving toward the door when Jason spoke. "Your mother isn't here."

Andrea turned back to face him. "Where is she? At Sarah Murray's?"

"She's in Brattleboro."

"I didn't know Mama knew anyone in Brattleboro. . . ." The expression on her father's face caused her to break off.

"She was ill," Jason said defiantly. "You ask Dr. Sills. He can tell you how ill she was."

"Brattleboro," Andrea repeated. "The asylum for the insane." She whispered the words, afraid to say them aloud.

"She was ill," Jason said again. "Your going away like that, without a word. Millicent took it hard."

"Oh, no!" Andrea walked back to his desk and leaned over it. Her breast was heaving with emotion, the first she'd shown since she entered the house. "Oh, no! You won't put the guilt of this thing on me. If Mama went insane, it happened long before I left. It's your doing, Jason Whitby. I know it, and you know it."

He was crying. "Andrea, listen to me. There're things you don't know about, things you don't understand."

"Don't," she said. "Stop sounding like a fool, like a silly old woman." Rage was making her tremble, but her voice didn't falter. "I came back here to claim what's mine, to be your ally. Now you tell me I don't understand. Stand up. I said stand up, Papa!"

He did as she commanded.

"Now compose yourself. And get your coat. You're going

to Brattleboro and bring Mama home. If she doesn't sleep under this roof tonight, then neither do I. Ever again."

"Andrea"—he tried again, not wanting to plead but doing so nonetheless—"she really is ill. She says all manner of peculiar things. And now she's been in that place almost six months. She's bound to be worse."

"Then bring a nurse home to take care of her," Andrea said. "I told you I'd give you grandsons. I don't intend that they should grow up with a grandmother locked away in an insane asylum. If Mama's ill, she'll be cared for here. Just like always."

Millicent proved to be no trouble. She stayed quietly in her room with a nurse, who sat by the bed. She knew she was home, and she recognized her husband and her daughter, but she didn't seem to understand that it was spring of 1870 and Andrea had returned with a husband after a long absence. For Millicent time had stopped. When Andrea went to her mother's room, Millicent would read aloud from the Bible she kept close at hand and speak about the glories of the world to come. Of Patrick she took no notice at all.

His adjustment to life in the big house was marked by the same surface calm. His only demand was a simple one. "I need a place to work," he told his wife when they'd been in Whitby Falls three days.

"But you'll have an office at the quarry," she said. "Papa will see to that. Perhaps a study here, too, if you wish. I can rearrange the sewing room if that suits you."

"No, the sewing room won't do. I must have a laboratory."

"Oh." She glanced at the locked wooden trunk he'd carted all the way from New York. "A corner of the basement, perhaps? Will that do?"

"That will be fine," Patrick said.

He cleared an unused section of the coal cellar. When the space was prepared to his satisfaction, Patrick moved his trunk into the basement and set up his laboratory. Andrea never came down to see what he was doing. Neither did anyone else. Patrick had created his own world, the only one in Whitby Falls that belonged to him, not to his wife.

At night, lying beside Andrea in the Chinese bedroom, he felt the chasm between them yawn wider. No matter what Andrea did to arouse him, and she did try, Patrick remained impotent. Just as he had been since the first morning in the Astor House.

Andrea recognized it would be folly to reproach him for his failure. "Why?" she whispered after the first celibate week. "Don't you find me desirable, Patrick? You said you loved me."

"I do love you," he answered. "That's the hell of it, lass."

"I don't understand."

"Neither do I, not really. Just be patient. Talking about it won't help. Maybe time will. I need a while to get used to all this."

"Whitby Falls, you mean?"

"Not just the town. Your place in it."

Andrea sighed. She understood more than she admitted, but she didn't blame Patrick for what he felt. She had made all the decisions. If she'd misjudged him, the fault was hers. Besides, there was plenty of time. She wasn't even eighteen yet.

Patrick tried to understand the thing that had happened to him, but despite his reassuring words about the healing power of time, he was terrified. Twin fires burned in his gut—shame that he was suddenly less than a man, anger that she had not even bothered to lie to him. Those conflagrations were feeding on each other and threatening to destroy him in the process.

Andrea had no time to dwell on the problem of Patrick's impotence or its implications for her carefully planned future. She had other things to worry about.

"Has Jay Gould contacted you?" she asked her father soon after her return. "About some land?"

Jason's eyebrows raised. "How did you know about that? He wanted to buy the Skillet. I heard from him around a month ago."

"I hope you didn't set an unacceptable price," Andrea said. "He's going to run a railway spur through Whitby Falls. It will be excellent for business."

"I didn't set any price," Jason said. "I can't sell him the Skillet. Hugh Villette has an option on it."

"Hugh Villette! What on earth possessed you to give Hugh Villette an option on the Skillet? And what does he want with it, anyway?"

Jason told her the story. "He has until November to come up with the two thousand," he ended.

"That's seven months," Andrea said. "Will he make it?"

"I didn't think he could," her father said with a wry smile. "That's why I agreed, as I told you. But he foxed me, no point in denying it." He seemed to take a kind of perverse satisfaction in that fact, and Andrea withdrew from thinking about why.

"Hugh's taking red slate off the Skillet," Jason explained. "Getting a premium for every square he sells. And he was lucky. We had an open winter, so he and Jackie have dug slate every day since they took the place on. He just might do it, after all."

"Doesn't that bother you?" Andrea asked. "Hugh Villette has no right to the Skillet, or to any Whitby land! None at all."

"It's done, all of it," Jason said wearily. "And the deal with Hugh is legal. Let it be."

5.

By May, Hugh knew he was going to fail. He couldn't possibly reach the goal of two thousand dollars by November.

Jackie thought they'd do it and crowed gleefully over the prospect. "Jesus God Almighty, Hugh! We're going to make Jason Whitby eat his fancy legal papers!" Jackie sang while he hauled blocks of slate to the makeshift shanty where Hugh did the slitting, and he laughed when they loaded the squares of finished tiles into the wagons that took them to the railroad in Castleton.

The wagons, and the mules that pulled them, came as a by-product of the stick at Whitby Quarry. When Jason converted Hugh's invention to steam, he dramatically reduced the number of teamsters he required. Villette was able to employ the residue. So three men had joined the brothers, and they shared Jackie's enthusiasm and his confidence.

The miracle being enacted on the Skillet was a thing all Whitby Falls discussed and watched and enjoyed. Andrea's return, as mysterious and unexplained as her departure, heightened the drama. A real threat to Jason and his quarry would be a threat to them all. But a slight prod, a gentle hint that there remained some small distance between Whitby and Almighty God, was a good thing. Besides, Villette was creating more jobs.

"How's Hugh?" the storekeepers would ask when Lise did her shopping. "How's it going? All right?"

"Yes, thank you," she would answer with a smile. "We've been lucky with the weather."

"Glad to hear it," they'd say. "And nice to see you looking so well."

Lise would leave, her proud, swollen belly quivering with delight, her head filled with laughter and dreams.

Jacques Villette accepted the realities once he got over his anger at the destruction of his still. Hugh was pursuing some mysterious master plan. Somehow the boy was going to beat Jason Whitby. Jacques had never conceived a workable scheme to achieve that end, though he'd thought about it often enough. He was prepared to make some sacrifices to help Hugh.

"I do a bit with you and Jackie up there," he had told his son when the operation began. "Know nothing about slate, but I can be some use. But a still, too," he added. "Your *maman* and me, we are used to the applejack to see us through the winter."

"No still," Hugh had said resolutely. "We're through doing this town's dirty work for 'em."

"Not for the town," Jacques explained. "For us only. A gallon a week. That's all."

Hugh accepted the compromise. If he didn't, Eve would be even more surly and difficult to handle. At least drunk she was placid.

However, when Hugh recognized that he was destined to fail, it was Eve who first guessed the truth. She came and stood beside him one June night when he was sitting beneath the oak tree with a pad of paper and a pencil.

"You do the figures," she said nonchalantly, "but you are not happy with the numbers."

He was suddenly enraged. "You'd like that, wouldn't you?" he demanded. "You want me to lose."

"No, I do not want you to lose. You're my son. But I know Jason Whitby. I know how he is."

"It's nothing to do with him," Hugh said. "It's the slate."

"What about it?"

"There's only about twenty feet of the red stuff left. After that, the seam peters out. There's another one, but it's gray. Just like all the rest of the slate around here."

"Do the others know?"

He shook his head. "I suspected about a month ago. I could tell just from the way it looked in the ground before we hauled it out. I did some test blasting in another section. Jackie and the others don't know anything."

"They do not smell the slate the way you do," his mother said. "Nobody does. What about her?" She jerked her head in the direction of the cabin and Lise.

"I can't tell her. Not now." Lise was due to give birth any day.

"No, you cannot. Still"—Eve sighed—"you almost did it. You tried. That is something."

He wasn't consoled by her unexpected kindness. "Not for me it isn't," Hugh muttered. "For me it's nothing at all."

Just then there was a sound from the cabin, and Eve realized before Hugh did that it had been a scream from Lise. Not a loud wail, just a little cry of surprise. "Her time comes," the woman said quietly. "We go to her now."

Hugh was allowed to sit beside his wife and hold her hand for an hour before he was banished to the outdoors while Lise and Eve went about the business of bringing the child into the world. His brother and father joined in the vigil, and Jacques produced a jug of applejack.

They drank a lot, but Hugh didn't get drunk. He was too tense, torn between elation and failure. "I remember the night you were born," Jacques said. "And Riley. Not you, though." He turned to Jackie and laughed. "I think I am real drunk that night. Don't remember nothing."

Jackie laughed, too. Then he said, "Sometimes I wonder about Riley, about how he is." His voice was slurred by alcohol. "He was sweet on Andrea Whitby, you know. I could tell you things you wouldn't believe. I wish I could ask her if she knows anything about him."

"You leave Andrea Whitby alone," Hugh commanded. "She's trouble."

"Yeah." Jackie chuckled. "I bet she married that big

Irishman just 'cause his name was Whitby, too. That must be why she brought him back here."

"Hell," the father said, taking a long pull on the jug, "wouldn't you come back if you were the heiress?"

Talk of heirs made Hugh gag, and he moved away to sit by himself in morose silence. He could hear the muffled sounds of Lise's struggle, and he was proud because she wasn't making a huge fuss like some women did. What about his part of the bargain?

"You'll be a fine lady in a fine house," he'd promised her. "Our child will have a future to look forward to." Now the red seam was running out, and it was his own fault, because he hadn't checked carefully enough before they started digging. He'd just gone ahead and made his big plan and signed the agreement with Jason Whitby, feeling proud and sure because he'd tricked the great man.

"Come in, Hugh," his mother called from the doorway. "You are papa to a nice baby boy."

They all went and admired the red, squalling infant, and Lise told them sleepily that the baby was to be called Henry. She and Hugh had planned that months before.

"You understand, don't you?" she'd said when she mentioned the idea. "It's nothing to do with how I feel about you. It's just that he was good to me when nobody else was."

Hugh had remembered the log boss and the fact that he'd killed to protect Lise and nodded. His son would need to be that tough.

Now he looked at the baby, and it pained him that little Henry would require toughness more than most. His father had failed to provide him a stake in life.

A week after the child was born, the red slate came to an end. The workers on the Skillet stared at the mottled gray blocks they were now exposing and looked at Hugh in disbelief.

"It's a different seam," he told them quietly. "A new one. See, the angle's slightly different."

"What about the red seam?" one of the teamsters asked. "Can't we find where it went, Hugh? You could blast it open again, couldn't you?" His voice was husky with the faith he wanted to have.

"It's finished," Hugh said. "There isn't any more red

slate.'' He threw down his mallet and his chisel and walked away.

Word spread through the town. By nightfall everyone knew. "Too bad." They sighed and shrugged their shoulders. "Figured, though. Can't expect that kind of luck to hold."

At the big house Andrea was exultant. "Call in the option, Papa. Call it in now."

"I can't," Jason said. "Hugh has until November to pay. It's not July yet. That's the way Lliam drew up the papers."

"For the love of God, lass," Patrick said to his wife. "Villette's lost, and you've won. Can't you wait a few months to collect the spoils?"

Andrea looked down and didn't say any more. Patrick finished his dinner in silence. Later, alone in their bedroom, he said, "I'm sorry if I sounded harsh earlier. I know you've been upset about Villette's operation. I just don't know why."

"The land belongs to us," Andrea said. It was all she ever said.

"You've got enough, lass. The little bit he's trying to buy can't make so much difference."

Patrick wanted to understand. He'd been trying to puzzle it out for weeks, not just as an intellectual exercise but because Andrea felt real pain over this thing, and her pain was the most accessible thing about her. It was the thing that made him believe he could breach the chasm between them. "It's not just the land," he said again. "It can't be. You hate the Villettes. Why?"

"I don't want to talk about them." Andrea removed the pins from her silver hair, and it spilled over her shoulders.

He touched it gently, "You're beautiful, love."

She turned to him, and the predatory look in her eyes was so like a blow, it winded him. It was the glance of the female spider ready to devour her mate as soon as he'd performed his function. "Sorry," he said, and turned away. "I didn't mean to raise false hopes."

Sarah Murray had never forgiven Jason for what he'd done to Millicent. Her bitterness was in no way appeased when Millicent was brought home from Brattleboro. "She's worse," Sarah had told her husband. "A thousand times worse than she was before he sent her to that terrible place."

Lliam tried to placate her. "You can't know that, my dear, not for sure. It may be that Millicent would have gone downhill regardless of where she was."

"I know," Sarah said, and pursed her lips. She didn't dare voice the rest of her thoughts. If Lliam knew about Jason's shameful behavior, of the other women he'd been with over the years, he'd understand.

The situation festered in Sarah's mind. Each week when she returned from visiting her old friend, she would shake her head and ponder the injustice of it all. "Poor Milly," she'd whisper over and over again. "Poor, poor Milly. Jason deserves to be punished. He really does."

For a time she thought Hugh Villette was going to give Jason his comeuppance, and she was delighted. Particularly when Lliam confided in her what few others knew, that Jason had lost out on a chance to sell the Skillet to Jay Gould for a big price because of the option Hugh held.

Lliam told her because he hoped the story would appease her sense of justice and make her worry less over Millicent. For a while it had the desired effect. Then word of the finish of the red slate reached Sarah. It presented a different opportunity.

All her children were full-grown and married, with children of their own, but Sarah still had a trunk full of baby clothes—things she'd knitted and sewn with her own hands, things she couldn't bear to part with. She doled them out to her daughters and daughters-in-law as they produced offspring, but the supply was nowhere near exhausted. On a warm July afternoon she gathered a selection of the tiny garments into a basket and headed toward the Villette cabin.

"I came to see Lise," she told Eve.

The Canadian woman looked at her suspiciously. "What you want with her?"

"Why just to congratulate her, naturally, and to see the new baby." She held out the basket tentatively. "I've a few things here I thought she could use. I mean, my own children are all grown, so—"

Eve was about to send her away when Lise appeared at the door. "Come in, Mrs. Murray. It's kind of you to visit."

She ushered Sarah through the door with the confidence of a practiced hostess. "Little Henry's sleeping." The new mother gestured to a cradle in the middle of the floor. "Best time to see him. At least he's not wailing."

Sarah laughed. "They're all like that. Boys especially." She looked around and hoped her surprise didn't show in her face. Sarah had heard numerous stories of the filthy, slovenly ways of the Villettes. This was nothing like what she expected. The cabin was poor, and the dirt floor must be horribly damp in winter, but it was clean and tidy. Her eyes fell on a stack of magazines—*Harper's Bazaar*.

Lise looked embarrassed. "It's nice to look at the pictures and dream," she said shyly. "They only cost a dime."

"Yes." Sarah's voice was firm and full of reassurance. "It *is* nice to dream. And when you work hard, you can believe your dreams will come true. I hope you don't mind accepting these little gifts for the baby. They're not new, but they're clean and in good condition. I know how hard Hugh's trying, and I thought . . ." Her voice trailed away.

"Thank you, Mrs. Murray. I'm delighted to have the things." Lise reached for the basket.

Sarah gripped her hand. "Listen," she whispered. "There's something I want to tell Hugh. He's not here, though, is he?" She glanced over her shoulder with something like fear.

"Hugh's up on the Skillet, Mrs. Murray. Working hard, just as you said. Sit down, please. I'll get us a cup of tea. Then you can give me the message for Hugh."

She took her time making the drink, giving Sarah Murray time to compose herself. Then she sat beside her guest and said easily, "Now, what do you want to tell us?"

Sarah looked around again as if she were afraid of being overheard.

"Eve's gone," Lisa said. "She doesn't like company. And Mrs. Murray, I know how to keep a secret. I grew up in an orphanage. I had to learn."

The older woman leaned back and looked at the girl. An orphanage. Yes, it figured. And a new baby. And a husband who suffered a piece of terrible luck just when he needed the good kind. And Jason Whitby, who always had everything his own way, even had his daughter come back after she'd had every good reason to run away.

It was the dirt floor that did it, though. The thought of the baby who'd be just old enough to crawl when winter came and a dirt floor that would be cold and wet. Lliam would kill her if he found out, but he wouldn't. She could trust Lise. Sarah was sure she could.

"There's someone from New York wants to buy the Skillet," she said in a conspiratorial whisper. "Jay Gould, the railroad man. Mr. Whitby couldn't sell it to him because Hugh has an option. I just thought—I mean I hoped—that Hugh could do something if he knew that."

Lise pursed her lips and thought for a few seconds, then set down her cup and placed her hand over Sarah's. "I'm not sure," she said. "Maybe he can. I'll talk to him. And don't worry. I won't tell anyone how I know. Not even Hugh."

They talked of all the possible methods of approach, and finally it seemed the best hope was a direct, frontal attack. Hugh would go alone to see Mr. Gould in New York. Win, lose, or draw, it was the Villettes' only chance.

No one else knew where Hugh was going or why. "Business," he told them. "Back in a few days, maybe a week."

He was back after forty-eight hours. Lise saw him trudging down the path to the cabin with the jacket of the black suit she'd made him slung over his shoulder, an unreadable expression on his face.

No one else was home. She ran out to meet him. "Well, did you see him? Did you see Mr. Gould?"

"I saw him." The only thing his voice betrayed was exhaustion.

"Well? For God's sake, Hugh, tell me!"

"He bought my option on the Skillet." Hugh spoke the words slowly, as if he couldn't quite believe them himself. "His lawyers wrote up a lot of papers, and I signed them, and that was it. Jay Gould has an option to buy the Skillet for two thousand dollars."

Neither of them moved. "He thought it was real funny," Hugh continued. "Mr. Murray never put in a clause saying my option wasn't transferable. Mr. Gould laughed and laughed about that."

Lise held her breath. She was almost afraid to ask the next question. "Hugh, how much did he pay for the option?"

"Nothing."

She stared at him. "Why did you agree?" It was too much

for her to take in. Her voice was a faint whisper. "How could you, Hugh? It was all we had."

He smiled then, a slow grin that spread from his mouth to his dark eyes and soon lit his whole face. "He didn't pay any cash." Hugh reached into his pocket and withdrew a folded document. "I've got land instead. Land that the railroad owned. I traded the option on the Skillet for four acres. The border runs parallel to Whitby Falls. Us and Jason Whitby, we're abuttors."

Lise pressed her hands over her cheeks. They were burning, and her eyes were blurred with tears. "Oh, my God," she whispered. "Oh, Hugh." Then, suddenly as the thought occurred, she asked, "What's there? What's on that land?"

"On it?" Hugh was whooping now. He threw his jacket on the ground and waved the deeds in the air and yelled, "Slate! That's what's on it. Slate! And it doesn't matter if it's red or gray or green, because it's ours, Lise! Yours and mine and Henry's!"

They fell into each other's arms and kissed and clung and laughed and cried, and finally Lise asked, "What are you going to call it? What's going to be the name of your quarry?"

"I'll tell you," Hugh said. "I thought about it all the way home, and I know. It's going to be Villette-Whitby Falls. I'm not going to let Jason Whitby forget that we're as much a part of this place as he is."

1876 . . .

Patrick

Chapter Six

1.

Patrick Whitby had finally come to think of himself by that name. Kelly was a distant memory; five years was a long time. But not long enough to make him think of Whitby Falls as home. Each time he returned from one of his frequent New York trips, Patrick felt himself a stranger.

He clucked softly to the horses and reined in. The buggy rolled to a halt. He often stopped at that point on the journey from Rutland station. Looking at the town below, he would prepare himself. The morning sun shimmering on the earth and the trees promised fierce heat to come and limned the jagged outline of his resting place.

He saw the area they called the Skillet, scarred with the remains of the slate quarry Hugh Villette had once operated on the site. It was deserted. All that fracas about the railroad and the option and Jay Gould had come to nothing. Gould now owned the land, but there was no spur, no track heading east into Whitby Falls and beyond. Spite—that's what the whole thing had been about.

Patrick sighed. That was usually the motive behind happenings in this small, self-contained universe. Hugh Villette's new house, for instance. He smiled ruefully. Villette had positioned the thing so that, in effect, it was an extension of Main Street. Seen from a distance, the elaborate white turret of Hugh's house dwarfed the classic simplicity of Jason Whitby's.

Technically, the Villette place wasn't even in Whitby Falls. But for the inhabitants of the town, Villette, his quarry, his house, his wife, and his four children were part and parcel of their world. Most of them admired what Hugh had accomplished, even Jason Whitby, however much he tried to hide it. Only Andrea would never bend. Andrea still hated.

Patrick sucked in his breath and tugged on the reins. He had to face her. The next day was the Fourth of July, 1876.

The Centennial. There would be a celebration, a picnic. The Whitbys would be hosts. He was expected to be present, as part of his unacknowledged agreement with his wife. He must do nothing to embarrass Andrea or Jason. At least not in public. The horses moved obediently down the hill.

Andrea Whitby stood behind the curtained window of the drawing room and looked up Main Street. She expected Patrick to arrive that morning, but she wouldn't make a public display of herself by waiting for him on the front porch. Besides, it made little difference. When Patrick was home, he spent all his time in the basement fiddling with "his work."

Did he have a laboratory in New York, too? She'd never asked about that or about the stuff downstairs in the old coal cellar. Sometimes she went and stared at the assortment of bottles and tubes and wires, but she could make no sense of them. Certainly she never descended to the laboratory when Patrick was home. It was one of the understood silences between them.

Like their silence about what they had each done in the years before they married. Neither did they talk about the future. The empty, hollow shell of their marriage simply went on from day to day. They didn't argue or recriminate or question. They just lived with their individual pain.

Jason had once asked if she and Patrick were going to get a divorce.

"Don't be ridiculous," Andrea had said. "Why should we do that? It would be a scandal."

Her father had stuttered and looked embarrassed. "I just thought. I mean— Well, child, you two still haven't produced that grandson you promised me." He'd tried to laugh, as if it were a joke.

"There's plenty of time, Papa," Andrea had said airily.

She was then twenty-four, and Patrick was twenty-eight, and there was still time, but Andrea knew things were unlikely to change. Patrick was unlikely ever to be a real husband to her. He expected me to be a virgin, and I wasn't, she'd tell herself. That's the reason. Patrick doesn't know about Riley and the gazebo and the baby. Maybe she should tell him. An explanation might change things; certainly they could be no worse. But it was impossible. She couldn't talk about the child she'd aborted or about Jason and Eve.

In the white house where the Villette family lived, the Fourth of July had receded in importance. That afternoon they would bury Jacques. He had died in his sleep a few days before. Eve wouldn't let either of the town's two ministers near the house. "We are no Protestants," she'd said firmly. Insisting on some weird rite dredged from her memories of Quebec, she stretched Jacques out on his old bed in the cabin and lit a candle at his head and feet and kept vigil for three days and nights. "A proper wake," she said. "Like home."

Lise knew more about such things, having been raised in a convent, but she'd didn't point out the errors in ritual. With Hugh and their four children and their almost-finished new house, Lise had too much to do to be bothered by her mother-in-law's peculiarities.

That morning, Riley Villette left Poultney and headed north, along the riverbank, toward Whitby Falls.

Riley had been two weeks in Poultney, but none of his family knew it. Had Jacques not died, they would never have known. Riley was only counting the days until he could leave Vermont.

He had come because Uriah Stephens asked him to. Uriah wasn't merely Riley's employer. True, he paid Villette eleven dollars a week to act as his secretary and personal assistant, but more important, he was the younger man's idol. Stephens had made the world take shape for Riley. His vision of the dignity of work, of laborers' rights and the mystical bond between working men, was the stuff of heady dreams. Stephens's Noble and Holy Order of the Knights of Labor had become mother, father, and religion to Riley Villette.

He had little hope, however, of organizing the slate workers into one of the craft-oriented assemblies of the Knights. "They're not the right sort," he'd told his mentor. "Vermont's not the right sort of place. Cities, Uriah, that's where we have to concentrate. Not a rural hinterland like Vermont."

Stephens recognized the validity of the argument; but Riley was Vermont born and bred and had worked in the quarries. It was an opportunity too good to ignore. In his single-mindedness, Stephens could not see that there were other reasons why Villette didn't want to return. He pressed hard, and Riley gave in. Not Whitby Falls, however. He'd go to Poultney. He knew some people there.

The man Riley had in mind was a fellow named William Williamson only a few years older than himself. They'd gone to school together. Riley remembered that the older boy had moved to Poultney and found work in a quarry there. He figured that was an attempt to evade the powerful grip of Jason Whitby. If so, it gave him a talking point.

Will Williamson remembered him, offered hospitality, and listened, patient if uncomprehending, while Riley explained the goals of the Knights. He honored, too, Villette's request that no one in Whitby Falls be told of his presence, recognizing that Riley didn't want to talk about his family. He mentioned Hugh's quarry once. Riley looked away.

"Suit yourself," Will had said with a shrug. "That's your business."

After two weeks, when Riley was about to conclude that his original assessment had been correct and Vermont slatemen weren't ripe for a union, Will brought him other news.

"I been to see my folks," he announced on Sunday afternoon. "Thought you'd like to know. Your pa died this morning. Funeral's on Tuesday."

2.

The Villettes were gathered by the river. Riley saw them when he was yet some distance away. As he came nearer, he noticed the coffin and the open grave. He'd assumed the funeral would be in town, had even wondered which of the two churches they had persuaded to bury his father. Instead, they were putting Jacques into the ground a dozen yards from the cabin. Riley dismounted reluctantly. It was ghoulish.

Hugh was reading from the Bible, "I am the resurrection and the life. . . ." He looked up and saw his brother, but he didn't stop reading. The others looked at Riley, stared for a moment, then turned back to Hugh. The elder brother's voice droned on, giving Riley an opportunity to examine the mourners.

Eve looked little changed except that she was wearing a proper black dress. In all his life he'd never seen his mother in such a gown. It seemed to him absurd. Riley looked for his sisters, but none of them was there. The only other female was a pretty girl whom he didn't recognize. She held a baby in her arms, and two boys and a little girl stood silently beside her.

Hugh closed the Bible and handed it to Eve. Then he turned and took a pair of shovels from where they leaned against the big oak tree. He kept one and handed the other to Jackie. "There's a third shovel if you want to help," he said.

Riley stepped forward. No one spoke as the brothers heaped earth on the coffin. When the hole was almost full, Hugh motioned to his two sons and gave them his shovel so that each little boy could add a bit of dirt to his grandfather's grave.

That's why he had an extra one, Riley thought. He didn't expect me. It was for the kids. It seemed a strange preoccupation for the moment, but nothing of the event was real to him.

Finally, it was done. They laid aside their tools and moved from the graveside. Riley went to his mother. "I'm sorry," he said, putting an awkward arm around her thick waist.

Eve shrugged. "He died happy. Just went to sleep and didn't wake up. How did you know? Never you come home in seven years. How come today?"

"I was in the area. I heard."

She shrugged again. "Is a good thing," she said. "Papa would be pleased."

Hugh shepherded them all to a waiting buckboard. Riley was surprised. He'd imagined they all still lived in the cabin.

"You'll come back to the house with us?" Hugh asked. It was by way of a greeting.

"Yes, of course. Where is it? I heard about your quarry. I didn't know you had a house."

"It's not far. Ride behind us. There's no more room in the buckboard."

It was a funny-looking place. Riley followed the others up the hill to where the white house stood alone and tried to think why it was so strange and unbalanced.

"It's not finished." Hugh climbed down and joined his

brother by the front door. "Jackie and me are building it ourselves. Takes time."

Inside, Riley was formally presented to Lise and the children. She nodded gravely at him, then disappeared into the kitchen. Eve made no motion to follow her. Instead, she went and sat by the window with a glass of applejack.

"Where are the others?" Riley asked.

"Betty and Celia are married, living in the Oregon Territory. They write every Christmas. They're okay. Don't know about Maryann. She went to Boston a few years back."

"You're doing all right." Riley looked around at the comfortably furnished sitting room. "I've been in Poultney. They say you're quarrying the best slate for miles around. Biggest stick in Vermont."

Jackie joined them, glass in hand. He was grinning. "Hugh invented the stick. Me and him, we put up the first stick in this valley. At Jason Whitby's number-three pit. Then Hugh foxed him out of land for a quarry of our own." He slapped his brother on the back and drank deep of his applejack.

"You got this land from Whitby?" Riley was incredulous.

"No." Hugh shook his head. "Not this. Another piece. It's a long story. I'll tell you later. What about you? Want to come home for good? There's work for you if you want it. You know that."

"I know. Thanks, Hugh, but I've got work of my own."

The older brother grimaced. "Somebody told me you were in Philadelphia, working with that madman Uriah Stephens."

"That's right. He's not a madman. He's the voice of the future."

Hugh poured himself a drink and said quietly, "I sure as hell hope not."

"Let's not quarrel," Riley said. "Not today. We see things differently, that's all. I'm glad for you, Hugh. People say you've worked hard. You deserve your success."

"Yes," Hugh agreed. It was a simple statement of fact. "Here's a picture of what the house will look like when it's finished." He held out a sketch that featured gables and turrets, elaborate carving, and endless porches. "Lise saw it in a magazine, and we copied it out. You like it?"

Riley stared at the drawing. "It's pretty ambitious."

"Exactly," Hugh said. The brothers smiled at each other.

At dinner, Jackie was full of talk, a contrast to the subdued mood of the rest of them. "Hey, Riley," he said suddenly. "Forgot to tell you. Andrea Whitby's married, but she's still got the same name. Can you beat that?"

Riley didn't look up. "Is she living here?" he asked. His voice was without expression.

"Sure is. Right in the big house like always, with her hard-as-nails father and her loony mother. No kids, though. That Irishman she's married to ain't around long enough to make her a mama, I figure. Always gallivanting off to New York."

"Maybe Andrea's barren," Lise said. "Some women are. It's a shame, Jackie, a tragedy. You shouldn't make fun of her."

Riley stared at his plate.

"Listen," Hugh said to change the subject. "Who's in charge of the fireworks tomorrow?"

"You are," Jackie said. "I mean, everybody expects you to be, Hugh. You've done it the last three years." He chuckled. "Rest of 'em like to look, but they don't want to be too close when the bang comes."

"Big doings, then," Riley said. "For the Centennial, I mean."

"Yes," Hugh agreed. "I thought we might not go, with Papa just buried and all. But I'll have to if they're counting on me for the fireworks."

"You're established, then. Prominent businessman in Whitby Falls. That how it is, Hugh?"

"Yes, that's how it is."

"You will stay for the Fourth, won't you?" Lise asked Riley. "There's plenty of room."

Riley knew no gracious way to refuse.

The Green was strung with banners and ribbons and flags, a sea of red, white, and blue. There was a Ferris wheel and a carousel, even a band. Riley recognized a number of the oldest Welsh immigrants among the players. He wanted to examine the town itself, see if it had changed. He couldn't. There were too many people, too much movement and shouting and laughing. The Green was a vivid kaleidoscope in constant motion. The population had grown.

Their tastes, however, were the same—cider and lemonade and doughnuts and ice cream for the children, endless supplies of applejack for the men. Just like Andrea's birthday parties.

He didn't want to look for her, but he couldn't prevent himself. When he spotted her, standing between her father and a tall stranger, he felt a vise tighten around his gut. She hadn't changed at all, except to become more beautiful. She was laughing, and her head was thrown back, and even at a distance he could see her white teeth and her golden skin.

"Oh, Jesus," Riley muttered. "Don't let it start again."

He didn't know if it was a prayer or a curse. He'd lived so long with the pain of the memory, the bitterness of the betrayal. Six years now. He'd thought it was over. That's why he'd agreed to come to the Green that day. But the sight of her made it all alive again. Nothing was over; it never would be. Not for him.

Riley turned to the table where they were pouring applejack. "Hey, Riley Villette!" the man tending the kegs said. "Good to see you, boy. Welcome home." He handed over a glass, and Riley drank it in one gulp, then waited for another.

"You Villettes," the man said, laughing. "You always could drink the rest of us under the table." He refilled Riley's glass three times, chuckling all the while. "Your pa could make the stuff better'n anyone in Vermont, and the rest of you can put it away."

Riley looked at him with loathing and walked away. Canucks. Hard-drinking, good-for-nothing Canucks from the cabin. That's all they'd ever be in this town.

Riley remembered the things Andrea had said. If he hadn't been the father of her baby, if it hadn't been half Canuck, she wouldn't have murdered it. He'd understood everything about Whitby Falls after that. Hugh was crazy to think he could change it.

He looked again for Andrea but didn't see her. His head was swimming, the hot July sun intensifying the effect of the alcohol in his blood. He turned toward the big house. He was going to tell her what he really thought. Tell her he was glad she was barren now after she had murdered his child.

She won't be there, though, he told himself. She's not at home. She's out there in the crowd with her handsome husband and her no-good bastard of a father. Mrs. Whitby now. Trust her to manage to keep even the name.

It doesn't matter if she's not there. The idea came slowly to his benumbed mind. I'll write her a letter and leave it on the piano. She's sure to find it on the piano.

He knew the door would be open. No one in Whitby Falls ever locked a door. The hall, cool and silent, was a welcome relief from the heat and the tumult outside.

I'll find paper and a pen in the study, Riley thought. He had never been in Jason's private office, but he knew where it was.

He turned left and entered the room, his head racing with all the things he was going to write for Andrea to read.

She was standing by the window, and she turned when she heard the door open. The light was behind her, making a splendor of her silver hair and outlining her tall, graceful shape.

"What are you doing? How dare you come here?"

Riley was choking. He couldn't breathe. His words were a struggle for sanity. "I . . . want . . . to . . . tell . . . you . . . that I know." The sounds were not speech but the guttural moan of a tortured animal. He kept walking toward her, his hands extended as if he needed something to grab on to, to keep from falling.

"Get out," she whispered. "Get out of my house and get out of my town."

"Not your town," he muttered. "Town belongs to everybody. Belongs to me, too. All of us . . . born here."

"You're drunk." Her mouth twisted with the ugly words. Riley kept groping toward her. "I warned you," she said. "I told you what I'd do if you ever came near me again."

He didn't hear her. The ringing in his head was too loud. His hands closed on her arms, pinning them to her sides.

Andrea didn't struggle. She wouldn't give him the satisfaction. She just stared up at him.

"Whore," he said softly. "Beautiful bitch whore. Murderer." Then he was saying nothing, because his mouth was pressed over hers.

Riley didn't know it was really happening. It was the nightmare all over again. He pulled her down, and she lay on the floor beneath him. He clawed at her skirts and ripped her petticoats, and finally she was exposed.

"No . . . please, no. Riley, for God's sake, don't do this. . . ."

It wasn't possible. Andrea couldn't believe it was real. He

smelled the same; he felt the same. She hated him for what he'd done, what he was. For what he'd known and never told her. At the same time, she was trembling with the old longing, the old passion.

"Oh, God! Oh, Riley . . ." Of their own accord, her hips arched to meet his. When he slid himself inside her, all the once-learned responses, all the lessons he had impressed on her virgin flesh, were awakened as easily as opening a book and finding the print oblivious to the passage of time. The same sensations, the same feelings. Andrea shuddered beneath him with pent-up pleasure that exploded in the first seconds of penetration.

"Bitch," Riley shouted even as his own climax came. "Bitch! Whore! Abomination!"

Andrea heard the word at the precise moment when the tide of her response was ebbing. She pulled away from him easily. Riley lay on the carpet, limp and exhausted and very drunk. He was sobbing.

She struggled to her knees. The room was spinning. She clutched at her father's desk, gasping for breath. Her hands groped for purchase on the smooth mahogany surface, tried to find the leverage that would pull her to her feet. Then her fingers closed around Jason's letter opener.

It had been a Christmas present years before, an ornate conceit of pearl handle and long brass blade, a dagger. She pulled the thing toward her and stared at it. It was vengeance and truth and an end to misery. She raised the weapon in the air and plunged it into Riley's back.

He exhaled once, loudly, with a sound like air escaping from a burst balloon, and sobbed a few more times. Then he was still. Gingerly, she reached out and touched the spreading red stain on his white cotton shirt.

Her fingers were sticky with his blood. Andrea stared at them. They didn't look like her hands at all. They looked like stranger's hands seen from a distance. She touched her cheeks. Am I dead and my body a corpse? No, Riley is dead. I killed Riley, and he's dead.

Slowly, she stood up, rearranged her clothes, and walked out of the study. When she opened the door of the house, the sound of music and merriment flowed up Main Street to meet her. "Listen, everybody! I killed Riley Villette!" She shouted the words and waited on the elegant, white-pillared front porch.

3.

In the weeks that followed the Centennial, a lot of things happened. A man named Professor Bell exhibited something called a telephone in Philadelphia. There were reports from Germany of a wonderful new engine powered by gasoline. The Republicans, frantically trying to cleanse themselves of the scandals of Grant's second term, nominated a gentleman of upstanding reputation, Rutherford B. Hayes, to run for the presidency. The Democrats chose Sam Tilden, famous for breaking up the notorious Tweed ring.

There were places in America where such events caused excitement and attracted attention, but not in the Slate Valley of western Vermont. The *Rutland Herald* had only one front-page story: the trial of Andrea Whitby for the murder of Raoul (Riley) Villette.

The courtroom was packed every day; people stood in line for hours to get seats. Reporters from as far away as New York and Boston crowded into the gallery reserved for the press. It was a zoo, a circus, a sideshow. The main attraction, waiting in the wings, was death by hanging.

"Ain't gonna hang her," some people said. "Not a woman. Give her life."

"Got to hang her. Got to prove them Whitbys is just like everybody else. No special privileges for the rich."

"You're forgetting one thing. They may find her not guilty."

A lot of folks said that, and it was an uneasy notion in the back of Hugh Villette's mind. If the jury believed her plea of self-defense, her story that Riley had attacked her, Andrea might be acquitted. Hugh thought about that a lot.

Jason lived the days and nights behind a façade of stoicism. Each morning he rode beside Andrea and Patrick on the trip to the courtroom. Each night he accompanied them home to Whitby Falls. The five hundred dollars' bail set by the court he paid in cash. He wanted to hire a suite in a hotel to spare them the journey back and forth to Rutland. Andrea refused. She wanted to remain at home. Apart from that decision, Andrea was a zombie.

In the first days, the time of the inquest, Lliam Murray was her attorney. Then, when they knew there would be a trial, he said, "You need someone else, Jason, a criminal lawyer. Someone accustomed to this kind of thing."

"Who do you suggest?" Jason might have been asking about a carpenter or a blacksmith. His tone of voice and his eyes betrayed nothing.

"Harry Winslow, I think, from Montpelier. Good man."

"Good for this kind of thing? Better than someone from out of state? Someone famous, maybe?"

Lliam leaned forward. "Don't do that, Jason. You go hire yourself some smart-aleck Philadelphia lawyer, and it'll be the finish of Andrea. They'll resent it."

"Who will resent it, Lliam? The people of Whitby Falls? Do you think I care about them now?"

Murray shook his head. "I don't mean them. I mean the judge and jury, whoever they turn out to be. You know how outsiders are viewed up here. It would be her death warrant. You want Harry Winslow from Montpelier," he repeated.

Jason leaned back in his seat, thinking for a few minutes. Then he went to the door of the study and summoned Patrick. "Come in here. Lliam says we need another lawyer. Recommends a chap named Winslow from Montpelier. What do you think?"

"I don't know." Patrick's eyes were glazed. He couldn't believe any of this. He'd gotten through a quart of Irish whiskey since the inquest ended.

"What the hell does that mean, you don't know? You're her husband, goddamit!" Jason's voice wasn't as angry as his words. He'd expected this. He just needed to share the responsibility in case things went wrong.

"I don't know," Patrick repeated. "I guess Lliam is a good judge. We'll do what he says."

Winslow was a small weasel of a man with a hooked nose and black hair slicked back from his forehead. In some ways, he inspired confidence. He spoke to Andrea alone first, then to her husband and father and Lliam Murray.

"Gentlemen, I'm sure we all understand the realities of this case. The lady is still in a state of shock, naturally. I can't get much information from her. But''—he was toying with a gold watch chain hanging from his vest—''that's not what it's really about, is it?''

"What is it about?'' Patrick asked. The others stared at him, then looked at Winslow.

"Influence,'' the Montpelier lawyer said. "About in-flu-ence. And the standing of Mr. Whitby in this community. That is what will settle this unfortunate business.''

The Irishman was bewildered. He thought he understood America, but this was some arcane ritual he couldn't share. Something about the special, insular world of Vermont. He had never made a real effort to become part of that world, and now he could contribute little to saving his wife. It was too late to change that.

And he wanted to. Oh, dear God, how he wanted to. He sat in the courtroom and watched her, and the sight tore at his insides. Everyone else thought she was proud, even haughty. Tall, beautiful, cool, removed. Those were the descriptive words that appeared about Andrea in the press. Even Wins-low said, "If you could bend a bit, my dear, show a little feeling, a little more remorse.'' Andrea stared at him with unseeing violet eyes and went on as before.

Patrick was the only one who knew the turmoil churning behind the mask. He could see it, smell it, sense it in her every gesture.

"She's going to crack!'' he shouted at Jason after the fourth day of the trial. "Damn it, man, don't you see it? We've got to do something.''

Jason knew about cracking. He was aware of Millicent lying upstairs oblivious to everything that was happening, safe in her cocoon of unknowing. "I'm trying, Patrick,'' he said softly. "It's difficult. These things are delicate.''

Patrick looked at him, then walked out of the room and opened another bottle of Irish. He carried it upstairs to the Chinese bedroom and sat down beside his wife, who was stretched full-length on top of the pale blue quilt. Her eyes were closed. He could see the delicate tracery of veins in the fine skin and the shadow of long lashes on her cheek. "Andrea. I've brought you something, love. A bit of Irish. 'Twill do you good.''

"No, thank you,'' she said quietly. She looked at him then and reached out her hand but didn't touch him. "I'm sorry,

Patrick. I'm really sorry. That day in Castle Garden, I thought I had a lot to offer you. I never expected all this. Too bad. Who knows what you might have found at the Labor Exchange?''

"Oh, Christ," he said. "Andrea, tell me about it." He was pleading with her, for the first time, though he'd felt like it often enough. He took her hand in both of his and held it. How many years since he'd touched her? he wondered. "Tell me what happened, love. Maybe I can help."

"There's nothing to tell. He attacked me, and I fought him off." She turned her face to the wall. "I'm sorry, Patrick," she said again. "It's too late."

Paul Harper, the district attorney, wasn't particularly ambitious. He liked his life as it was. But he was competent and reasonably honest. He didn't intend the fact that the defendant was named Whitby to change anything. He had prepared his case painstakingly. He would do things as they should be done, by the rules. Witness after witness who had seen Riley Villette on the afternoon of the killing. More witnesses to prove that the weapon was a familiar item on Jason Whitby's desk. Yet more who had heard the defendant announce that she'd killed the victim. Thorough. By the book.

"Mr. Harper. I'm Hugh Villette. This is my brother Jackie."

The district attorney nodded. "I know who you are, gentlemen. What can I do for you?"

"I, that is, Jackie . . . We think we've got evidence. Something important."

Harper looked around the crowded courthouse corridor. "Come to my hotel," he said. "In an hour. Room one-twenty-seven."

He had a pot of coffee waiting. Hugh wished it was something stronger. "This case," Villette said by way of opening. "How's it going?"

"As expected," Harper said. "It's a bit sensational, perhaps. Not unusual, unfortunately."

Jackie sat forward in his chair. "What do you mean, 'not unusual'. . . ?"

"Man has a bit to drink, gets carried away. Andrea Whitby's a beautiful woman."

"Are you saying"—Hugh's voice was strained—"that you believe her story? That Riley tried to rape her and she killed him in self-defense?"

Harper shrugged. "It's not unusual, gentlemen, as I said."

"She stabbed him in the back," Jackie shouted. "How did that happen if it was like she says?"

"Lower your voice, Mr. Villette. The hotel is crawling with reporters. As to your question"—Harper took a sip of black coffee—"that's the puzzling thing, really. That's why the lady was ordered to stand trial, at least in my opinion."

"Your opinion!" Hugh stood up and began pacing. "Your opinion is that she's innocent. She's a Whitby, so she must be. That's how it sounds to me."

"I have a job to do, Mr. Villette. I intend to do it. The rivalry between your quarry and Mr. Whitby's doesn't enter into it. Do I make myself clear?"

Hugh sat down, kept folding and unfolding his hands. They looked odd and out of place; workman's hands showing below the cuffs of a gentleman's shirt and suitcoat. Harper kept looking at them and avoiding his visitor's eyes.

"Listen," Hugh said after some seconds. "I'm sorry. I didn't mean that. I'm just upset."

"I understand, Mr. Villette." Harper poured himself another cup of coffee. "Back at the courthouse you said something about new evidence."

"Not me," Hugh said, "Jackie. He's got something to say."

Jackie looked at his elder brother. They had agreed he wouldn't talk unless Hugh decided it was wise. What Jackie knew could be twisted to help Andrea if the D.A. chose to use it like that. Now Jackie waited. Hugh nodded. The younger man cleared his throat.

"About that rape business," he said. "There was no need. Riley, he was getting whatever he wanted from Andrea years ago. When they was kids."

Harper set down the cup and saucer and stared at Jackie. "Are you saying they were lovers, Mr. Villette? I've talked to dozens of witnesses. No one has said anything like that. How do you know? Can you prove it?"

Jackie ran a finger around the tight collar of his dress shirt and loosened his tie. "I don't know about proving it. I saw them. That's how I know. Used to spy on them in the summer house down behind the Whitby place. Just for laughs, you understand.''

"You're an eyewitness," Harper said. "Is that what you're telling me?"

"Yeah, I guess that's what you call it. An eyewitness."

"Now Mr. Villette, I'm sure you realize you're under oath," Harper said. "I'd like you to tell the court your story just the way you told it to me."

Jackie squirmed once or twice, then looked at the jury. Hugh had told him to do that. "They're the ones that count," Hugh had said. "That jury has to know the truth if Riley's going to get justice. You tell them."

"Well," he began slowly, "It was some time ago, before Riley left for New York and before she, er . . . Mrs. Whitby, ran away. Sixty-eight."

"The year 1868, Mr. Villette?"

"Yeah, the year 1868. I was coming down from Herrick one day. I'd gone up there looking for beaver, but there wasn't none. Anyway, I was coming down, and I heard talk, laughing. I went to see who it was, and it turned out to be Riley and Andrea."

"The deceased and the accused," Harper said to the clerk. "Did they see you, Mr. Villette?"

"Naw." Jackie laughed. "Riley would've killed me. I watched 'em, though. Just so I could tease him about it later."

"And what happened? Between the deceased and Mrs. Whitby that day on the mountain."

"Nothing."

Harper raised his eyebrows.

"Nothing that day, I mean," Jackie amended. "But I followed them home, and before they got to town, they separated. Andrea—I mean Mrs. Whitby—she went ahead. Riley waited until she got home before he went into town."

"I take it you mean they were attempting to keep their meeting secret," Harper said.

"Yeah, sure. Jason Whitby, he'd of killed Riley if he caught him sniffing around Andrea." Warming to his story, Jackie forgot he was supposed to be formal and dignified in the courtroom. "Anyway, after that, I used to spy on 'em all the time. Just for laughs, like I said."

"All the time, Mr. Villette? What does that mean? Every day? Every week?"

"Two, maybe three times a week. They always got together Sunday afternoons on the mountain. In between, whenever they could. Then it got to be fall, and it was turning cold, and they started meeting in the summer house. The old gazebo thing down behind the Whitby place."

"Are you saying, Mr. Villette, that you observed the deceased and the accused every single time they were together?" Harper glanced at Winslow. The defense lawyer smiled at the prosecution's attempt to anticipate his cross-examination.

"Naw, course not. I can't know for sure if I saw them every time, can I? But I saw them plenty of times. Particularly once they started using the summer house. I'd go down there and peek in every chance I got. I was just a kid, you understand, just seventeen. I hadn't never seen nothing like that before."

"Like what, Mr. Villette?" Harper moved to his right so that the jurors would have a good view of the witness. "What did you see in the summer house?"

Jackie looked around him and blushed. There were several women present in the courtroom. The twelve men of the jury were staring at him, and he concentrated on them. "I saw Andrea and Riley doing it. Lots of times."

A ripple passed through the chamber and became a muted roar. The judge gaveled for silence. Andrea Whitby didn't look up. She just stared at her gloved, folded hands. Neither Patrick nor Jason moved.

Harper waited for silence, then said, "The ladies present must excuse me. This is a court of law, and clarity is vital. Mr. Villette, are you saying that you saw the deceased and Mrs. Whitby having sexual congress? Is that precisely what you mean?"

"Yeah." Jackie nodded. "Doing it. Like I said."

This time there was tumult. Half a dozen reporters fought their way out of the chamber and raced for the telegraph office. The smart ones waited. Despite the judge's repeated gaveling for silence, there was still noise and confusion when Jackie Villette was excused from the witness box. Only when Harper said, "I call the defendant, Mrs. Andrea Whitby, please," did silence resume.

Andrea didn't hear him the first time. Winslow had to lean

over and jostle her arm. "You've been called, Mrs. Whitby. You have to take the stand."

"She can't," Patrick whispered furiously. "Can't you see that? Do something. Stall them, for Christ's sake!"

Andrea gave them no opportunity to do anything. As soon as she realized what was expected, she rose and walked alone toward the front of the room. If she heard her husband whisper her name, she didn't acknowledge it.

Watching her approach, Harper saw a stunningly beautiful woman in a dark mauve dress. She wore a small hat of pale straw with feathers dyed to match her gown. Stupid of Winslow, Harper thought, to let her look like that. There would be no sympathy from the men of the jury for a woman who looked so desirable. They'd all know they couldn't have her, and they'd resent it—a natural male reaction. Winslow was a damn fool.

He waited until she was seated. It was her second appearance. She'd taken the stand the first day and given her abbreviated, incomprehensible account of what had happened. "He attacked me, and I killed him in self-defense." That was the only thing she would say. Now Harper looked at her carefully. She had the same blank expression she'd had since the trial began.

"Mrs. Whitby," Harper began, "I remind you that you are still under oath." She nodded. "Then, since you understand that, I've only one question. Do you deny what Mr. Villette has said here this afternoon?"

She shook her head.

"I must have a verbal reply, Mrs. Whitby, for the record. Is Jack Villette's story the truth?"

"Yes," Andrea said quietly. "It is the truth." Then she fainted.

4.

"What happened?" Andrea opened her eyes, recognizing her bedroom and her husband. Where were the courtroom; the jurors; the lawyer looking at her as if she were some new species of vermin?

"You fainted," Patrick said. "The judge granted a three-day recess for you to recover."

"Recover." Andrea spoke the word with a hint of wonder. "Does he think I will? In three days?" She laughed, and the sound filled the blue and gold room with ugly, mirthless echoes.

"Stop it!" Patrick seized her shoulders. "For God's sake, Andrea, we've no time for hysterics. We've got to talk."

She closed her mouth, and the laughter died as quickly as it had been born. He let her go. "It's too late for that," she said.

"No. Past time, I grant you, but not too late."

"I feel funny. My head's spinning."

"Dr. Sills gave you something. Laudanum, I think."

Andrea sat bolt upright in the bed. "Don't let him do that again. Promise me, Patrick! No laudanum. He's kept my mother passive for years on laudanum."

"We're not talking about your mother. We're talking about you. You're changing the subject, Andrea."

"Not changing," she admitted. "Avoiding."

"Well?"

"Well, what?" She sighed and lay down again. "There's nothing to say."

"I don't agree." He stood up, walked away, and stood with his broad back to the bed. "There's a lot to say, Andrea. This may well be the last chance to say it."

"Before they hang me, you mean?"

"No, I don't mean exactly that. They're not going to—" He couldn't say it. "It's not the trial I'm talking about, love." His voice had become a bare whisper. "It's us."

"There hasn't been an us for a long time, Patrick. Probably never."

"Is that the way you want it?"

She didn't answer right away. When she did, some of the icy reserve was gone. "I've forfeited any right to have an opinion about that," she said. "I am sorry, Patrick, as I've already said."

"Listen." He came and sat by the bed, taking both her hands in his. "It's sounds crazy—I know that—but in these last weeks I've seen a lot of things I never saw before. I've understood a lot."

She stared at his big, competent hands, clasped over hers.

"Riley and I," she whispered, "we started years ago. The way Jackie said. When we were children almost."

"Why didn't you tell me before, Andrea?" he asked. "All these years, this sham of a marriage. Why didn't you tell me?"

Her answer wasn't direct. "In the courtroom, when Jackie began telling his sordid little story for the whole world to hear, I know you believed him, Patrick. I glanced at you, and I could see it in your face. So did my father. I kept expecting him to jump up and shout something like 'That's a filthy lie!' He didn't because he knew it was true. So everyone knew. Why does it matter whether I told you before?"

"Because more than anything else, Andrea, I have hated the fact that you didn't consider me worth telling. You've never needed anyone or anything. That was your attitude from the day we were married. Andrea Whitby takes what she wants. She doesn't ask. God knows she doesn't apologize. There was only one thing you wanted from me, one thing you couldn't get for yourself: a child. I knew it that first night."

"So it was the one thing you refused to let me have. That's it, isn't it, Patrick?"

"You're making it simpler than it was. I didn't consciously decide. It hasn't been an act."

"Tell me something." He had to lean forward to hear her small voice. "Is it just with me? When you go to New York, are there other women?"

"Sometimes," he admitted. "Sometimes there have been other women."

"Why didn't you just leave me if you hated me so?"

"I never hated you, love. Never."

"Not even now?"

"Especially not now." Her eyes met his in astonishment. "You need me, Andrea. In five years it's the first time you've ever needed me. It changes everything."

Her lips parted, and she drew her tongue across them. He had a crazy desire to kiss her. Patrick poured a glass of water instead. "Here, the medicine's made you dry."

She took a sip, but her eyes kept gazing into his over the rim of the glass. Finally, she said, "There's a lot more to the story. Do you want to hear it? It's very ugly."

He paused for a moment before answering. "I want you to

tell it to me, Andrea. That's not quite the same thing. It's an important distinction.''

She turned away then. "I don't think I can. I thought maybe I could, but I can't. Go away, Patrick.''

"No!" He grabbed her shoulders again, and shook her. "I won't just go away and be quiet, damn it! You owe me, Andrea Whitby! You dragged me out of Castle Garden and into your life, and now, goddamn it, I want to understand. So talk, lady! Talk, or I swear I'll beat it out of you!''

She spoke not in fear but in fury. "Very well, the whole truth and nothing but the truth! Am I still under oath? You can be judge and jury, Patrick, since that's what you want. Riley Villette was my half brother. My father had an affair with his mother. It lasted for years. Only I didn't know that when I fell in love with Riley. I found out after he'd gone to New York, after I was expecting his child. My mother told me most of it, though I didn't understand right away. She told me my baby would be an abomination.''

Her head fell back on the pillows, and her breast heaved with the effort of breathing. Patrick's anger had disappeared. He wanted to stop forcing her to relive the whole thing, but he knew he must not. "What happened to the child?" he demanded.

"I killed it. Maggie helped me have an abortion.'' She was gagging on tears she tried to stifle. "I wanted to have the baby, to take care of it, but I couldn't. Do you know what people think of a woman who has a child out of wedlock? Do you know, Patrick?" She screamed the words.

"Easy, love," he said softly. "Easy. I know. What about Villette? Did he know about the baby?''

"He came to Desi's one night, and I told him. He swore at me and cursed me, and I hated him as I've never hated anyone in my life. He knew about my father and his mother, and he let me conceive his child. I told him if he came near me again, I'd kill him.''

At last she was crying, her face buried in the pillow and her whole body shaking with sobs. Patrick got up and left her to cry. For long minutes her weeping was the only sound in the room. Looking out the window toward the garden and the roses and the gazebo, he found himself thinking of human frailty and forgiveness.

When she was still, he went back to the bed and gathered

her into his arms. "The day he came here, the Fourth, did you expect him, Andrea? Had you made an appointment with Villette?"

"No. I didn't even know he was in town."

Patrick took a deep breath for the hardest question of all. "Did you mean to kill him?"

She didn't answer for some seconds. "When I did it, yes, I think I did. I hated him for what he'd done, not just to my body, to my soul. But I didn't plan it. As God is my judge, I didn't plan it."

"Right," he said softly. "Then I know how to proceed."

She was about to ask him what he meant when there was a knock on the door. Patrick went and opened it. Andrea tried to restore some order to her face and her clothes.

"Sorry, sir," Nelly whispered. "Now of all times. But I had to tell you."

"Tell me what, Nelly?" Patrick asked patiently.

"It's Miss Millicent, sir. She's gone. Went quiet sometime in the last hour or so. Nurse's day off, so I brung her tea. When I went to get the tray, she was gone." The woman pressed a handkerchief to her eyes. "She's had trouble breathing lately. I guess she just couldn't struggle no more."

The funeral was supposed to be absolutely private. Still, Main Street was full of strangers and reporters who cried out questions and comments when the Whitbys left the cemetery. They ignored them and walked on in silence. The locals stayed behind closed doors.

"Listen," Patrick told his wife after they'd reached the security of the big house, "we've got a week's more recess because of Millicent. There's someone coming. He'll be here day after tomorrow."

"I don't understand." She was dry-eyed but gaunt. "I can't see anyone now, Patrick. Please, not now."

"Not now," he reassured her. "In two days. It's important, Andrea. Trust me."

Jason saw the stranger as he walked to the front door. The August sun shone full on the man's mane of bushy white hair and his spotless white linen suit. Whitby couldn't make himself go to the door. Another reporter, probably, another vulture.

He continued to sit by the window and stare, imprisoned in his anger at the destruction of his world. He heard Patrick's voice in the hall. It was all right. Patrick was taking care of the intruder.

Jason's relief was short-lived. "Come with me," his son-in-law said as he opened the study door. "There's someone we have to see."

"You handle it." Whitby turned away and stared at the spot on the floor where Riley Villette's dead body had lain. They'd tried to make him stop using the study, but he wouldn't. The world could attack him as much as it chose, but no one would drive him from his own study.

"It's important, Jason," Patrick said.

Jason sighed and followed Patrick into the drawing room where Andrea and the stranger waited.

"My father-in-law," Patrick said to the visitor. "Jason, this is Zachary Katz, an attorney from Philadelphia."

Jason narrowed his eyes. "I've heard of you," he said.

"Yes." Katz was smiling. "I expect you have."

"Mr. Katz is the best criminal lawyer in the East," Patrick said. "That's why I telegraphed and asked him to come."

Jason looked from Katz to his daughter. Andrea was sitting very still, her hands folded in the lap of her black gown. She'd refused to wear black in the courtroom despite Harry Winslow's advice, but she was wearing it now for her mother. Jason turned back to Patrick. "Don't you remember what Lliam Murray said?"

"He was wrong. I've talked to Winslow and removed him from the case. Mr. Katz wouldn't come otherwise."

"Professional ethics, gentlemen, you understand." The stranger raised his glass of whiskey. "Who is Lliam Murray, and what did he say?"

"My local attorney and business associate," Jason said. "Born and bred here, like me. Like all of us except Patrick. Lliam warned us what a Vermont judge and jury would make of a fancy big-city lawyer, an outsider." He looked pointedly at the Philadelphian, running his eyes from the white hair down to the highly polished alligator shoes.

Katz seemed unconcerned. "Your friend Mr. Murray sounds like a wise man. That's good advice ordinarily. But"—he paused and examined all three Whitbys—"this is no ordinary case. Now madam, gentlemen, let us get to work. I've some things here to show you." He opened his briefcase and withdrew a sheaf of papers. "I've been doing a bit of homework since I received Mr. Patrick Whitby's wire. I think you'll find it very interesting."

That night, Andrea turned to Patrick as they lay side by side in the Chinese bedroom. How many nights had they been just so? she wondered. Sharing the same bed, not speaking, not touching. Years. And since the day of Jackie's revelations, the day she and Patrick screamed at each other, the day Mama died—how long had that been? Less than a week. It seemed like a lifetime. Everything was ostensibly the same, but everything was different. Both she and Patrick knew it. They were waiting, that's all. Now she lay her hand on his arm and said, "Mr. Katz thinks there's hope, doesn't he?"

"Yes." He rolled over and propped himself on his elbow. "He does think so, Andrea. So do I."

"I feel . . ." She hesitated. "I feel free. No matter what happens."

Patrick touched her cheek—a tentative finger drawn along the exquisite tracery of her delicate bones. "So do I," he said. "Where it matters most. Between us."

"Would you believe me," Andrea whispered, "if I said I love you?"

For an answer he kissed her. He tasted of Irish whiskey, but he wasn't drunk. Andrea could feel something pressing against her thigh. He wanted her, she realized. For the first time in five years her husband wanted her. "Take me, Patrick," she said quietly. "Please take me."

"Listen," he said. "You don't have to, not now. I can wait."

"No. Not unless you want to."

"What do you want, Andrea? What do you really want?"

"I want to be yours, Patrick," she said. "I want to be your wife."

He groaned and rolled over her. There was no preamble, no foreplay. Not this time. There was just the simple truth of his possessing her and her giving herself without restraint and without demands.

Afterward he held her and kissed her hair and her eyes and her cheeks and said, "When all this is over, when we've learned to know each other, it will be better for you. Better for us. The way it should be between a man and a woman."

"I know," she said. Encircled by his arms, she fell into the first dreamless sleep she'd known in a long time.

5.

The day the trial reopened, Katz met them in a private room just next to the judge's chambers. "They've agreed to Mrs. Whitby's change of counsel." He turned to Andrea. "I approve, madam. A good choice of dress."

"It's black for my mother," she whispered. "Not for them." She jerked her head toward the courtroom.

"My dear lady, listen to me. I am fighting to save your life. If you cannot help me, at least don't hinder me."

Andrea dropped her eyes. "Will I have to take the stand?"

"Not in your own defense, no. I think it best. Mr. Harper may call you again in the redirect. He has reserved the right. I've explained all that to your husband."

Patrick nodded. "Don't worry about any of that now, love," he said. "Come, it's time."

Zachary Katz led the way into the courtroom. Andrea walked between her husband and her father. The Whitbys and the attorney took their seats. There was a rustling among the spectators, a palpable effort to examine the famous lawyer from Philadelphia. Patrick ignored it and studied the jury. Twelve good men and true. "A jury of her peers," Katz had reminded him. "That's important, Mr. Whitby."

"I've been studying the makeup of the jury," the lawyer had said. "A few quarry owners, a few manufacturers, some shopkeepers. Only two laborers—that's good. Men of Mrs. Whitby's own class will be to our advantage. Mr. Winslow served you well in the selection of the jury."

They were his only words of praise for Andrea's former counsel.

"This case," Katz had told Patrick, "is not about what happened on the Fourth of July. On that day, your wife stabbed Riley Villette and killed him. To concentrate on it would be disastrous.''

Now Patrick remembered the words and looked at the jurors. We are gambling everything on whether Zachary Katz has correctly evaluated those twelve men, he thought.

''All rise,'' the clerk intoned.

Justice Walter Lakeland entered and took his place. An old man, experienced, hard but fair, he was a neuter in the equation. Everyone agreed Judge Lakeland wouldn't influence the proceedings one way or another. But he might not allow the kind of evidence Katz planned to introduce that day. If he did not, it was over.

''Let the record show,'' the judge said, ''that I have allowed the defendant to change her counsel. Mr. Zachary Katz, a member at the bar in the state of Vermont, is representing Mrs. Andrea Whitby.''

That he was a member at the bar in half the states of the union was one of the less flamboyant truths about him. Katz rose. His white hair gleamed; his perfectly tailored gray suit was spotless.

''Mr. Katz, is the defense ready to present its case?''

''We are, Your Honor. If it please the court, I call Mr. William Williamson of Poultney.''

A murmur of surprise rippled around the room. District Attorney Harper leaned back and tapped the end of a pencil rhythmically on the table. It was the pose he was to maintain throughout the presentation; it gave little away. He'd already called Williamson and established that Riley had stayed with him for two weeks before he went to Whitby Falls. If Harper shared the assembly's surprise at Katz's summoning the man, he didn't show it.

''Mr. Williamson,'' Judge Lakeland said, ''I remind you that you are still under oath. Proceed, counselor.''

''Mr. Williamson, this court has already heard you explain that the deceased was your guest in the two weeks preceding the Fourth of July . . .''

''The third,'' Will interrupted. ''Riley left my place on the third. He went up to Whitby Falls so's he could go to his pa's funeral.''

''Yes,'' Katz said smoothly. ''Thank you for the clarification, sir. One thing isn't clear, however. Would you tell us, Mr. Williamson, what brought Mr. Villette to your home?''

"You mean why'd he come? Because I was the only one he knew in Poultney. I'm from Whitby Falls. We knew each other when we were kids."

"Thank you, Mr. Williamson. I think we all understand that. What I'm getting at is, why was Mr. Villette in Poultney? Why was he in Vermont? We have learned that Mr. Villette was resident in Philadelphia these past six years. So what brought him to your doorstep, Mr. Williamson?"

"He wanted to talk with me about something." Will looked uncomfortable. The jurors looked bored.

"About what?" Katz asked.

There was a brief pause. "About forming an assembly," the witness said finally.

"An assembly? I'm afraid I'm not clear about that, sir. Please, enlighten me. What sort of assembly?"

"Of workers in the slate quarries. All of 'em in the state."

"Ah . . ." Katz rolled the exclamation over his tongue and stepped back. "I think I see. An assembly of slate workers to be members of the Knights of Labor? A trade union? Is that what you mean?"

There was a collective intake of breath, a few angry gasps.

"Yeah," Williamson said miserably. "That's it. But I told him," he added hastily. "I told him it was crazy. I didn't do nothin' except listen to him." He looked around as if demanding vindication.

"I'm sure of that, Mr. Williamson," Katz said soothingly. "You look a sensible sort of man."

Harper climbed slowly to his feet. "Your Honor, I object. I don't see what my learned brother from Philadelphia is getting at with this line of questioning. No one is disputing anything that happened before the day of the murder."

Judge Lakeland looked at Katz.

"Your Honor, with all due respect, Mrs. Whitby claims she was defending her virtue. My learned colleague here has attempted to discredit that claim, to insist that a past relationship between the defendant and the deceased makes it unlikely. I aim to prove that things had happened since the people in question were young and foolish. Sinister, subversive things. In the mind of Riley Villette. Now, it seems to me that in Rutland as well as in Philadelphia"—he turned to Harper and smiled—"this is admissible evidence in a murder trial. With Your Honor's permission, of course," he added.

"Objection overruled," Lakeland said. "Proceed, Mr. Katz."

After that it was a tour de force. A few times Patrick even wanted to laugh out loud. Katz paraded a series of meaningless witnesses across the stand, a few quarry workers, a professor from the University of Vermont, two men who owned nearby factories. The exercise had only one purpose, to give the lawyer an opportunity to tell the jury exactly what tenets were espoused by the Noble and Holy Order of the Knights of Labor.

He had with him a number of their supposedly secret documents, and he read from them in ringing, stentorian accents. "They admit to seeking to organize every department of productive industry . . . to establish by law industrial safety measures . . . to make further laws directing how much a man must pay his employees . . . to limit the workday to eight hours . . . to make it mandatory that women be paid the same wages as men . . ."

The indictments piled up. The air was thick with them and with the horror Katz was producing in his listeners. Finally, he came in for the kill. The university professor was on the stand.

"Now, sir," Katz said. "Do you tell us that these so-called Knights actually maintain a *strike fund*? That they put money aside to *pay* their members for illegally disrupting the peace of their employer's business?"

"Yes." The professor nodded.

"Thank you, sir. Your witness, Mr. Harper."

The district attorney shook his head. "No questions." He had not cross-examined one of the men whom Katz had brought forward. There was little point in it, and Harper knew it.

"Your Honor," Katz said, turning to the judge, "it seems to me apparent what happened in this case. A young woman made an admitted and tragic mistake in her youth. Later, her partner in that error returned and attacked her. In the intervening years the defendant had grown wiser, chastened, remorseful. She is, as you see her, a beloved daughter and wife, an admired and respected lady. Riley Villette, on the other hand—"

"Mr. Katz, you will have an opportunity to summarize," Lakeland interrupted. "Does that conclude your case?"

"It does, Your Honor. I thank the court." Katz sat down.

"Does the prosecution have any redirect?" Lakeland asked.

Beneath the cover of the table Patrick grabbed Andrea's hand. He could feel how cold it was despite the August heat and the silk glove.

Harper looked over at her, as if he hadn't quite made up his mind, even then. "Nothing more," he said finally.

Andrea exhaled softly. Patrick kept hold of her hand. From the rear he heard someone say, "Jesus Christ!" He was sure it was Hugh Villette's voice.

"Recess for lunch," Lakeland gaveled. "Summaries at two P.M., gentlemen."

Both men were brief. "You have heard my learned colleague," Harper said. "The gentleman from Philadelphia" —even now he wouldn't relinquish that weapon—"has tried to confuse the issue with a lot of rubbish about what the victim did for a living. Even what he believed. It has no bearing on this case.

"On the Fourth of July Andrea Whitby stabbed to death Riley Villette. She then stepped onto her front porch and announced the fact. Dozens of people heard her. The lady claims that the victim attacked her, that she was protecting her virtue. But you have heard how Andrea Whitby conducted a sordid, I may say a lurid, clandestine affair with the deceased. She has admitted that as well. Now we are asked to believe that she had an attack of conscience and that she killed to protect her honor. What honor, gentlemen? I leave you with that question. I trust you will demonstrate that in this state justice does not depend on unrelated trivia. I ask for a verdict of second-degree murder."

Katz rose. "No bearing on the case, gentlemen of the jury. That's what my distinguished colleague would have you believe. We have learned that Riley Villette was a leader of an organization seeking to undermine the very fabric of our society. To destroy those rights and freedoms which our forefathers fought so valiantly to secure. A secret society; I may say a diabolical society! With special rites and rituals and oaths. And with the avowed purpose of pitting working men against their betters, of inciting the laborer to strike, gentlemen. To strike!"

He moved up and down in front of the jury, an avenging angel with white hair.

"Now, is it any surprise that such evil caught up with the perpetrator? That on the one hundredth anniversary of the day when freedom was born in these United States, the poisoned, twisted mind of Riley Villette collided with the purified, strengthened resolve of the woman whom he had seduced when she was an innocent child?

"I remind you, gentlemen, that the prosecution has not attempted to convince us that the relationship between the accused and the deceased had continued. Nor do they offer any motive for this thing they dare to call murder. No, because Mr. Harper knows as well as all of us that when Villette appeared at the Whitby home, he was an uninvited intruder. That Mrs. Whitby was shocked and terrified. We all know what happened. Mrs. Whitby was alone in an empty house. Everyone who might have helped her was outside celebrating the holiday. Riley Villette attacked her, and she, recognizing the demented animal which he'd become, defended herself the only way she could. I know you will bring in a verdict of not guilty. Justice, in the great tradition of this free and sovereign state, will allow nothing less."

"Why are they taking so long?" Jason demanded. "Damn it, what the hell's the matter with them?"

"Patience, sir," Katz said easily. "Six hours isn't a long time in a case like this. They must be unanimous. You know that."

At last, the door opened, and a clerk stuck his head into the room. "They're coming in."

Andrea stood up. Patrick pulled her arm through his. "Chin up, love," he said. "We're in this together."

The courtroom was silent. Andrea looked at the sea of faces. They seemed surreal, distorted, not like human faces at all. She hadn't seen them before. Always she'd kept her eyes down, looked neither right nor left. This time she was holding her chin up, the way Patrick wanted. Her eyes met Hugh Villette's, and she gave a little gasp, faltered for a moment, then continued. Beside him sat Jackie; neither Eve nor Lise was present. When she turned to take her seat, Andrea could feel the eyes of the two Villette men boring into the back of her head.

"All rise."

Judge Lakeland took his place. The jury filed in.

"Gentlemen of the jury," Lakeland said, "have you reached a verdict?"

"We have, Your Honor." The foreman was the man who owned the carriage manufactory in Rutland, the man who had made the victoria for Andrea when she and Patrick first came home. He leaned forward and handed a slip of paper to the clerk.

The judge took the written verdict, but he didn't look at it. "Is your decision unanimous, and are you of like mind in the matter of the state of Vermont versus Andrea Whitby?" he asked.

"We are, Your Honor."

"Gentlemen of the jury, how say you?"

"We find the defendant not guilty of the charge of murder in the second degree."

There was an uproar. Lakeland gaveled for silence. "Does the jury find Mrs. Whitby guilty of any lesser crime?"

"No, Your Honor. We believe she acted in self-defense, and we find the lady innocent."

"The court thanks you. Case dismissed."

6.

She never went out of the house, even to take a walk or to ride into Rutland. A few people came to visit—the Murrays, the Sills—but Andrea refused to see them.

"You can't hide up here forever," Patrick told her. "This bedroom is a small place, love. It's not supposed to become a prison. You were acquitted, remember."

"I know. I just can't face it."

He sat beside her and took her hand. She smiled at him. "That doesn't sound like the Andrea I married," he said. "The girl I knew wasn't afraid of anything or anybody in the whole world."

"Sometimes she was," Andrea said. "She just never showed it. Anyway, she's dead and good riddance to her. There's a new Andrea now. Mrs. Patrick—'' Suddenly, she stopped. "Should I say Kelly?'' she asked him. "We can have it changed back if you want to.''

He laid his hand on her cheek, and she placed her own over it. "Thank you,'' he said. "That's sweet. But it doesn't matter anymore. Leave it as it is. We've had enough of courts and judges.''

"You're sure?'' she insisted. "There's a reason. It's important.''

"I'm sure.'' He'd thought of it, too, but decided it was silly and unnecessary. "What reason?'' he asked now. "Why is it important?''

"Because I'm going to have a baby. You're to have an heir.''

He was silent for some seconds; then he leaned down and kissed her. "It's our heir,'' he said. "The fruit of our love.'' He blushed. "Does that sound silly?''

"Not to me.''

"Good. I don't have roots, not the way you think of them, love. Kelly doesn't mean anything. Let the baby be a Whitby. It will please Jason.''

Andrea frowned. "I don't care whether or not he's pleased. But I can't hate him. A lot of everything is his fault, but not all of it. He's apart from it somehow, outside the rules—at least in his own mind.''

"Amoral,'' Patrick supplied. "Yes, that's Jason. But why are we talking about him? When's the big day, love?''

"In May. Toward the end, I think.''

"And are you just going to stay closed up in this room until then?'' he asked.

"It's what expectant mothers do in Vermont,'' she said, smiling. "I've a perfect excuse—my delicate condition. Besides, I'm not brooding, Patrick. You mustn't think that. I'm just not up to facing the sly whispers and the stares.''

He sighed. "I'd like to suggest we go away, but frankly I don't see how we can. The only money we have is the allowance Jason pays us. It won't support a household independent from this one.''

"Do you hate that, Patrick, being dependent on my father?''

"Maybe it will shock you, but no, I don't hate it. It's a nuisance at the moment, that's all. The way I see it, Jason is supporting my work until it's finished and pays for itself. He's doing humanity a favor."

"What are you working on?" she asked. "You've never told me."

"A light. A totally new kind of lamp for people to use in their homes. I don't like to talk about it."

"Very well. But when you've made it work, you must promise to show me before you show another soul."

"I promise."

Their daughter was born in early April 1877. At least six weeks premature by Andrea's reckoning. Unless . . . She pushed the thought away. It was Patrick's child. It had to be.

Patrick seemed to have no doubts. "She looks just like you," he told Jason gleefully. "Look at that mop of black hair." Patrick didn't mind that the baby looked nothing like himself. He thought everything about the infant remarkable and marvelous. So did Jason. Riley Villette had black hair, too, but Andrea didn't remind them of that.

"So," Jason said, "a grandchild at last. Thank you, my dear."

"Maybe a grandson next time," Andrea said.

"It doesn't matter." Jason was finished with that old struggle. "She's a Whitby heir. What are you going to call her?"

"We haven't decided," Andrea said.

Later, Patrick suggested Millicent, but Andrea rejected that. "She was such an unhappy person," she explained. "I don't want to wish that on the baby. What I'd really like," she added, "is Patricia. For you."

He swallowed hard, understanding her need to affirm his fatherhood, but didn't say so. "If we have a boy next, you'll have used up the name. We can't have a houseful of Patricia and Patricks."

He was laughing, but Andrea was in dead earnest. "We can call him something else. Please, Patrick."

"Very well. Patricia Whitby, then. Patsy, I guess."

"Yes, Patsy."

She still wouldn't go out. She took Patsy into the garden and sat with her there, but first she arranged with Jason to have a high fence built.

"You shouldn't give in to her about this," Patrick remonstrated with his father-in-law. "She can't just go on hiding."

"Leave her alone," Jason said. "She's been through enough."

At that moment Patrick almost asked if he'd stake them to a house in New York so they could move away from Whitby Falls, but he didn't. Jason faced the town every day. He went to the quarry and managed his affairs as if nothing had happened. Still, he wasn't God anymore, and he knew it. Jason wasn't just old; he was frail. The only time he really looked alive was when he sat with Andrea and the baby. Patrick couldn't suggest leaving.

Then, at the end of the summer, Jason released them from bondage. He died.

"Been an accident at number-three pit!" the man who brought the news yelled. "Cable snapped on the stick. Mr. Whitby's hurt bad."

It was bizarre that the first fatality they'd ever had at the quarry should claim Jason, not a workman, and that it occurred as a result of Hugh Villette's invention. "Been broken arms and legs before," Lliam Murray said. "One fellow even lost an eye. But killed outright . . . Nothing like that's happened in twenty-seven years, since we started. Damned stick. I never liked the thing. Told Jason that."

"It made him a lot of money," Patrick said. "It was a brilliant innovation. Jason was the first to admit it. The only thing that went wrong was that somebody got careless."

The cable that took Jason Whitby's life had been one of several guy wires holding the stick. When it gave way, the stick didn't even move. But the heavy wire rope snapped with a vicious force, hitting Whitby in the head. He never recovered consciousness.

"Had their share this past year, the Whitbys have," folks said.

"Some kind of justice," Hugh Villette was heard to comment. "Not a lot, but some. Leastways it was my stick that got the bastard."

"Villette's slate has been giving a lot of competition," Lliam told Andrea after the funeral. "Now it all belongs to you; you've got to know that. But we manage. We do all right. You can rely on an income of four thousand a year minimum, five or six if you're lucky.''

"That's enough," she told him. "But someone has to look after things. The quarry won't run by itself. Can you do it, Lliam?''

"Me? Well, yes—I mean, I could. But I thought Patrick—''

"Patrick's not a slateman; he's an inventor. As a matter of fact, he should be in New York most of the time, conferring with other men in his profession. But this last year, well, we didn't like to leave my father. If we move, Lliam," she continued, "if we only spend part of the year in Vermont, could you manage? I'll want records and books sent to me every month, you understand. And I'd pay you well for your services.''

"Sure," Murray said finally, "why not?"

Patrick and Andrea moved into a new apartment building on Fifth Avenue and Seventieth Street in October, when she was two months pregnant with her second child. From the drawing-room windows Andrea could look across through the "Children's Gate" to Central Park and see the trees turning color. When their son was born in May 1878, the park was filled with tulips.

They named him Edgar, for Andrea's grandfather, Edgar Turner. "It's better to skip over Millicent and Jason," she said. Patrick understood and agreed.

Eddie was beautiful, and on the nursemaid's day off Andrea and Patrick took their two children for walks. As they strolled together along Fifth Avenue, Andrea decided she was really happy. For the first time since she was a little girl, everything was perfect.

She loved her life, and she loved New York. The location of their building wasn't in the least central—people teased them about being up in the boondocks—but the apartment was large. Since they had eleven spacious rooms, Patrick could take two rooms as his laboratory. And the rent was only fifty dollars a month. Downtown, in the fashionable Thirties and Forties, people had to pay half again as much. Yes, Andrea decided, they'd done the right thing.

In 1879, when Patsy was two and Eddie just a year, the *New York Times* reported that a man named Thomas Edison had taken out a patent on an electrically powered incandescent light. Patrick read the story with his breakfast eggs and disappeared for a week. When he returned, he was unshaved and unwashed but sober, for all he reeked of whiskey.

"Do you want to go back to Whitby Falls?" Andrea asked. "Take over the quarry?"

"Hell, no! It's a setback, not the end of the world. I'll think of something else. A fertile brain, that's what your husband has, love, a fertile brain."

Patrick never set foot in his laboratory again, but their lives didn't change much. The Whitbys had their regular income and their children and a growing circle of friends. Andrea and Patrick were a popular couple. And at night, in the bedroom she'd decorated in shades of red, they had each other and the sweet taste of love.

Andrea was grateful for the peace and security of her life. Very rarely did she wonder about the buoyancy, the excitement, that had gone out of Patrick. Sometimes she couldn't help remembering the way he'd looked that first day at Castle Garden, ready to take on the world. That's why she had selected him. It was sad that he'd had to change. But she had changed, too. She didn't hunger anymore; she had what she wanted. Perhaps the only cloud in her sky was Patsy.

Once in a while Andrea would look at the little girl and see Riley Villette. A fleeting expression on the child's face. A look in her eyes. Then she would turn away and try to ignore the terrible guilt. But it didn't happen often.

"You're a pussycat, love," Patrick told her one day. "A silver pussycat. You'll always fall on your feet."

1886 . . .

Chapter Seven

1.

Sometimes it seemed that Lise's hair must grow again, as a symbol of all that was new and wonderful in the shape of her days. It didn't. The closely cropped cap of curls remained, and occasionally Lise would finger them in wonder and speculation. Was it a warning? Perhaps the present was a trick, a mirage to be whisked away by some new catastrophe, and she would again be the powerless and hungry child that lurked behind the current image.

More often Lise reveled instead in the opulent luxury of the big white house. Each footfall on the polished parquet floors and thick carpets was a caress; Lise walked her rooms with a lover's concentration. When the noise of the quarry came through the open windows that spring of 1886, she stood still, listening, and rejoiced. They were opening the tenth pit. Ten! More than any slateman in the entire valley could claim.

"It's endless," Hugh had told her. "I don't think there's an inch of our ground without good hard rock. . . ." "Our ground" now meant twenty-six acres—a vast expanse acquired bit by bit, studied, cherished, paid for with dollars literally hewed out of the earth.

To her husband, the slate itself was everything; to Lise, it meant security. She would no longer allow Hugh to return their total earnings to the quarry. "We mustn't neglect to have a stake," she had told him. "Like the old days."

The memory of the strongbox and how it was filled danced in his eyes. "You're my stake. You and the children and the pits."

"Maybe. But cash is important. You know it is."

It wasn't for him, but he understood her need. "I'll give you ten percent of the profits every year," he'd told her in 1882. "You invest that however you want."

"Can you give it to me every three months, or do I have to wait until the end of the year?"

He had laughed at her eagerness. "Every three months," he'd agreed. "Quarterly, like some of our customers pay."

Hugh kept his word. Oh, Lise knew the accounting wasn't wholly accurate. What constituted profit, after all? Hugh made that determination, and he used an erratic yardstick. What Lise got was ten percent of any money he didn't have earmarked for some other specific. Never mind, she told herself. It's something. I'm building a cushion for us, for the children. She would finger her curls then and grimace with determination.

Perhaps if she'd come to Whitby Falls by a different route, Lise would have recognized that the place for the money was a big bank—in New York. As it was, the idea never occurred to her. Instead, she went to Rutland and bought a strongbox like the one Hugh had in Canada. The original had disappeared years before, but the new one was its twin. Every three months she would take it from its hiding place under the floorboards of her sewing room and add the stack of bills Hugh solemnly handed over.

At the end of three years, she had $5,520. A stake.

On that May morning, Lise turned the key in the padlock and slipped it into the little drawer of her Singer sewing machine. The key nestled unobtrusively among the bobbins wound with colored thread. Then she lowered the box itself into the cavity between the floor joists and replaced the loose board and the carpet. Satisfied, she stood up and smoothed her dress of red bombazine. She caught sight of herself in the mirror: attractive, assured, pretty. Mistress of her world. Lise smiled with satisfaction.

Henry Villette, the firstborn, was two weeks from his sixteenth birthday. Short like his father and slight like his mother, he didn't have far to stoop to watch through keyholes—only a little farther than he had to bend when he was eleven and took up the practice. It didn't occur to Henry to feel guilty about spying. He was heeding his grandmother's advice. "Take care of yourself," Eve often told him. "No one else will."

Henry didn't spend much time with his father's mother; none of the family did. It seemed as much her choice as theirs. Eve sat in a rocking chair in the kitchen with a jug of hard cider at her side. As far as Henry knew, she slept there, too. He remembered his mother trying to change the pattern a few years back when servants first came to work in the white house.

"You'll be in the cook's way," Lise had said. "We'll move your rocker anyplace you like. Just so it's not in the kitchen."

"The cook . . ." Eve's chuckle reached Henry where he stood unseen behind the pantry door. "Imagine, you, a little bastard off the ice, with a cook." She had laughed some more.

Lise merely repeated her request. "Where would you like us to move your chair?"

From where he'd stood, Henry hadn't seen his grandmother's face, but he heard the scorn in her voice. "Stays where it is, my chair. You leave me alone, or I talk to Hugh."

Eve and her rocker remained in the kitchen.

Henry wondered why his mother gave in so easily. That wasn't like her, except where the old woman was involved. What did Eve know? The thought tantalized him. What would she talk to his father about? It seemed to him that Eve must have some hold on Lise. He longed to know what it was, but he never succeeded in finding out no matter how many keyholes he bent over. Still, he'd learned many interesting things, which gave him a feeling of power.

Sometimes, watching her children, Lise felt guilty that they didn't provide her with the sense of security they inspired in Hugh. She knew his reactions to their offspring the way she knew all else about her husband. In the hours when the two of them lay side by side in the dark quiet of the bedroom, Hugh spoke to her of the past and the future, confiding his dreams, as he had in the lumber camp in the north woods.

Together they had made most of those dreams come true. For Hugh the four children were a testament to that achievement. Lise never told her husband of the unease she sometimes felt about their sons and daughters, particularly about Henry.

When she stood at the window of her sewing room, Lise could see the front lawn and the terrace and the side of the house where Hugh had made a play yard for the children. She looked out now and spotted Laura on the swing that hung from a towering old elm. Her youngest daughter was ten,

Jane was twelve, and Hugh Junior was thirteen. She could hear the middle two, together as usual, but she couldn't see them. Then, out of the corner of her eye, she caught sight of Henry moving toward the tree.

Something fluttered unpleasantly in Lise's throat. Henry often made her feel like that. She didn't know why, and she hated her reaction. But it was real. She felt her spine stiffen as the eldest boy acceded to his sister's request for a push. The swing sailed out across the rich green carpet of grass. Laura's blond braids flashed yellow in the sun.

"Not so high, Henry!" the child shouted. "You know I don't like to go so high!"

"Scaredy cat," he called in response. "Laura's a scaredy cat!" He pushed harder, and the swing soared into the leafy branches of the elm.

Lise pressed her hands to her mouth. Don't say anything, she told herself. Don't interfere. It's natural for brothers to tease sisters. Laura has to learn not to be afraid of her shadow. Hugh Junior came into view. He was watching the tableau. So was Jane. They looked uneasy, but neither of them said or did anything.

Lise stepped closer to the window, opened her mouth to shout a command, then closed it again.

"Please stop," Laura wailed. Her voice rose and fell with the movement of the swing. "Please, Henry."

"What'll you give me if I do?"

"A penny. I promise. . . ."

"Not enough." Henry put all his strength into the next thrust. For a breathless moment it seemed the swing might turn full somersault. Laura's hands clung to the creaking rope, her terror visible even from the sewing-room window.

"A nickel!" She wailed desperately. "My allowance for next week."

"Three weeks," Henry said. "Your allowance for the next three weeks."

"Yes! Oh, yes! Just stop. . . ."

Henry was laughing as he grabbed hold of the swing and halted its wild flight. "You shouldn't ask for a push if you can't take it," he said. Lise saw him deliberately jerk the seat and tip the sobbing little girl onto the grass.

*　　*　　*

May was benign, but summer followed cool and rainy. Then, in August, the valley was suffocated by heat. Still, humid air descended on them, and the sun blazed. The farmers considered themselves blessed, while the rest of the population wilted in the torrid climate, so unusual in Vermont. Eve chose that unlikely moment to come down with a cold. "You better come, ma'am," the cook told Lise one morning. "The old lady's bad."

Lise found her mother-in-law coughing and sneezing. Her breathing sounded terrible. "Come along," she said firmly. "You have to go to bed."

"Don't tell me what to do," Eve said. "I need only a mustard plaster." Her words were interrupted by the hacking cough.

"You'll have it, but first you're going to bed." She lifted the jug of applejack from its place beside Eve's chair and started from the room.

"Hey! Where you go with my cider?"

"I'm taking it to your room. If you want it, you'll have to come, too."

Cursing, Eve stumbled to her feet and followed the younger woman.

Three days later, she was worse. "We've sent for the doctor," Hugh told his mother.

"Not that young smartass. He don't come near me."

"Not Doc Williams," Hugh explained. He'd had sense enough not to summon the man who'd taken over Josiah Sills's practice in 1883. "We sent for old Dr. Sills. I said it was for you. He'll come."

Eve made no further protest about having a doctor—a sign of how ill she was. Another sign was the level of cider remaining in her jug. She hadn't had a drink for over twenty-four hours.

In the cellar of the white house was the small still Jacques had built when the Villettes left the cabin and moved up the hill. It had been part of the truce between father and son, the acknowledgment that Hugh ruled but Jacques and Eve wouldn't be asked to change.

After Jacques's death, Hugh had taken over the distilling, turning out a jug or two a week. Ostensibly, it was for Eve, but he and Jackie secretly still preferred Vermont hard cider to any of the more fashionable liquor they could now afford.

Hugh wondered if he should send for Jackie. Was Eve sick

enough for that? Jackie was in Brattleboro. A few years past he'd bought into a small hotel there. The place never showed much profit, but it didn't lose money, and it kept his kid brother occupied. Hugh quietly made up any financial need.

He went to the cellar and stood for some minutes by the still. In some ways, the still was the most important thing in the house, at least to him. It was a reminder of all he'd been before. The sound of horses coming up the drive ended his reverie. Hugh sighed and went upstairs.

It wasn't Dr. Sills; it was a man come to begin the installation of electric lights in the white house. "Where do you want me to start?" he asked.

Hugh almost said, "In the kitchen." That's what he and Lise had agreed on. Instead, he said, "In the cellar. Come with me. I'll show you."

When he came upstairs again, Dr. Sills had arrived. "He's with her now," Lise said. "Who's in the cellar?"

"The man from the electric light company."

Lise looked at him oddly, but she didn't comment. A moment later, Josiah Sills joined them. "She's bad," he said simply. "Cold's gone to her lungs. Pneumonia now."

"Pneumonia?" Hugh said. "In this weather?" He wiped his brow with a handkerchief already drenched in sweat.

"Yes," Dr. Sills said. "Not surprising when you think of it. Eve always did do everything her own way."

Hugh nodded. Lise ushered them into the dining room and poured glasses of lemonade. "Sorry," she said, "no ice. The store in the icehouse is almost all gone."

"How did that happen?" Hugh demanded. He'd built that icehouse himself and saw to its stocking every winter. There was no reason for two weeks of heat to curtail their supply.

"Henry," Lise said. "He left the door open last Sunday. I didn't find out until Tuesday; by then it was too late."

Hugh looked embarrassed, a little annoyed with her for choosing this moment to mention the boy's lapse. "He must have forgotten," he muttered. "I was always forgetting things when I was his age. . . ."

The doctor drank his lemonade without comment. "There's not much I can do for Eve," he said when the glass was empty. "You know that."

They did. That's why they hadn't pressed him after he'd

delivered his diagnosis. "Anything to make it easier," Hugh asked, "so she won't suffer?"

Sills opened his bag and withdrew a small brown bottle. "Laudanum, ten drops in a bit of water whenever she's bad. It won't cure anything, but it will help her sleep."

Lise took the offering. "Thank you."

"Ten drops," the doctor repeated. "No more. It's dangerous."

Lise thought often of those words in the next week. The heat didn't break. Neither did Eve's fever. Despite that, the old woman was conscious and increasingly difficult. Her demands on Lise were endless. When she took to soiling her bed rather than asking for the bedpan, Lise suspected the lapse was deliberate. Still, Lise said nothing. Only sometimes she looked at the bottle of laudanum and remembered what Dr. Sills had said about the dosage.

Jackie came in response to Hugh's summons. He was strangely subdued, awkward, almost embarrassed. As if death were a shameful thing. Hugh took to spending most of his time at home, going to the quarry as little as possible. With Eve they all pretended not to know what they knew. "You're looking better," Hugh told her one afternoon.

Eve stared at him from eyes that burned with fever. She chuckled. The sound rattled in her throat and set up reverberations in her chest. Lise moved quickly to the bed. The spasm passed. Eve's still-heavy breasts lay over her quickly wasting frame like obscene caricatures of womanhood. Lise adjusted the sheet.

"Patrick Whitby's in town," Hugh said. "He and his two kids are staying at the old house." He never called it the big house anymore. And he seldom mentioned the Whitbys. But he knew his mother remained interested in Jason's kin. Gossip was the only thing that seemed to please her these days.

"She with him?" Eve muttered the words. No name was necessary. They all knew who "she" was.

"No. Just like always. Whitby and the kids, not Andrea."

"She never come back now. . . ."

Lise could barely make out the words. "What did you say, Mother Villette?" she asked, bending nearer the bed.

Eve's voice was suddenly loud and strong. "I say Andrea Whitby never come back. Never face this place where she done the murder."

The two women stared at each other. Lise felt herself go red. It was as if Eve had guessed about her daughter-in-law and the laudanum.

Eve was the first to look away. "What are they like, the Whitby kids? . . ."

"All right, I guess," Hugh said. Discussing the Whitbys made him uncomfortable. "The little boy's handsome. The older one, the girl, is too pudgy to judge."

"Riley's girl . . ." Eve whispered.

"We don't know that," Lise said. "Not for sure. It isn't—"

Hugh held up his hand. Eve's eyes were closed, her chest rose and fell beneath the sheet. "She's sleeping. Anyway, no point in arguing with her now."

"No, I know that."

Lise did argue with her mother-in-law, however. She couldn't help herself. When Hugh wasn't there, the old woman took to taunting her. "Blood tells," she said. "You wait. You'll see. That son of yours, that Henry. Bad blood in that one. You'll see."

"Don't you dare say that!" She turned away, ashamed at herself for the sharpness of her tone. Through all the years Lise had kept peace with the woman for Hugh's sake. Now she was allowing herself to lose her temper when it mattered least of all. It must be the heat. And the stench of the sick room that defied her efforts to keep it clean.

Lise dipped a cloth in the bowl of water she'd brought in five minutes earlier. It had already become unpleasantly warm. The scent of the lemon geranium leaves she'd added was masked by the acrid smell of urine and death. "Here," she said, "let me sponge you down. You'll be more comfortable."

Eve was strangely still. Lise turned back the sheet. It was damp with sweat; she'd have to change it again. Then something made her pause and look hard at Eve's body lying in the bed. The cotton nightgown had crawled up and was bunched around her hips. Sparse pubic hair barely covered the creased and folded flesh of what had once been her womanhood. Like the full and flabby breasts, it seemed a grotesque mockery of the past. Lise looked at the woman's face. Her eyes stared up at the ceiling, but they saw nothing. Lise understood. She pulled up the sheet and went to find her husband.

*   *   *

It nagged at her that Eve's last words had been a condemnation of Henry. All during the funeral Lise thought about it. Bad blood. Eve had meant her own bad blood. Lise understood that. She'd been telling the younger woman that she would lose in the end, warning Lise that she'd passed her ways on to her grandson.

"You mad at me for bringing in that priest?" Hugh asked the day after the burial. He'd insisted on getting a Catholic priest from Rutland to perform the service.

"No, of course not. What makes you think that?"

"Just 'cause you're so quiet."

"It's the weather," Lise said. "And everything. You were right to get the priest. Whatever she was, Eve was no Protestant."

"No." Hugh smiled. "Not much of a Catholic, either. I had to promise to put a new roof on that Irishman's church to get him to come."

Lise laid her hand on his cheek with love. "It was a good thing to do."

"I thought maybe you'd figure I was hurting your standing with the town. Whitby Falls has never had much use for Catholics."

"Nor for Canucks," Lise said with a grin. "That hasn't stopped us up to now. It never will."

"I've got a surprise," Hugh said. "I didn't want to tell you till after the funeral."

"Let me guess," she said. "Another pit."

"No, nothing like that. Better. It's about Henry."

She felt herself stiffen, but Hugh didn't seem to notice.

"I'm sending him to Boston. To Harvard. Our son's going to be a Harvard man. Pretty good for a couple of Canucks, isn't it?"

The pride in his voice brought tears to her eyes. She pressed her face to his chest so he wouldn't see them. "Pretty good," she said. She wanted to say much more, to warn him not to set his sights for Henry too high. She couldn't. Maybe Henry would distinguish himself at Harvard and prove her wrong.

2.

Harvard College was no part of the Cambridge of Maisie
Duggan. It was simply that place by the river where the
swells went and talked to each other in funny voices with big
words. For Maisie, Cambridge was the abattoir at the end of
the block, her parents and six sisters, and the house on Wye
Street where they lived, above the store in which they earned
their keep.

As the eldest, Maisie spent long hours behind the counter
of Duggan's grocery. She knew which customers could be
trusted to have their names and the amounts of their purchases
entered in the big ledger under the till and who must pay
cash. The customers knew that, too, most having long before
learned their place in the hierarchy of Wye Street. Only
occasionally would someone try to change their status. "My
man's got a job," a woman would say. "Working over in
Boston on that new road. I'll just take these things and pop in
and pay you when Friday comes."

"I'm sorry," Maisie would have to say. "We're not accepting any new accounts this month. My father's orders. You can
talk to him this evening if you like."

"No, that's all right," was the inevitable response. "I'll
just pay now and speak to your pa next time I'm in the shop."
A few of the chosen purchases would be silently returned to
the shelves, and a clutch of grubby coins would change
hands.

Maisie hated such exchanges. Left to herself, she would
have given credit rather than see the pained expression on the
faces of the refused supplicants. But on Wye Street, Abe
Duggan's word was law. As a child, Maisie had learned all
she needed to know about his method of enforcing his
commandments, the cold contempt in his eyes when he did
so. It was better to be embarrassed than beaten.

Maisie was glad enough of the Duggan name when it was
her turn to shop elsewhere. She could choose anything she
wanted and pay a month or more later. And when Sunday

morning came around, the Duggans all went together to the Methodist church two blocks away and took their accustomed places in the front pew. In such a circumscribed world, the local grocer was a man of station.

Abe Duggan always insisted that his wife and daughters wear black to worship. They had identical dresses of black bombazine with high, round necks and long, tight sleeves that they donned like uniforms once a week. The rest of the time, Maisie was free to dress as she liked as long as her frocks were what Abe called "seemly." That meant fitted almost up to the chin and down to the wrist, with no excess of frills or lace. The color was unimportant. Maisie made most of her dresses in vivid rainbow hues, and she always included a sash that tied in a big bow in the back.

She had bright blond hair so tightly curled that no matter how strictly she made her bun, wisps and strands always came loose and curled about her round face. Her mouth was round, too, full-lipped and marked by a prominent and perpetual pout that gave her a look of constant surprise.

She was small and plump, and when she tied the sash of her bright dresses, she looked like a series of circles set one atop the other. "Like the Lord cut her out with a biscuit cutter," one of her younger sisters said.

On the day that Henry Villette appeared in Duggan's Grocery, Maisie wore blue calico sprigged all over with pink rosebuds and bound at the waist with a wide pink sash. Had it been earlier, such splendor would have been hidden beneath the long brown apron she wore when serving behind the counter. As it was, the clock had struck six, and she had removed her apron and gone to lock the front door when the young man materialized on the threshold.

"Sorry," she said. "We're just closing."

"I only want some tobacco." He held out his pipe. "You can do that last bit of business, can't you?"

Something in his smile was engaging, and his unfamiliar presence intrigued her. "I guess so," she said. "Come in." She stepped aside, and when he passed, she noticed that his clothes were of a quality that no man in that district could afford.

"What kind of tobacco?"

"King's Choice, please."

"I'm afraid we don't stock that." It was a very expensive brand, unlikely to find many takers in this neighborhood.

"What do you have, then?"

She mentioned three names, and he looked puzzled. "I don't know any of those. Which do you recommend?"

"Well, Prince Rupert is popular." Maisie removed a small tin from the shelf behind her head. "It's twenty-five cents." It was the dearest tobacco in the store.

"I'll have three tins, then, since you say it's so good."

Maisie hadn't sold three tins of tobacco at once in all her years of serving customers. Her eyes widened, and her mouth became a more pronounced O. "That's seventy-five cents, you know," she said, placing the three tins in a neat stack on the counter. "We can't extend credit to any but regular customers."

"I'd hardly expect you to," Henry said, laughing.

He held out his hand with a bill in it, and when she took it, she saw it was ten dollars. "I can't change this, I'm afraid." Her wonder wasn't well hidden. The only time anyone ever gave her ten dollars was to pay a monthly bill of a few cents less. "Have you anything smaller?"

"Sorry. That's the one and only." He held out an elegant leather wallet and fanned it so that she could see it was empty. "Now what do you suggest we do?"

It seemed to Maisie that he was teasing her, and not in a very pleasant way. Perhaps he thought she'd give him the tobacco on credit, after all. Well, he had another think coming. "I'll get my father," she said. She didn't return the ten-dollar bill. "He'll be able to change this."

Maisie tugged on a rope hanging behind the door to the upstairs flat. A bell sounded overhead. "Pa'll be down straight away," she explained.

The strange young man leaned against the pickle barrel with his ankles crossed as if he meant to lounge there forever, his empty pipe clamped casually in his teeth. She was glad when her father came through the door.

"It's long after six, Maisie," Abe said. "Your mother's waiting supper." He was a tall, spare man with a patriarchal beard and eyes sunk deep in his head. The simplest sentence sounded ominous when he spoke it.

"I know, Pa, but this gentleman wants three tins of Prince Rupert tobacco, and he only has a ten-dollar bill."

"Very well," Abe said. He took the money and opened the fat wallet he carried. "Here you are, sir," he said, counting out the change. "Will that be all?"

"At the moment. Thank you."

While the stranger put away his money, Maisie looked about for the tobacco. She'd left it on the counter. It was gone. "Did you—" she began tentatively.

"In here," the young man said, patting his coat pocket.

Maisie felt a surge of relief. She'd feared he was going to try and make off with six tins for his seventy-five cents. It wasn't like her to be so suspicious, but something about this fellow made her uneasy. She crossed to the door and held it open for him. Then Abe's voice halted the stranger's exit.

"Where you from, sir?" he asked suddenly. "Not seen you around here before."

"No," the younger man said. "I'm a student. At Harvard. I took a walk and found myself outside your shop without tobacco. Sorry to cause you so much trouble."

"Not at all. Always glad to oblige." The friendliness of her father's tone astounded Maisie.

"Nice to see a small shop like this again," he said, turning back to the proprietor and his daughter. "I'm from Vermont, a place called Whitby Falls. This reminds me of home. Nothing like it over near the Yard."

"This your first year at Harvard?" Abe asked.

"Yes, sir." The politeness wasn't lost on any of them. A subtle alteration had taken place in the dim grocery store.

"And you're a bit homesick, right?" Abe's geniality flowed around the room like a sudden gush of water. Maisie was brick red with embarrassment at the flagrant, uncustomary fawning. "Tell you what, son," Abe said. "I expect you're hungry. Supper's waiting, like you heard me say. Come on up and have a bite with us."

"That's very kind of you. You're sure your wife won't mind having a guest so unexpectedly?"

"Not a bit. Glad to do our Christian duty, both of us. Come along." He stood aside to let the guest precede him up the stairs.

"Thanks again. I'd be delighted. My name's Henry Villette, by the way."

"I'm Abe Duggan, and this here's Maisie. Five more like

her upstairs,'' Duggan added with a grin that seemed to split his face.

Maisie walked behind the two men, gaping with astonishment.

"How come you invited that strange boy to supper?" Mrs. Duggan demanded later. It wasn't often she questioned her husband, and when she did, it was always in the privacy of their bedroom, with her iron-gray plaits hanging down her back and her voluminous white linen nightdress giving her the look of some enormous messenger from the spirit world. Mrs. Duggan was as fat as her husband was thin. She was a portrait of what her daughters would look like in the future.

"Don't be a fool, Mother," Abe said. "How many young men like him wander into Wye Street? Too good a chance to miss. I know who he is. Near dropped my teeth when he said his name. Villette of Whitby Falls. Biggest slate dealers in the nation, I expect."

His wife folded her arms and looked at him hard. "You're asking for trouble, Abraham Duggan. Gents like this Villette fellow don't make nothing but playthings of girls like ours."

"You're a fool," he repeated. "You think I'd let that happen? He's coming back to call on Maisie Saturday night. Don't worry. I know what I'm about."

That evening, Henry sat up late in his room. He perched himself by the window and looked down on the Yard, its trees bare and etched black against the October moon. In the distance he could see the Charles, also washed in moonlight. Henry held his pipe, but he didn't smoke it. He didn't really like the taste of tobacco; he only affected the habit to make himself look like the other Harvard men. It was a poor effort. So were the clothes he'd acquired at Brooks Brothers in Boston. Nothing could give him the assurance of his classmates, and no amount of swagger could make him easy with the other students. They shared things he knew nothing about.

Most of them were from Boston and had known each other for years. Their parents shared connections in clubs and banks and businesses; their sisters went to the same balls and cotillions and finishing schools. They could expect election to Hasty Pudding in their sophomore year and to the elite Harvard clubs once they were juniors. They talked glibly about the arcane subjects of the professor's lectures. Plato and Aristotle and the military career of Julius Caesar; abstract values attached to lines invented by some ancient called Euclid; poetry in Latin. It all meant nothing to Henry Villette. In the village school in Whitby Falls, nobody ever mentioned such things.

Just the day before someone in the common room had said, "Carthage must be destroyed," in response to a comment about the iron virtue of a barmaid at a nearby tavern, and everyone but him roared with laughter. Henry understood few of their jokes. The others had recognized that after the first week, and they left him alone. His poor performance in class didn't help.

No one expected Henry Villette to be invited to return to Harvard after the Christmas holiday, least of all himself. He felt sick when he thought about that becoming known in Whitby Falls. No wonder he'd enjoyed the attention paid him that night in the Duggan flat above the grocery store on Wye Street and impulsively asked if he could call on Miss Maisie Duggan.

Was her virtue also clad in iron? Henry wondered. "Carthage must be destroyed," he whispered aloud. Whatever the hell that meant. The other men never bothered to explain themselves. And they all implied that they knew everything about women, virtuous and otherwise. Henry was a virgin still—the only one at Harvard, he thought. Maybe Maisie Duggan could relieve him of that burden.

Henry tried to keep the impatience from his voice. "Aw, c'mon, Maisie. It's natural. All the girls let their boyfriends do it." He fumbled clumsily with the buttons at her neck.

Maisie pushed his hands away. "Not nice girls," she said. "I don't know about those fast women you Harvard men run with."

"Of course you're a nice girl. Don't you think I know that? That's why I care for you."

Maisie knew the argument was flawed, but she didn't know how to refute it. In truth, she understood little of this peculiar relationship. She hadn't a clue as to the reason for Henry Villette's courtship. But he'd been pursuing her relentlessly for six weeks, calling at the flat over the grocery store in Wye Street, finally prevailing on her father to allow afternoon walks without a chaperone, and then that day, taking her to Boston to see the big stores and ice skate on the pond in the Public Garden.

Their skates were slung in a corner, laces and runners tangled. They were sitting in a deserted boathouse where Henry had taken her to warm up. It wasn't very warm, however. And it was dark. "I'm cold," Maisie said.

"You wouldn't be if you'd just let me cuddle you a little," Henry wheedled. He reached for her again.

"Now, don't you start that all over! You're just making me mad, Henry Villette. Is that what you want?"

He sighed and struggled to his feet. "I want us to have a good time," he muttered. "But you're too stubborn." He gathered up their skates. "C'mon, let's get out of here."

The banks of the Charles were crowded with people enjoying the fine brisk Saturday. Half a dozen boys and girls were indulging in a mad snowball fight. Maisie looked at them wistfully. She was there, and she might as well enjoy it, pretend she was as carefree and privileged as the people around her. "Can't we go someplace for a hot drink?" she asked.

Henry started to refuse. What was the point in throwing good money after bad? Maisie's virtue was apparently as iron-clad as he'd first suspected. Then something made him change his mind—the wide-eyed way she looked at him, maybe, with all her emotions plain on her moon face. "Sure," he said magnanimously. "Why not?"

Impulsively, he took her to the grand marble-fronted Commonwealth Hotel on Washington Street. "In here?" Maisie asked incredulously.

"Right," Henry said with more self-assurance than he felt. "Most of us Harvard men come here." He'd never been in the place before, only heard it mentioned, but he marched straight to the front desk. "We'd like to have tea, please. Can you look after these?" He handed the skates across the mahogany counter.

"Of course, sir," the clerk said after one glance at the young man's expensive clothes.

Henry led Maisie through the lounge to a banquette covered in red plush and sat close beside her so that their thighs pressed together. He expected her to pull away, but she didn't. Henry felt some of his confidence returning. A waiter appeared instantly. "Tea for two," Henry said. His voice sounded deep and mature in his own ears.

"Could I have hot chocolate, please?" Maisie whispered. She loved sweet things.

"Chocolate for the lady," Henry amended. "And a plate of cakes."

When the food came, Maisie devoured it without pausing to speak. Henry sipped his tea and began rubbing his leg against hers. She didn't respond, but neither did she move. He watched her speculatively, fastening his eyes on her full breasts where they strained against the confinement of her bright green dress.

Later, he realized he'd learned an important lesson. Luxury aroused Maisie. He'd been going about his campaign the wrong way. It wasn't just the fact of their bodies touching, of the opportunity presented by dark, deserted boathouses; it was exposure to fancy things, to baubles. He'd been an idiot not to figure that out before. Carthage would indeed be destroyed. He chuckled aloud at the thought.

3.

The bracelet was only paste and enamel. Still, it delighted Maisie. Her mouth and her eyes were three enormous circles in the moon of her face. "Oh, it's lovely," she whispered, holding the thing up to the light coming through the grocery-store window. "But I can't take it," she broke off sadly. "A lady doesn't accept gifts from a gentleman unless—"

"Unless what?" Henry asked. He was grinning and leaning against the counter with what he hoped was casual grace. "When is it all right for a lady to accept gifts from a gentleman?"

"When they're engaged," Maisie said with quiet desperation. "So I can't take this. Here, Henry, put it away." She held out her hand, with the bracelet hanging loosely from her short, pudgy fingers.

"No," he said. "I won't." He closed his hand around hers and locked the gift into her palm. "Oh, it's not a real engagement gift. I can't say that. I've got three years left at Harvard.'' A month, probably no more, but it wasn't necessary to say anything about that. "Let's just call it a preengagement gift. Will you take it, then?''

"Preengagement . . .'' Maisie was confused. She was glad when her father came into the shop. She drew her hand out of Henry's with a guilty start, but she knew Abe had seen. And she was still holding the bracelet.

"Pa, Henry wants me to have this.'' She held out the bauble for Abe to examine. "He wants it to be a preengagement gift.''

"Well, that's fine," Abe said heartily. "That's a right beautiful present, that is. And I'm just delighted about you two young people. Now, why don't you run upstairs and show this pretty thing to your ma and your sisters? I'll just have a word with young Henry here.''

The word was a series of veiled and incoherent sentences about the future and how Maisie would make a fine wife and how Abe knew there was a good living to be made in slate. Henry tried to keep from laughing aloud. Instead, he bit hard on his pipe, grunted every few seconds, and murmured something about three years and finishing his education. Abe nodded sagely.

"Now," Abe said when Maisie returned, "we understand each other just fine. And you two young people can take the rest of the day off to celebrate." He walked to the door leading to the flat and bellowed, "Ethel! You come down here and take over for your sister so's she can have some time off to celebrate her engagement.''

"Preengagement," Maisie whispered. Her father ignored her.

Before they left the store, Abe said to his daughter, "You're a right lucky girl, Maisie Duggan. Don't you forget it. Don't you do anything to make young Henry here think he's made a mistake." The words were spoken with bantering humor, but Maisie knew they were in earnest.

Henry remembered Saturday's lesson. "We'll go across the river to Boston," he said.

"To that same hotel?" Maisie's voice was eager, as if she already imagined herself moving up in society.

"Sure, if you like.''

Once more they nestled into the plush chairs of the opulent lobby and breathed the rarefied air of the rich and privileged. Maisie was drunk with it.

Henry grew alert as the girl melted into voluptuous sighs and little wondering murmurs. "We'll take a walk, shall we?" he asked when the remnant of her hot chocolate was a dark ring at the bottom of her cup. "It's not too cold."

"Whatever you like . . . dear," she added shyly.

Henry smiled and patted her hand with affection. They wandered out into Washington Street and across the Common to the Public Garden. The sun was westering behind the dome of the capitol.

Dusk brought cold and few people in the park. "Getting a bit chilly, isn't it?" she said. "Shouldn't we start for Cambridge?"

"Guess so," he said. "Come this way. I know a shortcut."

Ten minutes later, it was dark and very cold. Maisie was losing faith in his shortcut, but she didn't want to say so. Also, he was increasing the pace, walking ever more briskly. She had to trot to keep up, and soon she was swallowing mouthfuls of icy air.

"You're getting tired!" Henry said with sudden solicitude, as if he'd only just noticed.

"Perhaps a bit," she admitted.

"Can't have my princess tired," he said at once. "We'll find someplace to rest for a moment."

She glowed with the term. Princess, his princess. That's what she'd be. If only she didn't make a mess of things. "I can go on if you like," she volunteered.

"You'll do no such thing," he said firmly. "I was a cad to allow you to become so exhausted." His tone was both masterly and protective. She quivered with joy.

"I'm so sorry, my dear, I must have taken a wrong turn. Don't know this part of town at all."

"I think the river's over this way."

She turned to her left, but Henry stopped her. He had hold of her arm with one hand, and with the other he was waving wildly. "There's a hansom. Just what we need."

Seconds later, she was ensconced in the back seat of a jogging carriage. The windows were curtained; the driver rode high up in front. They were in a secluded world.

Henry had removed her muff and taken both her hands in

his. Now he was tugging at her gloves. "I'll get you warmed up," he said, rubbing her flesh vigorously with his palms.

"Mmm, that feels lovely." Her fingers were starting to tingle, and she was perspiring, as if the back of the cab were the corner of her mother's kitchen nearest the coal stove. "I don't know why I'm so hot all of a sudden," she said.

"Reaction," Henry pronounced. "Like mountain climbers get. That can be dangerous. Won't do to have you pass out." He undid the buttons of her coat without asking permission.

"How do you know about mountain climbing?" she asked in awe. "Have you ever done such a thing, Henry dear?"

"Just a bit, in Vermont," he said with diffidence. "We're mountain folk up there, you know." He could read her thoughts as if they were spelled out on a blackboard before his eyes. He was as intrigued as she with the notion of himself as hero. The vision was seductive, but he didn't forget his more immediate goal. "You're still flushed," he said, pressing his hand to her forehead. The flesh felt smooth and damp to his touch. "You've got to have more air, Maisie dear." He loosed the buttons of her frock as deftly as he'd opened her coat.

"Henry! You mustn't—"

"Nonsense. It's for medical purposes. Besides, it's all right now. Seeing as how we have an understanding."

She was only slightly reassured, but everything had changed since that afternoon. She'd made a promise of a promise to obey.

Henry was rubbing her hands again. And then her cheeks and her neck. "That's better," he whispered in her ear. "You're feeling better now, aren't you."

"Yes, oh, yes. Ever so much better." It came out as breathless little sighs. So did her hesitant gasp when his fingers fluttered into the deep crevice between her breasts. "Henry, you mustn't—"

"Ssh. Stop telling me I mustn't this and mustn't that." He was mouthing the words against her cheek. "We belong to each other now. It's all right; it's natural."

Henry was leaning against her with more force. She felt herself slipping down on the seat, almost lying across it. He didn't make any effort to pull her back up. Instead, he stretched out next to her. Suddenly, his mouth was fastened tight to her lips.

Maisie's skirts were a veritable ocean of fabric. Henry used his leg to hike up the hem of her dress and petticoats. Finally, he could feel the thick white cotton stockings that encased pudgy, yielding thighs.

He braced himself with one arm. The other he let loose in that field of contact where their legs were pressed together. Maisie jerked her mouth away from his. "Henry, stop!"

"Don't tell me to stop," he said softly. "It's right and natural now, Maisie. You know it is." He hesitated, then added, "Unless I'm mistaken about how things are between us . . . about our understanding." The threat was plain.

Maisie understood. Her whole future was hanging in the balance. She could stop his exploration of her flesh with a syllable and at the same time end the promise of glory symbolized by the bracelet. Or she could give Henry what he wanted. And that would seal it. They'd be committed to each other. Maisie remembered her father's advice. She could feel Henry's impatience, the rapid beating of his heart pressed against her breasts. Still, she couldn't speak.

"Have I misunderstood your feelings, Maisie?" he asked after a few seconds more.

"No," she said quickly. "Oh, no! It's just that I don't know—"

"Ssh, you don't have to know anything. I'm the fellow. I know. Men know about these things." Henry felt triumph course through his veins even as he lowered his head to the velvety softness of her neck and shoulder. He felt a desire to suckle, and he opened his lips and let his tongue play over her skin, sucking up the delicious smooth flesh and holding it in his mouth.

Maisie lay very still beneath him. Then she felt his fingers tugging at her bloomers, and soon the thin cotton protection had disappeared, and he was touching her in that place where she had never even dared to touch herself. It wasn't a caress; it was an exploration. She felt a slight stab of pain and screwed her eyes tightly shut, swallowing a gasp.

Henry wasn't sure exactly where the entrance was. He probed with his fingers again. The cracks and crevices of her were hot and dry and revealed no opening. Until he lowered his hand an inch or two. His thumb slipped inside her, and he moaned with the pleasure of discovery, still keeping his mouth pressed to her shoulder.

Maisie felt another twinge of pain. She conjured up a vision of herself in white satin walking up the aisle of the Wye Street church. She'd have a big bouquet of roses. When the thing that felt so big and hard was suddenly inside her, when the tearing ache came, it was much worse than the other little pains had been, but she didn't cry out. She held tight to her vision of splendor, imagining the line of hansoms waiting outside the church. More than Wye Street had ever seen at one time.

All the while he jerked up and down on top of her, she clung to that picture, elaborating every detail in her mind.

Then it was over. He gasped twice and heaved himself upright. For a few seconds the only sound in the cab was Henry's heavy breathing. "Better fix yourself up," he said at last. "We're just going over the bridge."

Maisie sat up and saw the moon glimmering on the Charles. Ahead of them, Cambridge was a dark smudge on the horizon. She fumbled with her bloomers and her petticoats.

The family was waiting for them. Mrs. Duggan looked as if she'd been worried. It was nearly eight o'clock. Abe beamed at the couple with satisfaction. "Had a good time, did you? And ready for a bit of supper now. Sort of a celebration. Ma cooked a chicken. Seeing as how our Maisie's got herself engaged—"

"Preengaged," Henry and Maisie said at the same time.

"Well, it's all the same, isn't it?" Abe didn't wait for an answer. "C'mon upstairs. Food's waiting."

"I can't stay. Sorry," Henry muttered. "Got a lot of studying to do."

The women looked disappointed, Maisie most of all, but Abe jumped in with a brusque laugh. It sounded unnatural coming from the depths of his prophet's beard. "Guess we just gotta get used to having a Harvard man in the family," he said. "Well, you go on home now, Henry, and we'll have our little party some other time."

"Yeah, sure. Some other time." He turned to leave, then turned back. "See you soon," he said in Maisie's general direction. "Been a nice day. Thanks." Neither of them met the other's eyes.

Talk of study was, of course, absurd. Henry had given up studying his first week at Harvard. But he did have an urgent errand.

He walked with a spring in his step, conscious of a pleasant tingling somewhere below his waist, and a sense of victory in his head. One goal had been achieved, cleverly, with fore-thought and planning. The next was within his grasp. He'd not be sent back to Whitby Falls with his tail between his legs. Not Henry Villette.

The address he sought was four blocks behind the Yard, a rabbit warren of tenements far below Wye Street on the social scale. He had been there once before, the previous month, when the existence of the flat and its occupant was whispered into his ear in return for a five-dollar bill.

A lot of money, five dollars. But not as much as the man Henry knew only as George quoted for his services: thirty-five dollars.

In fact, Henry's expenses had been extraordinary of late. The conquest of Maisie had cost a "Chinese packet." He didn't know the origin of that expression, just that it was used by all the Harvard men. He knew the state of his bank balance, however. Precarious. He'd had to write home to Papa for an advance on next term's allowance. It had arrived, thank Christ. Only it had taken damn long to get there. It was almost too late. The paper on the Socratic method of argumen-tation was due the next day.

Henry recognized the sagging stoop of the house and turned in. He climbed four flights of stairs. There was only one door. The paint was peeling off in long snakelike strips. He knocked. Three fast, two slow, three fast. As he'd been instructed.

"Jesus Christ, it's after ten." The man looked to be around fifty. He was coatless and collarless, beard mangy and unkempt, breath reeking of alcohol. "Well, come in, now you're here. I thought you'd changed your mind."

"No. It took a while to get the money. I told you it might."

He followed his host into a tiny room littered with books and empty bottles. There was a scarred table with a plate of cold and congealed baked beans. They looked as if they'd been there forever. Henry drew himself apart with distaste. The man named George noticed.

"Fastidious, eh?" he said with soft mockery. "A gentleman.

Not exactly a gentleman of honor, though. Wouldn't you say?"

Henry ignored the jibe. "Is it ready?"

"Of course it's bloody ready. It was ready a couple of hours after you first came. Brilliant ideas, exquisite synthesis, original thought, all pouring from my pen like a stream. All yours for thirty-five measly dollars. Kingdoms have been won and lost on the production of such prose, and you can buy it with filthy lucre." His words were thick with irony and drink. He thrust a pile of foolscap sheets at Villette. "Not so fast," he said when Henry reached for them. "Let's see the cash."

Henry took out his wallet and laid thirty-five one-dollar bills on the filthy table. "There's your payment. Let me have the stuff."

Henry took the closely written sheets and peered at them in the light of the single gas jet. "I can hardly read this. You might have taken a little more trouble with the writing."

"That's your problem," George said. His grimy hand hovered over the stack of money. "You want it or not?"

"I want it." Villette folded the manuscript and tucked it carefully into his inside pocket.

"Hope you don't mind seeing yourself out," George muttered. "It's the butler's night off."

Villette returned to his room in the Yard, locked the door carefully, and seated himself at the desk. Then he began laboriously copying into his own hand the dissertation prepared by George.

4.

The top of Herrick Mountain was obscured by clouds that thrust long purple shadows down the snow-covered slope. Fingers, Lise thought, reaching into our life. She didn't know what made the obscure, slightly threatening thought surface. She wasn't usually given to introspection.

She studied the diamond ring Hugh had given her for their

seventeenth wedding anniversary the month before. Its colors were apparent only when she held the stone to the light in a particular way. After a moment, she dropped her hand with a soft sigh. In the next room she could hear Hugh Junior speaking to his sisters.

"I am so going to Brattleboro to live," the boy was saying. "With Uncle Jackie. I'm going to help run his hotel."

"You're only fourteen; you're too young." Laura's voice was still childish. She was the last little one in the family and aware of it.

"Fifteen next month," Hugh Junior said. "That's old enough. Uncle Jackie said so."

Lise opened the door to the small sitting room where the children were gathered. "Don't you want to work with Papa in the quarry?" she asked without apologizing for eavesdropping. "Papa wants you to. You know that, Junior."

"Don't call me that," her son muttered sullenly. He was staring at his boots, so Lise could see only the top of his dark head.

"Sorry," she said quickly. "I forgot. H.J., then. Why don't you want to stay here and work with Papa?" She looked to her daughters for support, but both Jane and Laura refused to meet her eyes.

"He doesn't want me to," H.J. said. Defiance had marked much of his speech since Henry went to Harvard, since he demanded that they stop calling him Junior and substitute H.J. "Papa only cares about Henry."

"He cares about you both," Lise said. "That's what he's worked for so hard all these years."

H.J. didn't reply. Lise understood. Henry was the eldest, the firstborn; Hugh Junior had always felt himself in his brother's shadow. She would talk to Jackie next time he came home. Jackie must stop encouraging H.J.'s rebellious streak. "Get ready for dinner," she said. "Papa will be home soon."

From the day they moved into the white house, Lise had enforced strict rules about "dressing for dinner." It wasn't, of course, the formal elegance she saw pictured in the magazines; that would have been ludicrous in Whitby Falls. Lise had an instinct for how far she could go, how much of her dream of being a "fine lady" could be realized in this time and place. She instituted a ritual of changing into clean shirts and ties before dinner and party frocks for herself and the girls.

Lise liked to look at her family when they assembled at the long mahogany table beneath the crystal chandelier. That chandelier was the last gas lighting remaining in the house. Hugh had electrified every other room. "Not the dining room," she had told him. "Leave the gas in there; it's softer, more elegant." Hugh thought it a nuisance. There was the work of lighting each of the prism-draped jets from a long taper, and inevitably it burned away before the job was done. But he always gave in to Lise's dreams. He understood so well their origin.

Only on rare occasions did Hugh reject one of Lise's social dictums. "Don't want nobody putting food on my plate," he'd insisted years before when his wife suggested having a servant at the table. "In my house I help myself to what I want." Lise had surrendered gracefully. Now Hugh scooped a generous portion of creamed chicken onto a mountain of mashed potatoes. "Any news from Cambridge?" he asked as he reached for a biscuit.

"Nothing today," Lise said.

She herself always went to Phoebe Anderson's General Store to collect the letters. It was Hugh who had lobbied the state government in Montpelier to make deliveries of mail to Whitby Falls. No longer did residents of the town have to trek to Rutland for their post. But the officials had balked at house-to-house delivery. Too expensive, they'd insisted. So Phoebe Anderson's had become a sub–post office. She even sold stamps. It was a change almost as revolutionary as the coming of electric light. Lately, Lise had wished for a return to the old system. If they only got their letters from Rutland once a week, she wouldn't have to tell Hugh every day that his son at Harvard hadn't written.

In fact, they had received only two letters from Henry since he went to Cambridge three months before, both written in the first week of the term, the other a request for an advance on his allowance. Neither said much. "I expect he's figuring that since he'll be home for the holidays soon, there's no point in writing," Lise said now.

"Then he's been figuring that for a long time," Hugh muttered.

*　　*　　*

The following day, the thirteenth of December, there was a letter, a thick creamy envelope, with the Harvard seal on the flap, addressed to *Hugh Villette, Esq.* Not from Henry, surely. Lise felt her heart beat faster, and a film of sweat developed beneath her thick woolen gloves.

"Cold today," Mrs. Anderson said, watching Lise. "Too cold for December. Gonna be a hard winter."

"They're all hard winters," Lise snapped. She tucked the letter into her muff and didn't meet the old woman's eyes. It wasn't Phoebe's fault if what promised to be bad news arrived through her hands. "Have you wood enough?" she asked in an effort to atone. "Don't you do any chopping, Phoebe. Hugh will send you cut logs from the quarry."

"Got plenty of wood," Phoebe said gruffly. She wasn't to be bought off with charity. What she wanted was her curiosity appeased. That was her right as postmistress, she had decided when she took on the job. Lise Villette should have said something about her fancy letter. "Always have had plenty of wood," Phoebe repeated. "Even in Jason's day."

Lise didn't know what Jason Whitby had to do with the conversation. It wasn't unusual, though. The locals always linked up Jason and Hugh, an acknowledgment of where and how the patriarchal mantle had passed on. "Very well," she said with barely concealed exasperation. "But you remember what I said. You're not to do any chopping. Just send word if you need something."

She left the General Store and started up Main Street, past the Murrays and the Sills, past the deserted Whitby place, shuttered and bolted for the winter. Lise glanced at the brick house. The envelope secreted in her muff felt like a heavy weight, and she had a sudden recollection of herself in her russet serge bridal dress passing for the first time between those white pillars. "Not cash, sir," Hugh had said, "land." And that had started it all. Why was she so sure that the news from Harvard was likely to be an ending?

The letter was addressed to Hugh. She had no business opening it. Lise stared at the sealed envelope where it lay on her tea tray. She drew one finger across the surface, pulled her hand away, but left it suspended in midair. Indecision was not usually one of her faults. Swiftly, she rose and locked the sewing-room door, returned, and slit the envelope with her scissors.

Her eyes raced over the page. Then she dropped into her chair, still holding the sheet of paper. ". . . considered best if young Mr. Villette does not return after Christmas . . ." No explanation, no alternatives posed, just the barely disguised command to get out. She had feared it for months without knowing why. Still, the reality was terrible. Lise buried her face in her arms, but she didn't weep. She hadn't wept since she was a small child. She'd learned to fight instead. But how to fight the unassailable institution of Harvard College? How to protect Hugh from men who wielded more power than even Jason Whitby had dreamed of?

Protect Hugh. That's why she had opened the letter. Hugh believed in Henry, believed in his dreams for the boy. Hugh didn't understand about Eve's bad blood, about the mark of Cain she had so gleefully passed on. How could he? Eve was his mother. And Henry was his son. Her son, too, but that was different. She didn't need Henry to be other than he was to feel love and pity for him. He didn't personify her hopes for the future. Hugh did that. Hugh and herself. Theirs was an elected union, not a whim of nature. That was the thing to be protected above all else.

Lise stood up and rolled back the carpet. She lifted the floorboard and retrieved the strongbox; then she unlocked it and put the letter and the envelope inside.

"I don't know why you have to go to Boston just now," Hugh said with a tinge of petulance. "You never needed to go so far to shop before."

"It's just a logical idea," Lise said. "With Henry there I can spend a few days going around the stores, and then the two of us can come home together. Besides, I need a change. I haven't been away from Vermont since we were married."

"You need a change from me," Hugh said, turning his face to the wall. "I'm not much of a husband for a smart little thing like you."

She laughed at the sadness in his voice. "You're an idiot," she said, laying her hand on his bare and brawny shoulder. Hugh always slept in only the bottoms of his long johns. She'd made him some beautiful nightshirts, but he left them in the drawer. "You must realize it's ridiculous to say things like that after all this time."

"I've always known it," he insisted. "Known you were too good for me. I just hoped it wouldn't matter."

"Listen, you oaf!" She rolled him over with the surprising strength of her small, compact body. "I love you. I've always loved you, and I always will. I just want to go to Boston and buy some fancy presents for Christmas. I want to spend some of that money you keep making."

"You're sure?" he asked, reaching for her. "You're telling me the truth?"

"Of course I'm telling you the truth. When have I ever lied to you?" She buried her face in the matted hair of his chest. Just this once, she thought to herself; just this once, my love.

Hugh didn't answer. Instead, he was kissing the back of her neck and pressing her closer to him with his big and capable hands.

"I'm sorry you force me to discuss this unfortunate affair in detail, Mrs. Villette." Professor Cody, white-haired and rosy-cheeked, had an air of permanent benignity, and he was obviously uncomfortable. "The president, the dean, and I—we all hoped to spare you and your husband as much as possible."

"Thank you," Lise said. "But it's Henry I'm concerned about."

"Naturally. Of course I understand your motherly feelings, dear lady. But as it is—" He spread his pudgy fingers in a gesture of hopelessness.

"But are you quite sure, Professor? This 'plagiarism,' I believe you called it. Isn't there a possibility you're mistaken?"

"None whatsoever. The style and content are irrefutably the work of a man well known to us. To be honest with you, madam, he is a former member of the faculty. So you see—"

"How is he allowed to do this? To entice young boys to pass his work off as their own?" Lise looked Cody straight in the eye. It seemed to her that Harvard was as much at fault as Henry.

"One can hardly use the term 'allow.' The poor fellow's not in possession of all his senses any longer. Drink, if I may speak frankly. A pity. A brilliant career thrown away." Professor Cody shook his head sadly.

"And what of my son?" Lise demanded. "What of his 'brilliant career'?"

The man stared down at his desk, refusing to meet her eyes. "If I may say so, madam, young Mr. Villette does not seem to us the stuff of a scholar. We thought so long before this incident. But we were prepared to give him another term, to find himself, as it were. In the light of your husband's generosity to the college, it seemed only fair. But now—"

"Give him another chance, Professor. Please." Lise leaned forward. "Surely Henry's not the first student to give way to temptation."

"I'm sure he's not." Cody sighed. "One might rather wish he'd been less clumsy about it, made an effort to disguise the source of his material. But this flagrant cheating . . . I'm sorry, madam, there's no other word for it. And no place at Harvard for your son."

Lise sank back in acknowledgment of the futility of her plea. "Does he know?"

"Not yet. As I said, we wanted to make it as easy as possible for you and Mr. Villette. The college does appreciate your generosity. We thought to inform the young man the day after tomorrow, just before the end of term."

"That won't be necessary." Lise rose and held herself very straight. She gave an impression of being much taller than she was. "I shall tell him myself. Will you send for him, please?"

"I tried to locate him as soon as I heard you were here," the professor said, coming out from behind his massive desk. "I'm afraid he's not in the Yard at present. I can offer you the guest drawing room if you care to wait."

"No, that won't be necessary. Can you show me Henry's room? I will wait there."

"Listen, Henry, you told me you'd decide today about meeting your folks." Maisie paused at the door to the grocery store. The hansom was already turning the corner and disappearing.

"Yeah, sure."

"What does 'Yeah, sure' mean? Am I gonna meet them, or ain't I?" Her voice was peevish, her round mouth pinched unpleasantly around the words.

"Course you are. Right after Christmas, maybe."

Right after Chritmas. At least that was something to tell

Pa. Enough to stop him nagging her. "All right," she said, attempting a smile. "After Christmas. In January." She opened the door and preceded Henry into the store.

"You coming up?" she asked her fiancé. Lately, the line between preengaged and engaged had faded in Maisie's mind. She had taken to thinking and speaking of Henry as her 'fiancé.'

"Can't," Henry mumbled. "Too much work at the Yard." He loathed the way the senior Duggans looked at him now. Their familiarity and jovial attempts to include him as one of the family made his flesh crawl. Everything about the place made him uneasy. The smell of cheese and pickles and sawdust was overwhelming. He'd stop coming altogether except that there were always those few minutes in the back of the cab as a reward.

Maisie seemed to be thinking of those same moments. She looked at him archly, her pale eyes half closed in an expression of shared secrets. "I love you," she mouthed silently. Then she tittered.

"Me, too," Henry whispered. "See you."

He then escaped with a sense of relief.

Lise was seated on the single chair in his room. It had a hard, straight back, and his mother sat in it as if she never intended to move. Henry stared at her in astonishment. "What are you doing here?"

"I came in response to this." She held out the letter announcing his expulsion from Harvard College.

Henry crossed the small space between them and took it. His knees trembled, and he sank to the bed. Maybe it was from the Duggans. Maybe they'd written to his mother announcing the so-called engagement. After he'd read the first paragraph, he realized what the letter said and who had sent it. "Jesus," he croaked. "Jesus Christ." There was no passion in the oath, only despair. He let the sheet of paper fall to the floor and buried his head in his hands.

Lise waited a moment before asking, "Have you nothing more to say? No explanation?"

"How the hell did they find out?"

Lise crossed to where her son sat and purposefully jerked his head back by the hair. It was dark and curly like her own. She twisted her fingers in it and slowly and deliberately slapped him across the face; over and over again, until her palm stung with the effort. Finally, she let go and stood, arms akimbo, watching him.

He hadn't cried out, but his eyes were filled with tears. They woke no pity in her. "You stupid, ungrateful fool!" she hissed through clenched teeth. "How dare you do this to your father! Everything he's worked for, struggled to give you . . ." Her voice choked, and she was silent. "What's the use?" she said finally. Eve's grandson, a lazy, cheating, useless clod of a man. "Pack your things," she said. "We're getting out of here right now."

"Where's Papa?" Henry asked.

"At home. He doesn't know anything about this. He's not going to."

"What are you going to tell him?"

"I haven't decided yet. That's my concern. From now on, you do and say only what I tell you. Otherwise, you'll never see another penny. Now pack."

They left the Yard half an hour later and took a cab across the river to the train station on Beach Street. Henry moved in stiff, uncomprehending despair. Maisie Duggan never entered his mind.

5.

Lise told Hugh that she'd arrived to find Henry down with a bad grippe and whisked him home. It was not a difficult fiction to sustain, since Henry took to his bed immediately. A week later, he still hadn't risen. "Should we have the doctor?" Hugh asked.

"Not necessary," Lise said brusquely. "It's only a bad cold. He's young. He'll recover soon enough."

Soon enough, indeed. Lise had no illusions about the lasting effects of the shock her son had received. She saw no genuine remorse in Henry, only self-pity. In a few weeks he'd be his old self, not at all improved. And what would she do then? How would she explain the boy's failure to return to Harvard? She didn't have an answer to that, but for the moment she didn't need one. Henry was in hiding, and everyone else in Whitby Falls was busy making ready for Christmas. Especially Hugh.

From his earliest days as boss, Hugh Villette had established his own style. He wasn't Jason Whitby, he said frequently. He had no need to control every aspect of his workers' lives.

There was the matter of housing, for instance. Three new streets had grown up around the Villette pits. The quarry owned the land and built the homes that stood on it, but there was a fixed price for each one. Any man who wanted to could buy his house, and Villette would finance the mortgage. He paid the best wages in the Slate Valley, and there were no company stores on Villette land. Folks who wanted credit made their own arrangement at Anderson's or Howard's or Phillip's. If a man ran into trouble—a long illness or a fire or any other kind of bad luck—he could approach Hugh Villette for a loan. Usually, he got it, at only slightly higher interest than was charged by the bank in Rutland. It was a business arrangement, not serfdom.

In other ways, however, Hugh couldn't avoid a role as local squire. Whitby Falls required such a figure. Hugh was chosen to speak at local functions; he was expected to be present at all christenings, marriages, and funerals; he was unofficial arbiter of village disputes, the ultimate authority on questions too weighty for instant analysis. Villette enjoyed the game. And he enjoyed watching Lise play her part in it. His wife set the standards of taste in Whitby Falls, and an invitation to dine at the white house had become the seal of social acceptance in their small world. What Lise wore was the latest fashion; what she approved was worthy. Wine with meals, for instance, and whiskey for the menfolk rather than cider. What she frowned on was reprehensible; because Lise had never learned to dance, dancing wasn't in fashion at Whitby Falls parties.

During the week before Christmas, the Villettes called personally on every family in town, from the humblest worker to the Sills and the Murrays. They held open house on Christmas Eve and Christmas Day. This Christmas of 1886 was no exception. Lise had little time to brood about her eldest son or worry about what she'd tell his father after the festivities were over.

*   *   *

Maisie waited two weeks before she did anything. Two days after Christmas, certain truths were apparent to her. First there was the extraordinary fact that Henry hadn't appeared in all that time, not even to wish the Duggans the joys of the season.

"Peculiar, I'd say," Mrs. Duggan pronounced with a sniff. "Mighty peculiar, considering."

"Considering what?" one of the younger girls demanded.

"Considering he's supposed to be preengaged to our Maisie."

"He's gone to Vermont, to his family," Maisie said stiffly. "I knew he was goin'. He said so weeks ago. They expected him. And I'm to meet them after he comes back."

"How you going to do that once he's in Cambridge and they're up in Whitby Falls?" asked Ethel.

"I'm going up there," Maisie said, her voice quick and breathless. It was a plan she'd evolved. She didn't know if it coincided with Henry's ideas. "I'm goin' up to Vermont for a weekend. Henry's ma is gonna invite me."

That silenced Ethel and the other sisters, though it had less effect on Mrs. Duggan. "Still seems mighty strange he didn't come to say good-bye before he went. Considering."

Maisie made no comment. Neither did Abe. But she could see the way her father was watching her, the things he was speaking with his eyes. She'd had her great chance, and she'd better not have messed it up. Abe was counting on being able to say, "My son-in-law's in slate. Perhaps you know the company, Villette-Whitby Falls. . . ." Counting, too, on the money Maisie would send him each week from the generous household allowance she'd receive as wife of the Villette scion.

And apart from that, and from recognizing deep down that *it was* very odd that Henry hadn't called before he went home, there was a more dramatic revelation. Only Maisie knew about it thus far, but the others would suspect soon enough. She was going to have a baby. She hadn't had "the curse" since early November. Not since the first time Henry got under her skirts. That's how she always thought about it; he'd "gotten under her skirts." What he'd done there was something she never considered in detail.

It had not hurt after the first couple of times. Maisie reckoned there were seven occasions in all, maybe eight, and early on she'd understood that it was something women endured and men enjoyed. It made her feel part of a secret female fraternity of patient suffering. Just like endless work while the menfolk sat around, just like having cramps and headaches once a month, and just like bearing children. Maisie had no illusions about that. She knew that letting Henry get under her skirts had introduced the possibility of being in a family way.

The idea had not really alarmed her. After all, she and Henry had "an understanding"; he'd said so straight out. And he'd given her the bracelet that was never off her wrist, even when she slept. What if she did start a baby? They'd just have to get married quicker than they planned. Maisie didn't think that a bad idea at all. Abe would like it, too. She knew that's what Pa meant when he'd told her to take advantage of her good luck. But Henry's wordless disappearance had introduced another possibility. Maisie knew what Abe would make of that, what the whole world of Wye Street would make of it.

Two years before there was talk that Jenny Howell had gotten herself in trouble. Jenny had not been heard from since, and the Howells were left strictly alone. Now they couldn't even claim credit at Duggan's Grocery Store. And they'd been good payers, too. Maisie thought hard about the way Amanda Howell skulked around the neighborhood since the business with her daughter.

The Wednesday after Christmas, Maisie determined to make her move. That day her parents took the youngest four children on one of their visits to Mrs. Duggan's maiden aunt in Providence, Rhode Island. They'd be gone for a week on a journey that entailed discomfort and expense. They bore it willingly, because the aunt was reputed to have a fortune buried beneath her mattress. The Duggans were not about to miss their opportunity. Neither, Maisie decided, must she miss hers.

"Do you know which is the Villette house?" Maisie asked the boy driving the trap she'd hired to bring her from the Poultney train station to Whitby Falls.

His name was Jeb, and he had a bad case of acne and filthy nails. Despite the snow and the cold—never in her life had Maisie seen so much snow—the boy wore no gloves. When she looked at his hands, Maisie felt the flesh crawl on the back of her neck. Maybe if she didn't find Henry, if they didn't get married right away, she'd have to give herself to boys like this.

"Sure," Jeb said in answer to her question. "Everyone in these parts knows the Villette place. That's it up on the hill. The big white house."

He gestured with his whip, and she half turned to stare at the edifice. It looked like a castle. Nausea rose in Maisie's throat. How could she knock on that door and ask for Henry?

Jeb drew up beside Phillips's dry goods store. He didn't help her down. Maisie half slid, half jumped to the ground. The snow was packed solid on the road. She wasn't wearing boots. There had been no snow in Cambridge, and it hadn't occurred to her that there would be any in Vermont. She was clumsy with fear and unfamiliarity, struggling to hold her footing on the slippery road. She hadn't walked far before the wet and the cold penetrated her Sunday shoes. And she was conscious of Jeb's little rabbity eyes boring into her back, watching her. After a moment, she heard the trap drive away.

No one paid her any attention, at least not openly. She realized that in such a small town any stranger was noticed, just as on Wye Street, but apparently the custom was to leave them strictly alone. Another time she might have thought that unfriendly. That day she was grateful.

Finally, the front door of the big white mansion loomed at the end of a long, straight driveway. Maisie hesitated. She could go around the back. It wouldn't be so scary knocking on the kitchen door. But it was the wrong thing to do. All her instincts told her so. She took a deep breath and moved forward in her sodden shoes. There was a great brass knocker. She grabbed it and let it fall before she could change her mind. The sound of the summons seemed to echo down the valley.

"Yes?"

"Are you Mrs. Villette?" Maisie tried to stop her voice from quivering. "I'm Maisie Duggan, a friend of Henry's. . . ."

The woman looked scornful. "Course I ain't Mrs. Villette. I'm the maid. You want to see Mrs. Villette?"

"No, oh, no," Maisie said quickly. "It's Henry I want. Henry."

"He's sick. Been sick since before Christmas. Ain't come down from his room."

"Please. It's very important. I came all the way from Cambridge. I'm sure he'll come down if you'll just tell him I'm here. Maisie, like I said. Maisie Duggan."

The maid pursed her lips and stared at the girl. Round little thing she was, like a ball of butter. And shaking with cold. Too bad neither of the senior Villettes was at home. Gone to Rutland for the day, both of 'em. She'd have to decide for herself about this visitor.

The pause lengthened. The girl's eyes filled with tears. "Oh, all right." The older woman stepped aside. "I'll tell him. He ain't sick as all that. You just wait in here."

She didn't consider placing this Maisie Duggan in the big drawing room, not with her wet shoes making puddles wherever she walked. The room in which she left Maisie was a tiny extension of the back hall, the place where tradesmen left deliveries. It had a slate floor to cope with their filthy boots. "Be right back and tell you what he says," the maid said, leaving Maisie alone.

6.

It wasn't the maid who appeared a few minutes later. It was Henry, looking as if he had indeed been ill. His face was white, a stubble of beard glazed his sunken hollow cheeks, and his eyes were glassy with fever or shock. "What the hell are you doing here? You crazy or something!"

Maisie didn't register the indignation in his tone. She was suddenly overwhelmed with joy at the sight of him. "Henry! Oh, Henry!" She threw her arms around his neck and clung on. She'd been sniffling with the cold before; now she was crying in earnest. "I knew everything would be all right once I found you."

"All right?" He struggled unsuccessfully to free himself. "What the hell do you mean, all right? What are you doing here? Why'd you come?" he repeated.

"I had to see you," she muttered into his chest. "You

went away without even saying good-bye. Everybody was asking me why you disappeared and when I was going to meet your parents and everything. They made it sound like you weren't coming back at all. What do they know, anyway? . . ."

Her words were tumbling out in a high-pitched wail.

"Keep your voice down, for Christ's sake," he said, and managed to disengage her arms. "It's none of your business where I went and why. You got no right to go poking your nose in my affairs."

Maisie paled. "I have," she said tremulously. "I have every right, Henry Villette. We're preengaged. We got an understanding. You said so yourself."

"That was okay in Cambridge," he muttered. "It's nothing to do with up here."

"That's not fair!" Maisie made herself lower her voice to match his. "That's not a fair thing to say. Not considering—" She broke off and stared at the floor. There were puddles of water wherever she'd stood.

"Considering what?" Henry demanded. A knot of fear was forming in his stomach, a terrible suspicion of what she might have come there to say. As if he didn't have enough bad luck. "Considering what, Maisie Duggan? You tell me the truth."

"Considering I'm gonna have a baby," she whispered. It was the first time she'd spoken the words aloud.

Henry swallowed hard. There was a lump in his throat, and he could feel his Adam's apple jumping. "You sure?" he asked.

Maisie nodded.

Henry stared at her for a moment. Her pudgy cheeks were streaked with tears; her nose was red and running. Christ, whatever had made him chase after Maisie Duggan, of all people? Suddenly, he had another thought. "Maybe you are pregnant. What's that to do with me? How do I know it's my kid, anyway?"

"Oh!" she gasped. "Oh, Henry! You know; you must. There's never been anyone else. Not before, not since. You know how it was the first time. . . ."

The memory of that groping struggle in the back of the cab filled Henry's mind. It had become a sour recollection that filled his nostrils with a stench. "Yeah," he admitted. "I know how it was. What you want me to do about it, anyway? It's done now.''

''But it doesn't matter. That's what I'm trying to tell you. We'll just get married like we planned, and everything will be all right.''

''I'm not going to—'' He corrected himself just in time. ''I mean I can't marry you, Maisie. Not just now.''

Maisie's lip hardened into a straight, firm line. She'd been half expecting this. He'd been saying two or three years from the beginning. ''We got to get married right away, Henry. We can't wait. Not with a baby coming.''

He ran his fingers through his hair. ''Maisie, I don't know how I can do that. Tell you what.'' He was thinking as quickly as he spoke, remembering snatches of conversations overheard among the sophisticated Harvard men. ''You can have an operation. No one need ever know you was pregnant at all. That's the answer. I can find out the name of the doctor. I know somebody in Boston will tell me. . . .''

''I ain't doin' no such thing,'' she said. Her words were firm, but there was a hint of wavering behind them. ''I ain't gonna murder my baby, Henry Villette. You just forget that.''

''Well, then, you can do what you like,'' he said. ''I don't care. You can't prove it's my kid, anyway.'' If she didn't want to take advantage of his generosity, it was her lookout.

Maisie knew better than Henry about such operations. In Wye Street, they'd been whispered about since she was a child. She knew how much they were said to hurt, how terrible they were. But she knew, too, that after the operation you weren't pregnant anymore. And she'd flirted with the solution for the last few days. All the while she had considered in some secret, unacknowledged corner of her mind that Henry might not agree to marry her right away. ''Even if I was willing,'' she said very low, ''that operation costs a lot. I ain't got no money. I had to take ten dollars from the till to come up here. Pa'll kill me when he finds out.''

''Does he know you're here?'' Henry suddenly thought of Abe Duggan's arriving behind his daughter, demanding to speak with Henry's father.

''No.'' Maisie shook her head. ''Not him and not my ma, either. They're in Providence visitin' my ma's auntie. Only one that knows I'm gone is Ethel. She don't know where.''

That was the first good news he'd heard all morning. Henry didn't say anything, just hung his head in deep thought.

"What are we going to do, Henry?" Maisie ventured timidly after some seconds.

"I'm thinking it out," Henry said. "You sure you haven't got any money? No little savings of your own put by?" She shook her head again. Damn! Just now when he had no funds, either. Lise had shut off the supply. There was one way, though. It was a big risk, but it might work. Maybe it would solve more problems than just Maisie Duggan. "Okay, tell you what. You get out of here now. . . . Where you staying, by the way?"

Poultney, she told him. That was a help. It was a good thing that she wasn't right there in Whitby Falls. "You go back there," he instructed. "Tomorrow I'll come down and meet you at the train station. I'll have the money for the operation then."

"What time tomorrow?" She was sniffling again. The words were muffled.

"Eight in the morning, just before the early train goes. By the far end, away from the ticket window. You know where I mean?"

"Yes."

"Good. C'mon. I'll let you out the back door so you won't see anybody."

Lise went to her son's room soon after she returned. "They tell me you had a caller. Who was she?"

"Just a girl. Someone I knew in Cambridge."

He was sitting in a chair looking down at the garden, buried in snow, at the outline of the quarry with its three towering sticks in the distance. His eyes looked particularly bright, as if he were feverish. Lise stepped closer and lay her hand on his forehead. His skin was cool to her touch, and she withdrew. Sometimes of late she'd thought Henry really was ill, but not that evening.

"You'd best be telling me the truth," she said, returning to the subject of the girl. "If there's any more trouble, tell me about it."

"Don't be silly," he said gruffly. "She's just a girl. There's no trouble." She was getting ready to ask more questions, so he countered with one of his own. "Have you told him yet?" There was no need to say who "he" was.

"No, not yet."

Henry noted the fleeting indecision that crossed his mother's face. "You'll have to, you know," he said. "You can't keep me locked away up here forever." He was taunting her with his failures, as if they were her fault. He enjoyed seeing the pain that caused her. It seemed to him it *was* her fault, in some way at least.

"Don't you start telling me what to do, Henry Villette," she said. "You've made enough trouble to last a lifetime. You just behave yourself. When I'm good and ready, I'll tell your father what's happened."

Later, she filled a huge copper tub with hot soapy water and immersed herself in it by the gas fire in the bedroom. Lise did her best thinking soaking in the bath. Hugh called them her meditations.

"You're meditating," he said with a grin when he came upstairs. "I'll go away and leave you to it. Come back in a quarter of an hour and scrub your back." His smile was a declaration of love and a promise. Lise wanted to cry.

She wouldn't, though. She wouldn't let that wretched boy drive her to tears. She'd figure out some solution; she'd not given her mind to it until now, what with the holidays and everything. Now she'd think about it. She leaned back and began examining one plan after another. The aim of them all was the same, to protect Hugh from the full weight of his son's heresy.

Henry's plan had been born full-grown in those moments in the back hall with Maisie, an answer to his own problems as well as hers. He had, in fact, toyed with the notion previously, during the hours he'd spent brooding in his room. He'd shied from the idea through fear, nothing more. If he was caught, it might be terrible. There was no telling about his mother. She could do the most incredible things; she could be as hard as any man alive. Sometimes even his father couldn't restrain her. That's why the plan he was now prepared to put into operation had waited all these weeks. Until Maisie, he'd not had the guts. Now it looked as if he was damned if he did and damned if he didn't. He knew that eventually Maisie would take it in her head to approach his folks. If she did that, everything was finished, and he'd never be free again.

He slept fitfully for a few hours, then rose at four. He'd taken the precaution of filling his jug with water the night before. Now he washed and shaved in silence, the first time in days he'd done either, and dressed himself in his best Cambridge clothes.

He thought of packing a suitcase but decided against it. He might have to move fast—better if he traveled light. Besides, he didn't know what kind of clothes gentlemen wore in Mexico. Probably he'd need a whole new wardrobe. Tight black trousers and jackets with embroidery up the front. He'd seen a picture of that kind of outfit once. And read a story about a huge *rancho* with an enormous house filled with servants and endless fiestas with beautiful girls in ruffled dresses wearing exotic flowers in their hair. No doubt it would cost a lot of money to buy such a place, not to mention the clothes, but that didn't matter. There was a lot of money in the strongbox.

Henry had learned years before to avoid the one board in the hall that creaked. He reached the door of the sewing room without disturbing the silence of the sleeping house. A tiny night-light burned on the landing of the circular stairs. Everything else was darkness. It was the dead of winter, and the sun wouldn't be up for an hour or more. He put his hand on the doorknob and held his breath. This was the biggest hurdle. What if his mother had locked the sewing room? She never did, but what if she had? The brass knob turned; he waited a second and pushed. The door swung open.

Henry never forgot to notice little details that might mean something to him later. Now he knew exactly which corner of the carpet to roll back, which floorboard to lift. He'd watched the process only once, but it was enough.

It was too dark to see anything, and he didn't dare risk a light. He felt a moment's panic. What if there were spiders under the floor, or beetles? Henry hated bugs. He steeled his resolve and plunged his hand into the opening. Then he drew back with a yelp of pain. He froze and waited. Someone may have heard. Again, he held his breath and strained his ears for any sound. There was nothing. He put his knuckles in his mouth and sucked them, tasting blood. He'd thought that the hole was deeper than it was. His hand had smashed into the heavy padlock of the strongbox. Gingerly, he reached for the thing again. This time he retrieved it without mishap. Carefully, he set the strongbox on the floor beside him and replaced the board and the carpet.

The padlock didn't respond to his tugging. Locked. He'd expected it would be. But he remembered where she'd put the key. The only problem would be if she'd changed the hiding place. Silently, he moved toward the sewing machine, the strongbox clutched tightly under his arm. There were a dozen or more drawers in the cabinet of the Singer. He knew only that he wanted one of those in the upper right-hand corner. The first he tried was locked, and he felt the sour taste of fear coat his tongue. Time was passing. It would be light soon; the cook would be awake; someone would be starting coffee in the kitchen.

Cursing under his breath, he tried another drawer. It opened easily, but his fumblings inside revealed no key. He considered abandoning the search. He could find a way to open the damned thing later, in Boston, maybe. He could buy a file or a hacksaw. But that was the difficulty—until he unlocked the strongbox, he was stone-broke. He had no money to buy even a railway ticket.

The next drawer was full of wooden bobbins wound with thread that tangled in his fingers. He continued pawing through the jumble and finally touched something hard and metallic and flat. With a sigh of satisfaction he took the key and slipped it into his pocket. Henry quietly let himself out of the room and out of the house. The hard-won treasure was snuggled safely beneath his Brooks Brothers greatcoat.

He had to walk to Poultney. It was too risky to take a trap and horse. His whole plan involved their not missing him till much later in the morning. These days he never went down to breakfast and seldom rang for a tray before ten. Sleeping late was meant to be part of his "cure." By the time anyone knew he was gone, he'd be halfway to Boston on the early train. No matter who might discover his absence, Henry knew it was his mother who would mount the search, but until she found out about the money, she very well might attach no significance to his not being in the house.

Henry hoped that's how it would be. After all, he deserved a little good luck. He'd had so many rotten breaks lately. It was as if he were cursed or something. Unbidden, the thought of his grandmother came to his mind. Eve believed in curses. Henry shivered. He didn't want to think about Eve's stories just then.

It hadn't snowed for almost a week. The ground was packed hard and worn smooth where men and horses had plodded the well-traveled route. He didn't have a bad walk at all. He just had to keep going. It got light, but the sun didn't appear. More snow later that day. Good, that would slow down his pursuers.

He stopped only once, when he was well clear of the village. He went behind an enormous old maple and made sure no one was about. Then he took out the strongbox and the key and fumbled the padlock open. He'd worried that maybe it was the wrong key; maybe it opened not the money box but the locked drawer. By the time he'd thought of that, it had been too late to do anything about it. He was jubilant when he discovered his fears were groundless. The padlock sprang open instantly.

What if she took money out sometimes? The thought dropped into his head from nowhere and remained to torment him. What if there wasn't any money in there now? But he'd seen the bills, stacks of them. That was over a year before; maybe they were all gone. He hesitated, lacking the courage to lift the lid. "Oh, Jesus, let me be lucky, just this one time . . ."

He thrust back the cover. Neat piles of currency winked up at him. The stacks, banded together with thread, were divided into equal lots. He picked one up and ruffled through it. There were no bills of less than a hundred dollars. Henry couldn't contain himself. He whooped aloud. A fortune! Jesus Christ! It was a bloody fortune! He was on his way to Mexico. Ahead was a life of guitars and bullfights and wine and women . . . He removed a hundred-dollar note, locked the strongbox once more, and put the money and the key in his pocket. Then he resumed walking.

Maisie was waiting for him just where he'd told her to be. She looked rounder than ever. Her eyes were puffed and swollen, her nose red. She kept raising a damp handkerchief to her face and sniffling into it. "You okay?" Henry asked.

"I'm fine." Her voice caught on the words, a half-formed sob gurgled in her throat. "Henry dear, look, I've been thinking. Maybe we can—"

"Later," he said gruffly. "We haven't time to talk now. Train will be in any second." He was flushed and panting with the exertion of his ten-mile hike. He kept his arms pressed to his body, and Maisie could see he was carrying something, but she couldn't see what. "How much money you got?" Henry demanded.

"Only a bit." She was learning to fear his temper. This wasn't the charming, cajoling Henry she had known in Cambridge.

"How much exactly?" he asked in frustration. "Let me see."

She opened her small purse and withdrew some crumpled bills. "Six dollars and thirty cents."

"It's enough," he interrupted. "Thank God for small favors." He snatched the money from her hand, and she looked startled.

"Henry! It's all I've got left!"

She was going to start bawling again. He couldn't allow that. It was the wrong time to attract attention. "Look." He plunged one hand in his pocket and kept the other locked around the strongbox under his coat. "This is all I have. It's a hundred dollars. I can't give the ticket seller a hundred dollars to change, Maisie. You understand that?"

She nodded, staring round-eyed at the note.

"Here," Henry said with all the charm he could muster. "You keep it. It'll pay back the ten dollars you borrowed from Abe and pay for the operation, too. It's yours, Maisie. A gift."

She was too moved to speak. Henry was good to her still. Just like when he bought her hot chocolate and the beautiful bracelet. She folded the money carefully and placed it in her purse.

"You wait here," Henry said. "I'll get the tickets."

He returned a moment later, and they stood side by side, peering up the track. Somewhere a clock chimed. Half past eight. The train was late. "I've been thinking . . ." Maisie tried again. "About that operation. Maybe I don't have to have it. Maybe we can get married secret-like, and I'll stay with my folks till you get sorted out. You wouldn't have to keep us, Henry. Not me or the baby. Not till you get on your feet. . . ."

He withered her arguments with a look. She retreated behind her sodden handkerchief. Five minutes went by. Henry strode off to the ticket booth.

"Why isn't that train here?" he asked.

The agent didn't look up.

"It's late, you know," Villette insisted. "That train is damned late."

"Yup."

"Why's that?"

"Damned if I know."

"But you must know. You're in charge here. You took my money for these tickets." He waved the two bits of cardboard in exasperation.

"Yup," the man said again.

"Well, I want to know when that train is going to get here!" He was making a fool of himself, attracting attention that he'd wanted to avoid, but he couldn't help it. Freedom, romance, adventure—all were just within his grasp. As long as the train came soon.

The telegraph machine behind the man started to chatter. " 'Scuse me," he murmured. Then he said, "Here's your answer, young fella. Been some kind of freeze up in Rutland. Be a while before they get that sorted out, I reckon."

"How long?"

"Now if I could say that, I'd be the richest man in Vermont." The ticket seller chuckled and turned to where a pot of coffee bubbled on a potbelly stove.

Henry moved down the platform in despair. "There's trouble further up the line," he told Maisie. "God knows when this damned train will get here."

"I know a boy that drives a trap," the girl ventured. "Maybe we can hire him to take us to Boston."

Henry examined the idea for a moment, then rejected it. Boston was too far for a trap and horse. "We'll just have to wait," he said finally. "There's nothing else to do."

The convent upbringing had made Lise meticulously neat. When she walked into the sewing room, she knew instantly that someone had been meddling. A bobbin of yellow silk lay on the floor. It had partially unwound and shed a web of thread across the carpet.

Lise picked up the bobbin and rewound it thoughtfully. Then she opened the drawer and noticed that the rest were not in the precise pattern in which she inevitably kept them. And the key was gone. She caught her breath and pressed her palms to her cheeks, stood motionless for a few seconds, then turned and ran down the hall.

Only after she found Henry's room empty did she go back to the sewing room and look for the strongbox. She wasn't surprised to find it gone. She'd understood everything as soon as she noticed the missing key and surmised the worst when she didn't find her son in his bed. She glanced at the little enamel clock on the mantel. It announced eight forty-five.

Lise deliberated only a moment. She raced downstairs and collected her coat and her handbag from the front hall. Hugh was long gone; he wouldn't be back until lunchtime. That gave her just under four hours to avert disaster. "Will," she called aloud. "Will, come here!"

Will was the cook's husband and functioned as odd-job man. He had a lame leg and didn't move quickly, but he was reasonably honest and usually sober. "Saddle me the landau," she told him. "Use the gray and Tess." They were the fastest horses in the barn. "Hurry. I've no time to lose."

Will shuffled out to the stable. Lise followed and had hold of the reins before he tightened the last harness strap.

Rutland, she decided. He'd have gone to Rutland to catch a train. "Move," she called to the animals. "For God's sake, move!" The first train would have left by now. Her only hope was that Henry hadn't made it and that he was in Rutland waiting for the eleven o'clock. She couldn't know for sure, but she must try. It was that or tell Hugh everything and see the pain and the disappointment spread across his beloved face.

"Ain't been a train out of here this morning, Miz Villette," the Rutland stationmaster told her. "Darned points was frozen solid. The boys just about got 'em loose now. Be one leavin' in five minutes," he added brightly. "That any use to you?"

"Perhaps. Listen, you know my son, don't you? Henry, my oldest boy?"

"Sure do, ma'am. Seen him around town with his pa lots o' times." His eyes narrowed slightly. He smelled gossip. A man could take a bit of pleasure from the problems of the high-and-mighty folk. "Thought Master Henry was off to Harvard," he added.

"He was," Lise said quickly. "But he became ill and had to come home. Now he's gone. And he has a high fever, delirious; doesn't know what he's doing, poor boy. I'm worried sick. I thought maybe you'd seen him this morning, waiting for a train. He's so anxious to go back to school; he doesn't realize how ill he is." She lay her gloved hand on the stationmaster's arm, a gesture of comradeship and appeal. "I'd be so grateful for any help."

"Well, ma'am, you just let me think a minute." He patted her hand with sympathy. It never hurt to do a favor for an influential lady like Mrs. Villette. "I'm dead sure he ain't been in Rutland. Not all that many people been in the station this morning. After the holidays and all, things is kind of quiet. But if he meant to get to Boston, like you say, he could of gone to Poultney. Next stop down the line."

"Have any trains left Poultney?"

"Can't have. Everything goes through Poultney makes up here. No, ma'am, anyone waiting for a train in Poultney is waiting still."

A steam whistle pierced the air. "That's the first train goin' now," the stationmaster said. "It'll be in Poultney in fifty-five minutes."

"Then I'll be on it," Lise said, running toward the track. The man ran after her. "See to my trap and horses," she called over her shoulder. "I'll send someone to collect them later today."

"Sure will, ma'am. Don't you worry about nothin', Mrs. Villette. Hope you find your boy." He waved to her departing back as if she were going on a holiday.

They steamed into Poultney station, and Lise spotted Henry at the far end. He was huddled into himself, arms clasped to his chest—a wounded animal, she thought, a beast gone to ground. Lise didn't see the girl next to him. She was preoccupied with getting off the slowing train and putting herself between it and her son.

He saw her as soon as she started up the platform. For the merest second it appeared that he'd bolt. Then he seemed to crumple. Lise felt a surge of pity. That he knew the game was up was apparent; his features were blurred with failure and disappointment, his shoulders bent like those of someone in chronic pain. "Good morning, Henry," she said.

Lise noticed the girl when she tugged at the sleeve of his coat. "C'mon, Henry, we got to get on the train. We ain't got time to be sociable."

"You go," he said without looking at her. "Go on. I've got to stay here."

"But I can't leave without you. . . ." The girl's lips started to tremble.

"Who is this young woman?" Lise asked.

"A friend from Cambridge," he muttered.

Lise stared at him in exasperation, then turned to the young woman. "I'm Mrs. Villette, Henry's mother. May I ask your name?"

The girl's eyes widened with shock. "Maisie," she stuttered. "Maisie Duggan." The conductor shouted his last all aboard. Maisie looked from mother to son. "Henry," she half wailed. "Henry! Ain't we goin' to Boston?"

He hung his head and said nothing. Lise answered. "Not by this train in any case. Perhaps you'd best tell me why you came to see my son, Miss Duggan."

Maisie opened her mouth, but no words came.

"It's none of your business why she came," Henry said with the hopeless bravado of the condemned man. "Get going," he told Maisie. "You got the money; you don't need anything else. Get out of here."

The train started to move. Maisie took a hesitant step toward it. "Please wait," Lise said quickly. She began to understand the drama, to see how it might be used to serve her own ends. "There will be another train shortly. You can take that if you wish. I think it might be useful if we talk first."

Maisie sighed and sank back on her heels. She nodded, and Lise recognized the acquiescence of the naturally servile. She'd seen dozens of such girls in the orphanage; born victims, everything she'd fought so hard not to be. "It's too cold to stand here and talk," Lise said. "There's a hotel nearby. We'll go there. First, Henry, give me the strongbox, please."

He withdrew it from beneath his coat without protest.

"Thank you," Lise said, taking the box. "Shall we go?" She led the way without once looking back.

In the hotel dining room Lise found a secluded table. "A pot of coffee," she told the waiter. It came, and she poured with the same gracious authority she exercised in her own home. "Now"—she turned to Maisie—"I would like you to tell me why you came to Vermont seeking my son."

Maisie remained tongue-tied. In desperation, she rolled back her glove and thrust her pudgy arm beneath Lise's gaze. Lise ran one finger over the gaudy bracelet. "Did my son give you this?" she asked finally.

Maisie nodded.

"And was it a token of something? Some commitment?"

"Yes," the girl whispered. "It was to show we was preengaged." Her chirping little voice cracked on the words. They seemed to Maisie such an impossible claim in the face of this elegant lady with her grand manner and her certitude.

Lise concentrated all her attention on Maisie. "And did you come here to protest a . . . shall we say a breach of promise? Was it action at law you were threatening, Miss Duggan? Is that what caused Henry to take this?" She tapped the strongbox on the chair next to her.

"Oh, no! Nothing like that. I swear it. I didn't threaten nothin'. I don't even know what that thing is!"

"It is a large sum of money," Lise explained. "It doesn't belong to Henry. He stole it."

"I didn't!" He came to life at the mention of the dreaded word. "I was borrowing it, that's all. It's your fault, anyway. You cut off my checking account. What else could I do? . . ."

"Be quiet," Lise said. She turned back to the girl. "Miss Duggan, I still don't understand. If you did not come here because of a presumed breach of promise, why did you come? What did you hope to achieve?"

"It's because I was . . . I mean I am . . ." Maisie could hold back her tears no longer. They squeezed out from between her reddened eyes and trickled off the tip of her nose.

Silently, Lise withdrew a handkerchief and passed it across the table. It was of incredibly sheer linen edged with hand-made lace. Maisie took it gingerly and blew her nose as quietly as she knew how.

"Are you trying to tell me you're expecting a child?" Lise asked. Her tone was matter-of-fact. Maisie nodded. "And you believe my son is the child's father?"

"I know he is; he's got to be. There ain't never been anyone else who . . . I mean, Henry said it was natural, us bein' preengaged and all. . . ."

Lise looked at the boy with curiosity. "Henry, have you nothing to say to all this?" He continued to stare at the tablecloth. "I see," Lise said at last. "Well, stop crying, Maisie. It's going to be all right. How far along are you?"

" 'Bout two months," the girl whispered.

Lise narrowed her eyes. That wasn't much time. It might turn out the girl was mistaken. No matter. Maisie Duggan was the answer to prayer, despite her obvious inadequacies. "You and Henry will be married within the week," she announced. "And right now we're all going home to Whitby Falls." A gurgle of pained protest issued from Henry's throat. Lise ignored him. "Where are your parents?" she asked Maisie.

"In Cambridge." She was still rubbing her nose and her eyes with Lise's handkerchief, uncertain whether etiquette demanded she return it used or put it in her own pocket. The older woman's proclamation had yet to dawn on her. "But they're not there now. They're in Providence visiting my auntie. So Henry said I could have an operation before they came back. . . ." She broke off. Maybe she shouldn't have mentioned that. Henry might not like it.

Lise turned to her son and looked at him with open disgust. "There will be no operation," she said softly. "Not now and not ever." She continued to stare at Henry while she addressed Maisie. "We will send your parents a wire informing them of the marriage. Now, we must find someone to drive us back to Whitby Falls."

"There's Jeb," Maisie said quickly, glad to be able to make a positive contribution at last. "He's got a trap. He's the one drove me to your house yesterday."

Lise nodded. "Go find him, Maisie. Tell him Mrs. Villette wishes him to come at once. Henry and I will wait here."

They rode out of Poultney fifteen minutes later. Maisie sat beside her betrothed with a growing realization that somehow this had turned out the luckiest day of her life. She hadn't been wrong to let him get "under her skirts" after all. She'd played her cards right, just as Pa said. Of the thoughts of Henry and his mother, she had no inkling. Both of them stared straight ahead and made the journey in silence. It didn't matter. The only important thing was that she and Henry were going to get married. Right away.

Maisie could see Jeb eyeing her slyly, puzzling over the fact that she rode between two of the powerful and famous Villettes. She couldn't quite suppress a giggle.

"But marriage," Hugh said, shaking his head. "It seems crazy, Lise. Jesus, the boy's not yet seventeen. And that Maisie, she doesn't strike me as much."

"Henry thought enough of her to make her pregnant," Lise said. "He was old enough for that. Don't you think it's a good idea he accept the consequences of his actions for once?"

"I don't know. . . . It seems so damned final. What about Harvard? What about all my plans for him? I was going to make him a lawyer, Lise. Bring him home to take over for old Lliam Murray."

"I know." She put her palm on Hugh's cheek with affection. "But he's not really suited for it, darling. You can take him to work with you in the quarry. You never went to Harvard, and look at all you've accomplished."

"Henry's different," Hugh insisted stubbornly. He pulled away from her touch.

"Henry's about to be a father," she reminded him.

Hugh slammed the door of the sewing room when he left.

In his own defense, Henry said nothing. For two days he wandered the house in a trance and paid little attention to Maisie's excited chatter. She was full of the details of the wedding dress Lise was making and of the reception to be held at the white house after the ceremony.

"Your ma says everyone in town will come. I don't see how they can manage that; it's such short notice and all. Just think, we'll be married four days from now."

Henry looked at her, then turned away. He went outside, but it proved no escape. Maisie followed him.

"You know, I thought the gown had to be pink or some other color. I didn't think I could have a white dress, considering. Your ma says it's gonna be white satin, anyway. With a train. Your ma's really something, Henry, I—"

"Shut up. Stop chattering, will you. And go away. I came out here to be alone."

"You mustn't talk to me like that, Henry. Not now."

"I don't want to talk to you at all. That's what I just said." He turned down another path. Maisie followed.

"What's that?" she asked, pointing at a thick hump rising like an igloo a few feet above ground.

"The icehouse."

"What's it for?"

"What do you think? For storing ice." He sighed with weariness. A long lifetime of Maisie's inane questions loomed ahead.

"Ain't it delivered? In Cambridge the iceman brings the ice."

"Well, this is Vermont. We cut it from the pond and store it in there."

"Don't it melt in the summer? And why's the roof so low? You must have to crawl to get in."

"It's mostly built underground. That's why the ice stays frozen."

Maisie walked closer to the door and tried the handle. "It ain't locked."

"No, why should it be?" Henry looked at her yellow-blond hair and her pink cheeks and her full bosom heaving with the exertion of the walk. "Want to see inside?" he asked softly.

Maisie nodded enthusiastically. Wisps of fly-away hair fluttered around her face.

"Come on, then." He stepped in front of her and pushed open the heavy door. It had iron clamps on either side. They were designed to take a heavy crossbar. He could see it propped against a nearby tree. Years before his father used to put that bar across the door so the children couldn't get in. All his growing-up years Henry had been told that the icehouse was dangerous.

"It's dark in here," Maisie squealed. "It's spooky."

Henry moved up behind her. He was near enough to smell the cheap scent she wore, sickly sweet, like the smell of death. He had a vision of Maisie frozen solid, with icicles over her lips, sealing them forever. In the shaft of light that came through the open door, he could see the long, lethal ice pick and the heavy tongs hanging on the wall.

"There's no ice in here," Maisie said. "Are you fooling me, Henry?"

"It's just not here yet," he said. "We don't start storing it until January." It would be at least a month before anyone came to the icehouse. Henry pulled his eyes away from the implements on the wall. They weren't necessary. He backed toward the door.

"Okay, I've seen enough," Maisie said, turning around. "Henry! Where are you?"

He was standing on the top step, his slight form blocking the light. Then he was leaning on the closed door and struggling to keep his weight against it while reaching for the crossbar a few feet away.

"Henry! Don't tease me, please! I'm scared."

Maisie's screams were a muffled sound rising from deep in the earth.

"Open the door, son."

Henry looked up. His father stood a few feet away.

"I said open the door."

"I was just teasing her," Henry mumbled. He dropped the arm that had been reaching for the means to lock the door.

"Well, you teased her long enough," Hugh said quietly. He waited while Henry let Maisie out. She was shivering with terror, and Hugh chafed both her hands in his, making it seem a playful gesture. "Henry's a terrible tease; always was. You'll have to teach him better once you're married," he added with a laugh. Maisie managed a wan smile.

"Run along home," Hugh told the girl. "Lise sent me to find you. You're needed for a fitting on that wedding gown she's making."

Father and son were left alone. "I was only fooling around," Henry said under his breath.

"Don't do it again," Hugh told him. He was trembling now, too, white-faced with rage, but his voice was controlled. "Don't let anything happen to that girl. If it does, you and I will know who's responsible."

"Fellow can't even have a joke," Henry said.

Hugh felt his hands ball into fists, but he didn't move. "Too damn late for it," he muttered. Henry stared at his father, mute with misery. Then he bolted down the path.

Rage and anguish built inside Hugh Villette, an onslaught of anger and frustration such as he'd not known for years, not since the red seam on the Skillet ran out. "Goddam!" he shouted into the winter twilight. "Damn! Damn! Damn!" He lunged for the crossbar that could seal the icehouse and would have killed Maisie Duggan. It was half a tree trunk, but he lifted it as if it weighed nothing and slammed it with all his force on the frozen ground. The wood splintered into hundreds of fragments.

"You lied to me," Hugh said.

Lise looked at her husband's ravaged face and felt a band of constricting pain around her heart. "What did he tell you?" she whispered. "You've been talking to Henry. I can tell."

"I didn't talk to him," Hugh said. "I stopped him from . . ." He let the words die away. "Doesn't matter. But you lied to me."

"About what?" Despair made her voice shrill.

"About Henry. About what happened at Harvard. He was a failure, wasn't he? My God, he's a failure as a human being!"

"He's not rotten," she said, "just weak. An opportunist." She reached out her hand to touch him, but it was as if Hugh had erected a wall between them. "He cheated," she said tonelessly. "Submitted someone else's work as his own. I didn't want you to know. I wanted to spare you the disappointment."

"We can't let him marry that girl," Hugh said. "He'll make her life hell. Whatever she is, she doesn't deserve that."

"He won't abuse her. I'll see to it," Lise said. "They'll live here with us. I'll keep an eye on both of them."

Hugh thought of the afternoon and the icehouse. "It'll have to be a twenty-four-hour watch," he said.

"No, not once he realizes there's no getting out of his responsibilities. Think of the child, darling. Our grandchild."

"What makes you so sure it's our grandchild? Maybe she's the type that went with all the Harvard men."

"She's no whore," Lise whispered. "I'd know if she was. God knows I should."

A growl of protest choked in his throat, and he reached across the chasm that separated them to press her to himself. "Don't say that. Don't even think it. You're mine. The finest thing that's ever happened to me."

"I never meant to deceive you," she said at last. "Only to keep you from being hurt."

"I know." His lips grazed the top of her head and caressed her cap of silky curls. "What do we do about Henry?"

"Nothing. They'll be married. He'll go to work with you. It will be all right."

"Whatever you think best," he said, sighing. "You always have the best ideas. You always did, starting with the arm wrestle." She chuckled and reached up to kiss him. "Anyway," Hugh said when they moved slightly apart, "there's still H.J. Maybe I'll get my Harvard lawyer, after all."

Lise knew she must inflict a clean wound with nothing left to fester. "No. Not H.J. He's no more cut out for it than Henry. I'm sorry, darling. That's the way it is. Don't let's fool ourselves or each other anymore. Maybe they're more Eve's and Jacques's boys than ours. We're a different breed. Henry and H.J. aren't like us, not even like we were."

Hugh walked to the sideboard, poured himself a drink, and downed it in one swallow. "You're sure about H.J., I suppose."

"As sure as you are when you say there is or there isn't slate someplace."

"That's pretty goddamned sure."

"I know."

He paused for a few seconds, then turned to her with a lopsided grin. "Okay, you win. They'll both be slate men like their pa. Who the hell wants a Harvard lawyer, anyway?"

Lise smiled back and held out both her hands. Hugh crossed and took them in his.

"You work them hard," she said. "The pair of them. We should have done that years ago, but it's not too late to start. You work them until they begin to appreciate where all this comes from." She nodded her head to indicate their hard-won kingdom. "We'll find a wife for H.J. pretty soon, too. And we'll keep the lot of them right here so I can make sure they're behaving. We'll do right by them, Hugh, in spite of themselves." In spite of Eve, she was thinking.

He nodded gravely.

1895 . . .

Chapter Eight

1.

Somebody coined the phrase "Gay Nineties," and it stuck. To Patsy Whitby, an avid reader of newspapers, it seemed debatable. There was economic chaos and a drain on gold; banks failed, and businesses went under in the hundreds. It didn't seem to Patsy very gay for the tide of jobless who marched on Washington in 1894. Coxey's Army, they were called. The nation, she decided, had a penchant for catchwords.

In 1894, when Patsy was seventeen, the Pullman strike brought the country's trains to a halt. Mr. Pullman had cut wages but not the rental for company houses. That wasn't gay either. Particularly not when federal troops marched into Chicago as strikebreakers. And if you were black and lived below the Mason-Dixon Line, you were suddenly confronted with a literacy test if you wanted to vote and a poll tax you probably couldn't pay. And the Supreme Court said "separate but equal" was just and the law of the land; to some people it seemed that the Civil War might as well have never happened. Patsy shook her head over all that.

Andrea decried her daughter's passion for the serious side of life. She suspected that Patsy was avoiding her own world because she wasn't comfortable in it. That seemed cowardly to Andrea. All the pretense at being an intellectual made Andrea nervous as well as angry. Riley Villette had been an intellectual.

"Look around you," she told her daughter repeatedly. "New York's an exciting place for a young girl. If you'd just lose a few pounds and pay some attention to your appearance, you could be enjoying it with all the rest."

"What about them, Mother?" Patsy pointed to a picture of immigrants huddled together in a tenement somewhere on Mulberry Street. "Do you think they're enjoying New York?"

"Listen," Andrea countered. "Your father was an immigrant. He managed. People who want to can get ahead."

267

Patsy shook her head again. "You don't understand. People like you, who have always had everything they want, how can they understand?"

Always had everything she wanted . . . Andrea almost told her then. What would Patsy think if her mother told her about the words on the wall in the roominghouse on Houston Street. *"Oh, God! That bread should be so dear and flesh and blood so cheap."* Andrea never said anything, however. She couldn't. Patsy would not allow a story to go unplumbed. She'd dig and dig until she knew everything.

Years before, when Patrick told his children the bare facts of the trial, Eddie accepted it without question. His mother had been unjustly accused and acquitted. Patsy had probed and demanded and nagged for detail until Patrick forbade her to mention the subject again. It was always thus—Eddie pleasant and tractable, Patsy anything but.

Most of the time the family kept the peace. The three other Whitbys buttressed Patsy, absorbed her temper and her obstinacy, presented a united front, did things together. Like going to see the unveiling of the Statue of Liberty in the harbor. "There," Andrea said in triumph. "That's the first thing the immigrants will see when they come here now."

"Do you think that matters, Mother?"

"Patsy, please! Spare us."

So it went. But it was hard, even for Patsy, to totally ignore the glamour of New York. Broadway, for instance, was oblivious to financial panic or scandals in Washington. *The Knickerbockers* played to a standing-room-only house; so did *The Belle of Bohemia*. For her eighteenth birthday, in 1895, Patsy was taken to a performance of *The Mikado* at the Fifth Avenue Theater.

She liked the operetta; Gilbert and Sullivan appealed to her sense of the absurd. And she had a new gown, bottle green, because her mother said dark colors were slenderizing, and an evening coat trimmed with fox fur that she wore even though it was a warm night. The coat covered most of her bumps and bulges. The rest of the family looked gorgeous, of course; they always did. Everyone waxed poetic about handsome Mr. and Mrs. Whitby, he so dark and she so silvery fair. And now Eddie had outgrown his gawky period. He was tall and ruggedly built, like Patrick, but he had Andrea's coloring.

Even the violet eyes. In his first top hat and tails, her little brother was positively handsome.

"By the time you go to Princeton in the autumn, you'll be insufferable," Patsy told him.

"Well, you already are," Eddie retorted.

Patsy didn't say anything. It was probably true. If only she didn't always feel like an outsider. She wasn't tall and beautiful; she was short and dumpy, at least thirty pounds overweight. And her eyes were dark and ordinary and her skin pale, not golden like Mama's. If only they'd let her go to a university as she wanted to do. Radcliffe, the new girls' college at Harvard, or the even newer Bryn Mawr. Her parents said the idea was ridiculous.

"You're not to think of yourself as some stuffy old maid, Patsy," her mother said. "I won't have it. You really are pretty, prettier than you think."

"College isn't sensible for ladies," Patrick agreed. "Besides, darling, you'll have a lot more fun staying home."

Patsy suspected there was another reason behind their objections. The Whitbys weren't millionaires, not like the Morgans and the Astors and the Vanderbilts. The Whitbys would have all they could do to pay Eddie's tuition at Princeton. No one had said that to Patsy, but she knew it.

On the night of *The Mikado*, she decided to drop her campaign for college. Maybe it wouldn't be so terrible, coming out in the autumn, being one of the debs. Maybe she could lose weight that summer, find a new hairstyle. Just possibly her dance card wouldn't stay empty at every party.

Andrea didn't harbor any preposterous ideas of Patsy making her debut at one of the balls of the Family Circle Dancing Class. Those events were strictly limited to the Four Hundred. The Whitbys weren't climbers; they had neither the pedigree nor the wealth to aspire to such rarefied heights; Andrea accepted that. Patsy would come out at a ball the society pages would largely ignore, a ball sponsored by the thousands of families like them; established, confident, moderately well off, not fabulously rich. Of course, it would be held at Delmonico's, just as the F.C.D.C. balls were. But it would be less lavish and unremarked by those who concentrated on the doings of the upper crust.

For Patsy the affair's minimal publicity made it no less

terrifying. "Patsy's dreading the autumn," Patrick told his wife one Sunday evening in August when they strolled in Central Park. "She's miserable about it."

"She's being silly," Andrea said. "She'll have a marvelous time."

Patrick eyed her speculatively. "Why are you being so insistent about Patsy? Maybe we should think again about letting her go to Radcliffe."

"Are you mad? We can't afford it. Besides, she should be here having fun. When I think how I threw away my own youth . . ." Andrea broke off. By the time she was eighteen, she'd been married to Patrick, but that wasn't what she regretted. She didn't want him to think it was.

"I know what you mean, love," he said softly. "But none of that's got anything to do with Patsy. She's worried about silly things like not looking good in a white dress and not being asked to dance. Foolish, maybe, but important to her."

"If she'd stop nibbling cakes and candies from morning to night, she wouldn't have to worry," Andrea retorted. "The truth is she's afraid to compete with girls of her own class. That's why she hides behind this false passion for art and literature and a lot of political nonsense."

Patrick swallowed hard. There were things he didn't want to say. But he loved his daughter, and as far as he was concerned, she *was* his. "Andrea, that's what's behind all this, isn't it? The kind of person Patsy really is and what that makes you afraid of."

"I don't know what you mean," his wife said. She walked briskly forward and studied the ornamental fountain as if each droplet of water were of vital importance. She's not Riley's child, and she won't be like him, Andrea kept repeating to herself. I won't let it be so.

Patsy kept nibbling despite her mother's warning. "Your father thinks you aren't looking well," Andrea said firmly. "He thinks you need a doctor. Really all you require is sensible eating habits, Patsy. You and I know that."

"Daddy shouldn't worry about me," Patsy said. "Neither should you. If you'd both simply leave me alone, I'd be fine."

"Your ball gown's going to need to be refitted," Andrea said.

Patsy turned to her mother with misery in her bloated face.

"I don't care!" she shouted. "Can't you get that through your head? I don't care!"

"She screamed at me this afternoon," Andrea told Patrick. "Like some fishwife from Fulton Market." Her hands were trembling. "It was so horrible. I didn't know what to do."

Patrick sat down heavily on the side of the bed. "We've got to do something. We can't let her go on being so unhappy. You're sure we can't afford college?"

"It's not just that. It's what such a thing says about her. Girls who go to college have acknowledged that they're going to be old maids. I don't want her to throw her life away, Patrick."

"All right, say she doesn't go to college. Does she have to come out?"

"What else can she do? Sit in this house while all her friends go to parties and balls? You think that will make her happy?"

"No." He paused, then leaned back on his elbows and stared at the ceiling. It was intricately molded plaster with a ring of cherubs eternally chasing each other across its gilded expanse. "When I was Patsy's age, I wanted to travel. So I set off to see the world. Or at least the part of it that interested me. What about that, love? Can we send her on a tour of Europe?"

Andrea was silent for a few moments. "It wouldn't have to be terribly expensive," she said finally. "Not an old-fashioned grand tour with a procession of carriages and servants."

He grinned. "Maybe we can hire an art professor to take her through Florence and Venice and Rome. Study the old masters."

Andrea looked shocked. "Not a professor! No man would do as a chaperone. A lady, though. A companion. There are agencies that supply that sort of thing. I'll look into it tomorrow."

"Hadn't we better ask her first? Patsy may not want to go to Europe any more than she wants to be a deb."

"No. I'll arrange everything," she answered. "Then I'll tell Patsy about it."

The companion was a lady named Miss Wilcox, genteel, English-born, and poor. The agency explained that the previous year she had taken a group of seven young ladies on a tour such as Mrs. Whitby was proposing. Miss Wilcox had both experience and excellent references. She also had a thin, spare frame and a nose long enough to allow her to look down it effectively.

Patsy rolled her eyes at her mother when she met the companion. "She's horrid," she whispered when the woman walked over to the window to study the view.

"Ssh!" Andrea cautioned. "She'll hear you!"

"So wise of you to live up here, madam," Miss Wilcox turned to face mother and daughter. "The air's so much purer than lower down the avenue."

"And a good deal less expensive," Andrea said, ignoring any hint of sarcasm. "We aren't millionaires, Miss Wilcox. If you and Patsy take this trip, you must be sensible about your expenses."

The Englishwoman's face made plain what she thought of people so vulgar as to discuss money. "Of course it's mademoiselle's mind we wish to enrich." Her eyes traveled the girl's excessively full figure. The rest of her was already sufficiently nourished.

Patsy's cheeks reddened with anger and embarrassment. "I'm Miss Whitby," she said sullenly. "I'm not French; it's silly to call me mademoiselle."

"It gives an air of grace, *ma chère*," Miss Wilcox said. "Of elegance. All the best people use a bit of French to lighten their speech. You do speak that beautiful language, do you not?"

"I do." Patsy was defiant. "I won the medal for French in my class at school."

"Patsy was a fine student," Andrea said quickly.

"Quite." Miss Wilcox turned again to the window.

Patsy shot her mother a look of desperation. Andrea rose and assumed her most businesslike air. "Thank you for calling, Miss Wilcox. I think we must both consider this a bit more. It means nine months when you and my daughter will be living in the closest possible proximity. It does require careful thought."

"Certainly." The woman drew on her white kid gloves and started for the door. Her dress of stiff gray taffeta rustled when she walked. "Good afternoon, mademoiselle," she said. "I'm sure that if we do travel together, we shall become good friends and you will find the experience immeasurably broadening."

"Oh, my God!" Patsy sank to a chair and leaned back, exhausted.

"Don't use such oaths," Andrea said. "And don't sprawl. Both habits are vulgar."

"My God," Patsy repeated, ignoring the reproach. "You sound just like her. Mother, you're not serious about this? You can't be."

"I am very serious," Andrea said. "And you had better be, too. Look, Patsy, your father and I have cast about for a solution to your dilemma. A dilemma you fashioned for yourself, I must say. Now, make your choice. Do you wish to tour Europe with Miss Wilcox or to come out when your friends do?"

"I've acquaintances, Mother, no friends. There is a difference, in case you haven't noticed."

"You are evading the issue. A deb or a traveler, Patsy, which is it to be?"

"Hobson's choice," Patsy muttered. "Between a rock and a hard place, as Daddy sometimes says. Or 'the devil or his tail,' another of his quaint Irish expressions." She reached for a bonbon and licked at the sugary violet coating. "Daddy can be very colorful sometimes. Don't you think?"

"Patsy! I'm at the end of my tether. Truly I am. Now, put down that candy! You really are your own worst enemy."

"Ah! Another trite but true saying. All right, Mother, all right." She knew she'd gone as far as she dared. Besides, she didn't like herself when she was like this. She didn't even understand why she did it. "I'll choose my mode of execution. Hemlock."

"What does that mean?"

"Socrates, Mother. A Greek philosopher, 469 to 399 B.C. Were they Gay Nineties for him, do you think? No, don't answer. And don't look like that. Miss Wilcox," she said firmly. "She's more like hemlock than any alternative available. I will go to Europe and be broadened. Immeasurably broadened." She giggled, but it had a shrill sound. "I don't need that, do I? I'm quite broad enough." Patsy popped the bonbon in her mouth and stared at her mother with sad dark eyes.

2.

England was cold and wet and depressing. Seen through the gray fog that blanketed that particular September, neither Oxford nor Stratford-upon-Avon had charm. Miss Wilcox chose small guesthouses that specialized in providing bed, breakfast, and evening meal to the visiting impoverished. They were all alike; dreary brick houses away from the center of things, cold and damp with small, stingy fires lit for a few hours in the evening and stodgy but ample food.

Patsy consoled herself with huge servings of steak and kidney pie, its thick suet crust enclosing chunks of fatty meat and bursting with floury gravy. When dessert came, she always asked for seconds of treacle pudding or jam roly-poly. Her spoon flew over the bowls containing these sticky, oozing sweets with a dexterity born of practice.

"Really, mademoiselle, it simply isn't ladylike," Miss Wilcox protested.

"I'm in exile," Patsy told her. "A prisoner of war. I need to keep up my strength. Besides, if you don't approve, you can always write to my parents. Doubtless they can be persuaded to cut short our tour."

It was the ultimate weapon. Miss Wilcox could ill afford to have the excursion shortened. Her pay would end when the trip did. "Suit yourself, I'm sure," she said haughtily.

The dragon, as Patsy called her companion, won a round in London.

A genuine art lover, Patsy was looking forward to the Tate and the British Museum and the National Gallery. To make it better, the fog lifted. Sunshine lit the elegant streets and parks of London. On the very day they arrived, they were treated to a glimpse of Queen Victoria riding in her coach along the Strand to Buckingham Palace. No eighteen-year-old could fail to be cheered.

"Well, Miss Wilcox," Patsy said. "This is more like it! How long are we staying in London?"

"Two weeks." The dragon smiled with satisfaction. Patsy felt a tremor of warning.

She could not have guessed the subtlety of the woman's attack. Their guesthouse was in outlying Maida Vale, a bastion of the middle class. The landlady was a small brown wren of a woman given to vague metaphysical yearnings. She was also a vegetarian. Her establishment served only raw salads, goat's milk, and brown bread. It was patronized by twittering women who shared her belief in the ability of diet to put one in touch with the spirit world.

Patsy raged, but the dragon was adamant. There were no alternatives; every other tourist facility in London was either booked solid or beyond their budget. The girl might have bought food elsewhere, but she had no money. Miss Wilcox had been given charge of all the finances. Patsy had to endure, and she did, but the riches of the London art world were lost in the constant cramp of hunger.

"Don't you ever dare do that again," she hissed through clenched teeth when they were aboard the cross-channel ferry headed for France.

"Do what?" Miss Wilcox said innocently. "Isn't this salt air bracing?"

Patsy turned aside and went below.

In France, Miss Wilcox didn't have to organize a starvation diet. It came with the national passion for superb food. Because no Frenchwoman would allow her kitchen to produce stodge in place of expensive choice ingredients, the dinners in their Paris boardinghouse were remarkable for both quality and quantity. There was a great deal of the former and very little of the latter. Breakfast was milky coffee and one roll. Lunch was a necessarily frugal meal that Patsy and Miss Wilcox ate in one or another little café. In the evening, when they returned to their lodgings, Patsy ached with hunger and misery.

Dinner was always the same: a bowl of exquisitely seasoned consommé, one chop delicately perfumed with fresh herbs, a tiny portion of beautifully prepared and presented vegetables, and for dessert, fresh fruit and a bit of cheese. It was the ordinary fare of the natives, and the other guests raved about the meals. Patsy cried herself to sleep.

It did have a slight effect, however. Her face lost its bloat, and if none of her girth really lessened, at least she didn't huff and puff after walking five minutes. "You are looking well, you know," Miss Wilcox said one night. She was smiling, really smiling.

Patsy was desperately lonely. "Do you think so?" she asked. Her voice was barely audible.

"I do. And listen, I saw something today I think would suit you. In the window of that little shop on the corner. I'll show you tomorrow."

They were staying in a section known as the Chaillot Quarter. Pedestrian and respectable, like all Miss Wilcox's choices, it had suddenly become the center of a raging controversy. A man named Eiffel had lately built an enormous monstrosity within view of the placid, uneventful streets of Chaillot. He called it his three-hundred-meter flagpole and boasted that France was the only nation in the world to possess such a thing.

The Chaillot district was also home to numerous small modistes. It was to one of these that the dragon led her reluctant charge. "Look." She pointed toward a discreet display in the window. "That evening cloak would flatter you." It was dark blue velvet, a rich, sumptuous thing, and it fell in graceful folds from shoulder to hem.

"I hate clothes," Patsy said sullenly. She was sorry she'd agreed to come.

"Please." The expression in Miss Wilcox's eyes was startling; it was genuine friendliness. "Try it on. It's right for you, I know it is."

"I thought we were on a strict budget."

"We are. But we can manage the cloak if you like it."

Patsy allowed herself to be led inside. The companion spoke with the modiste. The cloak was removed from the window and draped over Patsy's shoulders.

"Voilà! Regardez, mademoiselle," the woman pointed to a full-length glass. "Charmant. Très charmant."

It really was. The color suited the girl, reflecting the highlights in her dark hair and eyes. Her ungainly weight was disguised, and with her face slim enough to show her high cheekbones and graceful neck, she did indeed look charming.

"We'll take it," Miss Wilcox said without further discussion. Not such a dragon after all.

* * *

Later, it occurred to Patsy that it might have been better if Miss Wilcox had never smiled and the cloak never been bought. She was wearing it in Milan on the November evening when they went to La Scala to see Verdi's *Aida*. That was the night a drunken Milanese cabdriver nearly ran Patsy down and an agile, slender young man sprang to her rescue with florid Italian curses for the driver and voluble Italian sympathy for the signorina.

"I'm sorry," Patsy said. "I don't speak Italian."

The young man smiled. His teeth were a wondrous white in his swarthy face; his black eyes danced. "But you are English! I spent some happy years in England."

"No, American. From New York."

"But that is yet more marvelous! I have longed to visit your New York. Please, ladies, allow me to accompany you to your hotel. To apologize on behalf of my country for that fool of a driver."

"Thank you, sir," Miss Wilcox intervened quickly. "But we don't know you and—"

"Of course. *Santa Madonna* I am so stupid!" He clapped a dramatic hand to his forehead and smiled again. "Permit me to introduce myself. Count Francisco Antonio Bellotini di Moro. Your humble servant." He bowed low and summoned his coach without waiting for their reply. It was a handsome vehicle emblazoned with arms. "Ladies." He bowed again and motioned to the door the footman was holding open. "Please," he said softly, pleading with exquisite black eyes.

Miss Wilcox hesitated a moment. By the time she opened her mouth to speak, Patsy had one foot on the step and the footman was helping her into the count's coach.

"Now, where am I to take you?" the Italian asked. "Which hotel?"

They gave him the name of the small and undistinguished hostelry where they were staying, and Patsy watched his reaction. She knew about European fortune hunters who thought every American was an heiress.

The young man betrayed no flicker of surprise. "Ah, I know the place. You have chosen well. It is quiet and good value. Just the thing for two ladies on their own."

Patsy didn't speak during the journey through Milan's streets. The count carried on an animated conversation with Miss Wilcox about the architecture of Milan's many churches. "Of course," he said finally, "here in the north it has always been business that excited men's passions, not art."

"And you, Count di Moro," Patsy said, "are your passions excited by art?"

He turned to her, and his face was serious, as if he had missed the sarcasm behind her words. "I am excited by life, signorina," he said gravely. "All of life."

"Such a charming young man," Miss Wilcox commented after he dropped them at their hotel. "So thoughtful for his years."

"He's probably dirt poor and fortune hunting," Patsy said briskly. "One hears such stories all the time."

"I don't think we should be so quick to judge others," the dragon replied. "It's not Christian behavior."

The next day a note arrived from Count di Moro. It was an invitation to join him for an afternoon tour of the countryside. He would call at two, the note said, in hopes that they would consent to accompany him.

"Isn't that lovely!" Miss Wilcox was enthralled.

"He has a lot of nerve if you ask me," Patsy said. "Not even giving us an opportunity to refuse."

"But why should we? He is a nobleman, after all." She folded the thick creamy stationery with its impressive letterhead. "Do wear your blue cloak, Patsy," she added as if it were an afterthought. "It's so becoming."

Patsy didn't come down from her room until she was sure that both the dragon and the count would be waiting in the lobby. Then she appeared in a brown walking suit with a short, tight jacket that displayed every lumpy curve she possessed. It was decidedly not becoming.

"*Buon giorno, signorina.*" If Francisco Antonio Bellotini di Moro was nonplussed by her appearance, he didn't show it. "We have a beautiful day for our tour. I trust it will erase all unpleasant memories of last night from your mind."

It was hard not to like him. He was cheerful and attentive, and he paid as much attention to Miss Wilcox as he did to Patsy. Franco—he had insisted on the familiar name—seemed to genuinely enjoy showing them the sights. "Of course," he explained, "I am a visitor to Milan, just as you are. My home is in Rome. You must come and let me show you the eternal city. Now, there is true beauty!"

The first three days Patsy tried to put him off. She made numerous references to the fact that her father was an Irish immigrant, that they lived in the most unfashionable part of New York, that she and her companion were traveling on a limited budget. And she wore the most unflattering outfits she owned.

"You do seem to be making an effort to be disagreeable," Miss Wilcox said. "I don't know why you must be your own worst enemy, Patsy."

The girl flinched at the phrase her mother used so often. "I just don't want Franco getting any silly ideas," she said. "These Italians, they're all a little mad."

"Not Franco," the dragon insisted. "He's a fine young man."

She was smitten with him. Patsy snorted with disapproval, but she didn't say any more. Neither did she change her ways.

When they had been his guests for five days running, Franco wrote to his mother in Rome. "I have met a nice American girl traveling with an English companion," he told her. "The signorina is no beauty, but she is pleasant. She has been at great pains to impress upon me that she isn't rich. You know how these Americans are. Frank to the point of vulgarity. And defensive. Nonetheless, I think it would be advantageous if you invited them to stay with us in Rome."

The note from the contessa reached them a week later. By that time, even Patsy was beginning to believe in Franco's friendship. "We must go, of course," Miss Wilcox said enthusiastically. "Aren't we lucky, Patsy? We've been asked to spend Christmas in Rome with a noble family. I've never had such an experience before!"

She seemed to view her difficult, cumbersome charge with new eyes. Perhaps the Whitby girl possessed some attraction she had failed to notice.

The Villa di Moro stood in its own gardens above Trastevere beside the Gianicolo, one of Rome's legendary seven hills. It was built of the same yellow stone as most of the city. As much as anything, Patsy realized, it was the color of that stone that gave Rome its unique warmth and glow.

"Not just that," Franco said when she mentioned it. "It's the angle of the sun. I don't think the same thing can be true anywhere else in the world." He grinned. "At least in the world I've seen. Is New York a golden city?"

Patsy laughed. "Some say it is. The streets are paved with gold. Haven't you heard that?"

"Yes, but is it true?" They were in the garden, and Franco reached for a branch of oleander. It carried one pale pink, out-of-season blossom, delicately scented of vanilla. "Smell." He held the flower out to her. "It's beautiful."

"Yes," Patsy agreed. "And no."

"No what?"

"The streets aren't paved with gold. That's a myth. A cruel one, I think."

Franco stopped walking and looked at her. "And have other myths become obvious, too? Look, *cara*." He turned her gently back toward the villa. Its graceful terrace was perfectly proportioned, a stone poem in a leafy green frame.

"It's lovely. Is that what you mean?"

"No, Patsy. I mean that it is neither decrepit nor, what is your English word, fabulous."

"I don't understand." She moved away from his touch on her arm to where a carved nymph was endlessly pouring water from a jug into a small lily pond. "It doesn't seem like a week before Christmas," she said. "It doesn't even seem like winter."

"That's because Rome is enchanted. Twelve months of the year. But you're changing the subject. I think you do understand what I'm trying to say."

She blushed. It was ridiculous, but she really did feel her cheeks redden. "I think I do," she said softly.

"It's very important, so I will speak it plainly."

"Say," she corrected. "Not speak."

"Very well, say it, then. I am neither a pauper nor a man of fabulous wealth, *cara*. My family is old and respected, and we survive comfortably. So all your efforts to make me know you weren't an heiress, they were unnecessary."

"I thought you were a fortune hunter," she admitted quietly. "I didn't want you to be disappointed."

"Or yourself." He spoke the words so close to her cheek she could feel his breath. With one finger he traced the curve of her eyebrow.

"Franco"—there was naked pain in her voice—"why are you pursuing me? Do you enjoy being cruel?"

He drew back with an oath. "I have done nothing to deserve that, Patsy. It is you who are cruel."

She couldn't stop. "Look at me! Look at yourself. You are handsome, titled, and, according to you, not in need of a fortune. So why should you bother with a fat, ugly girl from New York?"

"Because," he said softly, "that's not what I see. I see a lovely woman, intelligent, generous. Hiding behind a façade she has made for herself. The most unflattering clothes, the unkindest wit. I'm not fooled by that, Patsy. I see you for what you are, and that is what I care for."

She lifted her face, her cheeks wet with tears. Franco leaned forward and brushed the tears away. Then he kissed her. For seconds her lips were still beneath his. Finally, she moved her mouth, and his arms went around her waist. It was her first kiss, and it was set in a beautiful, mysterious garden, bestowed by a handsome and romantic foreigner. Patsy's defenses couldn't stand up to that.

"Oh," she breathed when at last he pulled away. "Oh . . ."

"Thank you, *cara*," he said gravely. "I am honored."

A gong announced luncheon. Silently, they returned to the house.

Patsy lived the next days mainly in wonder. The memory of Franco's kiss filled her life, but it was not repeated. He was the soul of propriety, still giving Miss Wilcox as much attention as he did her young charge. The senior di Moros were equally gracious, equally charming. Franco was their only child, and they seemed to view it as a particular pleasure to entertain his friends.

"You say your father is Irish," Contessa di Moro said to Patsy one evening after dinner. The ladies were alone in a high-ceilinged circular room with marble walls and tiled floor. Candles gleamed in heavy gold sconces.

The girl tried to pay attention to her hostess, to brush away the gossamer veils of the dream that had enfolded her since the day of Franco's kiss. "Yes, that's right," she answered. "He's from Dublin."

"And he was a poor boy, a commoner?" The countess spoke precise, unaccented English learned from a textbook. It was without coloration of vocabulary or tone.

Patsy felt a tingle of fear. "That's right," she said evenly. "I explained all that to Franco when we first met."

Miss Wilcox stirred in her seat, trying to warn Patsy with her eyes. The men were still closeted with their cigars and brandy. The Englishwoman wished desperately for them to come in and end the scene. The door remained closed, almost as if the di Moros had arranged things beforehand.

"I know that," the contessa was saying. Her elegant gray hair was beautifully coiffed. She wore a jeweled comb over each temple, and the candles made the gems sparkle each time she moved her head. "There is one thing that puzzles me," she continued. "May I be frank, my dear?"

The girl nodded. Her hands were clenched into fists in her lap.

"I thought that all such Irishmen as your father were Catholics. But you are not. How is that?"

Patsy felt an almost irresistible urge to giggle. "Religion hasn't been very important in my family," she said. "Daddy was raised a Catholic. Then he simply stopped being one. I was educated by nuns, however."

"Ah!" The woman sighed with satisfaction and leaned back in her chair. "That's very good. And you have no prejudice to the true church?"

Patsy's lips twitched. She mustn't let herself laugh with relief. "I guess I'm a Christian," she said slowly. "It seems to me that Catholicism is a particularly rich and ancient form of Christianity."

"It *is* Christianity, my dear," the woman said. "Everything else is heresy." But she was smiling as she spoke.

"It is very important to my parents," Franco said, "that we be married in the Catholic Church, that our children be raised as Catholics. You understand?"

Patsy stared at him. She didn't doubt that the contessa had reported the previous night's conversation to her son, only that he was really saying these things. Casually, as if they were accepted facts. "Are you asking me to marry you, Franco?" She spoke too loudly. Her voice echoed down the allée of cypresses.

"My dearest Patsy, when I kissed you the other day, did you not know then?" He took her hand and raised it to his lips. "Do you wish me to kneel and ask formally for this hand which I wish to possess?"

She shook her head, still unable to respond.

"Anyway," he went on, "that would not be correct, not what the English call 'the done thing.' My father must ask your father for your hand. He will write tonight, if you give permission, *cara*. Say that you do. I cannot wait any longer."

"Yes," she whispered. "Oh, yes." You're a fool, a voice shouted in her head. This can't be real. You are still fat, Patsy Whitby. Stop believing you're Cinderella. "Franco," she said, pulling her hand away. "All those things I told you before are true, you know. My parents will not be able to give me a big dowry."

He chuckled softly. "Still, *cara*? After everything I have said?" He took her face in his hands and gazed into her eyes. "I think when we are having our silver wedding anniversary you will be telling me that you are poor and I must hunt fortunes elsewhere."

She had to laugh. He pulled her to him then, letting her mixture of giggles and tears play themselves out against his chest. "Listen," he said. "One thing I must tell you. My father will expect a dowry of some sort. As a gesture, a token. It is the way things are done in Italy. You won't worry about that, will you? And there should be some small allowance paid to you regularly by your family. For your own use, you understand. It's our custom."

Patsy barely heard him. She only felt his strong arms

around her and smelled the scent of winter jasmine that filled the air.

They decided to spend Christmas at their second villa in the Frascati hills. "There's a plan behind that, I think," Franco told Patsy. "I believe we're to be given the place as a wedding gift."

Her eyes widened. A villa in Italy. She was to be mistress of a mansion.

"Don't expect too much," Franco cautioned when he saw her expression. "It isn't as grand as this." He gestured to the house behind them. "It's always been just a summer place. No gardens, either. Olive groves and vineyards. We can make a garden if you like. You can use your allowance for that," he teased. "The great fortune I am supposed to be hunting."

She looked away. It pained her now to think of the doubts she'd had about him. "Don't remind me, darling. I was awful."

"Never," he said. "Never awful, my dearest."

Miss Wilcox loved every minute, as if she herself were the bride-to-be. "The contessa told me they'd like to announce the engagement on Christmas Eve. In Frascati. She only hesitates because she doesn't think your father's reply will have arrived by then. I said that was merely a formality."

"Oh, yes! Do convince her of that, Miss Wilcox. I'll tell her, too, if it will help. Of course Daddy will give his permission. Christmas Eve—that would be so beautiful."

Later, the contessa questioned her about it. "You are sure, my dear? I would not dream of offending your parents in any way. But you are so far from home . . ." She had a habit of letting her sentences end without being finished, leaving a thread for her listener to pick up.

"Yes," Patsy agreed. "Very far. And they won't be offended, contessa. They'll be thrilled. I've written myself to tell them all about it."

The woman smiled. "Then we should go ahead and set the date of the ceremony, should we not? April, perhaps?" A small frown darkened her smooth forehead. "Since the wedding is to be Catholic, I thought it best if it take place in

Rome. To spare your mother and father any embarrassment. Of course, if you prefer—''

"Oh, no! That's just what I want. Rome, not New York. And April is perfect.''

A wedding in beautiful, golden Rome. In spring, with the gardens full of flowers and the air heavy with the scent of lemon blossoms. Franco had told her all about it. "At that time of year the sun strikes the dome of San Pietro just so. It is a vision, *cara*, a rainbow. Wait till you see it.''

They left for Frascati in three carriages. Franco and Patsy were alone in the first, and he was the driver. "We Italians aren't so stuffy as the English or the Americans. I want you to myself for a little while." Behind them, Miss Wilcox rode with the senior di Moros. The third carriage brought servants and luggage.

It was raining, but gently, and the air was warm. The silvery mist struck Patsy as sensual, satisfying. These days she was receptive to such impressions. Food wasn't as important as it had once been. Sometimes she didn't even finish her pasta. Her clothes fit less tightly now. She wasn't slim, and heaven knows, she wasn't pretty or fashionable, but she could feel things. The touch of fabric on her skin, the caress of a fur collar around her neck. The rain was like that. It fell on her face as she walked to the carriage and became part of a tactile universe she had only just discovered.

They had been traveling almost an hour, laughing and chatting and sometimes being silent, but always wrapped in the togetherness of their private world, when she glanced back and didn't see the other two carriages. "We seem to have outdistanced them," she said.

"This is because we are young and speedy and they are old. Besides, I am a better driver than my father's servant." He chuckled and reached for her gloved hand beneath the light robe that covered her knees. "Do not be afraid, *cara*. I've already declared my honorable intentions. Anyway, they'll catch up.''

They didn't. When Franco turned in to the driveway of the Villa Bellotini, the two following carriages were nowhere in sight. "Never mind. The key is hidden in a flowerpot by the front door. My mother has left it there since she stopped having a resident staff in this place.''

Patsy looked up at the austere façade of the house. It hadn't the grace of the villa in Rome, but it suited its site among the wooded hills. "Why did she do that?"

"An economy. A few years ago, after the shares her parents left her reduced in value. On the London exchange, by the way. Only a madman would invest money in Italy."

"The contessa's income has supported this place, then? Always?"

He was fumbling with an enormous iron key. The rain had swelled the door, and it was reluctant to budge. "Always. It is the custom. Villa Bellotini is the wife's responsibility. Besides, it once belonged to my mother's family. Now"—he turned to her suddenly—"you're not going to start all that again, are you? By American standards it costs a pittance to maintain this place."

He was angry with her for the first time since she'd known him. Patsy looked chagrined. "I'm sorry."

His smile was like sunshine after rain. "You are also soaked. Here, I've finally got this open. Come out of the wet at least."

She stepped into the rectangular hall and craned her neck to gaze up at the skylight. The villa spread to either side along matched stone staircases.

"It looks bleak now," Franco said. "But when the sun is shining and there are flowers, it's beautiful."

"I think it's beautiful now. The proportions are perfect. Not bleak at all."

"Come, I'll show you your room." He led her up one of the staircases and along a broad corridor that looked down into a courtyard. "This was my mother's room when she was a girl," he said. "She was determined you should have it. Later, after April, we'll have the *sala di matrimonio*." He pronounced the phrase slowly, almost as an invocation.

"After April," Patsy agreed. Her eyes caught his and held them. Her heart was racing, and her hands were trembling inside her muff.

Franco broke the visual current between them. "Get out of those wet things. There's sure to be a dressing gown in that cupboard. Your luggage is all in the third carriage, I'm afraid."

"I'll find something."

"Yes. There's wood downstairs. Maybe even a bit of coal. I'll get some and start a fire in here."

He left, and she stood in the center of the room and turned around in a slow pirouette so she would miss nothing. This was to be her home, this strong and beautiful house with its centuries-old stone walls and its extraordinary play of light and shadow. From the window she could see the vineyards. They were stark and bare now, each vine trained to wires that marched in harsh procession up the gentle hills. In Rome, the di Moros drank only the wine from those vineyards.

From the earth to the table. Possessed, owned, held. She and Franco, their children, all of them, would be nurtured by the oil and the wine produced on their own land. It made everything in New York, in all of America, callow and ridiculous. A rented apartment, maids hired from agencies. How different from a house and land of one's own, servants who were born under your roof, who were part of your world.

"Are you decent?" Franco called from outside the door.

"Come in," she answered.

He did so with his arms filled with logs, then looked at her sternly. "You are supposed to be changing from those damp clothes. You'll catch cold, *cara*. What kind of Christmas will that allow?"

"I was admiring."

"You can admire later. Now, get behind that screen and undress while I start a fire. I'll find something for you to put on."

She did as he said. She was soaked to the skin. The rain looked gentle, but it was penetrating. Patsy took off everything. She could smell the fire and hear the logs crackling. "Have you a robe for me?" she called. "Hurry, I'm freezing." She reached her hand over the top of the screen to take whatever he had found for her to wear. Nothing happened until she felt something warm slip over her shoulders.

"I brought you this quilt," Franco said. "It was the best I could do." He was standing behind her, nuzzling her neck, only the silken quilt between them.

"Franco . . . Don't. We mustn't. Your parents . . ."

"Ssh. My parents are not here. Neither are yours. We have only each other to please, *cara*. Turn around so I can kiss you."

She tried to wrap herself in the quilt and turn at the same time. The maneuver was only partially successful. Her arms and shoulders were bare.

"You wear my love well," Franco said softly. "Every day you grow more beautiful."

"I'm not beautiful." She dropped her eyes. "Don't tease me, Franco. Please, I can't bear it."

"I'm not teasing. I mean every word. Come." He guided her to a long mirror on the opposite wall. "Look at yourself," he said. "Really look."

She saw only the same Patsy Whitby she'd always seen. Plain and homely. Then Franco removed the pins that held the simple bun at her neck. Black hair in deep, shining waves fell over her shoulders. It was beautiful. She could see that for the first time. Always before she had looked and mourned, because it wasn't her mother's silvery glory. Now she saw the way its ebony highlights reflected the pale whiteness of her skin and the darkness of her eyes.

"You see," Franco whispered. "I am not lying to you, *cara mia*. You have lied to yourself. For years, I think. Now I am showing you the truth. And there is more."

He reached up and loosened her grip on the quilt, let it fall to the floor. Patsy stood naked and too mesmerized to feel shame. She was hypnotized by the reflection of her pale skin in front of his dark suit. Franco reached around her and gently cupped her breasts in his hands. They were heavy and full and snow white, except for the dark amber ring around nipples that were turgid with the coolness of the room and the heat of his touch.

"They are what a woman's breasts should be," he whispered into her hair. "Plentiful, waiting for me and for our children. I would not want you otherwise."

He continued to hold her bosom in his hands. His fingers looked dark against her whiteness. Patsy couldn't take her eyes from the mirror. When he touched her nipples, she gasped, but he didn't stop. He squeezed them gently, and they tingled and grew more swollen.

"Franco, no . . ." she managed to whisper.

He moved his hands as if he were obeying her, but he didn't pull away. Instead, he caressed her hips. "They are made for bearing children," he said in her ear. "Do you think I would prefer a thin, hard woman? A barren woman?" She couldn't reply; she was choked with feelings she couldn't understand. And with gratitude.

His knee was prodding her legs, forcing them apart. He

pulled her closer, and Patsy could feel her buttocks pressing against the smooth cloth of his trousers. "Do you feel that?" he whispered. "I am hard for you, *cara*. Some people think a man should never say such things to a woman. That is wrong. I want you to know how much I want you."

She still could say nothing. His fingers moved lower down her body and tangled themselves in the black curly hair between her thighs. "Here," he said, "in the most intimate part of your beautiful woman's body, you are moist. Because you want me, too. It is right, *cara*. Truly right."

He released her suddenly, and she wanted to cry out for him to continue. "Go to the bed," he said very softly. "Turn it down."

She did as he told her, conscious the whole time of his eyes studying her nakedness. She folded back the satin spread and exposed the heavy linen sheets. Franco took off his clothes. Slowly, without hurrying.

When he was naked, she dropped her eyes.

"Do not turn away from me," he said. "I want you to look, Patsy." He crossed to where she was standing and put his hands on her shoulders, holding her at arm's length so that she was forced to examine his body as he had examined hers.

She could see how broad his chest was—before then she'd thought of him as slight—and how it tapered to a hard, flat belly and narrow hips. She could see, too, the erect, pulsing evidence of his manhood and his desire.

"Would I want you thus if you were not beautiful?" he asked.

She shook her head.

"Say it," he whispered. "Say, 'Franco loves me, and I'm beautiful. . . .'"

"Franco loves me, and . . . I'm beautiful." Her voice broke on the words. She was crying. Hard, rough sobs made her shoulders shake and closed her throat.

"Cry," he said. "Cry for joy, because we belong to each other." He moved her closer to the bed and made her lie down. Then he lay over her, supporting his weight on his hands. His slim, swarthy legs stretched between hers. "Now," he said, and he lunged downward and pierced her in one long stroke.

The pain was sudden but swiftly over. Franco ignored her gasp and thrust again. And again.

Patsy did not feel pleasure. She was quivering with exultation. Franco loves me, and I'm beautiful. The words played over and over in her head. They were a symphony, and when he moaned with release, his cries were a magnificent and perfect counterpoint.

4.

"I don't know what to think." Andrea stared at the letter. "Can it be true?"

"Funny kind of hoax, if that's what it is," Patrick said. He ran his finger over the engraved letterhead. "Count di Moro. I've never heard of him, but then, what do I know about Italian nobility? And why does he say here, '. . . my son the count . . .'? How can they both have the title if the father's alive?"

Andrea shook her head impatiently. "I don't know. Some peculiar Italian custom. They're mad for titles, one hears." She rested her chin on her hand and stared at the piece of paper. "The obvious explanation is that they're fortune hunters."

Patrick shrugged. "Not much of a fortune. He says a dowry of three thousand dollars and an income of fifty dollars a month. That's not exactly up to the standards of the Four Hundred."

"What, then?"

He rose and walked to the sideboard, then poured himself another cup of coffee. "Listen, we're being rather unfair to Patsy, aren't we? Is it not possible this di Moro lad loves her? Recognizes her worth?"

"I suppose it is. Yes, of course." Andrea sighed. Her violet eyes said something very different.

"Let's just not do anything for a bit. We should hear from Patsy herself before too long. If it's not a hoax, that is."

The girl's letter arrived two days later, brimming with happiness and enthusiasm. Franco was wonderful, they loved each other, she knew it sounded preposterous, but it was true. "I'm a changed woman with him," she wrote. Andrea smiled. A woman, no longer a girl? Perhaps.

There were three closely written pages singing Franco's praise. Then, at the end, the one grave note. "I'm sure you understand that for the sake of the di Moros it must be a Catholic wedding. Surely that won't disturb you, Daddy! Under the circumstances I'd like to be married in Rome. We've been talking about the spring. You will come, won't you? And Eddie, too. I shall die if you aren't all here to be happy with me. . . ."

They read the letter and didn't say much, but the doubts lingered. Patsy married to some dashing Italian nobleman? Difficult, ungainly, unlovely Patsy? They knew her virtues, but could they believe a strange young man had recognized them as well?

Patrick went to his study, Andrea to the old nursery the children had shared when they were little. Like most of the rooms in the apartment, it looked out on the park. She could picture them sailing boats there in the spring, sledding across the East Meadow in winter—Eddie a blond picture in his sailor suit, Patsy already dark and lumpy at six. Oh, Patsy, why couldn't you look like me or like Patrick? Why oh why did you have to look like him? Doubt had shadowed her daughter's life. In some obscure, mystic way Patsy's existence was distorted by a fear she knew nothing about, guilts born before she was. I did it to her, Andrea thought. Papa and I and the Villettes.

Her head was throbbing. She pressed her fingers to her temples. In the end, did it matter? Patsy was hers, whoever her father might have been.

Andrea sped down the hall to the study and threw open the door without knocking. "Listen, I've decided. I have to go to Italy right away. I have to see her, Patrick, now, before it's too late. She could be so hurt. I can't bear to think about it."

"I know, love," he said. "I've already been on the telephone to the steamship line. We'll both go. There's a sailing to Genoa in twelve days."

The *Laurencia* was an Italian ship, boasting thick black coffee and mountains of pasta and charm. Patrick took Andrea below deck and showed her steerage. Traveling east, it was occupied only by a few Italians going home for a visit. He spoke of how different it was when full of people going to America; the way it had been when he crossed.

"Dreadful," Andrea said.

"No, not entirely. Exciting. Hopeful, too. Everyone with a dream and sure it will come true."

Apart from steerage, there were three classes. The Whitbys were in first, along with other couples very like themselves, or much richer, and a few prelates in red or purple.

"I've been making inquiries," Patrick told her the third day out. "Among the Italian clergy. The di Moros are well known and respectable."

"Are they rich?" It was a purely practical question.

"Their Eminences won't speak about that openly. But I get the feeling they're not impoverished."

She frowned. Inconclusive.

Genoa after sixteen days. "I'm told the trains to Rome are miserable, even in first class, but I don't see what else we can do," Patrick said.

By the time they reached Rome, Andrea was drawn and pale. Tiredness had the effect of making her beauty more ethereal. Patrick handed her down from the railway carriage and looked around. They had wired from Genoa. Someone should be meeting them.

"Daddy! Daddy! We're over here." Patsy descended on them. The painful contrast between the girl and her mother struck her father instantly. Not seeing them together for a few months, he'd forgotten.

They hugged and kissed and amid a jumble of luggage and scurrying porters were presented to a dark young man with enormous black eyes and an incredible smile. He called Patsy "*cara*" and was solicitous of her every need. Andrea stared at Franco and at her daughter. She looked at Patrick, and he was staring, too.

Patsy's eyes were shining, and her cheeks were flushed; she'd even lost a little weight. But she was still Patsy. No miracle had occurred to turn her into a raving beauty. Beside her elegant fiancé, she looked a pudgy, clumsy mongrel, paired with a greyhound.

"What did he say to you?" Andrea asked.

Patrick sat up in the enormous mahogany bed hung with gold velvet curtains. He stretched and squinted at the sunlight through the shuttered windows. "I take it you mean Count di Moro the elder?"

"Of course. I tried to wait up for you, but it got so late. I fell asleep. You must have talked till after two in the morning."

"Close to three, actually. And he said very little, except to repeat what was in his letter. That they understood how hard it must be for us to marry off our daughter in a foreign land, that he hoped we believed they loved Patsy as if she was their own. That kind of thing."

"And money? Did you make him understand, Patrick? Do they realize we have limited resources?"

"It took a while to get him to that. Delicate and circumspect, very Italian. We laid our cards on the table finally. He seems to have no illusions about the Whitby funds. Patsy apparently made a point of telling them that from the beginning. She suspected Franco of fortune hunting as soon as they met."

"Not now." Andrea turned her face to the wall. It was hung with blue and gold brocade. "Now she's besotted with him, with all this."

"And he with her. Or haven't you noticed that?"

"I've noticed. From the look of it he dotes on her. Oh, Patrick! I want to believe it. If you only knew how much I want to." She buried her face in his shoulder, and he stroked her hair. "I think I'll kill him if he hurts her."

"Careful, love," he said softly. "I suspect we are more likely to hurt her than Franco is."

"More wine, Signora Whitby?"

"Thank you, contessa. A little more, perhaps. It's delicious."

"It comes from our own vineyards. I'm pleased you like it."

Andrea sipped the pale gold wine. They were on the terrace alone. She and Contessa di Moro had looked for an opportunity for a private talk, and at last they had it. "Tell me," Andrea said. "Do you produce a great deal of wine?"

"To sell, you mean? Oh, no!" The contessa's silvery laugh hung tinkling in the air until, it seemed, she dispersed it with her expressive hands. "Only a small vineyard in Frascati. At our villa there. A few hectares of grapes, a few of olives. Just for the family. My husband and I are planning to give the Villa Bellotini to Franco and Patsy as a wedding present. But they must promise to share the wine and the oil with us!" She laughed again.

"Patsy says it's a beautiful place," Andrea said.

"In its day it was," the contessa said frankly. "It is in much need of repair now. Our hope is that Patsy will, how do you say it, put things right."

Andrea ran her finger around the rim of her glass. It was fine Florentine work, delicate and beautiful. "Contessa, I must be very frank, and you must forgive me for being thoroughly American."

"I like Americans," the contessa said, smiling. "I always have."

"Patsy's income will be very limited," Andrea blurted out. "You and the count and Franco must realize that."

The other woman sat back in her chair and studied her guest. "You are indeed frank, Signora Whitby. I never imagined myself discussing such a matter. But let me, too, pretend to be an American, just for a little while. The sums my husband detailed in his letter to Signore Whitby, they are acceptable?"

"Well, yes, of course. But—"

"But there is no need for buts! I know, dear lady, that you have come here because you fear for your daughter's happiness. As a mother, how can I not understand—"

"As a mother, then—" Andrea said quickly. She was angry, but she couldn't have said why. "Please, tell me the truth. Is Franco in love with Patsy?"

"He cherishes her. We all do." The contessa rose. The time of intimacy was over. "You must excuse me, Signora Whitby. Guests will arrive at eight. There are things to see to."

"Yes. Contessa, if I've offended you, I'm sorry."

"You have not. Please, you must not worry yourself about such a thing. Only . . . Well, I would have thought you could see for yourself how happy they are. How well suited. And it makes strong children, you know, this blending of the blood. . . ."

She left, and Andrea sat alone on the terrace listening to the birds and sipping the wine that came from the vineyards of the Villa Bellotini.

Andrea saw little of Rome in the first two weeks. Her days were filled with shopping and fittings for Patsy's trousseau and her nights with numberless friends of the di Moros. The wedding day was brought forward to the tenth of February.

"It's better than having you make the journey again in April," Patsy said. "Besides, Franco and I don't want to wait."

Andrea guessed that they hadn't waited. She'd never say so to Patrick, but her instincts told her Patsy and her fiancé were lovers. The sooner they were married, the better, then. That is, if it was wise for them to marry at all. "I can't find any reason to oppose it," she told her husband. "Not without hurting Patsy dreadfully. But I'm terrified for her."

"I know," he said. "But it's Patsy's life, love. Maybe this time we've got to give her the freedom to make her own mistakes."

"Damn that Wilcox woman! Why did she let this happen?"

"She's bowled over by Franco and his family," Patrick said, laughing. "I suspect she'll find work for years to come on the strength of having married off one of her charges to Italian nobility."

On the last day of January Andrea determined to confirm her doubts or end them. In the afternoons, Franco usually went out. When he returned, it seemed to Andrea that he had the look of a man with a secret. Patrick insisted that was absurd, but she couldn't shake off the idea. That day she intended to know. Patsy was busy with the dressmaker. Patrick was to accompany Franco's father to a gunsmith's to see some new kind of hunting rifle. No one would miss her.

Andrea waited a few minutes after Franco left the house, then slipped out behind him. From the front gate she could see him descending the hill, a man sure of himself and happy with his world. She followed at a discreet distance.

Franco strolled the streets of the district known as the Trastevere as if he were in no particular hurry. Andrea easily kept him in view. Around them, climbing the rise to the Gianicolo, were the villas of people like the di Moros; a few yards away, squalor and poverty. In this place, to be born poor was to die poor, locked out of any other future by class and accent and custom. No wonder people flocked to the New World.

And now Patsy was making the journey in reverse. Why couldn't she relax and let her daughter be happy? Andrea asked herself. Why must she be so suspicious? Franco passed the Quirinale and approached the Fontana de Trevi. A woman broke from the crowd around the fountain and hurried to meet him. Andrea paused and studied the pair.

The woman was a few years older than Franco, but exquisite. The sort of companion one would expect young Count di Moro to choose. Andrea watched them. She made no attempt to conceal herself or her scrutiny. She even moved closer, but couldn't identify the woman. She wasn't someone invited to the contessa's parties.

They were smiling. Franco held the woman's hands in his and pressed them close to his chest. His top hat was tilted rakishly back on his head, and his walking stick was tucked under his arm. He was the young man-about-town wooing his love of the moment. No other interpretation was possible. Soon she cocked her head and said something that made him laugh. Then she withdrew her hands and moved away. As he stared after her, she turned and blew him a kiss.

Franco stood where he was until the woman was out of sight. When he headed back in Andrea's direction, he walked with a jaunty spring, swinging his gold-topped stick with the swaggering confidence of youth.

She didn't move. He was less than six feet away when he recognized her. "Madam Whitby! But I am astonished. How wonderful to find you suddenly in my path. You are escaping from the wedding fuss, perhaps. I confess, so am I. Come, we will have a *granita* and talk about your lovely daughter who is soon to be my lovely wife."

"Franco"—she stared into his eyes—"who was that woman? The one you met just now."

He smiled again. There was a slight hint of mischief in his expression. "So you saw us. She is beautiful, is she not? She is a principessa, one of many in Rome. I fear we aren't very selective in bestowing titles. I would tell you her name, but it would mean nothing to you. And a gentleman must be discreet."

"Franco, please, for the sake of whatever God you believe in, tell me the truth. What is between you and this principessa?"

His look was rueful. "You are a true American, dear Madam Whitby. Everything, how do you say it, 'cards on the table.' It is no accident your being here today, is it? You followed me."

Andrea nodded. "I had to know."

"Very well, you shall know. Though I would never say such a thing to an Italian lady. The principessa is my intimate friend. My very intimate friend."

Andrea exhaled in a deep sigh. She didn't know she'd been holding her breath. "Come," she said quietly. "We will have that *granita* you mentioned. We need to talk, you and I."

5.

Andrea studied the pale, iced confection in front of her. Extraordinary that the Romans ate sherbet in January. She toyed with the silver spoon.

"Please, Madam Whitby, you are not eating. It is very good, I promise you."

"Tell me," Andrea said, "why do you say madam?"

"Your English 'Mrs.,' it is hard on my Italian ears."

"Signora, then."

"Very well, Signora Whitby, if you prefer. I apologize for offending you."

"You have not offended me. And what I prefer is the truth. Not studied affectation, not artifice. Do you understand?"

"I understand, signora." Their eyes met, and Franco was the first to look away. "You are thinking that I have lied to you. Because of the principessa."

"Not to me, to Patsy. She's my daughter, Franco. I cannot stand silently by and see her hurt."

His manner changed abruptly. "You think I would hurt her? But I have done nothing to deserve such an accusation!"

She understood that they were dealing with a chasm of culture, a tear in the social fabric. "I am not accusing you, not the way you mean. To the men of your country, a mistress is something apart from a wife. I know that."

He shrugged. "Then why must we have this unpleasant conversation? It is not something a gentleman discusses with a lady."

Andrea reached out and lay her hand over his. "Franco, please, tell me the truth. Why have you asked Patsy to marry you?"

He did not answer immediately. When he did, his voice was thoughtful. "It seems to me a remarkable question. I'm trying to find the words to explain. Patsy is exactly the right sort of wife for me. I saw that as soon as I met her. When it became clear to me that I could make her happy, I asked her to marry me."

She wanted to accept that. To smile and change the subject, to ask him some idle question about Rome or the weather. She could not. "Franco, Patsy is in love with you. Are you in love with her?"

He paused again. "Signora," he said after some seconds, "Patsy is a dear, sweet girl. She is generous and intelligent; she has a sense of humor. I love her with all my heart."

"That's not what I asked. Are you in love with her?"

"You mean do I have the great passion, the beating heart, the belief that without this woman I cannot live? No, signora, it's not like that. But what I feel, it is not *interessato*. What you would call ignoble."

"I ask you again, why do you want to marry her? I thought it was money, but—"

"Ah, the fortune hunter. So we have that again." He signaled the waiter and asked for two coffees. They sat in silence. The coffee came, small cups of sweet, milky cappuccino. Franco twisted the saucer around and around on the marble table.

"Money is many things, signora," he said at last. "By your American standards Patsy's dowry and allowance are small. For us they are adequate. I am the only son of my father. I have an obligation to my family. In Italy today, in all of Europe, money is scarce. Property abounds but not cash. Thankfully, what Patsy brings is ample to meet the needs of the family; otherwise, I could never have considered marrying her. But I would not take a wife of whom I was not fond for three times as much. My parents would not expect it. It is not the di Moro way. Does that answer your question?"

"Your parents," Andrea said. "They know the—how shall I put it—the limits of your affection for my daughter? And they approve?"

"My affection for Patsy is not limited," he said gravely. "You do me an injustice to suggest it. My mother and father are very fond of her. They believe we will be happy together, that we will produce fine, healthy children to carry on the di Moro name."

Andrea nodded and took a sip of her coffee. "One last

thing, Franco. Then I promise the inquisition will end. This principessa—do you plan to continue your relationship with her after you and Patsy are married?"

"I will tell you the truth, signora," he announced. "Because you are a great lady, I think, and Patsy and I have a long life before us. The principessa and I have been friends for many years. It is not reasonable to think that friendship will suddenly end."

"Or that another won't take its place," Andrea added.

He smiled and laid down his napkin. "Enough, Signora Whitby. Come, we will hire a carriage to take us home."

It was almost dusk in the Piazza Navona when they left the café. The three fountains shimmered in the westering sun.

"This was once the Circo, the arena, I think you say, of the Emperor Domiziano. Chariots raced around this oval. Gambling with fate, Signora. All in this place. Rome never changes."

She smiled at him. "No, Rome never changes," she agreed. "Neither do people. We are what our heritage and our upbringing makes us, Franco."

He hailed a cab.

"Why did she tell you?" Franco looked at Patsy. Her eyes were red, and he knew she'd been weeping. "I don't understand your mother. It was cruel and unnecessary."

"She thought I deserved the truth," Patsy said quietly. "The right, as she put it, to make an informed decision."

"Bah!" He flung his hands into the air. "Informed decision. Your English, it is a cold language. Clinical. Your people, too. I am not like that, *cara*. I am a man with feelings and passion. You are more like me than like them. You will ignore all these stories, and things will be as they were between us."

Patsy shook her head. "I can ignore the past, Franco. I don't care about it. But not the future."

"The future! But that is exactly what I speak of. Our future, *cara mia*, our life together, the Villa Bellotini, the children we will have . . ."

"And the mistresses you will have." She managed a wan smile. "That is our future, is it not?"

"You are talking like a child." He moved closer and put his hands on her shoulders. "Look at me, Patsy. Do you imagine that I could be as I am with you, as we are together when we make love, if I did not care deeply for you? If I were not devoted to you?''

Patsy pulled away. "That first time," she said. "The day in Frascati. Your parents took their time deliberately, didn't they? They wanted to give you time to seduce me, to cement the arrangement, as it were.''

"Seduce you." There was a new coldness in his words. "Is that how you think of it? Did I force myself on you? Were you unwilling, Patsy?''

"No, I wanted you. I want you now.''

Franco ran his fingers through his hair. It was his gesture of ultimate frustration. "*Santa Madonna!* Then why are we having this ridiculous argument? Come, *cara*. We will get out of this house. It is full of people who wish to meddle in our lives. We will find someplace where we can be alone. Someplace where we can make love. I will make you forget all the terrible things your mother has told you.''

"No.''

"No? Do you not want to be with me? To be in my arms? I don't believe that, *cara*.''

"I want to.''

"Then why . . .''

"Because it isn't enough, Franco. Not for a whole lifetime. I wish it were. I try to tell myself it is. But I have an addiction to reality. It's one of my chief failings. You can ask Father Lucco. He's been instructing me in the Catholic faith. He knows all about my inability to believe the impossible.''

"The possible is not always what it seems," he said softly. "Most reality is gray, Patsy, not black and white.''

"Not for me.''

There was a long silence. They watched each other, waiting for the movement or the word that would change things, wipe away the past twenty-four hours and restore their world to what it had been. Franco admitted the impossibility first. He smiled at her and shrugged as if he were dismissing the present and acquiescing to the future. "Good-bye, *cara*," he said quietly. "Do not think you must hurry away. I'll be gone by nightfall. My parents will offer you hospitality as long as you wish.''

Patrick moved his wife and his daughter into the new Hotel Eden. It was off the Via Veneto near the Villa Borghese, on the other side of the Tiber from the Gianicolo and its di Moro associations. "I'll check on sailings, love," he told his wife. "We'll get the first ship out of here."

"Have you dismissed Miss Wilcox?" Andrea asked. Normally, it was a detail she would have seen to, but not now. She was pale and trembling, more upset than Patsy by the look of it.

"I did," he told her. "Stop worrying. As soon as we get her home, it will be all right. You'll see."

"But— Oh, God, Patrick! What if I was wrong?"

"You mustn't think about that. You did what seemed right to you. It was Patsy's choice, love. Don't forget that."

She waited until he left, then tapped softly on the door to the girl's room.

"I'm sorry if I woke you."

"I wasn't sleeping."

"Resting, then," Andrea said. "That's good. You need to rest, darling." Patsy had blue shadows under her eyes, and her skin was waxen. "Daddy's gone to see about sailings. We'll be home soon."

"How marvelous," Patsy said tonelessly. She was wearing a short-sleeved nightdress. There was an ugly red line where the fabric of the gown was too tight. "I guess a sea crossing's just what I need. All that lovely food. I can eat my way to oblivion. And to obesity. It hardly matters, does it?"

"Patsy." Andrea turned away. "Don't sound so bitter. I can't bear it."

"You can't bear it? What about me?" Her mother's shoulders shook. Patsy knew she was crying. "I'm sorry," she said softly. "It's not your fault."

"Yes, it is," Andrea whispered. "If I hadn't meddled, you'd be getting married in three days' time to a man you adored. I'm sorry, Patsy. Truly sorry."

"It's not your fault," the girl repeated. She stretched out her hand. "Here, look at me. I can't talk to your back."

Andrea turned. She took the outstretched hand and held it very tight.

"Listen," Patsy said. "I'm glad you told me. Not about what happened but about knowing. I'd have found out, you know, sooner or later. And I'd have been more miserable. And there might have been children. It would have been much worse."

"You're being very brave," Andrea said.

"Not brave, just realistic, as always."

"I wish you could understand. I didn't want to say anything, but I had to. In my life, Patsy, long ago before you were born, I've seen terrible things happen because people lived with lies, protected them, wove the web tighter. I couldn't bear to think of that happening to you."

Patsy smiled slightly. "You're a woman of mystery, Mother. You always have been. Even Eddie and me, we've never known all of it. I sometimes wonder if Daddy does."

"I'd like to tell you." Andrea's mouth barely moved. She had to force out the words. "I just can't talk about it."

Patsy tugged at her mother's hand. "Look, it's all right. It doesn't matter. Sit down. We'll talk about something else."

Andrea sat on the side of the bed and smoothed the girl's hair back from her forehead. "It's ridiculous," she said with a little laugh. "Here you are jollying me out of a bad mood. It should be the other way around."

Later, she told Patrick, "We mustn't take her home."

"What are you talking about? We have to take her home."

Andrea shook her head. "Think about it. She's miserable, Patrick, worse than she was when we first suggested she tour Europe. And we're going to bring her back to the same situation she hated before. I can see her future, and it's awful."

He knew she was right. "What about college, then? The thing she wanted from the beginning."

"She's not the same now. She can't just become a school-girl again. She's a woman, for better or for worse. What terrifies me is that she's going to become a fat, bitter woman. She'll hide behind humor and sarcasm, while inside she's screaming with pain. It's like handwriting on the wall."

"In God's name, then, what do we do?"

"Something dramatic. Something to change everything."

He was staring at her as if she'd begun to speak a foreign tongue. "What kind of dramatic, different thing?"

"I'm not sure yet, but I'm thinking about it. Just don't make reservations to leave until I've had a little more time."

The next day Andrea appeared on the doorstep of the Contessa di Moro.

"Signora Whitby, this is a surprise. But of course you are welcome. . . ."

"No, I'm not," Andrea said. "I know my presence here is an embarrassment to us both. But I need your help. I had to come."

"Sit down, please." The contessa gestured to a stiff gilt chair and took one herself. She sat precisely on the edge, unbending and unbent. "Now, how can I be of service?"

Andrea swallowed hard and summoned all her resources. "Your son, Franco, will find someone else. Someone just as suitable as Patsy, probably more so."

"I don't think—"

"No, let me finish, please. I'm speaking to you as one mother to another, like that day on the terrace. And as Patsy's friend. I believe you always meant to be her friend."

"That is true, Signora Whitby."

"Once, at a dinner party here, I heard two of your guests talking about a place in Switzerland. A kind of spa where one of them had sent her daughter to take the waters. It sounded rather like what we call a finishing school, but not exactly the same thing, I think."

"Ah, St. Moritz." The contessa's smile was faint, perhaps ironic. "Not exactly a 'finishing school,' if I understand the term."

"According to what these ladies were saying, it seemed a good place to lose weight. They were implying that Patsy ought to be sent there. I think they were right."

"It is a new fad, this emphasis on slim women," the contessa said. "I think Patsy is lovely. A bit generously proportioned, perhaps, but lovely."

"She needs . . . a renewal, contessa. A new start. If she does not have it . . . All this, it's been very hard on her."

The contessa said, "Wait here a moment, please."

She left the room. Andrea studied the curved marble walls, the golden sconces, the gilt furniture. All this centuries-old grace and elegance could have been Patsy's. If she hadn't interfered. She bit her lip to keep from weeping.

The Contessa di Moro returned. She handed Andrea an envelope. "Here, this is the address you want. I know very little about this Madam Frobisher, who takes in young ladies. Except that she is exclusive and expensive. And from the few rumors I've heard, most unorthodox. However, the decision is yours.''

Andrea rose. ''Thank you very much.''

''I hope it is of some help, Signora Whitby. Please, tell Patsy I wish her all the best. Both my husband and I do. You will tell her?''

''I will. Good-bye, contessa.''

''*Arrivederla, signora.*''

6.

Patsy passed from Rome's incipient spring into a lingering winter spread across a flat plain. Bologna, Modena, Verona . . . Then, suddenly, a world of white. Snow that blazed with the glory and abandon of a tropical summer. Patsy put on the dark glasses Andrea had given her before they parted.

''I'm told you'll need them, darling. A new invention, and all the rage.''

''I look like an owl,'' she'd said, ''or a creature from the moon. Whyever will I want them?''

''Snow blindness,'' Patrick had told her. ''Anyway, as your mother said, they've become fashionable.''

The train was Italian, which meant horrid. The carriage reeked of garlic and rough red wine. It was not the world of the di Moros, even in first class.

''I can take a second-class ticket,'' she'd told her parents. ''Miss Wilcox and I always traveled second-class.''

''Not this time,'' Andrea had insisted. ''You travel in style, darling.'' She'd put her slim hand under Patsy's chin and raised her head. ''Look up, not down. You're making a new start,'' Andrea said. ''And you'll do it by yourself. We're going home to New York, and we've dismissed Miss Wilcox.'' She smiled brightly. ''You're going to be just fine.''

Patsy protested no more. She was frightened, though, particularly now as the train chugged up the mountainous hills to Tirano, the last stop in Italy.

They stopped, and uniformed men swarmed over the carriage, demanding passports and customs declarations.

Madam Frobisher was tiny, slender, and exquisite. Swathed in furs, she had twinkling hazel eyes and black hair marked by a startling gray wing over each temple. "So, Miss Whitby? You are she?"

"Yes. Patricia Whitby."

"You are called Patricia?"

"Patsy."

"Good, I like that better. Paco, here is our guest." She summoned a man in a green loden coat and an enormous knitted cap. "See her trunks are brought to the house. Paco is my butler—cum-everything else. Don't worry about your luggage; he will lose nothing." She took Patsy's arm and guided her across the small station platform. It was awash in wealth and what the Italians called *bella figura*; elegance, grace, presence.

She must stop thinking in Italian phrases, Patsy told herself. There was no need now. Still, it was a good description. St. Moritz was a fabled playground of the rich and famous. The very air crackled with the excitement of their arrivals and departures.

"They are interesting, the privileged nobility," Madam Frobisher said. "Weak, often flawed, but interesting. I do not hesitate to say so, for I can see you aren't one of them."

"I'm sure it's obvious," Patsy said dryly.

"Not the way you mean," the woman said. "You do not reek of their decay, my dear. Neither do I. We can have as much money, and look as well, but we are of tougher stock. Mixed blood, not their endless inbreeding. Survivors." She flashed a brilliant smile. "I am confusing you. I will explain everything later. Come, we begin your regimen this instant. We will walk home. It is little more than two kilometers, just over a mile."

Her boots were of black suede and cuffed with fur. Patsy's were heavy leather. Madam Frobisher walked with easy grace, while her guest plodded along beside her.

Little houses with deep overhanging eaves and brightly painted trim stood out against the whiteness. Everywhere were enormous evergreens and the tinkle of sleigh bells. One came toward them, the soft swooshing sound of the horses' hooves on the snowy road mingling with the laughter of the occupants.

Patsy watched them drive by. "What do they come here for?" she asked. "They cannot all require a regimen."

Madam Frobisher laughed. "No, of course not. Some come for their health, most to toboggan or to ski."

"I'm afraid I know nothing of either."

"You'll see. They are wonderful sports. Soon you will know all about them."

"I don't think I want to," Patsy said doubtfully.

The woman smiled. "Not yet, but you will. You'll become an addict, like the rest of us. For now think only about your regimen. My house is in St. Moritz-bad, close to where you go to take the waters. Three times a day."

"What does it mean"—Patsy gasped as she struggled to keep up with Madam Frobisher's energetic pace—"to take the waters? I've never really known."

"None of you Americans do." She stopped in the middle of the road and examined the girl. "You are worth working on, Patsy Whitby. I can make you a great beauty. You have the bones for it. And the intelligence. Beauty is never stupid."

Patsy stared at her, mouth agape. Madam Frobisher laughed. "To answer your question," she said as she began walking once more, "to take the waters is simply to use the curative powers of the natural minerals in the earth. Here in St. Moritz the springs are red with iron. They have been known since before Rome was founded. You will drink to clean out the bowels and bathe to polish the skin and tone the muscles."

"This regimen"—Patsy was huffing; breathless with effort—"is that all there is to it? Just these miraculous waters?"

"Not miraculous, natural. And no, that's not all. You eat fresh, natural foods. And you breathe. Do it now." She stopped again. "With me, breeeeeethe. . . ."

Patsy didn't know whether to laugh or cry. She made an attempt at breathing. Or rather, breeeeeething, à la Frobisher.

The little woman cocked her head. The furs that framed her face were infinitely flattering. "You think I'm mad, don't you? An eccentric who has you imprisoned in this mountain fastness. I'm not mad, Patsy Whitby. Everything will be just as I say. Give me absolute obedience and six months. It's not just a question of taking off some pounds. I will make you think and feel and move like a beauty. Then you shall be one."

Patsy removed the dark glasses and narrowed her eyes. "I may as well trust you," she said finally. "The alternative is horrendous."

They moved off to the ever-present accompaniment of laughter and sleigh bells. Once, Patsy even heard someone yodel. "I thought that only happened in books," she said.

"In storybooks and in St. Moritz," Madam Frobisher agreed. "It is the same thing."

1896 . . .

Joseph

Chapter Nine

❧❦❧

1.

In the autumn of 1870, when Maryann Villette left Whitby Falls for Boston, she had a fixed plan for her future. Her vision of Camelot was the result of two conversations and an understanding of reality. Not for Maryann a romantic flight to the frontier. She guessed the likely lot of her sisters in the Oregon Territory; scrubbing and bedding, with not much pleasure in either. Maryann decided that since she was expected to spread her legs, she'd be paid for it.

Always she'd known herself no beauty. As a child, Maryann had compared her close-set, colorless eyes to Andrea Whitby's big violet ones, her crooked teeth to the flashing smiles of the other girls in the village. At first, she'd mourned her inadequacies; not even her thick brown hair was compensation when measured against Andrea's silver tresses or the ordinary blond of some of the others. Then, when she was thirteen, she developed her own startling asset—a figure exquisitely round above and below.

Maryann's breasts were like juicy pink watermelons, her buttocks glorious twin hillocks that trembled when she walked; between them she had a handspan waist. She realized very quickly that boys, even men, were bowled over by such attributes. Maryann reveled in their desire and usually obliged it. It was preferable to being viewed as just another Canuck. The main reason she'd lain with Jason Whitby was the superb satisfaction of reducing the great man to a groaning, straining creature imprisoned between her ample thighs.

After Jason threw her over, she pouted for a while, then let a number of other willing replacements heal her pride.

Her largesse ended only when she discovered that some girls earned money dispensing what she gave for free. A traveling salesman told her about the bordellos of the big cities. His stories about the fancy ladies he'd known in Boston were fascinating. After Maryann's first encounter with him, behind the railroad yard in Rutland, she made an appointment for a second meeting on the road to Poultney.

"What about New York?" she demanded as soon as he'd satisfied himself. "They got any of them fancy houses you was telling me about in New York?"

"Oh, yeah, sure they do. But New York's like a big jungle. So damn many people you can't walk down the streets. Boston's better; it's cozier."

"You're telling me the truth, ain't you?" Maryann demanded. "They pay girls to do it in Boston?"

"Sure they do. You don't think it's free, do you?"

"Now I know it ain't," she said smartly. "So you owe me a dollar."

The salesman hooted with laughter and paid.

Her plan ran into a temporary setback when she discovered she was pregnant. Whether the salesman or one of the lads from the quarry was the cause of her predicament, she wasn't sure. In any case, it appeared she'd have to wait until her baby was born to go to Boston. Then Hugh returned with his plans for transforming the easygoing life of the Villettes and his supply of cash. Maryann parlayed those facts into a railroad ticket, with forty-six dollars left over.

The Rutland and Washington Railroad had become the Delaware and Hudson. It took her to Albany whence she boarded the Boston and Worcester. Next morning the train steamed into the station at Lincoln and Beach streets in the city of her dreams.

Thanks to her previous research with the salesman, Maryann knew which was the best whorehouse in the city. She asked directions to Finney Court and eventually found it, a narrow lane between the immigrant slums of the North End and fashionable Scollay Square. She knew, too, that the door of the house she was seeking was painted blue and sported a brass knocker in the shape of a lady's boot. Her salesman had been fond of such detail.

The girl who opened the door was red-faced, rawboned, and foreign. Eventually, Maryann convinced her to summon her mistress.

"Are you Madam Pearl?"

"Who wants to know?" The woman studied her caller's curves with candor.

"My name's Maryann Villette. I want a job."

Madam Pearl tilted her head and narrowed her eyes. "What kind of a job?"

"I want to be a whore. I'm through doing it for free. I want to be paid."

Pearl stared at the girl in astonished silence for about three seconds. Then she threw back her head and exploded in raucous laughter. "Come in, honey," she said at last. "You're in the right place."

Maryann followed her hostess into a large room furnished with velvet chairs and gilt chandeliers. She nodded with satisfaction. "Yes," she said. "This is exactly like I pictured it. Now there's something you gotta know. It don't show yet, but I'm pregnant, so I won't be much good as a fancy lady until after the kid's born. Meantime, I'll work as a maid. Won't charge you a cent, and I'll do a better job than that foreigner you got now. After my baby's born, you gotta promise to let me be one of the others."

"How did you hear about this place, anyway? You're not from Boston, are you?"

"No, from Vermont. A fellow told me about you. Said this was the best house in the city. How about it? Am I hired?"

The woman pursed her lips and considered. "What about after the kid's born? You going to put it in a foundling home?"

"No. It's mine, it stays with me."

Madam Pearl thought for a moment. Girls with figures like Maryann's didn't appear everyday. "Okay," she said at last. "I may be crazy, but okay."

Joseph Villette profited by the unusual nature of his home life. By the time he was six, Maryann's son could tell the difference between a real gent and a four-flusher. At ten he was an accomplished pickpocket, and at sixteen he knew the finer points of every kind of confidence trick. Along the way, he also learned to read and write and developed a flair for drawing. Maryann encouraged those skills. "You may be smart as hell 'bout the way things really is," his mother told him, "but you gotta be educated, too. Otherwise, you'll be a punk all your life."

Joseph knew what a punk was, and he didn't want to be one. He recognized that one sure way to enter those undesirable ranks was to amass a lot of petty convictions. Joseph avoided trouble with the police as carefully as any minister's son. He had a naturally placid disposition; he could wait. The boy made himself useful at Madam Pearl's and bided his time.

Maryann gave up professional whoring when she was twenty-seven and the once-famous curves were turning to fat. After that, she was Pearl's second-in-command. It gave her more time to spend with her ten-year-old son, and she talked to him for long hours about every subject that interested her, including her past as a Canuck in Whitby Falls.

"Am I a Canuck, too?" Joseph asked one day.

"Only half," she answered, laughing. "Can't say for sure what the other half is. But I done right by you, Joey. Just look in a mirror and you can tell."

Her son was beautiful. He had brown hair like hers, but his eyes were an extraordinary aquamarine blue. For the life of her, Maryann couldn't place those eyes. "Nobody I was ever with had that color," she remarked often. "Must be somebody's grandmother or something."

In 1890, when Joseph was eighteen, Maryann died. She had influenza that winter, as did most of Boston, and she never recovered. The boy grew restless. Despite the affection of Pearl and the other women, his mother's death left a void in his life.

"I'll be leaving soon, Auntie Pearl," he told the aging madam shortly after Maryann's funeral.

"Yeah, honey," she agreed. "Expected you'd want to strike out on your own. Where's it to be? New York?"

"Guess so," he said. "That's where it's all happening, I hear."

"Take care of yourself, Joey. And remember, you always got a home here." She saw him off with a kiss and three hundred dollars.

At first, Joseph had felt like a wealthy man. Three hundred dollars was more than many men earned in a year. He took a room at the Hotel Plaza on Fifth Avenue and bought two new suits. He walked the streets of the city daily, and observed the life of the Astors and the Vanderbilts and the Morgans. There was no doubt in his mind—rich was the only thing to be.

Sometimes he'd stand for hours by the Vanderbilt mansion on Fifty-ninth Street, just a block from his hotel, and watch the comings and goings of society. It gradually dawned on him that such pastimes cost money; they allowed time to pass without adding anything to his funds. Three months after his arrival in New York, he had just fifty dollars left.

Joseph wasn't worried. He had sniffed out the location of the city's most notorious brothel. The Haymarket was society's soft underbelly. The most illustrious men of the Four Hundred paid visits to this house, known for the extreme youth of its girls and the innocence of their expressions. Rumor had it that for a price the Haymarket would even provide a virgin. Everyone knew about the place and its clientele, but no one talked about it. Joseph decided on a little judicious blackmail, helped along by his ability to make quick, lifelike sketches.

His plan was careful and apparently foolproof, and the day he sprung his trap, he thought he'd won. He paid a visit to the scion of a wealthy family, sketchbook in hand, and returned to the Hotel Plaza richer by two hundred dollars. Later that night, he stepped outside for a breath of air and was quickly flanked by two unsavory-looking characters who forced him into a carriage headed downtown.

Villette was prepared to fight, but it turned out unnecessary. His captors escorted him to an old and dignified house on lower Broadway. There Joseph met a man known as "the boss." He was unusual in both appearance and intelligence, and capable of recognizing such qualities in other men. The boss had been charged with disciplining Joseph, but instead he became his mentor.

After four years of training, the young man was put in charge of a complex and dangerous operation requiring him to travel halfway around the world and match wits with persons of much greater experience. Joseph performed admirably, and in the summer of 1896 he was detailed to bring the matter to its conclusion.

2.

Joseph wasn't much for small talk. The older man did most of the chattering.

"Jeez, it's hot in here. I got asthma; shouldn't be in places like this. Can't even open the damned window." He tried again, but the tiny opening had been painted shut years before. Everywhere else in the warehouse loft the paint was chipped and peeling; on the window it remained perversely intact.

"Leave it shut," Joseph said. "Somebody might notice."

"Who the hell's gonna notice? It's two in the morning, for Christ's sake."

"Stop complaining, Rudy. It goes with the job."

"Yeah, that's what I been thinking. I gotta get out of this racket."

Joseph chuckled. "You're well paid. Besides, what else could you do?"

"Nothin', that's just it. Now, if I was like you, I sure wouldn't be in no flea-bitten hole like this at two A.M."

The younger man rolled a cigarette and lit it, cupping his hand around the flame so there would be no telltale glow. "You think not?"

"I know it! Jeez, you're a Villette, ain't you? I read about yer old man in the papers. Just last Sunday."

Joseph had seen the feature story on the Villettes of Whitby Falls. "He's my uncle," he said. "I've never met him."

"Lousy luck," Rudy said. "That's my trouble, too. Lousy luck. That's why I gotta be nursemaid to this hunk of glass." He gestured to a small paper-wrapped parcel on the table.

"It's not glass," Joseph said quietly. "You can bet on that."

"You seen it?" There was a touch of awe in the words.

"Had to. I brought it back."

"All the way from South Africa?" Rudy was impressed. "The boss let you do it alone?"

"Yes." Villette didn't say any more. The room was hot and airless, but unlike Rudy, Joseph didn't squirm or pace. Composure was Villette's trademark. He was over six feet tall, broad-shouldered but very slim, with the controlled tension of a big cat. His eyes were catlike, too, the vivid aquamarine blue glittering in his tanned face. Nobody ever forgot his eyes. Sometimes that was a problem.

"Someone's coming," Rudy said. He moved closer to the package.

Villette stood up, unfolding his length from the chair. Rudy didn't notice him reach beneath his jacket. When the older man looked, Joseph was holding a gun.

"You think we'll need that?" Rudy asked nervously.

"I don't know," Joseph said. He walked to the doorway and stood to one side where he would see whoever came in before they saw him.

There was a knock on the door. Villette nodded. "Come in," Rudy croaked. His voice broke on the words.

The door opened. Two men entered hesitantly. Joseph stepped quickly behind them and slammed the door shut with his foot. "Hands over your heads," he said softly. The strangers complied. Villette frisked them, his movements practiced and efficient. "Okay," he said, slipping his gun out of sight. "Just checking, gentlemen. You understand."

"Yeah, sure," one of them said. "You Joe Villette? I heard about you."

"Joseph," Villette said. "Mr. Villette to you. Did you bring the money?" He knew they had. He'd felt the thick wad of bills in the shorter man's pocket.

"Right here."

The man withdrew the cash. Villette took it and threw it to Rudy. "Count it."

"All here, Joseph. Fifty thousand dollars."

"Good. Give them the package."

"Wait a minute." The protest, like the money, came from the shorter man. "We've got to check. Make sure we're getting what we paid for. We got orders."

Nobody spoke while the package was unwrapped. The stone lay in a fold of black velvet; glittering, enormous, a diamond for a sultan. Joseph wanted to laugh. The thing was ludicrous in this place and this company.

He waited while the taller man screwed a jeweler's glass in his eye, then nodded with satisfaction. "As promised," the man said. The jewel was rewrapped, and the two men left. Villette moved quickly and stood again beside the door, gun in hand.

"You crazy, Villette? It's over. They're gone."

"Shut up."

He stayed in place for five long minutes—motionless, listening. The only sound was Rudy's labored, asthmatic breathing. "Okay," Joseph said finally. "All clear."

"You must be crazy," Rudy repeated. "Put that thing away."

Joseph holstered the gun and said, "Two years ago, in

Chicago, I had to make a delivery something like this. The collection went off fine. Then the collectors doubled back and reclaimed their money. They didn't ask for it politely."

"Jeez," Rudy said. "I never thought of that."

"Relax," Villette said. "Here, the boss said I was to pay you." He peeled a few bills from the stack they'd exchanged for the diamond. "Next time there's something for you we'll be in touch."

Rudy left first. Joseph listened to his nervous footsteps pounding down the three flights of stairs.

A few minutes later, Villette went down to the street.

"So, Joseph, everything went well?" The boss sat back and studied the neat pile of currency on his desk.

"Yes, sir. I take it our client is satisfied."

The man smiled. "I've not heard otherwise. He was a bit impatient lately. Two years is a long time to wait when one covets such a prize as you delivered last night. But then, no one else could have procured it for him, not in any amount of time. I'm sure he knows that. You are very good at what you do, young man. Sometimes I wonder why you don't turn your talents in a more individual direction."

"I'm satisfied," Villette said.

The boss nodded. "Good. And you'll have a bonus for this job."

"Thanks. There's something else, though."

"What?"

"Rudy Heinz. He's no good to us anymore. He's a bundle of nerves, and he wheezes. Asthma."

"Very well. I'll see his name is struck from our rolls. In a manner of speaking." He leaned back and made a tent of his strange, beringed hands, peering at Villette over the top of the gesture. "I've been thinking about your next assignment."

The aquamarine eyes glittered, the only betrayal of interest.

"One of your talents, lad, is patience. I've always wondered how you acquired so much of it so young. Maybe a clerical background? A quiet vicarage in the country, perhaps? A minister's son? Am I close?"

Villette smiled. "I doubt it. Mama was a very accomplished whore, but she wasn't fussy. My father's name slipped her mind."

The boss guffawed. "Your frankness is admirable, Joseph.

Anyway, I knew all that before I asked you. All the same, you are a Villette, are you not? A member of the well-known Vermont family?''

Joseph shrugged. "I guess so. My mother was Maryann Villette. Hugh Villette, the one they call the slate king, was her brother. All these questions must mean you saw that piece in last Sunday's paper. But Vermont's a backwater. The Villettes may be big fish, but it's a pretty small pond.''

"Agreed. Nonetheless, I have reason to believe that certain people in Whitby Falls are interested in your uncle. I want you to pay your family a visit, spend a few weeks with them, observe.''

"What am I looking for?''

"I'm not quite sure,'' the boss said. "But I expect you will be, once you've seen it.''

3.

Lise had the pictures tacked up on the wall of her sewing room, above the pages she regularly cut out of *Harper's Bazar*. She loved to look at the sketches the artist had made of her huge white house with its half-dozen turrets and its numerous porches. "The Grandest House in Vermont,'' the caption said. It was, too; no one would deny it. Nice that the New York paper had recognized the fact.

She looked away from the clippings to the sheet of paper on her desk. It was the menu for a dinner party they were giving the following week. Such details were carefully arranged by Lise; her table was famous. So was her wardrobe. She copied the fashions depicted in her favorite magazine. Lise employed two local seamstresses, but she made the patterns and did all the cutting.

She was bent over a duplicate of a Worth gown when one of the maids arrived.

"Someone to see you, ma'am. It's a gent. Says his name's Joseph Villette.''

"Joseph . . . We haven't any relatives named Joseph.''

Jenny shrugged. "Shall I send him away?''

"No, put him in the drawing room. I'll be down in a moment."

Lise put away her sewing and checked her appearance in the mirror. She was almost forty-five, a grandmother, but she was as small and slim as she'd been when she trekked through the Canadian woods with Hugh. Nor was there any gray in her hair. She tugged once at her blue skirt, fluffed the collar of her white Gibson-girl shirtwaist, and descended the stairs.

Just before she entered the drawing room it occurred to her that the fellow might be a *Quebecois*. A Villette from Canada. What if he only spoke French? She didn't remember a word of it. One look at the strange young man reassured her that he was obviously an American.

"Hello, you must be Aunt Lise."

"I'm Lise Villette," she said. "I don't know about the title."

"I do." His smile was devastating. It made Lise want to smile back. "I'm Joseph Villette."

"So I heard. At least that's how my maid introduced you. But—" Her sentence was interrupted by Hugh's voice in the hall.

"Lise! I'm home. Where are you, darling?"

Lise stepped to the big double doors of the drawing room. "I'm in here. We have a guest. This young man says his name is Joseph Villette."

The years had made Hugh no taller, but they'd broadened him. He wasn't fat, but he'd become more than ever like a bull. Now he stood his ground and examined the stranger. "How's your name come to be Villette?" he asked.

"Maryann was my mother," Joseph said.

The senior Villette cocked his head and examined the lad. "Could be," he said at last. "Is she with you?"

"She died five years ago."

"Died," Hugh repeated. "She couldn't have been forty."

"Thirty-eight," Joseph said. "A short life but a merry one."

Hugh laughed. "I can believe it. Lise, why are we all standing here? Get someone to bring drinks. Let's go sit on the porch."

"What brings you to Vermont, Mr. Villette?" she asked when they were settled. The men had whiskey with plenty of ice. She had a lemonade. The boy took a long swallow and didn't answer. "After all these years, I mean," she prodded.

"Just passing through," he said, lowering his glass. "And please, call me Joseph, Aunt Lise."

"Right," Hugh said. "He's my nephew, darling. And I bet I know what brought you here, son. That story in the New York papers."

"It reminded me, that's all," Joseph admitted. "Mama spoke of you often. I've just never had the opportunity to come before. I must say, this isn't much like she described, though." He gestured at the elaborate house.

"No." Hugh laughed. "I bet it isn't. She tell you about the cabin? Papa's still out back?" Hugh was secure enough now to remember those things with humor, even with nostalgia.

"Yes," Joseph said. "All this is quite different. Big, too, just for the two of you, I mean."

"It's not just the two of us," Lise corrected. "Didn't you read the whole story? We've four children." She watched him carefully. Did he imagine there were no heirs to the Villette fortune? "Two daughters and two married sons. They and their wives and children live here, too. And there's Hugh's brother Jackie. He lives here when he's not in Brattleboro."

"He's bought into a hotel over there," Hugh explained. "You'll meet him later, though. He's here at the moment. You'll meet the whole family."

"I guess I forgot about the others," Joseph said easily. He flashed the bright smile again.

"Whitby Falls is changed, too," Hugh said. "It's a lot bigger than it was when Maryann left. More up-to-date. Got electric lights a few years back. I saw to that. Telephones, too. We're not the village hicks we were in the old days. Even have lots of visitors. Tourists, they call 'em."

Joseph turned his vivid blue gaze on his uncle. "Tourists?" His expression gave everything away.

"Sounds weird, huh?" Hugh chuckled. "I admit, we're not Niagara. But they do come. In summer mostly, to climb Herrick. A few to snowshoe in the winter. Then there are the geology fans. Professor types who come to study the slate and the granite and the marble."

"Is there a hotel?" Joseph asked.

"In Whitby Falls? Hell, no. They stay in Rutland and tour the valley by hired buggy. Fellow wants to make a living in these parts, he could do worse than open a livery stable." The senior Villette eyed his nephew speculatively.

"Interesting." Joseph rose and walked to the wrought-iron railing surrounding the porch. The town was spread out below him. "That's Main Street, isn't it? Which is the Whitby place, the one my mother always spoke of as the big house?"

"This is the big house now," Hugh said quietly. "Jason Whitby's dead. That was his house, that brick one with the white pillars in front."

"Who lives there?"

"Nobody. At least not often. The Whitby quarries are still operating. Old Lliam Murray manages them, but the family lives in New York. Some years they come for a visit. Patrick Whitby, that is, with his two kids. Andrea's not been back since the day she left. You know about that?"

Joseph shook his head.

"I'll tell you the details later, after supper. The short version is Andrea Whitby murdered my brother, your Uncle Riley, and got away with it. You should know the story; it's part of the family history. Why don't you stay for a few days? You'll find out lots of things."

"I'd like that, thanks." If Joseph was shocked by the mention of murder, it didn't show.

"That's settled, then," Hugh said expansively. "Last thing I told your mother before she left, she could always come home. Guess the same applies to her boy."

The dining-room table was enormous. Joseph took the place indicated, to the right of Lise, and made a swift head count. Thirteen, including himself.

"Fancy that," one of the women said with a titter. "We're thirteen tonight. Bad luck." She was a round-faced butterball of a woman, with elaborate blond curls and rather too much jewelry.

"Nonsense, Maisie," Lise said quickly. "In this house we make our own luck. This is Joseph Villette, Maryann's boy. Joseph, that's Maisie, Henry's wife."

The rest of the introductions were made. Laura and Jane, the Villette daughters, struck Joseph as the brightest of the lot. Certainly the prettiest. The daughters-in-law, Maisie and H.J.'s wife, Therese, were unremarkable in appearance, probably dull, too. He turned his attention to the men. There were three grandsons, two belonging to Henry, one to H.J. They were all under ten—nothing to know about them yet. Uncle Jackie was a well-meaning moron with a nervous laugh and a taste for hard liquor. Henry he disliked on sight; spoiled, self-indulgent, and tending to fat, just like his wife. H.J. was the only one with any possibilities. He looked like his father.

"You planning to stay in Vermont long?" H.J. asked halfway through the meal.

"Can't say for sure," Joseph said. He reached for the wine bottle and poured himself a refill.

"What brought you to these parts, Joseph? Saw that story in the papers, I'll bet," Henry said.

Joseph smiled artlessly in his cousin's direction. "I did read it, but as I told Uncle Hugh, it merely reminded me of all of you. Then I found myself nearby, so . . ."

"Know anything about slate?" the other man asked. "Ever been in a quarry?"

"Never. I'd be quite interested to see it. Perhaps you'll show me around. That is, if Uncle Hugh doesn't object."

"Object! Of course I don't. Henry, you take Joseph to the pits first thing tomorrow morning. Show him the whole place. Built it all from nothing, son. We're proud of it and don't give a damn who knows it."

Henry looked hard at his father. Joseph found something unnerving in the look, but he couldn't put a name to it. The meal continued, but it was left to the ladies to keep up the conversation.

Lise felt she had to say something, despite the fact that the stranger was beautiful and charming and Hugh obviously took pleasure in his visit. "We don't even know if he's Maryann's son," she said later in their bedroom. "He could be anyone."

"Of course he's Maryann's. He must be. Who else would know about her?"

"Why has he come? After all these years . . . The children didn't seem to like it."

Hugh tugged off his heavy boots and dropped them. They made only a dull thud on the thick carpet. "Of course not. They think he may be after some of what's theirs."

"Is he?" Lise asked quietly.

Hugh shrugged. "Maybe. He hasn't said anything yet. Looks prosperous enough."

"What does he do? Did you ask him?"

"He's a businessman, and he lives in New York; that's all he said."

"I don't know. It all seems very suspicious to me."

"Relax," Hugh said, putting an arm around her shoulders and bending over to kiss the top of her head. "There's no way he can hurt us, darling. And I don't think he wants to. After all, he's Maryann's boy. Far as I'm concerned, Joseph is welcome as long as he wants to stay."

"Does he look like Maryann? I only saw her those few days when we first got back. I don't remember. Were her eyes that color?"

"No. Maryann was no beauty. This lad's a regular lady-killer, and don't tell me you didn't notice." He grinned at his wife. "Still, he does remind me of her. Brown hair like hers, but it's more than that. Shape of his face, his smile. Little things. Jackie mentioned it, too."

"Jackie." Lise rolled her eyes heavenward. "Sometimes he makes me so mad. He asked me tonight if I thought this Joseph had Whitby blood. Imagine! He was practically foaming at the mouth."

Hugh crawled into the big bed and patted her place beside him. "Come here. And stop looking like the weight of the world's on your shoulders. I'll defuse Jackie. It's just that he's never gotten over Andrea Whitby going scot-free after he gave his evidence. You know that."

"What's it to do with Maryann's son?" She removed her thin cotton wrapper and lay down next to her husband.

Hugh ignored her question. "Do you want to?" he asked tenderly.

"Yes, please. But answer me. What's the trial to do with Joseph?"

Hugh reached over to the night table. "Crazy idea of his, that's all," he said while he fumbled in the drawer. "Jackie knows Maryann was Jason's woman."

Lise sat bolt upright. "You mean Joseph might be Jason's son?"

"He's not. Maryann told me so before she left. Swore she hadn't been with Jason for over a year. The night I dynamited Pa's still, she told me she didn't know whose kid she was having."

"Thank God!" Lise sighed and lay back. "Jason's son—that would be too much."

"Ready?" Hugh asked.

"Very much ready." She reached out and took the lighted cigarette he handed her, inhaled deeply, then blew out a stream of dark blue smoke. "I wonder if the maids smell it when they do the room in the morning," she said, giggling.

"Do you care?"

"Not about them. Not about the townspeople, either. I could make smoking a fashion among the ladies if I wanted to." She waved the scandalous cigarette in the air. "It's just the children. They aren't like we were, you know. They've had it too easy. All they think about is what people will say."

"Quite an operation," Joseph said at the end of the tour. "Biggest slate producers in Vermont, I'm told."

"Big enough," Henry agreed. "But I think we're at the limit. Not a hell of a lot more room to expand." He watched the newcomer out of the corner of his eye.

"Looks like there's plenty of land left," Joseph said. "What's the problem? No more slate?"

"Plenty more, probably. Leastwise that's what my father says. Nobody on this earth knows more about slate than he does. But the market's just got room for so much. There's only so many roofs you can make in any country."

Joseph grinned at him. "Ever been out of New England?"

Henry shook his head and turned away. Joseph could see the color rising in his neck.

"Pretty big country other side of these mountains," he said softly. "Pretty big world, if it comes to that."

"Maybe. We can't handle any more than we got on our plate right now."

Subtle as a sledgehammer, this lad. Joseph tried to keep his voice friendly and noncommittal. "Well, that's for you to say, isn't it? I wouldn't know."

"Right." Henry turned back to face his cousin. "You'd have had to be born and raised up here. Lived with the slate all your life. Then you'd know."

"What did Joseph think of the quarry?" Hugh asked his son later.

"What I expected. That it's big and profitable and he figures to get his share." Henry's voice betrayed both bitterness and fear.

"He say that?" Hugh asked.

"He didn't have to. What the hell do you think he came here for?"

Hugh rose from behind his desk and folded his arms. He looked as immovable as Herrick itself. "I don't know. But until I find out different, I believe he's come for a visit, just like he says. You believe that too, Henry. It'll be a lot better for you that way."

"I'm just trying to look out for all of us," Henry said.

"Leave that to me."

The boy got up and left the office. Hugh stared after him, then turned away with that mixture of anger and resignation he'd lived with since the business at Harvard.

Hugh came straight to the point when he and Joseph were alone later in the day. "My boys think you're interested in throwing in with us."

"I gathered as much. They don't like the idea, do they?"

"Doesn't matter a damn what they like. This is my quarry. I built it. If I say there's enough for one more, then there's enough."

"Thanks. But I'm not looking for work, Uncle Hugh. You can put their minds at rest. I have a job. Like I told you."

"What kind of a job?"

Joseph chuckled. "It's nothing you'd understand. I work for a man in New York. I'm just up here for a short holiday. Tell H.J. and Henry to stop worrying."

It was Hugh's turn to laugh. "No, I don't think I will. Let 'em worry a bit. Do 'em good. Keep 'em on their toes. Pair of 'em think it's all come down from heaven. Been told different all their lives, but that's still what they think."

For a moment Hugh remembered the icehouse and worried what Henry might do if he felt cornered. No problem, he decided. This Joseph could obviously take care of himself.

"What about the girls?" Joseph asked. "You going to take their husbands in when they marry?"

"If it looks like a good idea at the time, sure. Why not? But it may not work like that. Intellectuals, both Laura and Jane. Say they're going to be social workers, go help the immigrants in the slums. Sounds crazy to me, but their mother says I gotta let 'em try if they want."

"Aunt Lise seems a pretty special lady. She's probably right."

"More special than you can guess," Hugh told him. "And she's always right."

"That's laying a lot on her," Joseph said. "Nobody can be right always."

Hugh looked at him for a long moment. Finally, he said, "You stay as long as you like, son. Just ignore Henry and H.J. They'll get over being jealous. Specially when they find out they've nothing to worry about."

Joseph felt an unpleasant quiver somewhere deep in his gut. Hugh Villette was that rarity, an honest man. Joseph knew how dangerous that could be.

Three weeks later, his arms loaded with packages, Joseph stopped by the telegraph office in Rutland. He'd come to town to do a series of errands for his uncle.

"Let me help you, sir." The clerk hurried out from behind the counter. "Mr. Villette, isn't it? From New York?"

"That's right. Thank you." He watched the man deposit the bundles in the corner and return to his place. Such instant recognition always made Joseph nervous. It was a country trait, the mark of a small town. He wasn't used to it. In his line of work it could be a hazard. "I'd like to send a wire," he said.

"Sure thing, Mr. Villette. You just write out the message on this form here. I'll send it right away."

Joseph bent his head to the task, then pushed the paper across the counter. "You keep copies of these things?" he asked casually.

"Yes, sir! A whole week. Then we destroy them. Company figures if a customer wants to make an inquiry, he'll do it in seven days or not at all. I can hang on to this longer if you want." He looked like a puppy in his anxiety to please.

"No, that's all right. You can get rid of it right away, in fact. No chance I'll be making an inquiry."

The clerk nodded. "Just as you say, sir. Now, let me see if I've got this right." He read out the New York address.

"That's it," Joseph agreed.

"And the message is 'Material ready to be returned.' That the whole thing, sir?"

"Yes," Joseph said. "That's the whole thing."

*   *   *

"You're sure, Joseph?" The boss leaned back in his chair and drummed lightly on his desk.

"No, I'm not sure," Villette said. "It's a hunch."

"But you think there's a connection between Whitby Falls and the business in South Africa. It's stretching things, lad."

"Maybe. I won't know for sure until something more develops."

"And that could take months, maybe years."

"I won't give it full time," Villette said. "I'm suggesting that I'll keep an eye on things. Watch, between other assignments."

"Patience," the boss said, smiling. "Your great virtue, as I've always said. Very well, Joseph. If something does materialize, we'll want to have the biggest piece of the action, as our gambling friends say."

"All the action, sir." He grinned, and the perfect white teeth flashed. "I'm a Villette. Up in Whitby Falls it's my birthright to control all the action."

4.

Patsy's "regimen" was more or less complete by the end of the summer of 1896. "There!" her guide and guardian exclaimed one September morning. "Just look at yourself, exactly as I promised!"

It was by way of a graduation ceremony. They were on the sun deck that ran around the courtyard of Madam Frobisher's house in St. Moritz-bad. Patsy was stripped naked; la Frobisher wore extraordinary short pants like a little boy's, with a wisp of chiffon tied around her bosom. She would have been arrested immediately had she appeared in public. In fact, a great deal of what went on in her house, called Valkyrie, would have interested the police had they been admitted to the select circle of those who knew about the place. At first, Patsy had been terrified. Gradually, she had grown secure; ultimately she was amused.

An assortment of people came and went through the carved

oak door of Valkyrie. They came to consummate trysts, to pay secret gambling debts, perhaps to incur them. They came to involve Madam Frobisher's assistance in their perennial intrigues, their cataclysmic denouements or equally earthshaking preludes. They were those flawed superrich and titled of whom la Frobisher had spoken to Patsy the day she arrived, and the girl came to share Madam's evaluation. Interesting, like something exotic viewed in a zoo, but no part of reality.

Patsy had no desire to be like them, but her observations helped her to form a clear picture of who indeed she was. Madam Frobisher's regimen had done what Andrea had hoped it would do, stripped away the layers of fat behind which hid the real Patsy Whitby.

"I'm not bad, am I?" she asked shyly as she turned to examine her rear view. A long mirror reflected the courtyard garden as background to her nude form. "Still too much here, though." Patsy slapped her buttocks in disgust.

"Nonsense! You aren't a thin stick of a woman. No man really wants one like that, anyway."

Patsy turned to face her. "Is that what it's all about in the end? What a man wants?"

Madam Frobisher shrugged. "Depends. If a man is what you want, then that's what it's about." She narrowed her eyes and studied her charge. "Sometimes I wonder about you, *cherie*. All these months and you've expressed no interest in romance or amusement. Is it that men don't interest you? Girls, perhaps? I could arrange—"

"I've been concentrating on my regimen," Patsy interrupted. "Just as you told me to." There were things she'd never told Madam, despite their long talks. About Franco, about what he'd made her feel. It wasn't a painful memory, rather one that was too personal to share.

The older woman had a talent for knowing when to back off. She laughed lightly now. "Very well, I won't pry. But tell me, what next for you? Now that you're the beauty I promised you'd be."

"I'm not!"

"Hah! Don't contradict. I know more about beauty than you'll learn in a lifetime. That hair, that coloring . . . Step out of the sun," she admonished suddenly. "You're turning pink. Remember, ivory—that's your color. Ivory skin, black hair, black eyes. *Wunderbar!*"

She had never determined whether la Frobisher was French or German. Madam used both languages interchangeably with English. Perhaps she was Swiss. It didn't occur to Patsy to ask; she was not a woman one questioned. A woman who questioned, however. Sometimes relentlessly.

"You haven't told me what you plan to do next."

"I don't know. Go home to New York, I guess."

"Why?"

"I don't know," the girl said again. "It's just expected, I suppose. My parents are waiting for me."

"I had a letter from your mother the other day. She said you could stay as long as you wish. Why not spend the winter in St. Moritz? You've not had a real 'season' here yet. By the time you came in March, the best was over."

"But you said my course was finished—"

"With me, perhaps," the woman said. "I have done what I set out to do with your looks. But for you I think there is yet much to learn. Stay, Patsy." She reached out and touched the girl's alabaster shoulders. "Become comfortable with what you are, what you look like. Learn to see yourself, to feel yourself, as others do."

Patsy reached for a thin silk kimono. "What would I do here if I stayed?"

"As you've been doing mostly, except you don't need to take the waters anymore. But fresh air, exercise, and careful diet must be your constant companions, my dear, if the old Patsy is not to take over again. You could learn to ski."

"I couldn't! I watched a bit before the snows melted last spring. It's terrifying. Coming down the mountain with those things on your feet!"

Madam laughed. "It's magnificent. *Formidable!* And I know the very one to instruct you. He is beautiful. And he skis like a god. Just say you'll stay. I'll arrange everything else."

Patsy thought for a moment, then grinned and nodded.

In New York, Patrick and Andrea Whitby received, with relief and a pang of guilt, their daughter's letter announcing that she wished to spend the winter in St. Moritz.

"Is she all right, do you think?" Andrea asked anxiously. "She says so little."

"Madam Frobisher writes that Patsy has lost nearly forty

pounds, that she's beautiful," Patrick said. "She must be all right."

"Maybe it's all a lie. Maybe she just doesn't want us to know the whole thing's been a failure."

He shook his head. "I don't think so. Patsy's not the lying sort."

"What is this thing she says she's going to do? Skiing. I've never heard of it."

"Some Swiss sport. The Scandinavians do it, too. Slide down a mountain with boards strapped to your feet. Rather like sledding, but standing up."

"It sounds terribly dangerous. And not very ladylike."

He smiled slightly, but his eyes were grave. "Don't worry about it," he said. "She's happy, I think. And it's better if she isn't here right now."

Andrea sighed. "Yes, I thought of that right away. I must be an unnatural mother."

"No, just a realist. We'll have to go up to Vermont, love, and find out what's going on. We'll be bankrupt if we don't."

"I know what's going on." Her mouth became a tight, thin line when she spoke the name of the enemy. "Hugh Villette."

"I've told you before; it doesn't make sense."

"Yes, it does; he wants to punish me. He hates me. He's never forgiven the fact that I was acquitted."

"Good God, Andrea, it's twenty years! Why, after all this time? And why in such a petty, niggling way?"

"Because it's effective. We're almost bankrupt, as you just said. And he's bided his time, that's all. He's never forgotten."

"Neither have you," Patrick said softly. "You'll go to your grave feuding with the Villettes. I'll never understand that."

She didn't deny it.

At first, the letters from Lliam Murray hadn't been alarming. He was an old man, seventy-nine his last birthday. It was natural that he found the younger generation incomprehensible. "Hooligans and vandals," he'd written. "That's all the youth of today are. Think of nothing but how to make mischief. Steal anything that's not nailed down. I've had to post a night watchman at the quarry. First time in over forty years. You can't really afford to pay his wages, but there's no choice."

Patrick and Andrea had agreed the new employee was necessary and that his salary made an uncomfortable bite into their dwindling resources. It wasn't so much that they earned less from the quarry; it was just that they earned no more than they had a decade earlier. Murray ran the Whitby pits as Jason had run them; no changes, no modernization. Everything else was more expensive; only their income remained the same.

"Maybe Lliam's just too old to go on managing the quarry," Patrick had said. "And maybe he's imagining all these losses and pilferings."

"No," Andrea had insisted. "His bookkeeping is as accurate as ever. I've checked and rechecked. And he's thoroughly honest."

"I didn't say he wasn't. Only old. Never mind," he'd added. "We'll just tighten our belts a bit."

But it hadn't helped. There was no new business, and the losses magnified. The vandals, if such they were, moved from stealing tools and equipment to stealing the actual slate. "A load of five squares was in the yard," Murray wrote in late September, his handwriting spidery with rage. "Best-quality roofing tiles, intended for a customer in Chicago. When we came to work this morning, they were gone. Just disappeared into thin air. I've questioned Wolf, the night watchman, and everyone else. No one can explain it. No one saw a thing. . . ."

They were living on $250 a month these days. Profits were disappearing into the column marked miscellaneous expenses. It wasn't enough; with Eddie at Princeton, the upkeep of the apartment on Fifth Avenue, Patsy's allowance in Switzerland . . . It wasn't nearly enough.

A few weeks before Christmas, Patrick said, "It's now or never, love. Either we go up there and see if we can solve it, or we go under. What do you want to do?"

"I'll pack this afternoon," she said quietly.

Lliam Murray sent his buggy to meet them at the depot in Rutland. Then he watched it roll up Main Street and stop before the big house, Jason Whitby's house.

"Sorry about the way things are," he said. "I had a couple of women in to clean things up. They did the best they could."

"Yes, it's not your fault." Andrea stretched a gloved hand toward the faded wallpaper. Once it had been flocked red velvet; now it was colorless and showed a damp, uneven stain behind the tarnished brass of the mirror. She pulled her hand back, as if the stain might contaminate her. "Is Nelly still around?"

"Old Nelly Jones? She's been dead some twelve years. I thought you knew. I wrote you about it. We, the company, that is, paid for the funeral."

"I must have forgotten." Her voice was hollow, lifeless. As if the town and the house drained her vitality.

"You're tired," Patrick said. "Go up and lie down for a bit. You can see Lliam later."

"I told them to ready your old room," Murray said. "The Chinese bedroom. Is that all right?"

"It's fine, Lliam, thank you. Come back this evening. We'll talk then." She didn't wait for an answer but started slowly climbing the stairs. Patrick watched her for a moment, shot Murray a look of apology, then followed his wife.

They were upstairs when they heard the old lawyer let himself out. Andrea paused by the door to her mother's room, put her hand on the doorknob, but didn't turn it. Eventually, she walked on. When she came to the Chinese bedroom, she stopped. "You open it," she said to Patrick. "I can't."

"There are no ghosts, love," he said softly.

"Aren't there?" she asked.

5.

Eddie came up from Princeton for Christmas. He arrived on the twentieth, after having spent the first few days of his holiday with friends in New York. Initially, he was his usual cheerful self. By Christmas Eve he'd grown moody.

"What in hell are we doing in this place?" he asked his father.

"You don't like it?"

"It oppresses me. And mother looks like a ghost."

"You used to like it when you were little," Patrick said, ignoring the comment about Andrea.

"That was in summer, and as you said, I was little."

"Is it so different?"

"Why are we here?" Eddie asked again. "And why is Patsy still in Switzerland? What's going on, Dad?"

"Patsy's learning to ski. She's lost a lot of weight. She's recovering from that unfortunate business in Italy."

Eddie grinned for the first time in days. "Hard to think of Patsy on skis. Old lumps and bumps schussing down the slopes."

"She's not lumps and bumps anymore, I hear. And what's schussing? You know something of the sport?"

"Couple of chaps I know from Dartmouth told me it's caught on there. One of the foreign students introduced it, a Swedish fellow. Schussing is some kind of maneuver; I couldn't say what."

"Maybe you should learn to ski, too, while you're here." He glanced out the window. "God knows there's snow enough."

"I'm not interested in skiing, Dad, or in the country life. I repeat my first and second question. What are we doing here? What's going on?"

"There's trouble at the quarry."

"Sounds like a line from a bad melodrama. 'There's trouble at the mill, sir!' " Eddie rose and poured himself a brandy.

"It's not fiction, unfortunately," Patrick said. "It's fact. Things are disappearing with depressing regularity."

"Petty thievery? A few light-fingered workers are making us spend Christmas in the wilderness?" He sounded both incredulous and affronted.

"I'm not sure it's petty. Whole shipments of slate have disappeared. It's very expensive. We can't absorb that kind of loss."

The boy downed his drink and leaned back, hands folded behind his head, the picture of Ivy League chic in tweed knickers and a heavy beige pullover with a rolled neck. Patrick found the costume somehow inappropriate. So, too, his son's words. "I suggest, *Pater*, that you rid yourself of that senile old fool Murray and employ a foreman who knows how to deal with the laboring class."

"Lliam Murray has served us well. And besides, it's not that simple. The stealing is organized, planned. And it's increasing despite our having two night watchmen on duty now. I thought perhaps you might be able to help solve it."

"Me! What can I do? I don't know a thing about the quarry."

"You might care to learn. You live off the proceeds." Patrick saw the look in Eddie's eyes change from astonishment to anger, but he didn't wait for a retort. "A lot of the workers are lads around your age. I thought you might try to make friends. See what you could pick up."

"That's absurd. I'd have nothing to say to a laborer. And as for living off the quarry, that seems to me more your doing than mine."

Andrea came into the drawing room just then. "I thought we'd dine at nine this evening," she said brightly. "A bit late because it's Christmas Eve. Will that spoil any plans for you, darling?" She looked fondly at her son.

"I have no plans."

She picked up the waves of bitterness and anger eddying between the two men, fluttered her hands a moment as if to fend them off. The brief effort at ordinary mistress-of-the-household concerns died. "Sorry to interrupt." Deflated, she turned to go.

There was a sudden jangle of bells from beyond the window. Eddie rose to investigate. "There's a sleigh out there. An enormous one, filled with stuff. Looks like presents."

"The Villettes," Patrick said. "Delivering gifts to the local children."

"Ah, I see," Eddie said softly. "The beneficent squire placating the serfs. And what of us? Don't the workers in the Whitby quarry receive gifts?"

"They get a bonus," his father said. "In their pay packets."

"Nice touch the slate king's added." Eddie was still staring out the window. "A bit of personal involvement. That's old Hugh himself driving the sleigh. And a couple of his sons, I warrant. I recognize Henry, not the other one."

Andrea hadn't moved. Her hands were folded, and she was staring at the floor. "It's not his idea. In the old days my father and I used to do it. The sleigh was decorated with greens and bells, and I carried a red lantern.''

"Well, Mother, it looks as if you've passed on the torch. In a manner of speaking.'' He let the curtain fall back and turned away. Patrick took his son's place at the window.

"That is Henry with Hugh. I don't know the other. It's not H.J. Must be that nephew I keep hearing about. Joseph Villette. Lliam says he's been coming frequently this past year.''

Andrea's head jerked. "What nephew? You never told me about any nephew.''

"It's not important,'' her husabnd said quickly. "They say he's Maryann's boy.''

"Maryann . . .'' She gagged on the word and turned and ran from the room.

Eddie stared after her. "What was that all about?''

"It's a long story.'' Patrick sighed. "And an old one. It doesn't matter. Forget it.'' Their earlier anger was gone, stifled by the dead stillness of the house that seemed a tomb despite the presence of the living.

In the corner the fresh green of the Christmas tree was a useless reproach to the shabbiness everywhere else.

Eddie left two days later. He'd had an invitation to join some friends at a house party on Maryland's eastern shore, and his parents made no protest at his accepting it.

"He hates Whitby Falls, doesn't he?'' Andrea said.

"He hates the situation,'' Patrick amended. "The way we are just now. And he doesn't understand about the quarry.''

"No, how could he?''

"Indeed. That's our doing, you know. We've raised him in ignorance of his history. The worst kind of ignorance, the sort that thinks it's informed.''

Andrea didn't reply, but she did think about it. She went for a walk, perhaps the third time she'd ventured from the house since their arrival five weeks earlier, and she thought about everything. They had come to Whitby Falls to investigate a crisis that was ruining them, but all they'd really done was talk to Lliam Murray and to each other. Something they could have accomplished without traveling two hundred miles.

It was the house, the town itself that froze them, diffused their sense of purpose, enlarged their inadequacies. Both she and Patrick saw their failed past in that place. Now they were paralyzed by fear and a feeling of hopelessness.

Andrea stared at her pointed boots, at the scuffly marks they made as she plodded across the new-fallen snow. She turned to examine the trail of such marks she'd left behind her and found herself looking back at the village. From that vantage point it looked much the same as it always had, a green and white place, cupped in a declivity of soaring pines and towering Herrick Mountain. At her back she sensed something alien, something new. She whirled around.

The Villette house faced her. She had not realized she was walking toward it, had not looked up. Patrick had told her it was there. Years before, after one of his summer visits with the children, he'd reported that Hugh had finally finished building his house. Perhaps she had deliberately avoided seeing it until then. She could do so no longer.

Andrea let her eye wander over the gables and turrets, the heavy wrought-iron fences that edged each balcony and porch. A part of her, the part that wasn't aching and sore from the reopening of so many old wounds, understood and smiled. The thing was a rude and vulgar statement, something like Maggie Hoyt might have said in the old days. "Up yours!"

"Do you like it?" a woman's voice asked. "I don't think you've ever seen it before."

Lise Villette came up beside her. In the years when they had both lived there, when Andrea was still queen and Lise the pretender, they had spoken only when circumstances forced them to. And never with the tone of easy friendliness Lise adopted now. "Will you come in for a cup of coffee? Or tea, if you prefer."

"No, I won't come in." Andrea couldn't make herself say thank you.

Lise had her arms filled with bundles. She shifted them, but didn't make a move to pass the other woman on the path leading to the front door. "I heard you were in town. I thought about calling. It didn't seem possible somehow. But I'm glad you did."

"I didn't. I wasn't coming to see you. I just walked here by accident." It was important to Andrea that Lise understand that.

"We'd not die from it, you know," Lise said softly. "We could bury the hatchet."

"I don't think so."

Lise shrugged. The motion was barely visible beneath the fur collar of her heavy and elegant coat. It was as smart a garment as Andrea's, looking like it, too, might have come from a New York shop. Only Andrea wore a fur hat as well, a Russian toque that framed her face. Lise was bareheaded despite the cold. Her curls seemed to crackle with the static in the thin, sharp air. "We've heard about your trouble," she said. "I'm sorry. Maybe there's something we can do—"

"You're sorry!" The audacity of the comment took Andrea by surprise, more than the friendly invitation had done. "Isn't that kind. Well, when you're sorry enough, perhaps you'll end this vicious and vindictive campaign!" She shoved past the other woman and walked away without looking back.

Hugh came that same night. He knocked with his fist, making a demanding summons of the act. When Patrick opened the door, Hugh pushed him aside and stepped into the hall. "I want to talk to both of you. Get your wife."

"Who are you to give orders around here!"

"Don't be a fool." Villette's voice was harsher than Whitby's. Patrick still had that trace of an Irish brogue that mitigated against imperiousness. "Get Andrea. And let's go where folks outside can't hear every word."

Andrea came into the hall in response to the shouting, and froze. "What are you doing here?"

"I came to say something to you two. I'll say it here or in there." He nodded toward the drawing room. "Suit yourselves."

Patrick opened the door to the once-gracious room and waited until his wife and Villette had gone inside before following them and pulling it closed. He wondered for a moment if he should offer Villette a drink.

Andrea banished any social considerations. "Say what you want to say and get out of my house," she whispered through clenched teeth.

"That suits me," Villette said. "Lise told me about meeting you this afternoon."

Patrick looked startled. Andrea hadn't mentioned such a meeting to him.

"She told me what you said," Villette continued. "I just

came down here to tell you you're wrong. I'm not a crook. I don't care to be called a thief in my own town.''

''Your town!'' Andrea's perfectly formed mouth opened wide on the words. ''Your town . . .''

''Mine,'' Villette repeated. ''I made it mine, Andrea. Myself. I wasn't born to it, didn't get it as a gift, didn't turn my back on it and run away. It's mine, all right. You ask anybody in Whitby Falls; they'll tell you the same thing.''

Patrick watched his wife's beautiful, tortured face. He wanted to say something, to protect her, but couldn't. It was between Hugh and Andrea, the legacy of the years they'd shared in this place before Patrick knew either of them.

''Get out,'' Andrea said.

Hugh turned to go. Patrick stopped him. ''This business, the losses we've been having. If you're not behind it, who is? Has the same thing been happening in your quarry?''

Villette shook his head. ''It couldn't. Me and my boys, we run the place. Don't have somebody else do it for us. You're fools, both of you. The way you've done things all these years, it was bound to bring trouble.''

''Lliam Murray's honest,'' Patrick said.

''Never said he wasn't,'' Hugh answered. ''Old-fashioned, stuck in his ways, no imagination, but Murray is honest.'' He had his hand on the doorknob when he looked once more at the Whitbys. ''You think about it, it's crazy to suspect me. In a few more years, I'll have the handful of customers you got left. Because I quarry better slate and I do it faster and cheaper. I don't need to steal from you, and I don't need to murder anybody.'' He looked directly at Andrea. ''All I gotta do is wait and you'll give me your pits and your land. Just like Jason did in the first place. Whether he wanted to or not.''

On the first Wednesday of 1896, Patrick looked up from his makeshift desk in the Chinese bedroom to where his wife was lying on a faded chaise longue that used to be blue velvet. By mutual and unspoken consent they never used the study. They seemed to spend most of their days right there in the bedroom.

''I can't make the figures come out any different,'' Patrick said. He'd taken over the job of controlling the family finances only two months before, when Andrea said she was too tired to go on doing what she'd always done. "Maybe you should check them over," he added.

"No need. My result would be as bleak as yours, I'm sure. What do you suggest we do?"

"If we want to pay Eddie's tuition for this term and continue Patsy's allowance, there's only one thing to do. We have to give up the apartment in New York."

"Stay here, you mean? In this house, in Whitby Falls?"

"For the time being, yes. Just until things get straightened out."

"Do it, then," she said, and turned her face to the wall.

Chapter Ten

1.

Joseph and Hugh had achieved a slightly off-balance closeness. At first, Hugh felt guilty about his affection for his nephew. He knew it was born of the disappointment he felt in his sons. After a while, he relaxed and allowed himself to take half-forgotten dreams out of storage. Joseph became part of them. He was a young man to share things with, to trust. And he was kin. Not a son, of course, but the next best thing.

There were weaknesses in the bond, hollow places beneath the taut surface, but Hugh was unaware of them. They were created by things unsaid, unexplained, sometimes lied about. Only Joseph knew about those.

"What do you actually do, for God's sake?" Hugh had demanded one day when the relationship was about three months old. "Where do you go when you're not here?"

The aquamarine eyes had crinkled at the corners; the appealing grin had flashed. "I buy cheap and sell dear. I'm a middle man."

"Sounds crooked."

"Maybe. In New York, Rome, London—the kinds of places I go when I'm not here—everyone's a little crooked."

Hugh had laughed. "Okay. I'll buy that. Why do you keep coming up here, to this backwater? Sounds like you lead a pretty exciting life in all those big cities."

"Depends on how you see it. I come because of you," he'd added in a low voice that lacked its usual mocking edge. "Aunt Lise, all of you. You're the only family I have."

After that day the subject of what Joseph did when he wasn't in Whitby Falls was not discussed. Hugh knew his sons were resentful, and he watched Henry with unease, but nothing seemed to happen. Once or twice Lise was on the verge of uttering a warning, but he never let her speak.

Some five months later, in February of 1897, Joseph himself reopened the subject. "What do you think of this Klondike business?" he asked while he and Hugh were riding to Rutland. "Sounds like it's for real. Might be a chance to earn a dollar or two."

Hugh guided the horses around a snowdrift that nearly blocked the road. "Men have been chasing gold since Solomon's day. Most don't find any. You thinking of going up there?"

"Not to prospect. To investigate, maybe."

"What the hell's that mean? What are you going to buy cheap and sell dear in the Yukon? If they've got gold, nobody's going to sell it for less than the most he can get."

"True," Joseph agreed. "I just meant that where there's activity, the kind that generates money, there are always hangers-on, grafters, con men." He looked sideways at his uncle, wondering how much of what he'd said had been understood.

Hugh was oblivious to the scrutiny. "I was in the far north for a while, way up in Canada. It's a pretty bleak place. The Yukon must be worse."

"Some would say the same of Vermont."

"I guess they would. They're crazy. Cold here and plenty of snow, but it's different. Green, alive, beautiful."

"You really love this place, don't you?"

"Yeah," Hugh said without embarrassment, "I do."

"You think it possible speculators might move in here? Investors? Middle men?"

"What the hell for? There's no gold in Vermont."

As they approached Rutland, the sounds of the busy town made it harder to talk. "Natural resources, though," Joseph said over the increasing din. "Marble, granite, slate . . . maybe other things."

"They're too late," Hugh half shouted. "Me and the rest of us natives, we already own it all."

Joseph mentally kicked himself. His timing had been bad. He'd intended to bring the discussion to that point before they got to town. Now he didn't have an opportunity to probe what his uncle knew of the trouble at the Whitby quarry.

In New York a few days later, he told the boss, "Things are coming to a head a lot faster than I thought they would. The Whitbys were softer than I realized. It didn't take much pressure to bring them to the edge. A move will have to be made soon.''

"We shall see," the boss said enigmatically. "At least you shall, I have no doubt.''

"Yes," Joseph said. The word was sour in his mouth. He'd grown to dislike this operation and its ramifications. "I may do more.''

The boss shook his head. Beneath his chin, little rolls of fat wobbled with the effort. "No, Joseph, you will do nothing to alter things, not yet. It's too soon; you know that.''

Joseph didn't answer. The older man folded his pudgy hands across his protruding belly. "There's a small matter I wish you to take care of in the meantime. It will take you to Europe, but only for a month or six weeks, maybe less.''

"It's a delicate time. I shouldn't leave just now.''

"Only a matter of weeks," the boss repeated. "You sail tomorrow.''

Patsy had become a good skier, better than four months of lessons warranted. It was because she discovered in herself a wholly unexpected taste for danger. With the shedding of her excess weight she had developed an awareness of her physical self, and of the excitement of pitting that against the odds.

"You are mad," Diego told her when she skidded to a stop beside him at the bottom of the Zestert run. "You take crazy chances.''

"I like it." She laughed and dusted the powdery snow from her wine-colored ski skirt. It wasn't a skirt, really; it had a seam up the middle in imitation of a man's trousers, but it was full enough so that the seam didn't show.

Diego knew it was pointless to argue with her, just as he'd almost given up trying to arouse her romantic interests. This American girl knew her own mind. "Come," he said. "We'll have some lunch at Frau Gertl's.''

Diego took both pairs of skis over his shoulder and trudged off toward the little restaurant in the village. Patsy walked beside him, carrying their poles and making abstract patterns in the snow with their sharp tips.

Frau Gertl's was filled with men and women flushed with sun and cold and exhilaration, noisy with their laughter, and redolent with the odor of heavy food meant to ward off the chill of winter. Patsy ordered a small portion of bread and cheese and drank only one tiny glass of wine. Diego waded through a heaping plate of fried potatoes and sliced veal in a cream sauce, then waited until the smiling waitress had refilled his plate before beginning to eat again. He was from the Ticino, in many ways more Italian than Swiss; he drank wine, not beer. A huge jug of it disappeared with his meal. He was a boring luncheon companion, too busy gorging to talk.

Patsy's only interest in Diego was in his ability as a ski instructor. In the morning, before he was logy with food, he was a good one. She found his other attentions only mildly amusing. It was fun to measure her new appearance against the admiration in his eyes, but not exciting. Diego would view any woman as a challenge. The glances she received from other men in St. Moritz were better confirmation of what she had become. Patsy had finally accepted the truth that she could get a man if she wanted one.

She was thinking of that when she heard the distinctly American voice behind her. The familiar accent stood out among the babble of sound. She wanted to turn around and see who he was, and she had decided to drop her napkin as an excuse to do so when the voice moved closer.

Three men sidled by their table, deep in discussion, paying no attention to her or to anyone else. She spotted the American quickly. He was shockingly handsome, with the most extraordinary greenish blue eyes. They didn't focus on her. She wished they had.

"Take me home, Diego," she said suddenly when the strangers had left the restaurant.

"Now?" he asked in surprise. "I've not had my dessert yet." He was staring at a display of tortes and gateaux heavy with whipped cream.

"Please," she said. "I'm very tired suddenly, and I have a headache."

He sighed and paid the bill. The sum would appear on Patsy's account later. Weekly, Diego settled that account with Madam Frobisher; Patsy, in turn, paid her hostess. The ski instructor preferred it thus. He didn't wish to stain his relationship with his pupil by discussing money. Now he decided to include the price of a helping of kirschwasser torte in that day's expenses. There should be some justice for not having the opportunity to eat it.

At the door to Valkyrie she bade him good-bye, briskly, with no time wasted in thanks or plans.

"I'll see you tomorrow," he said.

"No," Patsy said. "I'm through with skiing lessons, Diego. I'm sure you'll find another pupil quite quickly." She didn't wait for his reaction.

Inside, she went directly to la Frobisher's room and knocked on the door. Madam was reclining on a satin sofa, a chamomile compress over her eyes. "Madam," Patsy said without preamble. "I've decided to go home. Right away."

"The season isn't over, Patsy," the woman said lazily, taking deep breaths between the words, reluctant to interrupt her own beauty regimen to talk with her charge. "Why be in such a hurry?"

"I saw a man today. At Frau Gertl's. A truly beautiful man. He was an American."

Madam Frobisher sat bolt upright and caught the compress as it fell. "You must be mad. How can you find him in America? It's a big country, child." She was laughing as she spoke.

"Of course I don't think I can find him. Anyway, for all I know, he has a wife and ten children. It isn't that. It's just that hearing him speak made me terribly homesick. I've been away almost two years. I'll be twenty in April. I shall grow old in Europe if I don't go home right away!"

"You are mad. And charming. Very well, *cherie*. I will make the arrangements."

She knew her parents were in Vermont; they'd written her about it. But until Patrick met her at the dock and they shared the long train ride to Rutland, she didn't know why or for how long.

He hadn't intended to tell Patsy much. With Eddie he'd tried the direct approach and failed. Moreover, when Patrick first saw her sweeping down the gangplank of the *Queen Charlotte*, he didn't recognize her. He spent the first hour in her company convincing himself that this dark-haired little sprite was truly his daughter.

Those big black eyes with the long curly lashes must have been there all along, only hidden by rolls of flesh. And the mobile, plummy mouth, that was just like Andrea's. How come he'd never noticed it before?

"You look marvelous," he said in tones of wonderment. "You're beautiful."

"I know," she answered with a grin. "Isn't it great?" She twirled to show off her figure, displayed in an emerald velvet traveling suit with a tightly nipped waist and a slim skirt swept back into a bustle.

"And you're happy," he added. "That will cheer your mother no end. It cheers me."

Patsy narrowed her eyes and studied her father as carefully as he was studying her. "Why do you need cheering, Daddy?" she asked. "The letter you wrote about the move to Whitby Falls didn't explain much. What's happening?"

So he filled the hours of the journey with details of the increasing losses at the quarry, her mother's conviction that Hugh Villette was behind it all, his disbelief of that easy explanation.

"Why is Mama so convinced it's the Villettes?" she asked after they changed trains at Troy. "If things are as you say, he has no reason to steal from us."

Eddie would have said, "steal from you." Patrick began to believe he'd found an ally. "Your mother's feud with the Villettes is long-standing," he said quietly. "I've told you some of that."

"The trial, you mean? The man who died?"

"Riley Villette, Hugh's brother. Yes, and other things."

The set of his mouth indicated he wouldn't say more. Patsy tried another approach. "What are you accomplishing by being on the scene of the crime, as it were? Doesn't that make it even harder for Mama?"

"Yes. It does. And we've accomplished little."

"Why, then?"

He hesitated. "It's . . . an economy. Seemed wise right now."

She cocked her head and stared at him. "Daddy, are we broke?"

He smiled wryly at her use of the modern, rather vulgar word. Patsy wasn't so much changed after all. "I think you might say so, lass," he admitted. "Not bankrupt yet but nearly."

"Why didn't you tell me before this?" she demanded indignantly. "Why did you let me go on frittering away money in Switzerland! I should have been home months ago!''

"Lower your voice." He lowered his own to make the point. "We didn't want anything to affect you or Eddie. We still don't want that."

"Where is he?"

"Eddie? At Princeton, naturally."

"Does he know about all this trouble?"

"A little," Patrick admitted. His daughter's interrogation was making him uncomfortable.

Patsy spent the rest of the journey staring out the window in silence. Schemes and plans raced through her mind as swiftly as the scenery raced by outside the train.

2.

An hour after they arrived Patsy contrived a time alone with her mother. "What are we going to do about all these difficulties?"

"I don't know what you're bothering your head about, darling. Daddy and I will manage everything." Andrea's tone was bright, almost gay. She was still reeling with the effect of seeing her daughter. Patsy wasn't just pretty; she was distinctive, extraordinary. There was about her a sense of exquisite wonderment.

"Don't patronize me, Mother."

"But I'm not!"

"You are," the girl insisted softly. "It's because you want to protect me. I know that. I don't want to be protected. I want to help."

Andrea's gaiety evaporated. "I'm afraid there's nothing we can do. He's won."

"Mr. Villette, you mean?"

"Yes, Hugh Villette."

"Daddy doesn't believe he's behind it. From what he says, neither do I."

"From what who says?" For a moment Andrea thought

that Patsy had somehow actually spoken with Hugh. "Do you mean your father or—"

"Daddy, yes."

Andrea sighed. "Your father isn't particularly worldly. He doesn't understand people like the Villettes."

"He understands more than you give him credit for," Patsy said.

"Perhaps. That changes nothing."

"But something must change. Surely you see that."

"We can carry on here. It's much cheaper than living in New York."

Patsy knew then how thoroughly her mother had accepted defeat. "All these years, you refused even to visit this place. Now you're willing to live here."

"Not willing," Andrea said with a wry smile.

"Well, I'm not giving in so easily."

Andrea took her hand. "Don't bother about it, darling. It's not your problem."

The girl leaned forward and kissed her mother. "Get some rest," was all she said. "You look tired."

The room that had once been Andrea's was now Patsy's. The dimity and rosebuds had faded, but for Patsy it was pleasantly familiar, the room she had slept in on every visit to Whitby Falls. She concentrated on the problems at hand.

It was the beginning of March, still winter in Vermont, but with a subliminal promise of spring. And Easter was early this year, the first Sunday in April. Eddie would be through with classes in a few weeks. They'd told her he was going to spend his holiday with friends in Maryland. She wrote a long letter to convince him otherwise.

". . . The short of it," she ended, "is that Mother and Daddy need you right now. I do, too." She signed it and found an envelope and slipped out of the house to the little post office tucked in the back of Anderson's General Store. When she was little, she had gone there clutching her penny and the letter she had written to Mama home in New York.

It was one of her strongest memories. In those days Whitby Falls had seemed a place that existed only in her imagination. It didn't change from year to year, summer to summer. Perhaps the town was real only when she and her brother and father came to visit.

For a moment she had that same silly notion again. Anderson's was unchanged: Huge wheels of cheese, endless barrels filled with pickles and salt fish and crackers, and behind the counter, Phoebe Anderson, looking as ancient as she always had. Patsy would have sworn the sweater she was knitting was the same one she'd been working on ten years before.

"I'd like a three-penny stamp, please."

The old woman grunted and finished her stitch before she laid aside the knitting and shuffled to the drawer in the back. She unlocked it, pushed the tiny square of paper toward the girl, and watched while she affixed the postage to her letter. Phoebe's rheumy old eyes still missed nothing. "Mr. Edgar Whitby, Witherspoon Hall, Princeton University," she read. She leaned forward and studied her customer. "I'll be blowed," she said suddenly. "You're Patsy Whitby, ain't you?"

"Yes. How are you, Mrs. Anderson?"

"Fine 'cept for my rheumatism. Why didn't you say who you was?"

"I didn't think you'd remember me."

"Jason Whitby's grandchild. Course I'd remember. Never thought you'd grow up to look like you do, though," she said bluntly.

Patsy giggled. "Neither did I."

Phoebe let this peculiar response pass unchallenged. "Heared you was in Europe. Didn't 'spect to see you back here. You married?"

"No." Patsy smiled again. The people of Vermont were unchanged, too.

"Smart, maybe. Men is trouble. They die, and you gotta go on and do it all yourself. How long you staying?"

Patsy bit her lip to suppress a giggle. "I'm not sure," she said. "My parents are here."

"Yes, I know." The old woman frowned. "Not 'cause they want to be; I know that, too. Running a place like this, you know everything."

Patsy recognized an opportunity. She leaned on the counter and looked intently at the woman. "Mrs. Anderson, do you know what's behind the trouble at our quarry?" The direct question was just as a native Vermonter would have asked it.

"Can't say for sure," Phoebe answered without hesitation.

"If I did, I'd tell your pa. I always liked him despite him bein' a foreigner. Nice lad, Patrick." To her, Patrick was still a lad.

"But you suspect something, someone . . ." Patsy pressed.

This time Phoebe didn't answer right away. She pursed her lips, walked slowly back to her chair with its threadbare cretonne cushions, and picked up her knitting. "There's lots behind lots in Whitby Falls," she said enigmatically.

"I don't understand." Patsy followed the old woman the length of the shop and perched on the edge of a pickle barrel near Phoebe's chair. "I'd like to understand, Mrs. Anderson. Will you help me?"

Phoebe finished the row she was knitting, moved the yarn to her other hand, and started a new one. Neither she nor the girl said anything for a while. Finally, she spoke, more to herself than to her questioner. "City folks think everything's simple in a little town like this. You can see it on their faces when they come to visit. Lots of 'em come now. Pass through, look at everything, poke their noses into everything. But they don't see it for real. Not like it truly is."

"How is it?" Patsy asked softly, unwilling to disturb the flow of talk but reluctant to let it get too far from her concerns.

"Hard," Phoebe said. "Real hard sometimes. Folks die. Some die early, hard, like I said. Your grandpa's first wife— Rachel was her name. She hung herself. Right in the kitchen at the big house." She looked up and stared at Patsy. "Anyone ever tell you that?"

Patsy shook her head. She wanted to mention that other hard death, the one she did know about. She wanted to say "Riley Villette" and see what response that would elicit. She was just working up the courage to do it when the bell on the front door jangled and a man entered. In the dark store, she couldn't see who it was.

"Afternoon, Mrs. Anderson," he said cheerfully. "My aunt sent me to fetch some sugar."

Patsy knew the voice, but at first she couldn't tell from where. Then he moved closer, and she caught her breath in shock.

"Help yourself," Phoebe said, nodding her head toward the sugar barrel. "You know where everything is. This here's young Patsy Whitby. Just come home from Europe."

"Hello." He turned to her, and the aquamarine eyes were more startling than she remembered. "I'm Joseph Villette," he said easily. "Hugh Villette's my uncle."

"I'm Patsy Whitby." She thought she'd stammered, and she hated herself for it.

"I know," he answered, smiling. "Mrs. Anderson just said that. First of the fabled Whitbys I've ever actually spoken to. I'm impressed."

His offhand charm suddenly made her angry. She was angry, too, that he'd chosen to arrive at the moment when she might have learned something. "I was just going," she said, and stood up. The top of her head barely reached his shoulder. She adjusted the woolen shawl she was wearing and started for the door. "Thank you for the visit, Mrs. Anderson. I'll call again soon."

Outside, the sun was blinding after the dim shop. It reflected glittering gold off the pristine white snow. She fumbled in her bag for the dark glasses. They were as useful here as they were in St. Moritz.

"Don't put those on," a voice said at her elbow. "I haven't had a good look at your eyes yet."

"My eyes are none of your affair, Mr. Villette."

"Maybe," he said. "They're beautiful nonetheless."

"So are yours," she said boldly. It offended her to play the shy flirt with this man. The absurd coincidence of meeting him here was an affront. "That hardly makes us friends," she said brusquely. "Good afternoon."

She tried to push past him, but he put out a hand to stop her. His touch, though feather light, restrained her. "Please, don't rush away. I know we're supposed to be blood enemies. Some old Montague and Capulet drama. It's all rather silly, don't you think? Come have a coffee with me. Please."

"It's not my old feud," she said. "I never said it was. But I doubt that your aunt and uncle would welcome me to their home."

"I expect they would, but I didn't mean that. Perhaps you don't know there's an ice cream parlor just down the road. Before you get to the old Sills place."

"You seem to know Whitby Falls well."

"I've been coming a lot this past year."

"It's too cold for ice cream."

"I agree. That's why I said coffee."

*   *   *

They ordered hot chocolate instead. Patsy told the man behind the soda fountain to leave the whipped cream off hers. Joseph asked for a double helping.

"In New York," he said, "I never think of drinking hot chocolate. Here it's delicious."

"You live in New York?"

"Sometimes. You grew up there, didn't you? Upper Fifth, across from the park."

"You seem to know a lot about me."

"Not as much as I'd like to know." The crinkles at the corners of his eyes danced.

"Are you flirting with me, Mr. Villette?"

"Of course. And my name is Joseph."

She couldn't resist an opportunity to take some of the sureness out of him. "You weren't in New York in the middle of February. Did you enjoy St. Moritz?"

He looked not just startled but furious. The flashing eyes became icy. "What do you know about St. Moritz?"

"A great deal," she said, smiling.

He was silent for a moment. When he spoke, his tone was menacing. "There are things it's best not to meddle in, Miss Whitby. Things it's best not to know."

She thought he was referring to the life-style of the people who frequented the Swiss resort, their amoral intrigues. "Knowing isn't necessarily approving or joining in," she said stiffly. It offended her that he thought her one of those mindless noblewomen she had observed for so long.

"How did you know I was in St. Moritz?" he asked.

"I was there for nearly a year. Studying and taking the waters. I simply noticed you one lunchtime in Frau Gertl's restaurant. I remembered because American accents were rare there."

He laughed, and so did she. They talked of other things; inconsequential chatter but pleasant. He walked her home. They said good-bye knowing they'd see each other again. They had to. Whitby Falls was a small place.

Only later, lying sleepless in the bed her mother had once lain in, did Patsy go over the encounter in her mind. There was something jarring about it, something that didn't ring true. He'd been enraged when she first mentioned knowing he'd been in Switzerland. Why? Mysteries. Nothing but mysteries. And perhaps related. She couldn't afford to overlook that connection. It was all she had. That and a story about the suicide of a woman dead almost fifty years were the total of what she'd learned that day.

3.

"Do you ski?" Joseph asked.

They were on snowshoes, tramping through the woods at the edge of the Little Whitby river. Patsy used the equipment easily, gracefully. Joseph was awkward. "Yes," she said, "I ski. Do you?"

"Nope. Never had the time to learn. I've watched, though, in Switzerland. It looks like fun."

"It is. Marvelous, in fact. I could teach you if there were any trails cut here."

"Good country for it, isn't it?" He paused and looked around at the towering pines and the snow and the mountain looming behind them. "I wouldn't be any good at it, though. I'm not the right sort apparently." He grinned and took another awkward step in the snowshoes to prove his point.

"You could be," Patsy insisted. "All it takes is deciding that you enjoy the danger. I think you might come to enjoy it very much."

He stared at her, his grin gone. "Why do you say that?"

"Something about you. I don't know, really. I just feel it."

He didn't answer but moved on ahead of her. She caught up to him easily. "We wouldn't need a real trail to teach you to ski. We could use that hill behind the schoolhouse."

"I don't have skis."

"I do. Two pairs, in fact. I brought them back with me."

"Someday, maybe."

"For sure," she said. "Not this winter, though. The snow's almost gone for this year. Look." She pointed to a bare patch by the river. A few sprigs of green marsh grass were poking their heads above ground. "Next week it will be Easter; after that, spring."

"Will you be here for Easter?"

"Yes, will you?"

"Not the holiday itself. I've business elsewhere. But I expect to be back a few days later."

Eddie wasn't in Whitby Falls for the holiday despite her letter. Patsy was furious with him and annoyed with herself because she was sorry not to see Joseph Villette at the sunrise service in the Congregational church.

The three Whitbys stood in the pew Andrea said was customary. It was the one in the front, just below the pulpit. The Villettes were across the aisle, also in the front pew. Neither Hugh nor Lise was present; just Henry and H.J. and their wives, children, and sisters.

"We have to go," Patsy had told her mother. "You're hiding in this house, acting defeated. Face them down, Mother. Don't let them win so easily."

Andrea had stared at her, remembering similar advice from Patrick years before about a different kind of hiding. Somehow it was more poignant coming from her daughter. "Very well," she'd agreed. "We'll go. Hugh won't be there, anyway. Not him and not his wife."

"Why not?"

"The Villettes never went to the Protestant church. In the old days they still thought of themselves as French Catholics. His children don't, though. They're . . . what's the word? Assimilated."

Patsy had shrugged. Her mother's preoccupation with Hugh and his family wasn't going to prove anything; she was convinced of it. But Joseph Villette knew something. Patsy told herself that's why she saw so much of him. And why she never mentioned him to Andrea or Patrick.

They sang the last Allelujah, and the service ended. There was an awkward moment when Patsy felt her mother shove her quickly into the aisle. Andrea wanted to leave before the Villettes did, Patsy realized—to lead the recessional, as it were. And she managed it. Andrea walked out just behind the minister, Patsy and Patrick in her wake, and behind them the Villettes. Patsy grinned. Score one for Mama. It was silly, of course, but she needed a few small victories.

Then, when they had all come as far as the door, they heard the explosions. A series of them, too close in succession to count. The sound shattered the silence, stilled the birds, shook the earth. It was wholly unexpected and unnatural. No one was working on Easter Sunday. No dynamite should have gone off in any of the surrounding pits.

"Oh, my God," Andrea said. "Oh, my God." She knew almost instantly what it was. Most of the others guessed, too. The men ran toward the Whitby quarry.

The explosions had been placed to destroy the pumps that kept the deep pits dry. Now three of the six pits were flooded, half the production area was unworkable, and God alone knew how long it would remain that way.

"Dynamite," Andrea said bitterly. "That's his style, all right. Hugh Villette knows more about dynamite than any man in Vermont."

"Mother, that's absurd." Eddie had come at last, but he was no more able to divert Andrea's fixation than Patsy or Patrick. "There was nothing paticularly clever about the charge. It didn't require special skills. Somebody just spread explosives around and lit a fuse."

"Besides," Patsy added, "all six pits were supposed to go up. Whoever did it bungled the job in half of them. Does that sound like an expert's work?"

"He was the only one not in church. Hugh Villette and his wife." Andrea left the room.

"She has a point," Eddie said quietly.

"Not enough of one to convince me," Patrick said. "I just can't believe Villette would bother."

Patsy knew of one other person who hadn't been in the church, who supposedly had not been in Whitby Falls on Easter Sunday. She didn't mention him. "Daddy," she said instead, "what about getting those pits drained? Getting them working again? How long will it take?"

Patrick looked suddenly embarrassed. "According to Lliam Murray, it'll take months. But—"

"But what?" Eddie was intrigued by something in his father's voice.

"I had, that is, I have, an idea. A way of rigging a series of pumps, making them work in tandem. More power, faster results."

"Sounds terrific! Can you do it?"

His son's unexpected enthusiasm made Patrick smile shyly.

"I dare say I can. It will take some experimenting, but in the end it will function, I think. Better than sitting around here wringing my hands, at any rate."

His children looked at each other briefly. Patrick could see in their eyes the memory that once he'd spent hours experimenting in the long-closed laboratory on Fifth Avenue. "I've still got some equipment here," he explained. "Locked up downstairs in the old coal cellar. I'll get at it." When he left the room, his walk was more purposeful than it had been in years.

"That's nice," Patsy said. "Something good coming out of this mess."

"I hope it works," Eddie said. Then, looking at her with full attention for the first time since he'd arrived that morning, "Sister mine, you're a gilt-edged, bona fide knockout. How did you do it?"

"My secret. I'm glad you approve."

"I do. Much better than having you messing up the family image. No need to hide you in the closet anymore." She flung a pillow at him, and he ducked. They both laughed, then were embarrassed by the sound of their merriment in the sad, tomblike house.

"You going to stay up here in the rural wilderness?" Eddie asked. "It's pretty deadly. You should be enjoying yourself, meeting people."

"I can't leave now. Neither should you. They need us, Eddie. They're in real trouble."

"I don't see what we can do."

"We can support them at least. And poke around, try to find out something. Besides," she added, "if this thing isn't solved, there won't be any money for us to do anything else. Not for your tuition, either."

He got red in the face. "It's not that bad surely."

"It is. Daddy told me. Will you stay? Help find out what's happening?"

"I can't. Besides, I already know what's happening. They're being harassed so they'll sell cheaply. It's an obvious ploy."

She ignored his explanation. "Why can't you stay? Is missing one term as critical as all that?"

"It is for me. Besides, this term's paid for. If you're right, the next one may not be."

Patsy sighed. Since he was a child, it had been the same.

Eddie was affable and easygoing as long as nothing challenged his comforts or his plans. "You've two years left, haven't you?"

"After this one, yes."

"What are you going to do?"

"Ever been in Maryland, on the eastern shore?" he asked.

"No."

"It's very rich, very beautiful. Millionaires and their ilk. But lots of them are newcomers. Not old money, not like the Astors and their crowd. Fellow I know at school is from there. Has a sister, a decidedly ugly sister. She adores me."

"Oh, Eddie." Her voice was soft, reproachful but not censorious.

"Sorry, pet, that's the sort I am. Are you very disappointed?"

"Just a little sad."

"I'll have to leave tomorrow. I'm expected back in Maryland. You'll stay on here? Hold the fort?"

She nodded.

Patsy thought a lot about Eddie's theory that someone was trying to buy them out cheaply. She mentioned it to her father.

"It could be, I suppose," he said. "It makes as much sense as anything else. But Whitby Quarry has been a less than huge success for years. An offer could have been made before, but it never was."

"Would you have taken it?"

Patrick shrugged. "We might have. Hard to say. We still might. If that's what's behind all this, I wish whoever it is would make his move. I wouldn't mind an alternative to consider."

"How's the pumping idea?"

His eyes lit up. "Good, I think. The first on-site test is planned for the end of the week."

Later in the day, she tried discussing the notion with Andrea. "Mama, Eddie thinks we're being harassed because someone wants to buy us out cheaply. What do you think?"

"I'm just waiting to see what Hugh Villette offers."

"You mean you've thought that was it all along? That Mr. Villette's intending to buy us out?"

"Of course."

"Has he ever said anything before? Ever tried to buy the quarry?"

"He didn't need to. He knew I'd never sell to him unless I had no choice."

Patsy crossed to where her mother was lying on the chaise longue, and knelt beside her. "I wish I understood more about the past. The things that happened before I was born. Remember that day in Rome? When you said you'd told me about Franco because you had seen people go on protecting lies for a lifetime?"

Andrea touched her daughter's cheek. The skin was silken, flawless. "What a beauty you've become," she said softly. "Yes, I remember."

"Must it continue, Mama? Must we still protect the lies?"

The violet eyes clouded in pain. "I've never lied to you, Patsy."

"I know that. You've simply withheld the truth. I understand, Mother. Really I do. I just think the time has come to explain."

There was a long pause. Patsy waited, then spoke hesitantly. "I was talking to Phoebe Anderson a couple of weeks ago. She said Grandpa's first wife hung herself in the kitchen downstairs. She implied that had something to do with something. But I can't see what or how."

Andrea showed no shock. "Yes, I heard that story when I was a tiny girl. From Eve Villette. She used to do the laundry here."

"Who?" Patsy had never even heard the name.

"Eve Villette. Hugh's mother. She was a vicious old hag. She told me about the suicide just to frighten me. I had nightmares for months."

"What about your mother?" Patsy asked. "How did she die?"

"She'd been ill for years. Dr. Sills dosed her with laudanum, and eventually her heart stopped."

"All these old ghosts, what have they to do with what's happening right now?"

"Nothing. Everything. I don't know." Andrea turned away. "I'm too tired to talk, darling. I'm sorry."

"You're making yourself ill, too," Patsy said desperately.

"You're just lying up here hour after hour brooding. It would make anyone ill."

"Don't worry about me. Just let me rest."

Reluctantly, Patsy left the Chinese bedroom.

She was meeting Joseph at four down by the river. She found herself glancing over her shoulder as she walked along Main Street, as if she suspected someone was spying on her. "I don't like sneaking around," she'd told him weeks before.

"Suit yourself," he'd said easily. "I'll call at your house if you prefer."

"No, that wouldn't do."

"Ah," he'd quoted, grinning, "what's in a name? A rose by any other name—"

"You're being silly."

"It's not me that's worried about what people will say. It's you."

"Not people. Just my mother and father. They're having a bad time right now. They're . . . vulnerable."

So they remained, as Patsy put it, "discreet."

He was lounging against a gnarled old oak tree, waiting for her. She paused above the bank and studied him. He was staring at the river rushing by in full spate, gorged with melting snow from the mountain. His jacket was open, as well as his shirt, and he wore no tie. She could see the tanned skin of his chest against the starched white cotton. Patsy had an overpowering urge to bury her face against that shirtfront, to know how it, how he, smelled. Clean, she thought, fresh. She shook herself and pushed the incipient feeling away. In months she'd not felt like that, not since Franco. Now was not the time to reawaken old urges, particularly not with Joseph Villette.

"Hi," she said, walking up beside him.

"Hi yourself. I wondered how long you were going to stay up there." He gestured back toward the place she'd been standing.

Patsy felt herself blush. "I didn't think you knew I was there. Why didn't you say something? That was rude."

"Sneaking up on people is rude. Anyway, I thought you might be changing your mind about our date. I didn't want to influence you."

"It's not a date," she said, blushing again.

"Our meeting, then." He smiled and took her hand. "C'mon, let's stop being silly. Let's walk."

She pulled away from him. "I can't stay long. My parents expect me home. What is that place? I never noticed it before." Patsy was staring at a pile of discarded, rotting lumber.

"The cabin where my uncle was born. The Villettes used to live down here, I'm told. My grandfather, Jacques, is buried over there. He had a still down here, too. But that's gone now."

She stared at the decaying boards and the thing Joseph said was a grave. Neither looked like what it was supposed to be. "What happened to the still?" she asked.

"Hugh blew it up. Dynamited it from the face of the earth when he came back from Canada to wage his great campaign to conquer Whitby Falls."

"You make it all sound ridiculous. To the people involved it was important." In some obscure way, she was defending her mother's obsession.

"Yeah, I know." He was angry. She'd learned to recognize the telltale tic at the corner of his mouth. "They dug the cesspool," he said. "Now they can't resist pawing over the dung inside."

"Don't say things like that! It's ugly. It's not even true. I have to go." She turned away. She'd planned to question him that day about where he was on Easter Sunday, jar him into giving something away. Instead, he had jarred her. She wanted to get away, to be free of his disturbing presence.

"Wait a minute," he said.

He reached for her unhurriedly. Patsy knew what was happening. He was going to kiss her. She wanted to run, but it was as if she were frozen. She felt his arms encircle her waist. They were hard, tough. So was his mouth. There was nothing soft or gentle about the kiss. It wasn't like Franco's at all. It was self-concerned and exploratory, all for himself, not an attempt to woo her.

"There," he said when he released her. "I've been meaning to do that for weeks. You can go now if you want to."

She turned and fled.

The next morning, very early, Patsy woke to the tinkle of stones on glass. Someone was throwing pebbles at her window. She got out of bed and looked out. Joseph stood below. He didn't say anything, just grinned at her. Behind him, the sun was a red disc on the horizon. He picked up a huge rock and made mock throwing gestures. She backed away. She'd have to go down. He'd wake the whole house if she didn't.

Patsy pulled on a robe, then thought better of it. She was not going into the garden with Joseph Villette in a nightgown and robe. Hurriedly, she slipped into her clothes. In five minutes she was standing beside him.

"What do you want?"

"To apologize."

"At this hour? Besides, it's not necessary."

"Yes, it is. I can tell by your tone. And I had to come early. How else could I see you without their knowing?"

"Very well, I accept your apology. Now go away."

"No, not just yet. Let's walk down the garden. There's some kind of shelter down there. I saw it." His breath showed in the frosty air.

"It's a gazebo. It has roses all around it in summer. I used to play there when I visited as a little girl."

"C'mon, then. Let's see if it's changed. Besides, you're well armored, I note."

He was mocking her again, running his eyes over her clothes, telling her he knew she didn't dare meet him in just a dressing gown. "It's cold out," she said by way of defense.

"Yes." He chuckled.

They walked through the neglected garden to the summer house. "The floor's still sound," Joseph said after some investigation. "And it's out of the wind. Come inside."

They sat propped against the wall. The low rays of the sun slanted through the broken latticework of one wall, and warmed them.

"I'm sorry about yesterday," he said. "I was in a foul mood. You're a sweet kid. I don't want to hurt you."

"I'm not a 'kid,' as you put it. And what makes you think you could hurt me?" She tried to sound haughty but sounded to herself just childish.

"How old are you?" he demanded.

"I'll be twenty this month. How old are you?"

"Twenty-six. An old man." He didn't wait for the objection she was preparing. He turned to her, and his eyes were suddenly serious. "Patsy, listen. You ought to go away for a while. Leave Whitby Falls. It would be better."

She stared at him, incredulous. "Where I go is none of your business. Besides, my mother and father are here. And you know they need me right now."

"There's nothing you can do." The words were stiff, spoken as if in pain. "I know what I'm talking about."

He wasn't touching her, but she could sense his nearness. She was torn between wanting to hate him and wanting to feel his mouth again. "I have suspected for some time," she said, "that you know a great deal. That's why I've continued to see you. I want you to leave us alone, Joseph Villette!" She began in hard, hollow tones and ended in a hysterical little wail. "Go away and leave us alone! What can you possibly want with our quarry? Want enough to blow it up . . . ."

He sighed and leaned his head back against the wall. "Jesus! I thought that's what you were thinking. I hoped you'd realize it was nuts."

"Don't swear at me. And don't deny the obvious. That makes you a liar as well as everything else."

"I'm not swearing at you. Just at the situation. Patsy, it's not what you think. It's much more complex."

He broke off and stared at her. "Oh, Jesus," he said again. Softly, almost to himself. Then he leaned over and placed his lips on hers—not hard and self-centered like the kiss the previous day. This one was sad and tasted of regret.

Patsy felt herself tremble. She was frightened and angry and hungry for him all at the same time. Without thinking about it, she thrust herself at him, and he clasped her very tight. They stayed like that a long time, their mouths searching. His hand strayed to her breast. She pulled away, gasping.

"Sorry," he said, that edge of mockery returned. "I didn't mean to alarm your maiden sensitivities." Whatever there had been of sincerity and self-revelation in his earlier remarks was gone. "Now go home and be a good girl. And don't allow yourself to get into a situation like this with a man again. You'll be quite surprised at where it may lead."

He didn't wait for her to leave the gazebo but did so himself, striding off into the early morning, his long, lanky frame hunched against the cold.

4.

Once Patrick Whitby began thinking about the quarrying of slate, everything changed. His first concern was to increase the power of the crude pumps, to make them capable of draining the flooded pits. He did this by linking them to each other and powering them not with wood but with steam. It sounded simple, and it was, but it involved him in endless days of hard physical labor. He was covered with grease; his hands, grown soft over the years, were first bloodied then callused; but his eyes shone, and he walked with a spring reminiscent of the early days. The change in him penetrated Andrea's self-absorption.

"You look like a boy again," she said one late April morning. "Like the day I first found you in Castle Garden."

"I'm enjoying myself," he admitted sheepishly. "Sounds peculiar, to enjoy a tragedy. But that's the truth of it."

"It sounds fine," she answered. "Why shouldn't you enjoy yourself? Exactly what are you doing?"

"First I'm working on a scheme to get enough power to drain the pits in record time, but it's more than that." He warmed to the interest in her violet eyes. "Did you know that the water is carted to the boiler house by mules? In this day and age, it's absurd! I'm going to change all that."

She didn't want to tell him it was futile, that Hugh Villette had beaten them. She only said, "Good. Let me know how it turns out."

Under Patrick's direction, the men dug trenches and laid pipes and created an interlocking network of waterlines that snaked up the sides of the quarry to meet at the boiler house. Patrick himself tinkered with the engine so they could handle the increased input and adjusted the carriages that moved along the cables suspended from the stick. He was sweaty and filthy and exhausted—and happier than he'd been in a very long time.

The workers watched all the activity with sullen disapproval. "All these years and finally he's doing something," they said. "Too late now, by a long chalk. And crazy. How the hell's he gonna get enough power to drive that water uphill?" They grumbled and counted their small savings and wondered how they were going to live when the Whitby Quarry closed, as it inevitably must.

"Villette will hire us," some said.

"He can't put us all on," others countered.

They were working at half pay. Lliam Murray had told them it was the best that could be done, and they accepted it because half pay was better than nothing. But they were counting the days until even that meager income would disappear.

Then, one fine May morning, Patrick switched on his juggernaut.

Murray suggested he dress for the occasion, appear in a formal suit and tie, as Jason would have done. "No," Patrick told him. "That was his way; it's not mine. Besides, I'm not sure anything will happen."

Actually, he *knew* his invention would work. He'd tested the model a hundred times in the past month. But he had awakened more than his creative memory in the last weeks. Patrick was remembering what it felt like to work hard with one's back and one's hands; to swing a pickax or haul a line as thick as your forearm, to feel your legs become jelly and your gut a screaming ache, and yet to go on working. It seemed fitting that the hand he laid on the switch which would start the motor was stained with oil and grease, and that the coveralls he wore were dirty.

"Ready?" he called to the lad manning the massive lever that would release the dam of water.

"Ready, sir," the boy answered smartly. His name was Gareth Jones, and he was the third in his line to work in the quarry. "Look sharp!" Jones shouted to those standing by other critical points in the system.

Patrick's hand was trembling. He removed it from the apparatus and wiped the sweat from his eyes, then rubbed it dry on his pants leg. Finally, he held his breath and flipped the small, innocent-looking switch. Nothing happened.

There was a collective exhalation of long-held breath, a murmur of resigned disappointment. Patrick ignored the sounds. He bent his head, got down on one knee, and worked for a moment with two tiny wires. He separated them gingerly, wiped them with a bit of soiled cloth, replaced them, and rose to his original position.

He glanced up. Gareth Jones was still watching him. This time Patrick only nodded. Then he flicked the switch again.

There was a dull thudding noise, hesitant at first, arhythmic. Then it became a steady roar, and the deafening sound of rushing water filled the valley.

The men cheered until their voices drowned out the sound of the machinery. From the edge of the flooded pits other men watched the water as it dropped from one notch to the next on the marking lines they held. "Mark nine," they shouted to those behind them, and the cry was taken up and passed along. Then, "Mark seven!" Until the numbers were jumbled by confusion and excitement.

People were pumping Patrick's hand as vigorously as his machines were pumping water. Few said much. They just grinned and touched him, and he quivered with their praise. "Let me through," he said finally to the crowd around him. "Got to check the steam engines."

There was no use yet for all the power he was generating. It just spun the wheels and pulleys and shook the frame boiler house. "Pity to waste all this steam," Lliam Murray said, looking at the mad, surreal dance of the equipment.

"We won't waste it for long," Patrick said in exultation.

Murray looked at him sadly. "You can quarry faster with all this; I see that. But there's only so much slate to take out of here. Only so many places to sell it. The old customers, lots of 'em, buy elsewhere now."

It was a veiled reference to Hugh Villette, but Patrick didn't rise to the bait. "Be patient, Lliam," he said softly. "I have plans."

His plans involved young Gareth Jones. He had watched Jones during the past weeks, and he'd formed an opinion. He was prepared to back it. He invited the boy to his house, and an hour before he was due, Patrick unlocked Jason's old study and went inside.

Everything was as it had been in Jason's day. Just once Patrick allowed himself to stare at the place where Riley Villette had bled away his life. Then he passed his hand over his eyes and wiped away the vision. Jason had not allowed the dead to defeat him. Neither would Patrick.

He'd expected to find the room thick with dirt, but the

original cleaning of the house had included the study. Lliam had not presumed the Whitbys' reluctance to use it. Now Patrick needed only to wipe the accumulated dust of five months from the desk top before he sat down. When Gareth Jones arrived, Patrick ushered him to a seat in the study.

"Ever been in Wales?" he asked the boy immediately.

"No, sir. Never been further than Rutland." The lad grinned. "My grandpa brought us over here, and we stayed."

"Do you want to go on staying?"

"In Whitby Falls, you mean? It's my home. I'll stay as long as there's work."

"Good. That's why you have to go to Wales. Have a drink, son. Let's both have a drink." Patrick poured a shot of Irish for each of them. When their glasses were empty, he refilled them and continued.

"There's a strike of slatemen in Wales. It's been going on for months, and it shows no sign of ending. I want you to go to England, contact the roofing contractors, and sell them Whitby slate to replace what they can't get in their own country."

Jones stared at his employer. It was a crazy idea. "I never sold nothing in my life," he said.

"I know that. But you've the look and the name of a Welshman. And you know slate. You can take a look at the stuff they're accustomed to getting, and tell them how ours is different, if it is. Show them how to work with it. They'll buy. According to this paper, they're desperate."

He passed a copy of the *New York Times* across the desk. It was dated a few weeks back. Patrick had been thinking about Wales almost as long as he'd been working on the pumping system.

Gareth read quickly, then looked up. "Could I have another drink?" he asked. Patrick smiled and poured a hefty shot into the boy's empty glass. Jones downed the whiskey in one swallow, coughed, then said, "Okay. When do I leave?"

"For New York, day after tomorrow. You sail on the *Brittanic* on Friday. She docks in Liverpool in twelve days."

Lliam Murray thought he was mad. So did Andrea. "We can't afford this, Patrick, not now," his wife told him. "Sending that boy on this trip will take every last cent we have."

Murray added the sobering fact that even with all six pits functioning, even with the new equipment, they couldn't take more than ten thousand squares of slate out of the quarry. There wasn't any more there. The veins were almost played out. "And what about them vandals?" he added. "How can you be sure they won't blow up the whole thing again?"

The last question struck Patrick as the most pressing. "I know you've been thinking about it a lot," he told his daughter. "And investigating a bit. How about it, Patsy? Any ideas?"

She shook her head. "None I can prove. None I'm even certain enough to discuss. I'm sorry, Daddy. I wish I could be more help. I admire what you've done and what you're trying to do more than I can say."

Patrick felt a tremor of satisfaction along his spine. "Thank you. And thanks for trying to help. You've been a great comfort all these months both to me and to your mother. We've been thinking, though. Would you like to go to New York for a while? Spend time with some friends, maybe. It must be quite dull for you here in Vermont."

"Leave now?" Patsy exclaimed. "Not on your life. I want to see you win, Daddy, and I'm sure you're going to."

She sounded just like Andrea in the old days. Patrick grinned. "Very well. But I still have to think of some way to protect against the kind of trouble we've been having."

"Why not mount a guard?" Patsy said.

"We've done that. Two night watchmen, in fact."

"They aren't enough. There's what, six acres of ground to cover? And it's all hills and holes in the ground and sheds and shacks . . . There's no way two men can guard all that. That's why they've been so ineffective."

"I know," he said ruefully. "But we can't afford any more. Can't afford the two we have, if the truth be told. Particularly not now that I'm backing this export venture."

Patsy thought for a while, twisted one black curl absent-mindedly in her fingers. When she spoke, it was slowly and with hesitation. "Do you think," she said, "the workers might help? Could they run a kind of revolving guard shift at the quarry nights? It's their jobs at stake, after all."

Patrick leaned back and eyed her speculatively. "Maybe," he said at last, drumming one finger on the desk in a kind of staccato emphasis. "But we can't be sure one of them's not been behind the trouble all along. Maybe more than one."

"But not forty, surely, or fifty!" She was intent on her idea now. "Fifty men to stand guard all night. They could watch everything, even each other."

"We've a hundred and twenty-five workers in all," Patrick said. "And they put in twelve hours of hard labor quarrying. How could they also do guard duty at night?"

"Some could. The young ones. Not every night, but maybe every other. A revolving shift, as I said. And they have wives, children. We can get whole families involved."

"We couldn't pay them," Patrick said. He wasn't really objecting to her plan, just working it out with her, thinking aloud.

"Not now," Patsy agreed. "But we could tell them they'd be paid later. When the quarry is profitable again."

That was just what Patrick did tell them. He called a mass meeting, but not on the Green, where it would have been held in the old days. The town didn't belong to the Whitbys in that way anymore. Patrick assembled his workers at the quarry and spoke to them for less than five minutes. "You all know what's been happening," he said. "If it continues, this quarry is finished, and so are your jobs. I need help. I'm asking for it."

They agreed to his scheme in less time than it took him to explain it. Within twenty-four hours they had drawn up a plan of the quarry, marked the vantage points the guards would adopt, and worked out a duty roster. It included wives and children, just as Patsy had said it must. They were paid at the same rate as the men. At least their IOU's read the same. "Asking them to do a man's work, got to pay them like men," Patrick explained. After he said it, he had a sudden sense of déjà vu. He remembered Zachary Katz standing in the Rutland courtroom and damning Riley Villette for being part of an organization that advocated equal pay for men and women. There was no time to puzzle out the morality of all that now. He needed to deal with Lliam's second objection to the exporting venture.

On that problem he received unexpected help. Hugh Villette came to see the new pumping system.

Villette arrived alone. He left his buggy at the top of the hill and walked the thirty yards to the office. He expected to find a clerk there or perhaps Lliam Murray. Instead, Patrick was alone, poring over a set of diagrams.

"I heard what you done," Hugh said. "Congratulations. It's a fine idea."

"Thank you. Is that all you came to say?" Patrick didn't share Andrea's beliefs about Villette or her hatred. Still the memory of their last bitter meeting was thick in the air between them.

"More or less." Hugh stared at the tips of his boots and turned red with embarrassment. "I been the first one with new ideas in this valley for so long I'm not used to telling any man 'well done,' nor hankering after what he knows."

Patrick looked up and saw the tension in his visitor, the effort the other man was making. "But you are now; is that it?" he asked softly.

"Yeah, that's it."

The two men stared at each other in silence. The years of hostility were a palpable barrier between them. Villette had made the first move; he'd come. Patrick knew it wasn't only curiosity; it was a statement—perhaps an olive branch. He felt a sudden overwhelming tiredness and a need to be shriven of the past.

"Here." Whitby reached for a piece of paper and drew a simple wiring diagram and a few sketchy lines. "That's all there is to it. It's no big mystery, and it's not patentable."

Hugh studied the sheet and nodded. "I think I see," he said at last. Patrick indicated he could keep the sketch. Hugh folded it carefully and put it in his vest pocket. Then he glanced at the plan Patrick had been studying when he arrived. It was a diagram of the Whitby slate veins—all the lodes they were presently tapping and some that had long ago been worked out.

"There's more slate here." Hugh drew a stubby finger between two of the pits outlined on the chart. "A lot of it, good stuff."

"You're sure?" Patrick asked.

Hugh smiled for the first time. "I know every inch of this valley. And I can smell slate."

"So I've heard. Why hasn't that vein been quarried before?" The place Hugh had indicated was in the heart of the Whitby holdings. It should have been among the first to be dug.

"Deep," Hugh explained. "Covered with maybe thirty

feet of worthless rock. Too deep to blast it free. You'd bring down the mountain.''

"Even you?" Patrick asked pointedly. "Could you blast it free?''

Hugh smiled again. "Not even me," he said. "Nobody's going to get that slate out just by dynamiting. If it were possible, I'd have tried to buy this quarry years ago. That's the only thing you've got that's worth having. Even if you do get orders from England.''

"You know everything, don't you?''

"That's the way it is up here.''

"Yes, I understand. Thanks.''

Hugh patted the pocket with the explanation of the pumping system. "Thank you. And like I said before, congratulations.''

Patrick began planning the tunnel before Villette was out the door.

5.

Patsy made sure she was always busy. For one thing, there was work to be done; for another, she didn't want time to think about Joseph. He had not returned to Whitby Falls in two months, not since Easter. Patsy told herself she wanted to see him because of what she believed he knew and her fears that vandals would strike again just when it looked as if they might revive the quarry.

Patrick had to worry about orders and production, learning as much as he could from Lliam Murray. Patsy took over supervision of the system of guards.

Each evening, after sunset, she'd take a lantern and walk to the quarry. There she'd let herself into the office with the key Patrick had given her and take the duty roster down from its peg on the wall. The sentries were already in place. They took up their posts as soon as the whistle blew to signal the close of the ordinary workday. So Patsy would mount an old mule called Hepsibah and ride the periphery of the quarry with the lantern and the list of names in her hand.

"Evening, Miss Whitby," the men, women, and children would say softly as she approached. "Fine night" or "Feels like rain."

"Good evening," she'd answer. "Everything all right? You have everything you need?"

"Everything's fine, ma'am," they invariably said.

She would raise her lantern and study the person with whom she spoke, assure herself that he or she was supposed to be in that spot at that time, and move on. Later, one of the others would ride Hepsibah around the same route and distribute hot coffee from a pair of gallon jugs slung either side of the mule. And later still, just before dawn, Patsy would make the trip once more.

"It's too much for her," Andrea told Patrick. "Too much for any woman. She's getting less than five hours' sleep a night."

"A lot of the local women stand a ten-hour guard," he said. "They don't sleep at all."

"That's different," Andrea insisted. "Besides, they take turns. No one person does it every single night."

"The workers need Patsy," Patrick explained. "They need to believe that we're involved. Don't you see?"

Andrea nodded and said no more until a few days later, when the letter from the New York attorney arrived. She gave it to Patrick with a look of infinite sorrow.

"What's this? You look upset."

"It came this morning, while you were at the pit."

"What does it say?"

"Read it."

He withdrew the folded sheet of paper and read it quickly, then once again, more slowly. It was an offer to buy the Whitby Quarry for twenty-six thousand dollars. "A generous offer under the circumstances," the would-be buyer, a man called Timothy Gottlieb, said.

"Who is he?" Patrick asked. "Any idea?"

Andrea shrugged. "None at all. It's a good address." The letter had been sent from 120 Broadway. "Anyway, he says he's acting for a client."

"Yes. An anonymous client, just as Eddie predicted. What do you want to do?"

She hesitated. "Twenty-six thousand dollars is a lot of

money. We could be reasonably secure for the rest of our lives if we invested it wisely."

"But it's less than the quarry is worth. A lot less."

"Lliam told me there are no more than ten thousand squares of slate left in all six pits. That does make it a generous offer." She sat down beside Patrick. Tiny lines of worry and age were beginning to appear on her face.

"I know," Patrick said. "He told me the same. But he's wrong. There's more slate, a lot more. And when Jones comes back from England, we'll have a place to sell it."

"How can you be right and Lliam wrong?" she asked. "He's been part of the quarry since my father opened it."

"And I'm new at the game. I admit that. But I'm right in this, love. I know I am." He didn't dare tell her that Hugh Villette had told him there was more slate. She wouldn't question Villette's judgment, but she'd insist he was deliberately misleading them. Patrick knew that wasn't so, but he couldn't prove it.

He tried another tack. "If the quarry really is all but played out, why does this stranger want it? Even for twenty-six thousand."

She sighed with weariness. "I don't know."

"What don't you know?" Patsy came in from her first tour of duty.

"I'll get your dinner," her mother said. "It's in the oven."

Patsy stopped her. "I'm not very hungry. Tell me what you were talking about when I came in. It sounded serious."

Andrea would have fobbed her off with an excuse, but Patrick felt that Patsy had a right to know. "Someone's just offered us twenty-six thousand dollars for the quarry."

"Hah! Then Eddie was right after all. It was just a scheme to make us sell cheap!"

"It's not cheap," Andrea said. "Not if there's almost no slate left to sell."

Patsy looked in puzzlement at her father. "But is that true?"

"Lliam Murray says it is," he answered. "There are plenty of folks who'd agree with him. People who know a lot about slate."

"Then why . . ." She couldn't continue. It was too painful to say the words. All this time and worry and effort, and they'd been beating a dead horse.

"I don't agree with the assessment, Patsy," her father said. "I think there's a lot more slate. And that we have a market for it in England."

Patsy looked accusingly at her mother. "You think Daddy's mistaken, don't you? You want to sell."

"I want peace," Andrea said. "I want a secure future for you and for Eddie and for us."

"Eddie's all right. He's making his own secure future. Why else do you think he's gotten engaged to that Maryland girl? Her family is dripping money."

"Oh, Patsy." Andrea's voice was strained with hurt. "You're always so quick to judge. Besides, there are still the three of us—"

"Speak for yourself," Patsy said bitterly. "I don't want to give in. I want to fight."

"Hold on, both of you." Patrick rose and faced his wife and his daughter. "There's more. You should know all of it before you cast a vote. The slate's there, but it's thirty feet below the level of the deepest pit. We'll have to dig a tunnel to get it out. It's too deep to dynamite it free."

"A tunnel . . ." Andrea stared at him. "No one has ever done that. Not in Vermont."

She suspected the source of his information. Patrick could see it in her eyes. His mention of dynamite had triggered her suspicions. He ignored them and went to the heart of the question. "I know it's a speculative venture. And a dangerous one. That's why I said you had to know about it before you decided anything. But I've worked on a plan for the tunnel the past two weeks. It stands an excellent chance of succeeding."

"And if you can get the stuff out, we'll sell it in England? That's the plan?" Andrea spoke softly, thoughtfully.

"Yes," he told her. "That's the plan."

"What about shipping?" Andrea said after some seconds. "How expensive will it be?"

"Cheap, I think. My idea is that most ships would be glad of the stuff as ballast. I haven't checked that out yet. I haven't had time."

Patsy looked from her father to her mother. "I could do that," she said quickly. "I could go and talk to the steamship owners."

"Not the owners," Andrea said. "The agents in charge of

cargo." Patsy looked at her mother with new respect. Perhaps she was not as changed by the past six months as she had seemed to be. "But," Andrea continued, "what about your work here? The guard duty? If we refuse this man's offer, there's every likelihood the harassment will start again."

Patsy bit her lip. "That's true. But I don't think I'm really needed. The workers and their families are really committed. They don't need a watchdog."

"But they need inspiration," Andrea said firmly. "You did say that, didn't you, Patrick?"

He nodded. "Yes, I did."

"Very well. I will do Patsy's tour, then, while she goes to New York to investigate the possibilities of shipping the slate we're going to take out of this miraculous tunnel you shall build, Patrick." When she turned to smile at her husband, Patsy saw that something had transpired between them in the past fifteen minutes. It had nothing to do with her and little to do with slate. She went to eat her supper alone in the kitchen.

It was good to be back in New York after an absence of two years. The day she came home from Europe, Patsy had gone straight from the dock to Grand Central Station. This time she would get to know the city again.

She didn't return to the old neighborhood. The Whitbys had given up the apartment, and Patsy had no reason to go to upper Fifth Avenue. She went instead to the Court, a small sedate hotel on Lexington Avenue and Nineteenth Street, and reserved a room for a week. Then she went out and walked, reconnoitering the terrain she planned to attack.

The cargo agents she must see were clustered fairly close together in the few blocks north and south of Fourteenth Street. She carefully noted their names and addresses in the notebook she carried, then continued walking, just for the sheer joy of it.

In some ways, New York was the most exciting city in the world. Living up in Whitby Falls these past months, she hadn't thought she missed it. But returning like this, on a glorious day in July, warm but not stifling as it could be this time of year, with her head full of plans and dreams—it was like champagne. The women were beautiful, the men handsome, the shop windows full of the most beautiful merchandise to be seen anywhere.

Patsy crossed the Bowery and started down Broadway. She soon passed beyond the section known as "the ladies' mile," with its emphasis on retail trade, into a stretch of elegant old houses. A century before, it had been the heart of the city, the only place for gentlefolk to live. It still retained much of that flavor. There were businessmen there now, professional offices mostly, but they kept a discreet veil over their commercial purposes, managing to blend with the many private homes still to be found. From the outside it was impossible to distinguish one from another.

Patsy glanced at one particularly arresting doorway just across the street. It was painted pale blue and showed up well against white stuccoed walls. The house looked as if at any moment a stolid Dutch burgher would emerge, as if it hadn't changed in the past hundred and fifty years. She was still admiring it when the brass number plate caught her eye: 120. The letter from the lawyer, Timothy Gottlieb, had come from that address.

Perhaps she should try and see the man, attempt to discover who his client was, why he wanted to buy the quarry. Then, just as she was deciding it might not be a good idea, the door opened. Instinctively, Patsy drew back into the shadow of the much taller building on the side of the street where she stood. It was unlikely that her gasp of surprise could have been heard from so far away. Or that the man hurrying away from the house had even glanced in her direction. He'd have recognized her, of course, if he had. Just as she had recognized him. The gentleman leaving number 120 Broadway was Joseph Villette.

Patsy stared after him for a few seconds, then she followed him down the street.

She was back at the Court Hotel by dinnertime. Too tired and confused to be hungry, she had a pot of tea sent to her room and soaked for an hour in a hot tub while she tried to make sense of the day's events, or rather, make them add up to something different from what they obviously totaled. Something she'd prefer to believe.

Joseph had walked six blocks south before turning into another house on the corner of Broadway and Spring Street. She had waited for over an hour, but he hadn't come out again. Finally, she had carefully moved closer to see if she could distinguish a name above the doorbell. There had been none. Eventually, when dusk was becoming dark, she had left.

It wasn't much, viewed in one light, but taken all together, it confirmed her worst fears. It couldn't be just another coincidence, like seeing him that first time in St. Moritz and later in Whitby Falls. Maybe that wasn't a coincidence, either. Maybe it was part of some horrid plot, some scheme to destroy her family, an extension of that inexplicable vendetta between the Villettes and the Whitbys. And this time the evidence was irrefutable. She had seen Joseph leaving the office of the lawyer who was trying to buy the quarry. Of course there was a connection. She'd have to be an idiot not to see it. The only questions remaining were what and why.

The Court was an old hotel still lit by gas. In the dull yellow glow the silver tea things had a rich, sensuous patina. Patsy stared at them, studying her distorted reflection in the bulbous metal creamer. Then there was a light, deferential knock; the maid had come to collect the tray. She rose and pulled on a kimono of thin silk, the same one she used to wear on the balcony of the house in St. Moritz. "Yes," she said, opening the door.

Joseph was slouched against the wall of the corridor. He looked casual and utterly relaxed despite his formal evening dress. He was absentmindedly twirling a silken top hat on one finger. And he was grinning. "I've been followed by the best of them, sweetheart. You're not quite in that league."

Patsy started to say something, stuttered in confusion, and pulled the front of the kimono tighter over her breasts.

"No need to apologize," he said, laughing. He straightened up and withdrew a small white card from the inside pocket of his tailcoat. "I've come bearing glad tidings. You are summoned."

She took the card and stared at it. There was no name, only an address—the number of the house into which Joseph had disappeared earlier. "Summoned by whom?" she managed to say. "For what?"

"Save your questions for tomorrow. Ten A.M. Be there; it's worth your while." Then he leaned forward and kissed her on the forehead. She pulled back, but not before she felt his lips graze her skin and smelled the musky scent of his aftershave.

He looked into her eyes for a moment. "Don't worry. It's

going to be all right. And don't be late. I'll be there, too."
He grinned again and put on his hat, tapping the crown with a
gesture of casual insouciance. "Good night, sweetheart." He
gave her a crooked two-fingered salute before walking down
the hall.

An Oriental manservant let her in. Patsy didn't know if he
was Chinese or Japanese. "Please to wait here, missy." She
was left in a long, narrow foyer with black and white tiles on
the floor and dark green damask on the walls. It was cool and
dim after the hot summer sun of the street.

In a short time, the Oriental emerged from the shadows at
the rear of the hall. "Please to follow me, missy."

She did, and was led toward the back of the house, then
ushered through a door the servant opened without knocking.
Patsy was blinded by light that streamed through a large
window at the rear of the room, only sightly filtered by the
sheer curtains that covered the glass. When she could focus,
she saw that all the surfaces in the room were also light
reflectors. Pale, honey-colored woods and gleaming brass.
Neither modern nor antique. Futuristic, rather. For a moment
she thought herself alone and let her glance range over the
place. In its way, it was beautiful, but it made her uncomfortable. Then she saw the man behind the expanse of desk.

He spoke as soon as she noticed him. "Please sit down,
Miss Whitby. It was good of you to accept my unorthodox
invitation." He gestured with a nod of his overlarge head
toward a chair.

Patsy took it and arranged the skirt of her navy blue linen
dress with care. It was a way to gain time. She was suddenly
frightened, but she made herself speak calmly. "I do not
know your name, sir."

"No. One of my peculiarities, I'm afraid. It's not important."

She started to rise. "I do not care to deal with an anonymous gentleman."

"Sit down, Miss Whitby. Joseph should be here at any
second. Doubtless that will make you feel more secure. He
had an urgent appointment. I apologize for the delay."

She started to say something, but the door opened again,
and Joseph came in. His timing was perfect. Too perfect. She
had the sense of being played like a fish on a line.

His manner belied that. "Sorry I'm late," he said to her,

as if their being there together was the most natural thing in the world. Then, to the man behind the desk, "Everything as expected, sir."

"No objections?"

"None I couldn't handle."

"Good. Now, we must enlighten our charming guest. I fear she questions my suitability as company for a lady."

The door opened again, and the Oriental came in bearing a tray. No one said anything while he served them coffee in delicate, pale blue porcelain cups with silver rims. It was the best coffee Patsy had ever tasted and the most exquisite china she had ever seen. She saw that the anonymous man held his cup awkwardly, and she realized that his arms were deformed. She dropped her eyes in embarrassment. If he noticed, he ignored it.

"Thank you, Moto. That will be all. We are not to be disturbed until I ring." The servant bowed his way out, and the door closed softly behind him. "Now, Miss Whitby, the explanations. First let me say I was reluctant to invite you here, reluctant to tell you any of this. But Joseph convinced me otherwise yesterday, after we became aware of your presence in the city. Your persistent interest, shall we say . . ." He smiled, and his small eyes were lost in rolls of wrinkled skin and fat. "It took courage to follow our mutual friend here. Courage or remarkable foolhardiness. Joseph Villette is not a man to be underestimated, Miss Whitby. But I believe you know that."

She set down her cup with a gesture of impatience. "I'm not sure I know anything. I keep waiting for these explanations you promise. But I am quite certain about Mr. Villette." She turned to him, and her black eyes flashed sparks. "He is a cheat and a liar."

Joseph smiled ruefully. Their host held up one misshapen hand. "Enough. Hear me out, please. Then you may form whatever opinions you wish. The trouble at your parents' quarry, the harassment to which they have been subjected, even the wanton destruction—we have known about it from the beginning, but we have been merely observers, not instigators."

"Who is 'we'?" she demanded. "And if you knew such terrible things, why did you not have the simple decency to warn us?"

"One question at a time, my dear. 'We' refers to my organization. Joseph first and foremost, but there are others. They are irrelevant to this discussion. As to informing you, that is not my role. I am a broker, Miss Whitby. A purveyor of goods and information to clients who employ me."

"And one of these so-called clients has seen fit to attack the Whitby Quarry? While you sat there and watched?" Disgust made her voice shake.

"As to my sitting here," the man said, "I have little choice."

He made a sudden effort and thrust his chair back from the desk toward the light in the window. It exposed him mercilessly. He had an enormous head topping an obese body, the distorted arms she had already noticed, and no legs at all. He meant to shock, and he did. When he was sure she had seen everything, he nodded to Joseph, who rose and pushed the chair back to its place by the desk.

"Joseph is my arms and legs, Miss Whitby. My eyes and my ears, on occasion. Still, I have certain uses." He waited, but Patsy was as speechless as he meant her to be. "You must understand a bit of background. For the last few years, money has been both a scarce and a devalued commodity. What there is of solid currency is in America, most of it in New York, but even here idiots are threatening to abolish gold as the standard for dollars. And in Europe there is almost no cash at all. So money becomes, as I said, both scarce and devalued. It is an extraordinary combination, and a dangerous one. In such circumstances, men of wealth seek another commodity to hold. Of late, some have chosen diamonds." He paused and looked at Joseph.

"My turn," the younger man said. "The largest concentration of diamonds in the world is in South Africa. Even there they aren't exactly dripping from the trees. But for those willing to pay, they can be had. A few years back, the boss and I managed to get a spectacular stone out of Johannesburg and into New York. It was bought by a chap who decided he wanted more. Just about then there was a rumor of diamonds in Vermont."

Patsy gasped. "That's absurd."

"Maybe," Joseph agreed, "but in our line of work we don't ignore such rumors. The boss sniffed around a bit. It turned out the chief interest centered around a little town called Whitby Falls. A dot on the map,'' he said softly. ''A backwater.''

''But by a humorous coincidence,'' the boss interposed, ''a place where Joseph could come and go without arousing suspicion . . .''

''How lucky for you both,'' Patsy said. She was startled at how protective of Whitby Falls she felt. ''Just a little rural no-place filled with hicks. Easy for you to manipulate, wasn't it?''

Both men ignored her comments. Villette spoke. ''Turned out that a chap named Rudi Vartek had been a frequent guest at the Bardwell Hotel in Rutland. Did a lot of touring the countryside.'' He paused to roll and light a cigarette, then asked her if she minded after it was lit. Patsy shook her head. ''Vartek is a South African mining engineer,'' Joseph continued. ''One of the most knowledgeable men in the world where diamonds are concerned.''

''And he's behind the terrible things that have been happening to us?'' Patsy asked. ''A man from South Africa?'' It was incredible. So much grief caused by a stranger from the other side of the world.

''Not directly,'' Joseph said. ''I doubt that Vartek knew anything about it. He went back to South Africa months ago. Vartek was in the employ of a cartel, a sort of ad hoc union of a few rich and mighty men. The names are unimportant; most of them you wouldn't recognize. They're the ones who decided to buy your folks' quarry.''

''They think we have diamonds?'' She almost laughed.

''Yup,'' Joseph said easily. ''You and two or three other places in the country. Seems Vartek told the cartel which spots were likely. He got around a bit while he visited the States—quite a tourist, our Rudi. Anyway, they hired an attorney to negotiate for them. A series of attorneys, in fact. They're big men, powerful. For them this venture is just one of many. You have to understand that. They gave the shyster a figure, their top price as it were. He'd get a percentage of the difference if he could buy the properties for any less. I think the rest is obvious.''

''Timothy Gottlieb,'' she said. ''Of 120 Broadway.''

''The same.'' He snuffed out the cigarette. ''Gottlieb hired some thugs. He figured that way he'd be sure to get Whitby Quarry below the cartel's maximum.''

"But I still don't understand . . . What role have you two in all of this? Yesterday, when I saw you, you were coming out of that man's office. So you must be—"

"Please do not jump to conclusions, dear lady," the boss said. "We are, as I said, brokers. We are not in the employ of the cartel. If we were, this whole matter might not have become so distressful. But as it happens, we have a client. The gentleman Joseph referred to earlier. A man as wealthy as any of the members of the cartel. And as willing to speculate in diamonds. I informed him of what I knew. He gave us a watching brief. We were to be observers. When the price was fixed for the sale of the Whitby Quarry, we were authorized to better it on our client's behalf."

She sighed and leaned back in her chair. "So either way we're pawns," she said. Joseph looked uncomfortable, but he didn't deny it. "Why have you told me all this now?"

"Because of the guards," Joseph said. "Your efforts and your father's. The tunnel he's planning, the export venture. It all adds up to making Whitby Quarry a going concern again, one that won't be for sale at a price either the cartel or our client would be interested in paying. They have no guarantees, remember, only Vartek's best guess. They are willing to back that just so far. There are plenty of places for them to invest. This was only a tangent. A side bet, you might say."

"And yesterday," Patsy asked, "what were you doing at that man's office?"

"Telling him pretty much what I've told you. That it's time to call it off. No percentage anymore. This morning I put the finishing touch on the man's education. If he persists, the boss has a file that can be made available to the police."

"Your client, too?" She asked the question tonelessly.

"We told him some weeks ago that the Whitby Falls scheme had ceased to be viable," the boss said. "We are at the moment pursuing other inquiries on his behalf." The boss leaned forward and awkwardly rang a large brass bell. "Now, you two young people must excuse me. It's time for my massage. Moto will show you out."

"C'mon, I'll buy you a soda." Joseph took her arm and led her up Broadway to Eighth Street. She felt numb. And still confused. It was all so farfetched, so macabre. South Africans, cartels. It was a world about which she knew nothing and, except for the way it had touched her and her family, cared less.

The shop into which he took her was small and pleasant. They walked up to the marble counter, and Joseph said, "Chocolate or vanilla?"

"Strawberry."

He grinned. "Ornery, just like all women. Two strawberry sodas," he told the clerk. They came, tall and pale pink and so cool the outsides of the glasses were frosted with moisture. Joseph spied a vacant booth, waited until she had slid in, then seated himself across from her. "Nice," he said.

"What's nice?"

"Being here with you. Drinking a soda. It has a Whitby Falls feel to it. I like that."

"Do you? Even though the place is only a backwater. A port of convenience for you, isn't it?"

"It's not like that anymore," he said. "I thought you understood that."

"I understand very little." She sipped the strawberry soda through two striped straws.

"You want to ask more questions? Go ahead. I'll answer if I can."

"You and that strange man you work for, you're crooks, aren't you?"

"That's not a question; it's an accusation. Never mind, I'll answer it, anyway. We sometimes bend the law a little, but we're not crooks. The boss is a broker, an agent, just like he said. I'm his assistant. Most of what we do is of little interest to the police, even if they knew about it."

"But you let all this go on," she said. "You could have told us months ago, and you didn't."

"Telling you wouldn't have stopped anything. Besides, I didn't care about you months ago."

"It isn't right," she said through tight lips. "It can't be legal."

Joseph finished his soda with a loud slurping sound and sat back. "Look, sweetheart, you want to know about crooks, just ask me. I can tell you anything your little heart desires. And a few things you'd never think of. But that's not because of the boss. All that started long before him. I'd probably be rotting in some prison right now if he hadn't taken me in hand."

He told her a little about Boston, his childhood, his one attempt at blackmail when he first came to New York. "I was a wet-behind-the-ears punk, and I thought I was a big shot. Lucky for me the mark I touched went to the boss for retribution, not to the cops. So he got his two hundred bucks back, and I got a chance to 'use my talents,' as the old man put it."

"You care for him, don't you?"

"He's the closest thing to a father I've ever had. After my mother died, I was strictly solo."

"Except for Lise and Hugh Villette," she said softly.

"That's a late entry," he said. "I only met them a year ago this month."

Patsy toyed with her straw and stared at the thick pink liquid in the glass. "Will you tell me one more thing? Your uncle, was he part of the cartel?"

Joseph hooted with laughter. The sound echoed in the half-empty ice cream parlor. "That's nuts. Hugh Villette wouldn't be able to play in that league if he owned every functioning quarry in Vermont. Not unless they all turned out to be diamond mines. Moreover, as far as my uncle is concerned, slate is the only thing worth digging out of the ground. If he came across any diamonds, he'd complain that they couldn't be made into roof tiles."

"And this South African, the one who said there might be diamonds in our quarry, you think he could be right?"

Villette shrugged. "It's a long shot. My head tells me it could be so. Vartek knows his stuff. But in here—" He tapped his flat stomach with one finger. "In here I say no. It just doesn't feel right."

"Well, we'll see, won't we?" She pushed the half-finished

soda away. "Daddy's going down thirty feet or better to dig a new vein. So we'll find out. Now I have to go. I've still got business to attend to."

He looked at her, puzzled. "I thought we settled everything this morning."

Patsy drew on her white gloves and smiled. "You think I came here to look for you, don't you? I didn't. I came to see some shipping agents about transporting our slate. It was just an accident that I saw you yesterday."

"Well, I'll be damned!" He grinned and didn't apologize for his language. "You're quite a lady, Patsy Whitby, quite a lady."

"One more thing," she said. "That day in St. Moritz— what were you doing there? Had it something to do with me, with this affair?"

"Not a bit of it. I was negotiating the sale of a painting. A gentleman from Boston wished to do business with a gentleman from Zurich. I'm a broker, just like I said."

They went outside, and Joseph flagged a hansom cab. He sat far away from her, looking tense and controlled. Patsy found herself studying his profile from the corner of her eye. He had a strong square chin and a thin aquiline nose. A Roman nose. That made her think of Franco. But Joseph had none of Franco's warmth or his gentleness. Joseph was hard and brittle. His humor was sardonic, not gay. She wondered why she was allowing herself to think of Franco, who had been her lover, along with Joseph Villette, who was—what? Her friend? Hardly. And not a suitor, certainly. Not even considering that he had kissed her twice. Patsy realized that she wanted him to kiss her now, and that he wasn't going to.

The cab rolled to a halt in front of the Court. Joseph paid the driver and accompanied her into the lobby. "How long are you staying in town?" he asked.

"Two or three days, maybe a week. As long as it takes to see the people I came to see. I'm needed at home as soon as I can return." She thought of her mother riding the old mule around the quarry, not knowing that it wasn't necessary anymore. Not if Joseph and his boss had told the truth.

"Maybe . . ." he began. "No, forget it. I'm tied up all the rest of the week."

The sentence didn't ring true. Patsy flushed as if it were she who had suggested they meet again and had been rebuffed.

"Good-bye," she said stiffly. "And thank you . . . I suppose."

"Don't metnion it." He was grinning in that mocking way he had, flashing the beautiful white teeth in the tanned face as if he knew their effect. "Take care of yourself, kid. I'll see you in Vermont."

"Perhaps," she said with as much dignity as she could muster.

Chapter Eleven

❦

1.

"So they'll be glad of the ballast," Patsy said. "Just as you suspected, Daddy. Here are the rates. They look favorable to me."

She passed her father a piece of paper with the figures. He took it, looked at it for a moment, then handed the list to Andrea. "Very favorable," he said. "Don't you agree, love?"

Andrea had taken to wearing reading glasses. She perched them on her nose and studied the numbers Patsy had brought back from New York. "We can make a profit, yes. If shipping costs are no higher than this. And if we get orders and have slate to sell."

"How's the tunnel coming?" Patsy asked.

"I'm still building the model," Patrick said. "But we'll be ready to start digging next week, I think."

"You look tired, both of you." Patsy rose and walked to the fireplace. There was no fire that night; it was muggy and airless inside and out. Still, she gravitated to the tall marble mantel as if in need of its support. "I have more news. Good news. It will make things easier."

Patsy took a deep breath. She'd worked it all out in her head, how much to say, how to explain. If she handled it well, there would be no need to tell them more than they should know.

"It's rather a long story," she began. "And complicated. I shan't bore you with all the details. I ran into Mr. Timothy Gottlieb while I was in New York. Quite by chance. Naturally, I took the opportunity to talk with him. He explained that it was a group of businessmen who were behind the offer to buy our quarry. They considered it a defunct operation and saw an opportunity to buy cheaply. They had some crazy idea that there might be diamonds in Vermont. If you can imagine such nonsense." She knew her laugh was nervous and unconvincing.

Andrea stared at her daughter over the top of the glasses,

removed them, and examined the girl more closely. "Did you believe such a ridiculous story, Patsy? It's not like you to be so gullible. And why all the harassment we've been subject to if it was only an ordinary business venture?"

"Oh, I talked to Mr. Gottlieb about that," Patsy said too quickly. "He thought it was the fault of one of the prospective buyers. Said the man's old, senile. Mr. Gottlieb promised there'd be no more trouble. They don't want to buy us out any longer, you see. I mean now that the quarry is functioning again, they realize they can't have it cheap. . . ."

"I'm afraid I have to repeat your mother's question," Patrick interrupted. "Why did you believe this incredible story?"

"Because Joseph said . . ." She stopped, clasped her hand to her mouth.

"Joseph . . ." Patrick repeated. "Joseph who?" Not a man given to intrigues, he asked the question in innocence, only seeing the possible implications after the words had been uttered.

"Joseph Villette, I warrant," Andrea said. Her voice was low, controlled, but her hands were trembling where they were folded in her lap. "Isn't that the man you mean, Patsy?"

"Yes." Her answer was barely audible. "I didn't want to tell you. I knew it would upset you. But I know it's all the truth. The guards, the worry, none of it's necessary any longer."

"Because Maryann Villette's bastard son says so," Andrea spat out. "Because he claims his uncle has called off his vendetta!" Her voice had risen, become shrill.

"Mama! Please, you mustn't let yourself become hysterical over a lot of old problems that have nothing to do with any of this! Hugh Villette's no part of any of it. It's about diamonds, just like I said. And this Timothy Gottlieb, he's the one who—"

"Stop!" Andrea rose and stood staring at her daughter. "Stop speaking these vile lies in my presence, in my house. You think yourself a sophisticated woman, Patsy, but you're a child. You know nothing of the things to which you refer. Now, I shall go to my room. I do not wish to hear the name Joseph Villette mentioned ever again."

Father and daughter stayed where they were, remaining silent for some minutes after Andrea had left. Finally, Patrick spoke. "You meant well; I know that. But I've told you before, there's a lot you don't understand."

"Then for God's sake," she exploded, "why don't you tell me! And why won't you at least listen to what I'm telling you? Do you want to continue all this worry and precaution? Even when it's no longer needed? Do you simply enjoy the drama?"

"Sit down, Patsy," he said quietly. "Here, beside me. Tell me what's happened. From the beginning."

She told him. "So that's it," she ended after a few minutes. "We're simply small fish as far as the cartel is concerned. They'll leave us alone now."

"It would seem likely," Patrick agreed. "Particularly if the actions of this Mr. Gottlieb have been documented. We'll relax a bit just to test things. But we won't say anything to your mother." He took her hand, holding it lightly but with love. "What about you, Patsy? And what about this young man?"

"There's nothing to tell," Patsy said, pulling away. "I know him, that's all. And I've told you my story, but you haven't told me yours."

Patrick shook his head sadly. "I can't, darling. It's not my story to tell. It's your mother's. I'm sorry. That's how it is. And if there is, in fact, nothing between you and Joseph Villette—well, it doesn't matter, does it?"

"No," Patsy agreed. "It doesn't matter at all. I won't embarrass you a second time by my awkward choice in men. No need to worry about that."

But Patrick saw the tense set of her shoulders as she left the room, the way she walked as if carrying the burdens of the world, and he did worry.

The following week they began tunneling. The vein of slate Hugh Villette had indicated ran between number-two and number-three pit. They made some test borings, and the indications were good but not conclusive. If the slate was there, it was too deep to reveal itself until they were committed to the risks of prying it out of the earth.

Patrick decreed that work would start from both ends. They would tunnel down and across, aiming toward each other. He had rigged all his own surveying equipment—they couldn't afford to buy any—but he was convinced his measurements were correct. If they were, the two tunnels would eventually meet. In the meantime, while they were transversing the distance of some two hundred feet, they would take out slate.

At first, when they sank the shaft, they found only worthless rubble. Endless loads of rock filled the carriages suspended overhead and swelled the waste heaps with alarming speed. But thanks to the increased power of the steam engines it did not take so long as to be impractical. Still, it was ten days before they could be sure of anything. Then, on the second of August, they hauled up the first "golden pheasant." It was useless, of course, the kind of block that couldn't be split into tiles, but it was a certain indication of what lay below. The men would have cheered when they saw it, but they were too tired.

The work was exhausting, terrifying. And the two ends were progressing at uneven rates, not in the measured tandem that Patrick had planned. He hurried back and forth between the two efforts, trying to discover the reason for the disparity. Hour after hour he was drenched in sweat, choked with rock dust, blind with fatigue. He was forty-nine years old and shaking with tiredness. Small wonder that, like the rest, he was beyond cheering when that initial telltale block of false slate was dragged to the surface.

By the following day, Patrick was refreshed. A night's sleep and the encouragement of his wife and daughter revitalized him. But the workmen were frightened. They were quarrymen, not miners. This venture down a narrow hole into the bowels of the earth terrified them. Patrick worried about their possible refusal to continue. "Hang in there, lads," he chivied them. "We've almost made it."

But even if it all went as planned, if the workmen reached the level of the lode without mishap, it was only the beginning. Then the real work would start, the quarrying itself. Not, as they were accustomed, in a wide, sloping basin where they could move and breathe and see the sun but in a narrow cavern of dark and danger.

They might have rebelled if Gareth Jones hadn't returned when he did.

No one expected him. It hadn't occurred to Jones to telegraph that he was coming home, successful beyond their wildest hopes. Jones simply docked in New York and took the train for Rutland, the sheaf of orders he'd obtained secreted in a shiny leather briefcase. He'd bought it in London, an impulse that cost him nearly a month's wages. But that briefcase gave Jones confidence. It was the badge of a businessman, not a laborer. He was swinging it jauntily when he appeared at the quarry on the fourth of August.

"Mr. Whitby! I'm back, sir! And I've got everything . . ."

Patrick stared up at the lad standing on the edge of number-three pit and gesticulating wildly to the cluster of men below. "Gareth! I didn't know you were back, lad! Hang on. I'm coming up."

Gareth Jones made his report right there in the open, where everyone could see—except Patrick. He was still blinded by sweat, and his efforts to wipe his eyes with his dirty sleeve just filled them with grit. He could hear, though. Every word.

"The strike at the Welsh quarries is bad, sir. I felt sorry for the workers. And guilty about being there. Those men, they've got rights; they're human beings. But I figured I'd told you I'd do it—took your money for passage and all. And the men who work for the roofing contractors, they need their jobs, too. So all in all it seemed best to do what I was sent to do."

The boy must have been rehearsing this speech for three thousand miles. "I understand, Gareth," Patrick said. "And I agree with you. So what happened?"

Whitby couldn't see it, but a slow-spreading smile illumined the boy's face. "I took orders, sir. Lots of them. I added it all up on the boat coming over. I sold just over eight thousand squares. And there's more to come later. I asked for a deposit, sir, just like you said. I got copies of the bank transfers all in here." He held up the new briefcase with pride.

Patsy couldn't leave it alone. For the first nineteen years of her life she had believed herself fat and ugly and unlovable. Then she had changed and seen in the eyes of many men her desirability. So why didn't Joseph Villette desire her? Why had he not come back to Whitby Falls, not seen more of her in New York, not wanted to kiss her again? Because of her family and his; that was why. Patsy became angry. One man had betrayed her trust. From now on she would call the tune.

She went again to talk to Phoebe Anderson at the general store. The old woman was willing enough to talk but only about her own interests. "Jason, your grandpa," she told the girl, "he was a hard man. Put his own wife in the crazy house. Course once Andrea came home, they brung Millicent back. But that was Andrea's doin', not Jason's."

"Where did Mama come home from, Mrs. Anderson? What year was that?"

"Don't recall the year exactly. Sixty-nine, maybe seventy. After she'd run away."

"To New York, you mean? Did my mother run away to New York?"

"Guess so. Least folks always said that's where she met your pa."

"But why? Had it something to do with the Villettes?"

Phoebe's small eyes clouded over. "Can't say nothin' about that. But Jason, he was a hard man."

Patsy tried to question her father. She went down to his workroom in the cellar and waited until he noticed her. "Daddy, I've been wondering, how did Mother happen to be in New York? That is where you met her, isn't it?"

"Yes, in New York." He ignored the first part of the question and bent closer to his model of the tunnel. "Seems to me we'll have to add extra support here . . . and here."

"Daddy . . ."

"Yes, darling?" He raised his head and looked at her.

His eyes, red and angry-looking, were swollen almost completely shut. Patsy had not noticed before how bad they were. "Your eyes," she said. "You'll have to do something. You must rest them, bathe them—"

"I will. As soon as the tunnel is finished. We're just starting to take out the good stuff, you see. The real slate. It's the dust that makes my eyes sore. It will pass."

He turned to his work, and she went away.

Talking to Andrea was even more difficult. Patsy tried it just once. "Mama, please tell me the truth. Living up here all these months, being so much closer to you and Daddy, it bothers me that I don't know."

Andrea heard the concern in her daughter's voice. "What is it, darling?" she asked quickly. "What's happened?"

"Nothing has happened. I'm just very much aware of all the undercurrents. All the things I don't understand. About you and Daddy and . . ." She paused, gathering all her courage. "And about the Villettes."

Andrea's face turned hard and white and very cold. Her voice seemed to come from someplace far away. "There is nothing to tell you about that," she said. It was all she would say.

When the idea came, the girl felt first guilty, then triumphant. The newspapers must have had a field day with the trial. And newspapers kept copies of old editions. Why hadn't she thought of it before! Patsy hitched up the buggy early one September morning and drove to Rutland.

"I'd like to see some back copies, please," she told the clerk in the *Herald* office.

"How old?" he asked in a bored tone.

"The summer of seventy-six. Right after the Centennial."

"They're stored away," he said. "Everything older than the last ten years."

"Yes, I realize that. But it's for the Historical Association, and we thought—"

He sighed and beckoned to an old man in the rear. "Clem, show this young lady the papers she wants to see."

He led her into the street, grumbling under his breath while he unlocked a battered, unmarked door. Patsy saw a set of steps leading into blackness. "Got a light just here," the man said, reaching for an old tin lantern. He put a match to it. "Kerosene. No electric down here."

Patsy clutched her skirts to keep them out of the dirt. They descended to a small room that smelled of must and decay. The lantern revealed rows of iron trunks with peeling faded labels. "July seventy-six, you said?"

"Yes, please. And August."

The man called Clem ran a withered finger along the labels, then grunted. "Here it is. June to September seventy-six."

Patsy tried to help, but he ignored her and wrestled the shallow trunk to a rickety table nearby. "Here you are. Help yourself."

Patsy stepped closer, reached into the pile, and saw that her gloves were already filthy. They looked smudged and wet in the dim light of the kerosene lantern. "I may be some time," she said. She did not want a stranger watching her while she read the truth about her mother and the Villettes. It seemed somehow obscene.

The man misinterpreted her meaning. "I can't just stay here while you look. I got work to do. You'll have to do it yourself." He took another lantern from one dark corner and lit it. "Here, I'll leave this with you. When you're done, see yourself out and come get me. I'll come back and lock up."

"Thank you. That will be fine." She turned up the wick of the light as high as it would go and began to lift the newspapers from their resting place.

2.

Patsy never went back to say she was finished with the papers. She remained in the cellar nearly two hours, reading and rereading the accounts of the trial. Eventually, she staggered up the stairs to the street and walked away.

She had never before known the exact dates, never realized their significance. Now she did. Riley Villette had been her mother's lover. They were together for the last time on the Fourth of July. Then, nine months later, she was born. So she was Riley Villette's bastard. Patrick wasn't her father. It had all been a lie. Twenty years of her life had been lived with Andrea and Patrick, and for twenty years they had lived a fraud.

"*I saw them doing it—lots of times.*" The *Herald* had quoted Jackie Villette's evidence, had reported that when called to the stand, the defendant, Mrs. Whitby, confirmed that the story was true. What had her mother looked like then? she wondered. Doubtless even more beautiful than she was now. And strong enough to stab a man to death, the man who was the father of her illegitimate child.

It started to rain. Not soft and gentle rain but a squalling thunderstorm that blew in over the mountains and punished the valley. Patsy was soaked to the skin, but she was unaware of it or of where she walked. Hugh Villette found her a couple of hours later, wandering in the woods by the side of the Whitby Falls road.

Hugh had gone to the bank in Rutland. It was a journey he made frequently, an ordinary part of his routine. Normally, he would have left for home two hours earlier, but the storm delayed him. Then, when he finally did set out, he saw the buggy tied up near the *Herald* office. Hugh recognized it as belonging to the Whitbys, and it seemed to him odd that Patrick would leave his horses untended in such weather. The animals were shivering, rain running off their backs into the muddy street. They had obviously been there a long time. Not my worry, Hugh told himself.

He hadn't reached the end of Center Street before he turned back. Some kind of feeling was in him for Patrick Whitby, some strange and unacknowledged bond forged over the last months. Maybe sympathy for the Irishman's troubles, admiration of his dogged efforts. Villette, always a man of instincts, knew that something was wrong. Otherwise, the horses would not have been left out in the storm.

He made inquiries at the hardware store and the lumberyard. No one had seen Patrick Whitby or knew of his being in town. Then Hugh went to the *Herald* office. "No," they told him. "Mr. Whitby ain't been in here."

"Hey," old Clem interrupted. "What about that girl? The one what just walked out and left the old papers. I thought I'd seen her before. I remember now. She's Whitby's daughter."

"Thanks." Hugh pushed a bill across the counter. "Take the buggy and the horses up to Quinn's stables. Tell him to board them until someone comes."

"Yes, sir, Mr. Villette. I'll do it right away." The younger of the two men hurried out behind Hugh and stared perplexed as the slate king jumped into his own carriage and raced down the street. The clerk was not quite thirty; otherwise, he might have been able to puzzle out the events of the day, just as Hugh himself had done.

"Okay, Miss Patsy, you're all right now. I'm taking you home." He led the sodden girl toward his buggy, and she hadn't the strength to resist. "Been looking for you the past hour." Villette rummaged in the back to find a blanket. "Figured you was walking home in this rain. It's let up now, but it's still pretty bad. You shouldn't have left your buggy behind."

She didn't react to his chatter or to the warmth of the blanket he wrapped around her shoulders. Only when he had seated himself beside her and started the horses moving did she ask, "Where are you taking me?"

"To your house, of course. Your pa will be worried sick thinking of you out in this weather."

"No." She spoke the word shrilly, with a rising note of panic. "No, no, no," she repeated, each exclamation higher than the one before. "I'm not going back there! Not ever!"

Hugh swallowed hard. The thought of a hysterical woman alone with him on the deserted road he viewed as a more explosive situation than any amount of dynamite. "Where do you want to go, then?" he demanded. "I can't leave you out here in the woods. Besides, like I said, your pa will be—"

"He's not!" She screamed the words into the wind. "He's not my father. It's a lie. All these years it's been a lie!"

"Oh, Jesus," Hugh said softly. Twenty years later and that bitch Andrea Whitby was still causing trouble. Still wanting everything her own way. She'd never told the girl. She'd let her find out for herself that she was probably Riley's. Hugh knew it; everyone that could count knew it. But this little thing didn't. Until she went and read the old stories and found out for herself. Now she was sobbing her heart out in his buggy, and he didn't know what to say to her.

"All right, girl," he muttered. "Just calm yourself. Please. It's all water under the dam. It doesn't matter anymore."

She didn't answer him, just kept crying so hard he was terrified she'd choke. Hugh looked at her and cursed quietly. Then he brought down his whip on the horses' backs and sped them forward. He'd take the girl home. Lise would know what to do.

"It's that damned Andrea Whitby. Same damned thing all over again. She's a genuine witch, that woman." He dumped the unconscious figure of the girl on the couch in Lise's elegant drawing room. "I picked her up on the road. She went to Rutland and looked at all the old newspaper stories. Andrea never told her. First she was hysterical; then she fainted. Says she never wants to go home again. I couldn't leave her in the woods, so I brought her here."

Lise nodded and told him to carry Patsy up to the yellow guest room. When she went for hot water and spirits and towels, it occurred to her that it was just like Hugh to put all the blame on Andrea. To Lise it seemed that Patrick was the more guilty.

*   *   *

"What did he say?" Lise asked her husband when he returned from the Whitby house.

"What could he say, poor bastard?" Hugh poured himself a stiff shot of whiskey and tossed it back. "Did you know he's almost blind? Some kind of reaction to the slate dust. Both eyes are nearly closed." He sat down heavily. "Didn't stop him from crying, though. When I told him what had happened, he sobbed like a woman. Don't blame him, the poor bastard."

"Did you see her?" Lise asked.

"No. Damn good thing, too. I'd have killed her, Lise. I swear I would. How can anyone make so much grief for so many people? It's been the same since the day she was born. Princess Andrea. That's what Riley used to call her. Some princess."

"She's had her share of suffering," Lise said softly. "More than her share."

"I don't think so. Nothing like."

Lise abandoned the futile defense. "What does Mr. Whitby want to do about Patsy?"

"He wasn't sure. He couldn't think straight. Just getting hit with it like that, out of the blue. He was just starting to worry where she was. Then I came and told him the worst. In his shoes I wouldn't know what to do, either. I said we'd keep her here for now. Tomorrow, maybe the next day, he'll come talk to her."

"Poor man." Lise shook her head.

"Funny thing, though," Hugh said. "He looked at me like I was crazy when I said about her thinking she was Riley's kid. 'She's mine,' he kept saying. 'Patsy's my daughter, my baby. . . .' That's when he started to cry."

Hugh looked close to tears himself. "Come to bed," Lise said. "You've had a hard day. We'll see what tomorrow brings."

Patrick went to the Villette place before nine the next morning. "She says she doesn't want to see you," Lise said frankly. "But go up anyway. First room on the left. She'll change her mind, I think."

Patrick climbed the stairs and felt the thick carpet beneath his feet, the silken mahogany banister under his hand. The door to Patsy's room was of mahogany, too. It was elaborately carved, but Patrick could not appreciate its detail with his limited vision and his mind filled with pain. "Patsy, please darling, let me in. I have to talk to you."

There was no reply. Patrick turned the knob. The door was locked. "Listen to me," he whispered urgently, his mouth pressed to the crack beside the door, as if it were a secret, as if everyone didn't know. "What you think, what you read— It's not like that. You're mine, darling, my child. I've always known you were. How can you—"

"Go away. I never want to see you or speak to you again. Go away." The words were not hysterical. They were just words.

"Please," he repeated. "Let me explain. It's complicated. You don't know everything." She didn't answer. Eventually, he turned away and descended the stairs.

"Perhaps in a few days," Lise said. "After she's had time to get over the shock . . ."

Patrick nodded. "Yes. I'll come back." Then he recognized his presumption. "I—we have no right to expect you to keep her. But I don't know—"

"Forget that," Hugh said gruffly. "She can stay as long as she likes. She'll be safe here. You needn't worry."

"I know. Thank you." The two men looked at each other and didn't say more.

Outside, the September sun was hot and blinding. Patrick fumbled in his pocket for the dark glasses that helped his sore eyes a little. And he remembered the day they had given a similar pair to Patsy, the day before she left for Switzerland in an effort to repair her shattered life. She'd been so young, so vulnerable, so hurt. He'd ached for her. He ached for her now. With a father's ache. That peculiar and unique pain one felt for one's child; like no other. Patsy *was* his child. He had never doubted it, never denied the testimony of his flesh and feeling. But Andrea always had. Now Patsy did, too.

He walked slowly down Main Street. He thought not of Patsy's flat voice when she dismissed him but of his wife's. "She's there?" Andrea had spoken the words in horror when he reported the news Hugh Villette had brought. "In that house? With them?" She had stared at her husband, willing him to say she had misunderstood. When he did not, she had turned away, shaking with sobs and refusing any comfort.

What would she say to him now? Patrick wondered. Nothing,

probably. She would close in on herself as she had in the old days, lock him out. They all locked him out. Patsy in her solitary pain, Andrea in hers, Eddie chasing the mirage of wealth as if it could banish suffering. Patrick sighed and opened the door to Jason's house. Not his, Jason's. Always. In the distance he heard the thud of dynamite. The tunnel. He thought of it once, then dismissed it as irrelevant.

3.

It didn't feel like autumn to Joseph; the morning was oppressively hot and humid. He drove the hired trap to the edge of Whitby Falls and looked at the town. It slumbered beneath a haze of heat. His gaze traveled from the white house to the Whitby place, and his heart started to hammer. Too late to start acting like a love-sick kid, he told himself. Still, he was grinning when he turned toward the Villette quarry.

"Hi, H.J. Where's your dad?"

"Oh, it's you. Ain't seen you all summer."

"No, I've been busy. Missed you all, though. How have you been?"

"Okay. Pa ain't here. He had to go see about a new account in Brattleboro."

Joseph showed no impatience with his cousin's hostile tone. "I'll just head for the house, then," he said. "See you later."

For weeks he'd fought the impulse to return and see her. Now he'd given in, and there was a spring in his step when he left the office. He didn't start for the town immediately. There was time. He looked once more toward Patsy's house, then started on foot up a path leading to the mountain. Joseph wanted time to absorb the feeling of Vermont and the future he hoped was waiting for him there.

"He's back," H.J. told his brother. "Came in about ten minutes ago lookin' for Pa."

Henry knew who "he" was. "I thought he'd given up,"

he muttered. These past weeks he'd stopped worrying about Joseph. Now the familiar sick panic knotted in his gut. "He say what he wanted?"

"Hell, he don't have to. Same thing he always wants." H.J. slammed his pencil on the desk.

"Yeah, well, he can't have it." Henry spun on his heel and walked out.

He spotted the hired trap near the west gate of the quarry and looked around for his cousin. Joseph was nowhere in sight. He wouldn't have gone to the house and left the trap behind. Henry turned up the path toward Herrick.

Joseph smelled the storm before he saw the first lightning flash. A wind came up, carrying the faint scent of burning ozone. Villette wandered to the edge of the trail. He was on a steep cliff. Below him, jagged outcroppings of granite tumbled down to the quarry and the town beyond. Thick black clouds raced across the sky. They were coming straight in his direction, and while he watched, lightning scissored blue in their midst. After a few seconds he heard the thunder.

"Jesus, it's magnificent," he whispered aloud. He knew he should be sensible and head for safety, but the beauty of the approaching storm mesmerized him. He remained poised at the edge of the cliff. A howling wind plastered his clothes to his body and swept his hair back from his face. Villette breathed deep and trembled with exultation.

From the shelter of a stand of pine Henry watched the other man. Hatred choked him. Look at him, so tall and handsome, so sure of himself he'll stand on a mountain in the middle of a thunderstorm. A goddam fool, like all city folk. No idea how dangerous it can be . . . Sweat trickled down Henry's face and dried instantly in the wind. He shivered. The muscles in his arms twitched with longing.

Less than six yards lay between him and Joseph. The ground was open and without cover, but the distance was short. Only six yards to cross and he'd be free of the threat that menaced his life.

Henry tensed and began edging his way out of the trees.

Joseph didn't hear anything—it was impossible to hear above the wind—he simply knew. He stood loose-jointed and waiting. The instincts of a lifetime melded with years of training to make his timing perfect. A fraction of a second before the lunge came, he stepped aside. His assailant hurtled off the cliff top. A loud crack of thunder drowned the falling man's scream of terror. The skies opened, and torrents of rain poured down.

Joseph dropped to his knees and tried to see through the sheets of water. He could make out a twisted form lying on an outcropping of ledge about fifteen feet below.

"Your brother's had an accident," he told H.J. He had not been sure which of them it was until he saw the younger man sitting in the quarry office. "Henry's fallen off a cliff."

H.J. stared in disbelief. Joseph stood in the middle of the room, dripping wet and breathing hard from his run down the mountain.

"Where is he?" H.J. finally managed through chattering teeth.

"About half a mile up the path behind the west gate. Better send some men to get him. Tell them to take ropes and a stretcher."

"Is he— I mean—" H.J. licked lips dry with fear.

"I've no idea. But if he's not dead now, he may well be by the time you decide to send help."

H.J. bolted from the office, and Joseph found the bottle of brandy his uncle always kept on the shelf by the window. He poured himself a double and watched the sun break through the clouds.

"It's just a broken leg," Lise told him. "Dr. Williams is setting it now. They'll bring Henry home later." She took off her shawl and dropped it on the couch. Then she walked to where Joseph stood in the middle of the drawing room. "What happened, Joseph?"

"Just what I told you, Aunt Lise. We were talking, the storm came up, Henry lost his footing."

"What were you doing up there? Why were you and Henry on the mountain?"

"I'd just arrived in town, and I went to the office looking for Uncle Hugh. H.J. told me he was in Brattleboro, and then Henry and I went for a walk."

"You and Henry. A walk." She turned away and pressed her fingers to her temples.

Joseph put his hands lightly on her shoulders. "Aunt Lise, everything's okay. Don't worry."

She turned to him, and he saw the pain in her eyes. "Henry's weak," she said softly. "He gets frightened, and then he does things. . . ."

"Ssh, it's over. We don't have to talk about it. I'm glad he's going to be all right. I know how they feel, both Henry and H.J. Uncle Hugh thought it was a good idea to let them sweat it out for a while. Now you tell them they've nothing to worry about. I don't want any of what's theirs. I just came up this time to see Patsy. I'm going over to the Whitby place now."

She gasped. "Patsy! Oh, Lord, you don't know. She's not at home. She's upstairs. She's been here a week."

Lise told him the story. She did not need to elaborate. Joseph had not forgotten what Hugh had told him about the murder and the trial and what had once been between Riley and Andrea.

"Jesus," Joseph said. "Why didn't they tell her before, not wait for her to find out like this?"

Lise shrugged. "How do you talk about something like that?"

He shook his head. "I don't know. Where is she?"

"In the yellow room. She won't see anyone, not even Patrick, and she hasn't come out since she's been here."

"Well, she will now," Joseph said.

He strode up the stairs two at a time and knocked firmly on the door. "It's me, Joseph. Open up."

Patsy cracked the door. "I'm not feeling like company just now," she said. "Please excuse me." She started to close the door, but she couldn't. Joseph's foot was in the way.

He forced himself inside. "We're going for a walk," he said. "Get a wrap. There's a chill in the air."

"No."

"Look, I'm not asking you. I'm telling you. Now do you come willingly, or do I carry you?"

"Who do you think you are!"

"Somebody bigger than you," he said quietly. "Might makes right in this world. Haven't you heard?"

She looked at him for some seconds, then managed a small, tentative smile. "You'd do it, too, wouldn't you?"

"You can bet on it, sweetheart."

She took a shawl and preceded him down the stairs. "Please," she said when they were outside, "let's go this way." She pointed away from the town.

"Suits me," Joseph said.

They walked in silence to the riverbank. When they stopped, they were in the place where the old cabin had stood. The place where he had kissed her that first time. "It's nice here," Patsy said softly. "Thanks for making me come. It's good to get out."

"You're a good girl," he said, grinning. "Always willing to admit when you're wrong. How long is it going to be before you do that with your folks?"

She stared at him. "Don't joke about it," she said in a strained whisper. "I can't bear it." She turned away from him, almost doubled over in pain. "You can't understand. . . ."

"Oh, can't I? Aren't you forgetting something, sweetheart? I've been a genuine, bona fide bastard since the day I was born. I don't even know who my father might have been, let alone have a choice of two."

She didn't answer him or turn around. He could see her shoulders heaving with silent sobs. Joseph reached for her and pulled her into his arms. At first she resisted; then she buried her face in his chest and wept. "Okay," he said after a long time. "That's it; that's enough crying. Now we make plans." He leaned down and kissed the top of her head, then laid his cheek on the soft, curly black hair. "I've thought about you a lot lately," he whispered.

Patsy stirred in his arms, moving her hands along the strong, hard-muscled width of his shoulders. "I didn't think you thought about me at all," she whispered shyly.

"Idiot," he said. "I thought women knew things like that. I've been in love with you since the day I saw you in that funny little store downtown with your head wrapped up in this thing"—he fingered the woolen shawl she was wearing—"and your nose shiny with the cold. It's taken me a long time to face it, but I thought you knew."

She leaned back so she could look in his eyes. "No," she said very softly. "I hoped, but I didn't know."

Joseph leaned forward to kiss her. Then, just before their lips met, Patsy gasped and pulled away. She moaned, and it was a wordless sound of realization and pain.

"What's the matter! For God's sake, Patsy, what is it?"

"You," she said in a strangled whisper. "Me. We're related, blood kin—"

"Oh, Jesus!" He took her shoulders in his strong hands and shook them. "Stop it! Stop making sticks for your own back. Maybe we are, and maybe we're not. You can't know for sure. And if it's true, so what? We're cousins if we're anything. What difference does it make!"

Patsy studied his face as if all wisdom, all truth, could be found there. "I don't know. I thought— They say—"

"*They* say a hell of a lot of things. Most of it's horseshit."

He'd meant to shock her with the word, and he did. "You're sure," she asked hesitantly after a few seconds. "It wouldn't bother you? You wouldn't worry?"

For an answer he kissed her.

The lovers said nothing to anyone. Lise and Hugh, preoccupied by Henry's convalescence, were content to ignore the circumstances of their son's fall—and Joseph and Patsy.

Joseph had only a week before he must return to New York. The pair spent as much time together as they could, unaware of any reality outside themselves. For a brief time they shared the wonder of their private dream, their discovery. On the third day, when they sat again in their favorite spot by the Little Whitby, Patsy turned to him.

"Make love to me, Joseph," she said.

He looked at her, his aquamarine eyes searching hers, his hands holding her face so she couldn't pull away. "I want you," he said. "I've never wanted a woman more. But I want you to be sure. Not frightened, not trying to prove something because you're still in shock."

"I'm none of those things," she said. She put her hands over his and moved them to her breast. Her heart was pounding, and he could feel her full breasts stirring beneath his touch. "Now," she said. "Please."

He nodded, then looked around. They weren't as private as they might be. "Come." He pulled her to her feet. They walked deeper into the woods. Then, when they had reached a place where the pines enclosed them completely and where the ground beneath their feet was soft with moss, he said, "This is a good place. Our place."

"Yes," Patsy said. She reached up and undid the buttons

of her frock. She'd worn no corsets; she seldom did. When she slipped the dress over her head, she was half naked.

Joseph stepped forward and cupped her breasts in his hands. Her nipples were turgid with the coolness of the air and with his closeness. He kissed each one delicately, as if in greeting. "Mine," he said.

"Yes. Always if you wish."

He let her go and took off his own clothes, spreading them on the ground as a makeshift mattress. His eyes didn't leave hers the whole time. When everything was ready, he untied the ribbons holding her petticoats and her pantaloons and let them drop to her ankles. She stood revealed and beautiful in a sea of white cotton and lace. Joseph held out his hand. Patsy took it and stepped free of the jumble of clothes.

They lay together on the pallet he had made. Patsy smelled the pine needles and the sun and the scent of Joseph. They explored each other's bodies with their hands and their mouths; their breath mingled. Gently, he parted her thighs, velvet smooth, firm and young and strong. When she clasped them around his narrow hips, he could feel the strength and certitude with which she yielded.

He wanted to be slow, to make it good for her, but he could not. Not this first time. He had imagined this many times, dreamed about it throughout the long weeks and months when he fought his feeling for her. Now the reality was a moment of acute truth. When he poured himself into her, he knew it as a promise, and he felt the spasms of her answering joy and her commitment. "Mine," he said again when it was over. "Always."

"You're sure?" Patsy whispered into his shoulder. He still lay over her, their flesh united in the moist aftermath of love. "Don't say it if you're not sure, Joseph. I couldn't bear it. I'd rather know now."

She had been rehearsing the speech, he realized. He raised his head so he could look at her. "Don't say that again," he said. "It doesn't have anything to do with us. Your parents, mine. Whoever they were. It's no part of you and me, what we feel."

"I don't mean only that," she said. She could not risk another betrayal. "You must know now. You're not the first. There was someone else. Two years ago—"

He silenced her by laying his finger over her lips. He

hadn't really thought about it until she said it. Now he knew that the ghost must be exorcised immediately and for all time. "I don't care," he said. "I don't care about anything that happened before I knew you. I only care about today, this minute. It's the way I am, sweetheart, the way I'm made. I've lived my whole life for the now. I can't change. I never will. Do you love me now? That's all I want to know."

"I love you."

"That's it, then. That's everything." He kissed her again, and it was not necessary to say more.

Joseph was due back in New York by the weekend. On Thursday evening he talked to Hugh. They were alone in the big drawing room with the double doors and the lavish decoration; the room that most epitomized everything Lise and Hugh had accomplished.

"I like this room," Joseph said. "It's impressive, makes me feel secure."

"Lise, too," Hugh said, smiling. "That's why she's spent so much care and money on it. I understand, but I don't feel the same."

"What makes you feel secure?" Joseph asked.

"Lise. And the smell of slate when it comes out of the ground. It smells like a million years of history."

Joseph stared at the tips of his shiny alligator shoes. "There are other things that come out of the ground," he said. "Things men will fight and steal for."

"Gold," Hugh agreed. "Stuff like that, I know. It's not the same for me. You can't build things with gold. It isn't part of anything real. It's just money."

"What about diamonds?" Joseph asked. "How do you feel about them?"

The older man laughed. "I bought one for Lise a few years ago, when we opened the tenth pit. She likes it. Far as I'm concerned, it might as well be glass."

"You aren't making it any easier," Joseph said with a sigh. "Pour yourself a drink, Uncle Hugh, and sit down. I've got a long story to tell. You probably won't like it."

When his nephew had finished speaking, Hugh sat silent for a while. Then he said, "What if it had been me, my quarry, they were attacking? What would you have done then?"

Joseph knew what he should say, but he couldn't say it. There had already been too many lies. "At first, nothing. It didn't mean anything to me, being your nephew. I had a job to do. That's all that mattered."

"I see. You said 'at first.' What about later?"

"I'd have told you. I'd have stopped it. You may not believe me, but it's the truth. I've come to understand, you see."

"What?" Hugh asked. "What do you understand?"

"About building things, building a life. Making a future. I didn't think any of that was important. I didn't want it to be. I just wanted to go on as I was. My boss, the man I work for, we're very close. He's been good to me. It took me a long time to realize that his way wasn't necessarily mine. I respect him, admire him. But I'm different. I'm a Villette. Vermont's in my blood now."

"It always was," Hugh said. "Your ma was Vermont born and bred. She passed it on to you." He was content with what he'd heard. He would not have been had the younger man made excuses. "You going to move up here?" he asked. He was hoping, though he didn't want to. All these months, comparing Joseph to Henry and H.J., he'd told himself it was wrong. A man's first loyalty must be to his own sons. After Henry's so-called accident, Hugh dared to flirt again with the secret dream. He imagined Joseph working beside him, a worthy successor. "You could come in with us. I'd handle the boys."

"That's not my plan," Joseph said. "It's more complicated than that."

Hugh recognized finality and let the dream die. He had Lise. A man couldn't have everything.

"There's this Whitby versus Villette thing to deal with. There's Patsy," Joseph added.

"What about her?"

"Patsy and I are going to be married," Joseph said.

"I suspected something like that. A Whitby marrying a Villette. It's probably a good thing."

"That's got nothing to do with it. I don't give a damn about some feud that started before either of us were born. All this melodrama you people have lived with for so long has nothing to do with us."

"I hope not," Hugh said. "There's been enough suffering. Anyway, what does Patsy want to do about her folks?"

"Nothing. Just go away and not tell them anything. She'll be twenty-one in April. She figures we can just live together until then."

"And you?" Hugh asked. "What do you figure?"

"They probably deserve better. And she'll come to regret it later on."

"Have you told her that?"

"Yes. She won't listen."

"You're right, though." Hugh stood up and walked to the window. He noticed a thin sliver of light in the Whitby house. It was the only sign of life in the place. No one had seen either Patrick or Andrea for over two weeks. "They're holed up in there like a couple of wounded animals," he said. "It stinks. It's no beginning for the two of you."

"What should I do?"

"Go to Patrick," Hugh said. "At least tell him how things are. He's a reasonable man, a good one. He'll listen."

"And her? His wife? What about her?"

Hugh sighed. "Andrea Whitby is a law unto herself. God knows how she'll react. I sure as hell don't." He turned, and his nephew could see in his face some vestige of the old fight he claimed to be ready to forget. "I don't care much, either," Hugh continued. "It's him I'm thinking about. Patrick. He loves his daughter. Far as he's concerned, she's his. He's raised her, worried about her, worked for her. He deserves to know how things are."

"Right." Joseph tossed back the glass of whiskey he was holding. "I'll go, then." But just before he went out the door, he said, "Uncle Hugh, come with me. Would you do that?"

"Sure," Hugh said without hesitation. "If you want."

"I do. I've never had a father. I'd like you to come."

4.

Patrick let them in, peered hard through his swollen eyelids to see who it was, then showed them into the study. There was no sign of Andrea. Joseph uttered a silent prayer of thanks. He would admit it to no one, but she terrified him. He'd only seen her once or twice from a distance. She had seemed to him the most inaccessible woman alive. He was glad that Patsy was so unlike her mother.

"Listen," Hugh said as soon as the three men were seated, "I wanted to tell you, Patrick. I've been up to the quarry a couple of times. Just to see how they were coming. They're working on the tunnel. Bit slower than they might if you were there, but they're working."

Patrick nodded. "It's good to know that. I should go. I know I should. But . . ." He made a gesture of helplessness. "My eyes," he said. It had nothing to do with his eyes. They all knew it, but no one said it.

"Have a drink," Patrick said, suddenly mindful of his duties as host. He took a bottle of Irish from the drawer of Jason's old desk. "There's brandy if you prefer."

"No," the Villettes said in unison.

"Irish is fine," Hugh added.

Whitby poured the whiskey, and they all took a sip. Then there was an awkward silence. Finally, both Patrick and Joseph began to speak at once.

"How's Patsy? . . ." Patrick began.

"Patsy and I . . ." Joseph said at the same moment. Then he added, "You first, sir." It wasn't just deference; he was glad of the opportunity to postpone the inevitable. This stooped and beaten man filled Joseph with pity.

"I just want to know how she is," Patrick said lamely.

"Fine," Hugh said. "Just fine." Then it struck him that it was the wrong thing to say under the circumstances. "I mean, I know she's still feeling bad about how things are between you, but—"

"I understand," Patrick said. "It was kind of you to come

408

and tell me. About Patsy and about the quarry. I appreciate it."

Joseph couldn't delay any longer. He cleared his throat self-consciously. Joseph had many times faced men with guns, men who were killers, men with enough money to buy the world; none had ever made him feel as insecure as this graying stranger with the trace of a brogue still in his speech and a lifetime of sadness in his lined face.

"I have something to say, sir," he began. "I came here to say it. I asked my uncle to come, too, because he's the only relative I have. It seemed fitting." He paused, but there was nothing in the other man's face except polite attention. No glimmer of understanding, no hint that he already knew what it was that Joseph had come to say. "It's Patsy and me, sir," he pronounced finally. "We love each other. We're going to be married. I hoped you might give us your blessing. For Patsy's sake."

"Aaagh!!!" The scream came from the hall; it rent the room, bounced off the walls. It pierced the men's eardrums and made fear knot in their bellies. It was the sound of elementary rage and timeless hatred. It was a primordial cry that harked back to the cave and that most ancient of taboos.

Andrea hurled herself into the study and stood in their midst. She had obviously been listening outside the door for some time. "You cannot do this," she said to Joseph. She had vented her hysteria in that one blood-chilling explosion of sound. Now she was icy calm.

Patrick tried to touch her, but she pulled away. His hand dropped by his side helplessly, and he sank back to his seat. He couldn't struggle with her anymore.

"You cannot do this," she repeated. Her violet eyes never left Joseph's face. "It is an abomination," she said. She repeated the word as if it said everything. "An abomination."

Joseph felt anger rise in his throat. "Why? Because you say so? Because you're staggering under a load of guilt you made for yourself years ago? I don't buy it, lady. Patsy doesn't buy it. So maybe we're cousins. So who the hell cares!"

Andrea kept looking at him as if he were some subhuman species. "You disgust me." Her voice was soft with menace. "You are revolting. You don't know anything, but you dare to involve yourself in our lives. You dare to speak my daughter's name." She turned to Hugh.

It was the first time in years that their eyes had met. In the brief exchanges they had shared since they were children, one or the other of them always looked away. Now the full force of her hatred shook him.

"Tell him," she said. "You tell him the truth. Tell him what your brother did to me. Tell him why I had to kill Riley." She sounded as if she were screaming, but still her voice was a low whisper. "Tell him why this thing he wants to do is an abomination."

"I don't know what you're talking about!" Hugh shouted the words into the teeth of her rage. "For God's sake, Andrea, can't you let it alone? Riley's dead. Let him rest in peace. Let the living go on." Tears rolled down his cheeks, frustration and pain and anger. He didn't acknowledge them, didn't even wipe them away.

"You coward. You can't face it. None of you ever could. But I can. I'll tell him." She whirled toward Joseph once more. "Jason," she said, "Jason, my father, was Riley's father, too. Riley and I were brother and sister. Riley knew, but I didn't. Then I found out. I saw Jason with Maryann, with your mother!" She took a step closer to Joseph, opened her arms in mock affection. "They were lovers, too. Jason and his daughter lay together, and you were born. Isn't it clear to you now? We're all one big happy family. And Riley was Patsy's father. Isn't it wonderful?" She was laughing. It was a terrible sound, even more frightening than her scream had been.

"Andrea, Andrea, please . . ." Patrick tried one more time. She pushed him away, and he fell back as if he'd been a paper cutout of a man rather than flesh and blood.

Andrea went on as if she hadn't noticed her husband or felt his touch. "That's why I had to murder Riley's child," she said. "That's why it had to be cut out of my body. It was an abomination. But Patsy . . . I couldn't murder Patsy. I couldn't. I tried to protect her. To keep her from knowing. I failed."

She hung her head, and the silver hair gleamed in the glow from the bulb overhead. It made a nimbus of light around her. It illuminated the spot on the floor where Riley had lain with the letter opener in his back. Andrea could see him as clearly as if he lay there still.

"You're crazy," Joseph said. The room had grown very still. His words carried in the silence. "You're crazy as they come. And all that stuff you're saying is horseshit!"

The word acted as an antidote to Andrea's tragic elegy. The other two men stirred.

"Joseph isn't Jason's son," Hugh said. "Sure, Maryann had an affair with Jason. We all know that. But she hadn't seen him in almost a year when she got pregnant. Maryann told me that herself. She swore it. Besides, look at him. Joseph's got nothing of Jason in any part of him. God knows who his father is. Maryann spread her legs for anybody that took her fancy." Hugh shot a look of apology toward his nephew.

"I know," Joseph said. "I know all about it. Maryann was my mother, and I loved her, and she was good to me. She always told me the truth, about everything. That's how I know Jason Whitby wasn't my father. She told me. And she told me he wasn't the father of any of you. She knew all about it, and she told me plenty of times. Everything this crazy lady has said is nuts."

"I don't understand about that part," Hugh said slowly. "What made you think Jason was Riley's pa, Andrea?" She didn't answer, and he grew angry. "Look at me, damn you! And explain yourself! What right have you got to say a thing like that?"

Andrea kept staring at the floor, at the ghost of Riley's dead body, as she spoke. "Eve and Jason were lovers. For years and years. My mother knew it. She tried to tell me why I couldn't have Riley's child."

"That's a lie!" Hugh shouted. "That's a filthy lie." Despite all the terrible things they had been saying, this thing struck him as unsayable.

"No, it's not," Joseph said quietly. "That part of it's true. My mother told me."

Incredulous, Hugh looked at his nephew. "Maryann told you that? She said Jason was Riley's father?"

"No. Just that Eve and Jason were once lovers. She was close to her mother, apparently. She knew more than the rest of you did. Eve admitted the relationship between her and Whitby, but she insisted he wasn't the father of any of her children. That was just a crazy idea he had. According to Maryann, Eve was real sure about it. Not a doubt in her mind. She let Jason believe it because it suited her, but you were all Jacques Villette's kids."

Hugh had been standing. Now he sank into a seat. "Well, I'll be damned," he said softly. "I'll be damned. I never knew that. None of us did. Except Maryann, apparently. But not me or Riley or Jackie. Jason Whitby and Ma. I'll be damned."

His whisper penetrated Andrea's consciousness as his shouts had not. "You didn't know?" She said it slowly, repeated it. "You didn't know? Riley didn't know?"

Hugh shook his head. "First I ever heard of any of it was tonight, right here in this room. I'd stake my life Riley went to his grave not knowing."

"Then—" She broke off and clasped her hands over her mouth.

"Then everything you've been saying is rubbish," Joseph finished for her. "The only possible relationship between me and Patsy is that maybe she's Riley's daughter. Maybe we're cousins. And maybe we're not. It doesn't matter. Get that through your crazy head, lady! You carry that load around with you if you want to. It's your funeral. Patsy and I are getting married. And if you ever come near her with your stories and your talk of 'abomination,' I'll kill you with my bare hands. I swear I will."

The door slammed behind him. Hugh waited a moment, looked at the Whitbys, each immobile in their private grief, shook his head, and followed Joseph.

Andrea went to her old room and locked herself in. Patrick spent the rest of the night alone. He didn't try to reach her; he knew it was futile. Eventually, he went upstairs and lay down fully dressed on the bed they usually shared. Finally, after the church clock chimed four A.M., he fell asleep.

He woke to glorious sunshine and chirping birds. The scent of new-mown grass floated in the open window. Patrick stumbled to his feet and fished his watch from his vest pocket. He squinted at it in the strong sunlight. It was seven-thirty. He could hear soft, tuneless whistling in the garden. A man was working with a scythe, cutting the tall grass that had been neglected all summer. Extraordinary. Patrick didn't know what to make of it.

In the hall, he smelled eggs and frying bacon. It was as if

he'd dreamed all the horrors of the past months, the terrible events of the night before.

Downstairs in the kitchen, Andrea stood at the stove. Her hair was piled carefully on her head, neat and tidy and still beautiful. She wore a gingham frock and a sparkling white apron. She was making breakfast. "Good morning, darling," she said brightly. "This will be ready in a minute. Sit down."

She had set a place for him at the scrubbed pine table, and he took it with timid, unsure movements.

"Listen," he started to say. "About last night, about Patsy and that boy. I was thinking—"

"This wretched old stove," she interrupted. "It doesn't heat up evenly on the left side. Maybe you can take a look at it one of these days."

"Yes, of course." He swallowed hard, his mouth dry. She'd heard him; she just wouldn't talk about it. Andrea wanted to pretend nothing had happened. Maybe she wanted to pretend Patsy didn't exist. Crazy. But better than hysteria, perhaps. For now, anyway. "How are you?" He squinted at her through his sore eyes and asked the question hesitantly, afraid of the answer.

"I'm fine. I slept well. Let me see your eyes." She cupped one slim, cool hand beneath his chin and turned his face to the light. "Better, I think. Still swollen but not so red. I've made a chamomile eyewash. You can use it after breakfast."

He was intensely conscious of the touch of her fingers. "I haven't shaved yet. I'm sorry. I thought—"

"It doesn't matter," she interrupted quickly, as if she didn't want him to say anything about what he thought. "You can do it after you've eaten."

She served him bacon and eggs and hot biscuits and fresh coffee. While he ate, she bustled about the kitchen, arranging things, dusting the shelves. "Aren't you hungry?" he said at last.

"Not just now. I'll have something later." She cleared away his dishes and brought a bowl filled with steaming scented water. It smelled faintly medicinal. "Wash your eyes with this." He picked up the little square of linen she'd provided, handling it awkwardly. "Here," Andrea said. "Let me do it."

When she was finished, he said, "That feels much better."

"I'm glad."

Despite his impaired vision, he saw the brightness of her smile. He didn't know what to think or say. The house shook with a slight tremor. It was after eight; the men were at the pit.

"You should go to work," Andrea said. "Even if you can't stay long. They need you. They may have questions about the tunnel."

"Yes," Patrick said. "It's over two weeks. There must be questions." He went to the hall and returned with something in his hands. "Look what I made," he said shyly.

He had fashioned a pair of close-fitting goggles with dark lenses and a frame that hugged his face. "They're better than the ones you can buy. They'll keep out all the grit."

Andrea looked at them carefully. "They're superb, Patrick. You should apply for a patent."

"Perhaps I will." He put on the glasses and looked out the window. The man with the scythe was nearby. "Who is that?" he asked. "How does he come to be working here today?"

"It's Sam. You know, the old fellow who used to look after the garden. I went and got him early this morning. The yard is a mess; something had to be done. The house, too. I'm going to clean it from top to bottom. One of the local women is coming in. Just for today. I know we can't afford regular help."

"Perhaps we can now," Patrick said. "With the tunnel and all . . . Things are getting better."

"Well, maybe I'll have her come again, then. We'll see."

He nodded, starting to feel quiet hope. It was only a fluttering in his stomach, but it was a beginning. "I'll wash and change," he said. "Then I'll go to the quarry."

"Yes," Andrea agreed. "You do that. When you come home, lunch will be ready."

Gareth Jones had become a kind of unofficial overseer. He'd taken on Patrick's role of reassurance and encouragement. "C'mon, lads," Patrick heard him say. "Put your backs into it. You can do it."

A half-dozen men were trying to force an enormous support post into place. It was a tree trunk some four feet tall and nearly as big around. They had set the bottom on a block of granite and were using broken slates to shim the top. The space in which they worked was narrow and uneven, and it was hard going.

"That's it," Patrick shouted when they made a final effort. "You've got it now!"

The slatemen stiffened at the sound of Patrick's voice. "Morning, sir," a couple of them said. The rest were silent.

"Good morning, boys. Sorry I've been absent so long. My eyes . . ." He gestured to his new glasses. "These help a lot. I'm going to make a pair for each of you."

"That will be great, Mr. Whitby," Gareth said enthusiastically. "Won't it, lads?" There were scattered grunts of assent. "Okay," Gareth said. "You just get on with it. I'll take Mr. Whitby around and show him what we've done these past few days."

The shaft at number-three pit still wasn't deep enough to allow them to level out and start working toward the other end of the tunnel. "It's a real problem, sir. I don't know why it's going so slow. I changed the blasting crew, brought over the lads that were working at number-two. It hasn't helped much."

Patrick picked up a piece of rubble from the difficult shaft and studied the seams and the grains. "It's specially hard rock, I think," he said. "Won't chip away as easy as the other stuff. We'll just have to go on. Slowly, but forward."

They walked from the work site toward the office. Jones told him how much slate they had removed from the other end where they were already quarrying. It was more than Patrick had estimated. There was no mention of diamonds; he'd known all along there wouldn't be.

The sounds of mallets and chisels echoed from the shanties where the slitters carved the slate into tiles. The quarry was humming. There was a good feel in the place, a good smell. The men were secure in their jobs for the first time in years. Success perfumed the air.

"I hope you've been careful," Patrick said. "You've not neglected the support system?"

"Damn careful, sir. Everything just like you worked it out." The model of the tunnel, created in the Whitby coal cellar, now had pride of place in the office.

Patrick removed his dark goggles. "Thank you, Gareth. Thank you very much. I won't forget this."

"It's all right," Jones said quickly. "It's my job that's at stake. I know that. The others do, too. We're just doing what we're paid for.''

"Thank you," Patrick said again. "What about Mr. Murray? Has he been coming?"

"Every day. Sometimes I don't see how he can walk, even with those two canes he's using now. He's past eighty. But he comes. Mrs. Murray drives the buggy and waits for him. He goes around and checks everything. Then he goes home.''

Patrick felt the sting of tears. "You've all been so good," he said. "So kind.''

Jones stared at the floor. "About all your trouble sir, I'm sorry." He cleared his throat awkwardly.

Patrick wasn't surprised. In Whitby Falls it was inevitable that everyone knew everything. The story of Patsy Whitby's taking refuge with the Villettes was bound to be talked about. "It's going to be all right now," he said. "Don't worry.''

"I've been thinking," Patrick told Andrea a few hours later. "About the workers, about how loyal they've been, how much help.''

She looked at him across the luncheon table, and for the briefest of moments he thought he saw dark things in her eyes. Then she was smiling, and he blamed the impression on his faulty vision. "Yes," she said. "They have been marvelous, haven't they.''

"We owe them money, you know. IOUs for doing guard duty, half wages before that. It's a lot of money when you tot it up.''

"Well, we can pay them eventually, can't we? After the shipments to England?"

"I had another idea." Patrick laid down his fork and took a sip of cider. It was sweet and fresh, the first pressing of the season. "The company's always owned their homes. I think we should assess each one, fair market value. Then measure that against the owed earnings of each family. Make the houses over wherever a man has two-thirds or more of the value coming to him in back pay. Let the others make up the difference until they all have a chance to buy their own houses.''

She listened to him in silence, staring at the meat loaf and mashed potatoes growing cold on her plate. "Yes," she said after a few seconds. "That would be the right thing to do. Now."

There was a false note in her voice, but Patrick didn't want to probe it. "It is the fair thing," he said. "I'll see to it. Lliam Murray's still able to take care of that sort of business. I'll let him do it."

5.

Patsy and Joseph spent the best part of the day talking. They were in Patsy's room, and no one disturbed them. The sound of their voices went on in a steady hum that Lise noticed every time she passed the door. Joseph told Patsy everything that happened the previous night, everything that was said. She listened without comment at first, then made him tell it again so she could ask questions.

"It's so complex," she said finally. "So ugly."

"It's only complex in your mother's head," he insisted. "The simple facts are that your grandfather had an eye for the ladies. He fooled around. But he was father only to Andrea. He worried about someone finding out. But he didn't let it ruin his life the way your mother did. She imagined all sorts of possibilities."

"But they were possible. They still are." Patsy looked at him in fear. "What if it's true? If we, you and I—"

"Stop it!" he said firmly. "Stop saying crazy things like that. I know it's not true. I heard the story years ago. My mother thought it was a joke. She laughed about it. She wasn't a fool. Believe me. Maryann was never that. Neither was Eve, from what I hear. They knew it was all Jason's guilty imaginings. So do I."

"You're sure, Joseph?"

"I'm sure. I couldn't feel the way I do about you otherwise. And my uncle, he's sure, too. I trust Hugh Villette's instincts. I trust my own. A lot more than the ravings of your nutty mother."

Patsy turned away in pain. "Don't say things like that. She's not crazy."

"Okay, she's not. But she's had to carry a lot of guilt. She killed a man, sweetheart. I don't like to remind you, but it did happen. And it's distorted her understanding of everything that's gone on since. Then again, maybe she has to believe what she does. Maybe that's the only way she can live with it."

Patsy bit her lip. "I just can't deal with it, not now." She lay her head on his shoulder, and he stroked her cheek. "What you were saying about instincts," she whispered, "I agree with that. I love you. I don't think I could, not this way, if—"

"Just hang on to that," he said, kissing the top of her head. "Let the rest go. Except your father, maybe." He spoke the last words quietly. "He wants to understand about us. Maybe you should see him."

He's not my father, she thought. But she only said, "Later. Maybe after we're married."

"Okay. Whatever you want."

They made plans. The long-term scheme was complex and daring. The life they envisioned meant breaking new ground. But first they would go together to New York and get married. "The boss can arrange things," Joseph said. "He'll find a cooperative judge. We won't have to wait until you're twenty-one."

Later, they joined the Villettes at dinner and told them what they had in mind for their future.

Everyone was silent for a moment or two. A brand-new idea took some getting used to. Hugh stared at his plate, then looked up. "It might work," he said. "But it's a risk. You know that. No telling if you can do it here in Vermont."

"We know," Joseph said. "But this is where we want to live." He reached over and took Patsy's hand.

"You can do that, anyway," his uncle said. "Without starting from scratch. The quarry, my quarry," he said with a glance at Patsy, "it's a big operation. There's room for you, Joseph."

There was a strangled sound from someone's throat. Joseph glanced around the table. Impossible to tell who had made the noise. Henry, H.J., and their families were all watching him with varying degrees of rage. He almost considered accepting Hugh's offer just to see them squirm. He looked at Lise. She was calm, prepared to back her husband. Joseph smiled.

"Thanks, I knew you'd say that. But it's not the way we see it. This idea of ours, we think we can make it work. We want to try."

There was a collective sigh of relief. Hugh studied the faces of his offspring, opened his mouth to tell them what he thought, then changed his mind. A man owed loyalty to his own sons. He caught Lise's eye and smiled. She smiled back. "Okay, do it your way. Good luck to both of you."

"Thanks," Joseph said again.

"I dare say the eastern half of the state's the right place to start," Henry ventured.

The eastern half, the Green Mountains. Away from Whitby Falls. Joseph grinned. Henry didn't want to take any chances.

For a few seconds there was an awkward silence. Then Hugh spoke.

"You'll make a million, boy. I'll make book on it." He looked around the table. "No takers," he said finally. "Looks like you and me's the only gamblers in the room, Joseph. And Lise and Patsy. Rest of 'em only bet on sure things."

Patsy and Joseph left for New York, journeyed in quiet through a constricted world, a crystal globe enclosing them. Through the prism of the crystal Patsy saw all else as luminous and multicolored. Surely more beautiful than ever it had been. And selective. It allowed her to see only what she chose, to ignore the rest.

In New York they went to Joseph's room, still wordless, still silent with wonder. "Why does it feel so different?" he asked finally. "You and me in this place. It feels as if I've only just met you."

"Because," Patsy said slowly and with great thought, "we have begun our now. Crossed into the future, as it were."

Joseph turned away, suddenly afraid. "This place, this room, you're going to hate it. You're used to better things. I've always lived as I pleased. Never thought about having a wife, a family."

Patsy smiled. "Are you having second thoughts? Now that you've 'compromised' me."

"Hell, that's not it. You know what I mean."

"I know I love you. Nothing else matters."

He turned to her with a muffled cry and held her very close

for a long minute. Then they were sloughing off their clothes with frantic, hurried movements, struggling to breathe, as if life were tenuous until they lay together.

The next day they went to see the boss. There was no expression on the man's face as he listened to Joseph's explanations. His wry laughter surprised Patsy when it came.

"And I'm the one that sent you up there," he said. "If I hadn't, you'd probably never have seen Whitby Falls."

"I'm glad you did," Joseph said. "It's just one more thing I have to thank you for."

The boss nodded his large head. "I suppose I have to say you're welcome. Sit down, both of you. Tell me some more of what you're planning."

They did, Patsy chiming in when Joseph faltered. The boss said nothing until they were through. Then, "If I were to tell you my wedding present would be a New York house, would it change your mind? Can I keep the two of you here?"

Joseph shook his head. "It's incredibly generous, sir, but no."

The boss smiled. "I expected that. What about you, Miss Whitby? You're convinced you want to bury yourself in the mountains? I can't persuade you to help me hang on to this clever lad?"

"We've discussed it, sir," she said. "We really have made up our minds."

He sighed, then spread his misshapen hands on the desk. "Quite right, too. I shouldn't want to share Joseph with me if I were you. Very well, we must see about getting you properly married. Then we'll examine the question of how much of the state of Vermont you can afford to buy."

Two weeks later, Andrea knew it was time to go. She had wanted to be sure things were tidy, arranged. As Jason would have liked. Now everything was ready.

She gathered her muff and her hat from the hall table and looked ruefully at the stain behind the mirror. She had been unable to do anything about that. Major repairs were beyond her.

She went into the drawing room. It was shabby still, as it had been since she returned to Whitby Falls. Nearly a year now. It had been almost Christmas when they came. She remembered the tree Patrick put up. It had looked sadly out of place in its faded setting. Would there be a Christmas tree that year? She wouldn't be there to see.

In the kitchen the years of neglect were less apparent. The scrubbed pine table had changed little since she was a child. Andrea remembered Nelly Jones making cookies on that table. They'd been sweet and chewy and flavored with maple syrup. If she closed her eyes, Andrea could smell them still. In the kitchen it was as if the intervening years had never happened.

There was an announcement propped on the mantel above the big fireplace. Once the Whitby women and their servants had cooked over that fire; now it was a relic. Cherished, though. Hard to imagine the room without its big fireplace. Andrea smiled at it fondly and fingered the announcement. It was the best paper, thick and creamy with a silken sheen. It told of the forthcoming wedding of Edgar Whitby to some girl whose name Andrea always forgot. She had to look at the engraved letters to recall it. Oh, yes, Cecily Kramer. What kind of name was Kramer? Had she asked Eddie when he came for a brief visit the previous month? She couldn't remember. It wasn't important, anyway. The Kramers were rich, and she hoped that would make Eddie happy. He thought it would. Might he be disappointed when she didn't attend the wedding?

She left the kitchen and climbed the stairs. It was her farewell to the house where she'd been born. She mustn't leave anything out. The bedrooms beckoned her, and she walked through each of them. The room that Jason had used for as long as she could remember seemed to her an empty shell. Jason had been too strong, too self-contained to leave anything of himself in the house. Millicent's room was different.

Andrea had avoided the chamber until that day. Now she entered it from a sense of duty; the obligation to pay final homage to the woman who had borne her. She was struck by how much of her mother remained. The scent of lavender-smelling salts seemed to linger, mingled with the remembered odor of laudanum. Andrea smelled Millicent's drugged and quiescent days. "Poor Mama," she said aloud. Then she closed the door.

She felt no need to visit the Chinese bedroom. The night before, lying beside Patrick, she had spent the wakeful hours saying whatever good-byes she owed there. She moved on to the room that had been hers until she married, the girlish room of dimity and rosebuds that she had rejected when she became Mrs. Patrick Whitby.

In that place she did not remember her own youth, only Patsy's. For a moment she reeled and had to hold on to the bedpost to steady herself. Thinking about Patsy always did that to her. Her grief had become a physical pain, beyond bearing. "Oh, Patsy, Patsy, Patsy!" Andrea cried her child's name aloud in the empty house. Her heart hurt, and her stomach. Her throat tightened with the rawness of all the silent, secret tears she had shed for her daughter.

Andrea shook her head and rejected any weakening of her resolve. It was too late; there was nothing she could do. Patsy was married to Joseph Villette. By now it was possible his child grew in Patsy's womb. That must inevitably be the penance. The child would be deformed, demented, a pitiful witness to the evil that had preceded it.

"You escaped, Patsy," she whispered aloud. "I thought it was a miracle that you were normal. But you have opened the wound again, and this time there will be no escape. . . ." Andrea took a deep breath to clear her head, then went downstairs.

The church clock chimed. She counted three bells. The middle of the afternoon. Everything was as she had scheduled it. Andrea went out the door and closed it carefully behind her.

There were few people on Main Street. The men were all working, the women taking a few minutes welcome rest before the children came home from school. She could picture those women as they sat behind the ruffled calico curtains of their cozy front rooms. With a cup of coffee, perhaps, or a cup of tea. They were good people, her people once. Just as they had been Jason's people. She had been heir to a great legacy, but it had been spoiled. It was all changed now.

She thought about the deeds she had signed the week before. Both she and Patrick had affixed their names to twenty-three pieces of paper; they had made twenty-three families the outright owners of houses that had, until then, been part of the Whitby inheritance. Those dwellings didn't represent the whole town anymore. Whitby Falls had grown; Main Street had lengthened and been joined by two more roads. The people who lived in the newer houses worked for

Hugh Villette. They had never been Jason's; they were not hers.

Andrea fought off her tears. Too late to weep over any of it. It wasn't her fault. It was not she who had destroyed the inheritance and the world it represented. That had started with Jason; it was the other half of her legacy.

A few snowflakes drifted down, settled on the bare earth, and melted. Soon they won't melt, Andrea thought. This is going to be the first blizzard of the season. She knew it with the certainty of her Vermont-bred instincts, but she wasn't cold. She had chosen her purple velvet traveling suit to wear that day. The one with the fur collar and matching fur hat. The one she had worn on her wedding day. It was old and out of fashion, but still warm and beautiful. It seemed to her appropriate.

She turned around to look back at the town before leaving it. She wanted to see it as she had known and loved it, but Hugh Villette's great mansion dominated the view. She averted her face and went on walking. A man passed her, a newcomer whom she didn't know. "Afternoon, Mrs. Whitby," he said politely. He even doffed his cap. Andrea smiled. That, at least, was the same.

She was flushed and breathing hard. The climb had been more difficult than she remembered. She hadn't been up there since 1869—twenty-eight years. It hadn't changed at all. It was growing dark, but she could see well enough to know that the ledge was the same. Even the stunted sapling growing out of the bare rock looked to be the one that had been there when she and Riley came.

For a moment she thought not of Riley but of Patrick. Would he find her note? Of course he would; she had left it on the desk in the study. Reassured, she dismissed her husband and thought about the boy who had been her lover. The tall, strong, dark boy who had trusted her and whom she had murdered.

"I'm sorry, Riley," she said aloud to the mountain. "I didn't realize that you knew nothing about Jason and Eve. If I had, I would have felt differently about what happened. At least I would have understood the things you said. I wouldn't have killed you. I know I wouldn't have." She was speaking in her normal tone of voice, with all the intelligent reasonableness she could muster. It was so important that Riley see her point of view.

"But it *was* an abomination. The baby, I mean. I was right to kill the baby. I guess you would say that I should have killed Patsy, too. Before she was born. I couldn't. I kept hoping that she was Patrick's. Then, when she was born and I knew, it was too late. She was so little and precious, and I loved her so. And she was normal in spite of you and me." Andrea broke off with a sob. For a moment she almost thought she heard a reply, but it was only the wind rising in the valley, heralding the snow.

She looked over toward the quarry. In the half-light she could see nothing but the outline of the big stick. No matter, she could imagine it all. The men working, cutting the stone from the earth, hauling it to the shanties. They were taking slate from the tunnel now. It was 175 feet long. Patrick had told her so the day before.

"What would you have thought of that, Riley?" she said aloud. "I guess you wouldn't have cared all that much. People interested you, and ideas. Not things. That's why you cared so much about what you called justice."

She stepped to the edge, felt dizzy, then laughed because it was so silly to be frightened now. "I care about justice too, Riley. That's why I knew what I had to do. As soon as I heard that you never knew about Eve and Jason, I made up my mind. It's taken me a bit of time, because there were things to see to. I couldn't just leave everything in a mess. And I had to help Patrick get himself straightened out. It's all done, Riley, so I've come. You shall have your justice."

She slipped her muff from her hands and laid it on the ground. Then, as an afterthought, she took off her hat. The wind was howling. It blew her hair free of its confining upsweep and scattered her hairpins. The exquisite silver cascade fell over her shoulders, as it had done when she was a girl. Andrea looked up. One star shone dimly in the evening sky. Then it was blotted out by the snow-laden clouds hurtling toward the valley. A small tremor shook the ground beneath her feet. A few seconds later, the sound of the blast reached the mountain. It was a fitting epitaph. She stepped over the cliff into welcome nothingness.

6.

Patrick left the quarry at six and trudged home through a curtain of white. The snow had started in earnest an hour before and already lay thick beneath his feet. His sturdy work boots cut a visible furrow through the powdery cover that blanketed Main Street. He spotted a flat, untouched tree stump and estimated the depth. Almost four inches. It would be a major blizzard if this kept up.

He was glad there was no wind. He didn't mind the snow as long as it was so soft and gentle. He paused for a moment before turning into the house. In such weather he couldn't see the mountain, but he sensed its presence. Such terrain once had unnerved him. As a young man he had hated the open country, craving the protective mantle of a city. It was less true now, though vestiges of the feeling remained. He wondered if Andrea would be willing to move back to New York once they could afford it. It might be possible. Gareth Jones would make a competent foreman for the quarry. Excellent, in fact.

The door was unlocked, and he stamped the snow from his boots and went inside. It was dark in the hall. Patrick pulled on the light. "Andrea, where are you, lass? I'm home." No reply. He called again, pitching his voice toward the kitchen and then up the stairs. Still nothing. Funny she would have gone out in this weather. Andrea went out so seldom. Even now when she was so much better than she'd been since the trouble started. Doubtless she'd appear any minute with an explanation.

Patrick let himself into the study, thinking of the bottle of Irish in the drawer of his desk. He needed that after his trudge through the snow and the chill of the house. He allowed himself a moment of pique. It would have been nice to come home to a warm fire and a hot meal on such a night. Andrea had been providing such comforts regularly of late. He felt cheated when they were absent.

Patrick didn't turn on the overhead bulb. He didn't like its harsh glare. He smiled as he fumbled for a match and lit the old gaslights. Sour grapes, no doubt.

Pale yellow light bathed the room. He walked to his desk. Then, as he bent to get the bottle of whiskey, he saw the envelope. His name was written on the outside in Andrea's elegant script. A note telling him where she'd gone and when she would be back, no doubt.

He didn't open the letter immediately; he allowed himself the luxury of pouring a drink first. Then he slid out the folded sheet of paper and held it close to his nose. His eyes were better than they had been. The goggles and the chamomile eyewash were bringing steady improvement. If he concentrated, he could make out the words.

> My dearest Patrick. I have known for some time the requirements of justice. In the light of what has happened, what I have been told, I'm sure you do, too—though you would never say so. Thank you for the good years— they were very good indeed. The bad ones have been all my fault, and I'm sorry. I leave you all my love.

He read the message twice. It made no sense. "I leave you all my love," he said aloud. Had she left him, then? But where had she gone? Why? Patrick stared at the words yet again. A convulsive spasm shook his body. "Andrea! Oh, sweet Jesus! Andrea!"

He ran through the house, turning on lights and screaming her name. In each room he was terrified lest he find evidence of what he suspected. The fear was worst in the kitchen. He remembered the story of the woman who had hung herself there, Jason's first wife. Patrick had to force himself to walk to the center of the dark room and pull the light cord. With every step in the dark room he imagined that he would collide with her body, that his face would brush against her skirts swinging in the air.

But the kitchen was empty, the stove and the fireplace cold and raked clean of ashes. He thought of the cellar and plunged wildly down the narrow, twisting stairs. He fell once and bruised his elbow. He rubbed it with his other hand while he whispered her name into the darkness. "Andrea, are you here, love? It's me. I want to talk to you, tell you you're wrong. It's over, done with. It was an accident, really. You never meant to kill Riley. You were just terrified because of what he did. . . ."

His explanations echoed in the dark. He didn't need light to know she wasn't there. The cellar was silent and empty.

Patrick climbed back upstairs slowly, feeling his body protest the effort. He was trembling, thought he was going to vomit, gagged on his bile and forced it down. In the front hall he sank wearily to the bottom step and leaned his head against the wall. He was still holding the note. He relaxed his fingers and let it drift to the floor. It lay there white and innocent, as still as his thoughts.

It was five days before anyone knew for sure what had happened, three more before they recovered the body. Sarah Murray put the Rutland police on the right track.

The sergeant in charge of the investigation interviewed everyone in Whitby Falls. "You understand," he told Mrs. Murray, "we can't know for certain that she's not still alive. The note she left her husband was unclear. She's been unbalanced, I hear. Depressed. And her mother died insane. We have to assume she may be anywhere."

Sarah would be seventy-four her next birthday, but she was still a rosy-cheeked, cheerful woman, spry and active. "Millicent Whitby wasn't insane," she said firmly. "She was just beaten down by Jason. She was my best friend. I know."

The policeman cleared his throat. "Well, that's as may be, ma'am. Not really the point, though, is it? Do you know anything about Andrea Whitby? That's what I'm here for."

Sarah sighed and leaned back in her rocker. "Do I know anything about Andrea? . . . Yes, I know a great deal. It's not likely to be of interest to you, however."

"Please, ma'am, I'm just doing my job. Now, if you can help . . ." He glared at her. "Obstructing the law is a crime, you know."

She laughed lightly. "Are you threatening me? Gracious, all these years and someone thinks I'm a dangerous criminal." The smile disappeared. "Andrea's dead," she said. "I have no doubt about it. No one in Whitby Falls doubts it. It was inevitable."

"But where is she?" He slapped his open hand on the table.

"Look on the ledge," Sarah told him. "The one about two hundred feet up Herrick, if you follow the east path that goes straight away from the town."

"What makes you think she's there?" the sergeant demanded.

"I only know what everyone else knows. They just haven't added it all up yet. That's where Andrea and Riley used to go when they were children, when this whole sorry mess began."

They found the hat and muff first; they were buried under nearly a foot of snow. A policeman pulled them free and shook the snow from the fur. They looked fresh and new, as if they had been safe in Andrea's lemon-scented closet all the time.

Patrick stared at the things when they were brought to him to identify. He reached out a finger and stroked them lightly. "Sorry, sir," the young policeman said. "I have to ask. Did—er, do these belong to Mrs. Whitby?"

"Yes, they're hers." Patrick spoke with great calm, a man viewing events from a distance. "She wore them on our wedding day."

The fellow went away and reported to his superiors. They began searching the mountain.

When the body was uncovered, it looked alive. The neck was broken, but the skin was still golden, the eyes still violet. Even the beautiful silver hair was as it had been. The snow and the cold had provided efficient preservation.

"Death by misadventure," the coroner wrote on his official forms. The ambiguity was a kindness. He could have specified suicide, but the name Whitby still carried weight in the valley.

Patrick accepted the reality after he saw the body. Only then was he ready to telegraph the news to Patsy and Eddie. To find his daughter, he had to go to Hugh Villette.

He went to the other man's office. "I suppose you know where Patsy can be reached. I have to let her know what's happened."

Hugh had considered notifying Patsy himself. He'd written her address on the memo pad on his desk. In the end, he hadn't meddled. Now he tore off the sheet of paper and handed it to Patrick. "This is where they live," he said.

"Thank you."

"Whitby—" Villette paused. The other man looked at him expectantly. "I just want to say I'm damn sorry. Anything I can do . . .'' His voice became husky and gruff. "Well, you just let me know, okay?''

"Thank you," Patrick said again. "There's nothing." He held the paper with Patsy's address. "Except for this.''

The church was crammed to overflowing. People spilled over into Main Street. Eddie said something about ghoulish curiosity, but Patsy shook her head. "It's not like that, not with all of them. She was something special here. This was her town. Her family built it.''

Eddie shrugged. He felt very much alone, an outsider. He wasn't yet married to Cecily Kramer, so she had not come. But he was thinking of her and of Maryland and of the faintly southern world she represented. It struck him as more gentle than this Yankee north with its unyielding tribalism.

Joseph moved closer to his wife and took her arm. Patrick was at the end of the pew, the seat on the aisle. He stared straight ahead, seeing no one. The minister spoke about the history of Whitby Falls, about the way the Whitby family had created civilization in the wilderness. He went on too long, and the congregation began to cough behind their hands and to shift in their seats. Finally, it was over. The minister had managed to say nothing about Andrea and the way she lived and died.

Six of the oldest slate workers were the pallbearers. All of them had known Andrea from the day she was born, had drunk their fill of hard cider at her birthday parties on the Green. Patrick walked behind them, his eyes fixed on some point in space. Joseph gave Eddie the place beside Patsy. Joseph was the only Villette at the service.

"I don't know what's best," Lise had said the night before. "I should like to pay my respects. So would Hugh. But it seems—''

"Yes," Patsy had agreed. "I know. It will just cause more talk. Don't go, either of you. It's better that way.''

"But you tell your father," Hugh said firmly. "You explain to him why. I don't want him to misunderstand.''

Patsy had looked away. It was Joseph who said, "I'll tell him. And I'll be there, representing the Villettes.''

"I thought perhaps Henry or the other children might go," Lise said, frowning. Her offspring had neither sympathy for the Whitbys nor understanding of the past. "They won't be there,'' she told Joseph. "You and Patsy are the bridge. Thank God there's a bridge at last.''

Despite all that, both Hugh and Lise were waiting outside when the mourners left the church. They followed the coffin the short distance to the cemetery and waited while the final words were spoken. "In baptism, she died with Christ,'' the minister intoned. "May she also be raised with Him. May she rest in peace.'' There was a muttered chorus of "Amens.'' It was over.

Eddie fell into step beside his sister as they walked back up Main Street. "This thing between you and Dad, what you think, I don't understand it. It's ridiculous.''

"I don't want to talk about it,'' Patsy said.

"But look at him! For God's sake, he's a wreck. At least say something.''

Patsy stopped in the road and turned to him. Her cheeks were wet with tears. "I wish I could. I can't, Eddie. I just can't.''

He shrugged and fell back to keep pace with his father. Joseph moved up beside Patsy. When Eddie and Patrick turned in to the brick house with the white pillars, the Villettes kept walking.

"Not much of a bridge,'' Joseph told his aunt later. "I'm sorry. I hoped it would be different. For Patsy's sake as much as anything. A thing like this, it festers.''

"She's hurt,'' Lise said. "Even now she can't understand, can't forgive. Give her time, Joseph. The wound will heal.''

In the city, Joseph still worked for the boss. It was his livelihood until he and Patsy could find a way to realize their dream. They lived in the rented room that had been his before they married. It was a sterile place, without personality or charm, but it was cheaper than taking a flat. Money was important now. Joseph had never saved. They needed to economize if they were to put together enough for a down payment on some Vermont land.

The Monday after the funeral, the boss summoned Joseph to his office. "Here, it's taken me a while to produce your wedding present. It wasn't easy to find just the right thing.''

He pushed a cardboard tube across the desk. Joseph looked at it with curiosity, then reached inside and extracted a roll of paper. It was a document, a deed, in fact. He ran his eye down the page and saw himself named as owner of a parcel of land in the township of Dover, Vermont.

"I don't know what to say, sir. . . ."

The boss cleared his throat. When he spoke, his voice was suspiciously hoarse. "Here, take a look at this map. I've circled your parcel in red. It's in the right area, fairly convenient to both New York and Boston. If anything in Vermont can be said to be convenient to anywhere."

Villette studied the map. "It's perfect. It's just what we've been hoping for. Patsy's been making all kinds of plans. This is just what she had in mind."

"Good. Well, I suppose you two better go make sure it's all right. You can take off a few days next week."

As it turned out, they didn't see their property for nearly a month. Patsy had a cold, and the doctor didn't want her to travel. She wasn't sure why the simple ailment made her feel so awful until she realized she was pregnant. Then it seemed to her imperative to begin plans for the move. "I want the baby born in Vermont," she explained.

They arrived in Dover on an icy December day. The Green Mountains rolled and swept across the landscape, lowered with snow and with smoke from the chimneys of the houses dotting the hills and valleys.

Joseph found a room in a tiny inn. It was just a private house, really, but it had two spare bedrooms for letting. He left Patsy there, drinking hot tea to dispel the chill, and searched out the lawyer whose name was on the bottom of the deed.

"Ah, Mr. Villette, I wondered when you'd be coming. It's not every day I sell a mountain."

Joseph was stunned. He'd had no experience in reading topographical maps. "A whole mountain?" He walked to the window of the lawyer's office and looked out at the peaks surrounding them.

"The better part of one," the attorney said. "Didn't you know?"

"It was a gift, a wedding present. Look"—he turned back to the man—"I'd like to get my wife. She's staying at that inn half a mile down the road. I'd like her to see it, too."

The lawyer stood up and collected his hat and scarf from

the wooden peg by the door. "Come along, then. We'll take my sleigh."

Together they looked up at the wooded slope. A hesitant snow blurred their vision. Overhead, a bird circled, then took cover in the sheltering pines. "It's magnificent," Joseph said softly.

Patsy didn't say anything. He watched her face, then encircled her waist with his arms, from behind, so that his hands pressed against her belly and the beginning life it contained. The lawyer walked away self-consciously.

"We're shocking him," Patsy said. "We'll get off on the wrong foot in this place. Our neighbors will think us shameless city folk."

"What do we care?" Joseph said. "We're rebels, you and I."

All around them was snow and pines, white and dark velvet green. It fused into one candescence and shimmered softly. The mountain, Joseph thought, will heal all wounds. Nothing can fester in this clean, fresh place.

1901 . . .

The
Mountain

Epilogue

Patrick had never before been in eastern Vermont. He passed slowly through Putney, then turned left on the road marked for Newfane. The motorcar behaved admirably, not balking at the twists and turns or the hard-packed snow softening in the mid-March sun. There were no other motorists; if the horseless carriage was catching on up there, it wasn't evident. Nonetheless, Patrick was glad he'd elected to motor rather than take the train. The leisurely two-week journey had given him time to adjust.

The Green Mountains were different from the Slate Valley and the western half of the state. They were somehow more Yankee, more a nimbus of Boston than of New York. He smiled at the thought. After thirty years he considered himself American enough to detect subtle differences in the style and character of the countryside.

In Newfane, he stopped to fill the tank with gasoline from the spare can he carried. A few children crowded around the automobile, openly curious. Behind them, older men and women stared surreptitiously. One bearded octogenarian approached Whitby with caution. "That thing any good?" he asked at last.

"Very good," Patrick said with enthusiasm. "It's going to revolutionize America. Just wait and see."

The old man showed toothless gums in a wide grin. "It'll have to do it mighty quick, then. I'll be eighty-three my next birthday. Can't wait much longer."

Patrick laughed. "Would you like to ride in it a short way?" he asked.

"Hell, no! That's for youngsters like you."

"I'm fifty-three."

"Youngster, just like I said. What you doin' up here?"

"I'm on my way to West Dover. I stopped to find out which road, in fact."

"That one there." The man pointed with his cane. "About ten miles as the crow flies." He cocked his head, resembling a brown, wizened gnome. "That thing fly, too?"

"Afraid not. It'll do ten miles in an hour, though."

The man watched as the Haynes-Apperson motorcar moved off. Its narrow wheels jounced over the rutted road, spewing slush. The driver's muffler and cap bounced up and down in counterpoint. "Crazy," the old man said.

Disregarding the route of the crow, the way to West Dover was skewed and ragged. It was close to four when Patrick rolled through the hamlet. "Go through the village and take the second turning after the last house," Patsy's letter had said. "Just keep straight and you'll get here eventually." When he did, the sun was dropping rapidly behind the mountain. It turned the snow blood red; the peak looked like a haystack afire.

His daughter waited for him, standing in the door of a small wooden house with deep overhanging eaves and no porch. The house had elaborately carved shutters and tiny balconies. It looked foreign and exotic but somehow fitting.

Patsy strode forward before he had turned off the car's motor and was waiting when he clambered down from the high, open driver's seat. "Hello, Daddy," she said quietly.

"Hello, darling." He stepped back a few inches. "Let me look at you. . . ." She stood motionless for his appraisal. She wore a rough country-tweed dress that fell awkwardly over a body swollen with her second pregnancy, but her ivory skin glowed with good health and vitality, and her dark eyes were warm and welcoming. "You look marvelous," he said after some seconds. "It's marvelous to see you."

"Yes, marvelous to see you, too." There was a brief pause, then, "Come inside. You must be tired and cold, riding so far in that thing."

"A little tired. Not the fault of the car, just age."

She started toward the open door, then stopped and turned to him. The weight of her unborn child made her ungainly when she reached out her arms. "Welcome to our home, Daddy." Her voice was husky, as if she were swallowing tears. "Thank you for coming. . . . I'm so grateful."

Patrick enfolded her awkwardly, conscious of the presence of the baby between them. "I'm the one that's grateful," he said.

They broke apart quickly; four years had made physical affection a strangeness between them. Once inside, the big front room eased their clumsiness. It was paneled in honey-colored pine, and a fire roared on an enormous brick hearth. Joseph waited beside it.

"A bit of Irish, sir," he said, holding out a glass. "A welcoming toast."

Whitby took the drink gratefully, raised it in salute, then tossed it down hastily. The whiskey burned his throat, then warmed his belly. "This looks a fine place," he said, glancing around. "Eddie didn't tell me how unusual it was, how charming."

"Eddie only notices the snow when he's here," Patsy said, smiling. "He considers each flake a personal assault on his dignity. Cecily likes it, though. She's learning to ski. They come once or twice each winter."

"Good for Cecily," Patrick said. "I never find much else commendable in her."

"She's all right. And she's good for Eddie. She makes his life utterly comfortable but doesn't take any nonsense."

"I suppose so. But damn it, the woman's so bloody ugly!" He flushed with embarrassment. "I shouldn't say that. I suppose it's unkind of me. But after all those years with your mother—"

He broke off. Patsy turned away with a flinch of pain. "Mama was born beautiful," she said softly. "But God knows, it didn't make her happy."

Patrick swallowed hard. It was one of the things he had come here to say, but he hadn't expected to say it so quickly, with such little preamble. "I don't want you to think that," he began. "You mustn't remember your mother only the way she was that last year. There were good times, happy ones. She remembered them. She mentioned them in her last note to me. 'Thank you for the good years. . . .' That's what she wrote."

"You gave her whatever she had of good years," Patsy said. She wasn't looking at Patrick or at Joseph, just staring out the window at the encroaching dark. "That's why I'm so ashamed. . . ." Her shoulders began to shake.

Joseph stepped beside her and put a hand on her cheek. "Don't, sweetheart. You promised, remember?"

"I remember." She wiped away the tears and smiled at her

father. "You don't have to explain anything. I'm just so glad you agreed to come and sorry it took me so long to invite you here."

He thought of telling her of all the letters to her he had begun, then torn up, but decided against it. "We won't talk about any of that," he said. "We're just going to enjoy being together." He looked around. "Where's the boy? I thought I'd see him first thing."

"He's in the kitchen with the cook. Under orders not to come until he's called," Joseph said. "I'll get him now."

He went out of the room and left Patrick alone with his daughter. Neither of them said anything, but the silence lost some of its tenseness. When the door opened again, a small whirlwind erupted in their midst.

The child was three, but he didn't toddle. He ran on sturdy, sure little legs and flung himself at his mother. She gathered him up into her arms. "This is Patrick Whitby Villette, your grandson."

Patrick stared in wonder at the little boy. His grandson was made in his image. Not just the brown hair and eyes but the shape of the body, the way he carried his head, the set of his shoulders. The child was a miniature of his namesake. "He looks just like me," Patrick said, awestruck. "Neither you nor Eddie ever did, but he does." He held out his arms, but the youngster turned away and buried his face in his mother's shoulder.

"He's shy with everyone at first," Patsy said. "He gets over it quickly. This is your grandpa, Patrick. You know the word we've been practicing. Can you say Grandpa?" The child mumbled something incomprehensible. "He can say it very well," Patsy insisted. "He just won't do it now, because I want him to."

Patrick smiled broadly. "Just like his mother. Stubborn as a mule."

Joseph took his father-in-law on a tour of the property. It was a vast tract. "We've only developed a small part of it so far," Villette explained. "But we're adding new facilities and cutting new trails every year. Next winter we'll be ready for our first guests."

"A ski resort in Vermont," Patrick said. "I thought you were mad when I first heard about it. It sounded like something that couldn't possibly succeed in America. But when I look at this . . ." He craned his neck and studied the grandeur of the scenery and the way the natural pine buildings complimented the landscape. "It looks so appealing, despite the ruggedness."

"That's the genius of the Swiss architecture," Joseph explained. "The first Vermonters were mostly English stock. They had no previous experience with this kind of mountainous country. Still, they came up with lots of good ways of living with snow. When that's combined with Alpine styles, it produces something even better."

"Something like St. Moritz, you mean?"

"Exactly. That's where Patsy and I got the idea."

"I went to St. Moritz," Patrick said. "During those two years I was traveling in Europe. I wanted to see it because Patsy had been there. . . ." He let the reference to the long estrangement trail away.

"I understand," Joseph said. "So does she. She feels terrible because it took little Patrick to convince her. When she saw him, how he was the image of you, well, it made all her fears ridiculous. But she has terrible guilts because she wouldn't believe before then that you were her father. Take it on trust, as it were."

Patrick picked up a handful of snow. It melted instantly in the warmth of his hand. "Life is short," he said. "It slips away without our noticing. Too short for guilt. That's what Andrea could never realize." He shook the slush from his glove and smiled. "How's your uncle doing? I haven't been back to Whitby Falls in a long time. Gareth Jones manages the quarry. He doesn't need me."

"Uncle Hugh's fine. So's Aunt Lise. We told them you were coming. They asked to be remembered."

Patrick nodded solemnly. "I remember them often," he said. "I'll never forget."

"Neither will they," Joseph said. They stood together in silence a few seconds. Then Joseph pointed to a sweep of level ground near where they were standing. "I've big plans for this stretch," he said. "We're going to lay out a golf course here this summer. And Uncle Hugh thinks it might be possible to blast out an artificial lake. We could dam one of the streams to fill it."

"For skating, you mean?"

"Yes, skating in winter. And fishing or boating in summer. The secret of a place like this has to be its year-round appeal. Otherwise, it's not economic."

"What . . . oh, yes. I see."

Joseph smiled. "C'mon," he said. "Let's go back. Patsy will be waiting. And little Patrick."

"Patrick Whitby Villette," the older man said. "You're making him a fine future, Joseph. A fine inheritance. Better than the past that produced him, certainly."

"I've thought a lot about that," Villette said. "It seems to me that's what life is all about. All of us striving to make something good for our children and believing we can do it."

They set out together for the house, stopping for a few moments to inspect the Haynes-Apperson motorcar. "It's quite a machine," Joseph said admiringly. "Makes you believe anything's possible."

Patrick looked at the mountain once more. After all these years he sensed the pull that lured people to places like Vermont. "Anything is," he said firmly. "Anything is possible in America. Make sure you tell your son that. Never mind. I'll tell him myself. Let's go home."

Generations of intrigue, romance and murder in these family sagas by...

Beverly Byrne

Available at your bookstore or use this coupon.

___	JEMMA	14375	2.75
___	FIERY SPLENDOR	12487	3.50
___	JASON'S PEOPLE	12455	3.95

from THE GRIFFIN SAGA...

___	THE OUTCAST	14396	2.95
___	THE ADVENTURER	14452	2.95

FAWCETT MAIL SALES
Dept. TAF, 201 E. 50th St., New York, N.Y. 10022

Please send me the FAWCETT BOOKS I have checked above. I am enclosing $.................(add 50¢ per copy to cover postage and handling). Send check or money order—no cash or C.O.D.'s please. Prices and numbers are subject to change without notice. Valid in U.S. only.

Name_____

Address_____

City_____State_____Zip Code_____

Allow at least 4 weeks for delivery.

TAF-36

4